"I love this novel. It has a wonderful, warm, true sensibility. I couldn't put it down and was sorry when it ended."
—Eliza Clark, author of *Bite the Stars*

"Joanna Goodman [is] an extraordinary talent. . . . [She] provides us with work of special genius." —*The Literary Review*

"*You Made Me Love You* manages to do a rare thing . . . give us a true picture of women."
—Michelle Berry, author of *Blind Crescent*

"A cross between *Four Weddings and a Funeral* and *Hannah and Her Sisters*. . . . Goodman has crafted exceedingly believable, multidimensional characters and strikes just the right tone between poignancy and melodrama." —*Quill & Quire*

"Brimming with strong characters, sharp dialogue, and good-natured humor about human nature, *You Made Me Love You* is a sheer delight to read. It will leave you smiling and wishing for more."
—Diane Schoemperlen, author of *In the Language of Love*

continued...

Written by today's freshest new talents and selected by New American Library, NAL Accent novels touch on subjects close to a woman's heart, from friendship to family to finding our place in the world. The Conversation Guides included in each book are intended to enrich the individual reading experience, as well as encourage us to explore these topics together—because books, and life, are meant for sharing.

Visit us online at www.penguin.com.

"A generously imagined panorama."   —*Publishers Weekly*

"Goodman's examination of the bond of family and her strong characters will resonate with many readers."   —*Booklist*

"The strength of Goodman's storytelling skills, and her sure touch with the canny observation and the revelatory bits of business, elevate the material beyond the disposable beach or airplane book to make for an engaging and satisfying read. . . . Textured, resonant domestic novels are alive and well, and *You Made Me Love You* is an enjoyable and well-crafted Canadian addition to that genre."   —*The Globe and Mail* (Canada)

"Readers who are Jewish and have sisters may get a special kick from this novel, the story of three Jewish sisters raised in Toronto. But its humor and insights into family life also give it a broader appeal."   —*The Gazette* (Montreal)

"Many will relate to the pull between pleasing your well-meaning parents and trying to live your own life. Goodman captures this dilemma amazingly well."   —*National Post*

Also by Joanna Goodman

Belle of the Bayou

You Made Me Love You

harmony

JOANNA GOODMAN

 NEW AMERICAN LIBRARY

NAL Accent
Published by New American Library, a division of
Penguin Group (USA) Inc., 375 Hudson Street,
New York, New York 10014, USA
Penguin Group (Canada), 90 Eglinton Avenue East, Suite 700, Toronto,
Ontario M4P 2Y3, Canada (a division of Pearson Penguin Canada Inc.)
Penguin Books Ltd., 80 Strand, London WC2R 0RL, England
Penguin Ireland, 25 St. Stephen's Green, Dublin 2,
Ireland (a division of Penguin Books Ltd.)
Penguin Group (Australia), 250 Camberwell Road, Camberwell, Victoria 3124,
Australia (a division of Pearson Australia Group Pty. Ltd.)
Penguin Books India Pvt. Ltd., 11 Community Centre, Panchsheel Park,
New Delhi - 110 017, India
Penguin Group (NZ), 67 Apollo Drive, Rosedale, North Shore 0745,
Auckland, New Zealand (a division of Pearson New Zealand Ltd.)
Penguin Books (South Africa) (Pty.) Ltd., 24 Sturdee Avenue,
Rosebank, Johannesburg 2196, South Africa

Penguin Books Ltd., Registered Offices:
80 Strand, London WC2R 0RL, England

Published by NAL Accent, an imprint of New American Library, a division of Penguin
Group (USA) Inc. Previously published in a Penguin Group (Canada) edition.

First NAL Accent Printing, August 2007
10 9 8 7 6 5 4 3 2 1

Copyright © Joanna Goodman, 2007
Conversation Guide copyright © Penguin Group (USA) Inc., 2007
All rights reserved

 REGISTERED TRADEMARK—MARCA REGISTRADA

LIBRARY OF CONGRESS CATALOGING-IN-PUBLICATION DATA:

Goodman, Joanna, 1969–
  Harmony/Joanna Goodman.
    p. cm.
  ISBN: 978-0-451-22133-9
1. Mother and child—Fiction. 2. Family secrets—Fiction. 3. Domestic fiction.   I. Title.
PR9199.4.G6658H37 2007
813'.6—dc22   2007008099

Printed in the United States of America

Without limiting the rights under copyright reserved above, no part of this publication may
be reproduced, stored in or introduced into a retrieval system, or transmitted, in any form,
or by any means (electronic, mechanical, photocopying, recording, or otherwise), without the
prior written permission of both the copyright owner and the above publisher of this book.

PUBLISHER'S NOTE
This is a work of fiction. Names, characters, places, and incidents either are the product of
the author's imagination or are used fictitiously, and any resemblance to actual persons,
living or dead, business establishments, events, or locales is entirely coincidental.
    The publisher does not have any control over and does not assume any responsibility for
author or third-party Web sites or their content.

The scanning, uploading, and distribution of this book via the Internet or via any other
means without the permission of the publisher is illegal and punishable by law. Please
purchase only authorized electronic editions, and do not participate in or encourage electronic piracy of copyrighted materials. Your support of the author's rights is appreciated.

For Miguel and Jessie

*Perfection is achieved, not when there is nothing more to add,
but when there is nothing left to take away.*

ANTOINE DE SAINT-EXUPÉRY

One

*H*er baby needs surgery. Only six months old and his first wound will be the incision of a cold knife in his tender pink skin.

She scoops him protectively into her arms and smothers his scalp with kisses, stroking the soft patch of dark down that is getting thicker and thicker by the day. He will have jet-black hair like his daddy, but he's got her eyes. Dark green, like a wine bottle. And the tiniest nose, red as a raspberry from all the crying, clear snot leaking onto his trembling lip. Soft, fierce arms that won't let go of her neck. This is her baby boy. He is almost perfect. Almost, but not quite.

Dr. Hotz, Evan's orthopedic surgeon, has reported some improvement in the right foot but very little in the left. She inspects both his feet now that the casts are off, but neither of them looks any better. The heel is still drawn up and the toes are still pointing down, with the same deformed high arch as before.

"Will surgery make them normal?" she asks.

"Hopefully," the doctor responds impassively. He looks bored to her. He always looks bored.

"Hopefully?" she repeats, her voice sounding high and squeaky, like she's just swallowed helium. She clutches Evan to her breast.

"Anne, it's not life or death," Elie reminds her. "It's only a cosmetic problem."

"Surgery is *always* life or death," she whimpers. "Especially for a baby."

"Mrs. Mahroum, I've done hundreds of these corrective surgeries," Dr. Hotz assures her.

Evan was born with severe bilateral club feet. The technician hadn't detected it at Anne's five-month ultrasound. In the delivery room her ob-gyn told her it was a common birth defect, but after twenty-two hours of labor the words "birth defect" made her weep inconsolably. It was one of several prenatal nightmares she'd had in her final months of pregnancy—the kind of worrying you do for worrying's sake but never truly believe will come to pass.

The nurses managed to stuff Evan into her quivering arms and calm her down with soothing promises that the "problem" would be easily fixed. Anne and Elie had no idea what lay ahead. No idea that at six days old their son would be put into two casts from his toes to his groin; that over the next five months they'd be bringing him in to have his casts changed every week; that they would spend the first half year of his precious life agonizing over the possibility of surgery.

Despite all the casting, Evan's feet are still completely twisted inward and look more like kidney beans than cute little baby feet. When he hoists himself upright into a standing position, which he's just starting to do, he stands on the top of his feet rather than on the soles. It looks excruciating, but he doesn't give up. No matter how frustrated he gets, he perseveres. Elie and Anne cheer him on, heartbroken and helpless, always pretending to celebrate each milestone. And when he sees them clapping he smiles triumphantly, wobbling heroically on those contorted little feet.

All she wants from Dr. Hotz right now is a placating, uplifting promise. *Yes, Mrs. Mahroum. Your son's feet will be normal after the next casting. Your son will be perfect. You will have a perfect son with two perfect feet. You will never even know that he was born deformed.*

"—because in the delivery room," she reminds Dr. Hotz, "the hospital pediatrician told us this was a *minor* problem that was *one hundred percent correctible* without surgery." She emphasizes "minor" and "one hundred percent correctible," hoping to convince him with her testimonial.

"I would have been reluctant to make such extravagant promises that early on," Dr. Hotz says cautiously. "The casting obviously isn't doing anything for him."

"But the pediatrician said—"

Elie puts his hand on her arm, his signal for "please restrain yourself." Evan is still crying. He will cry like this until they're out of the hospital and he's buckled into his car seat and they're driving away. Anne's chest will be in knots until his sobbing subsides and he falls asleep. Lately, she's only ever at peace when her boy is still and quietly resting. She had no idea love could be so excruciating.

"Mrs. Mahroum, the prognosis after corrective surgery is excellent."

"There wasn't supposed to *be* a surgery," she flares, wounded. "You said the casting would fix the problem. You said the tendons and ligaments were flexible enough to reposition."

"I said I *hoped* the casting would fix the problem," Dr. Hotz says wearily. "But both his feet are still very stiff and they aren't even close to flexing into normal position. You do have the option to wait."

"How long?"

He shrugs. "A few months."

"Do you think they might correct themselves on their own?"

"They might. You never know."

"Is it likely?" she asks impatiently, frustrated by his vagueness. Doesn't he get that this is her *son*? And that this decision will alter the course of his entire life? "Is it likely they'll correct themselves or not?"

"No."

She looks at Elie, confused. "What should we do?" she asks, more out of ceremonial obligation.

"Anne, it's your decision."

She turns back to the doctor. "I don't want to wait," she tells him, with a flutter of nervousness in her chest. "I just want him to *not* be in pain anymore!"

"Even if there's a chance his feet will heal without an operation?" Elie questions.

"I don't want to wait," she repeats, with growing confidence. "Especially since he'll probably need the operation anyway."

"Then I'll schedule the first surgery for next month—"

"The *first* surgery?"

"I'm going to do the left foot first," he says matter-of-factly.

She gets a sudden image in her mind of her tiny fifteen-pound baby sprawled helplessly on some gigantic operating table. The image leaves her cold. What if they give him too much anesthetic for his small body? What if he never wakes up? What if they correct his crooked little feet but he never wakes up to walk on them?

She has the urge to grab Evan and run out of the hospital, away from Dr. Hotz and her husband's recriminating eyes, and mostly away from what lies ahead for her baby boy.

"Other than time," she says, "is this our only option?"

Dr. Hotz nods. So much for the sublime reassurance she'd hoped for.

One of the most frustrating things about an affliction like club feet, which is inconvenient and painful but not life-threatening, is the infuriatingly self-righteous reactions she's gotten from the doctors. *Better his feet than his heart. You should be grateful it's not cancer. You should be grateful it's only aesthetic.*

Even Elie—who, by the way, has never once stayed up during the night with her, soaking Evan's limbs in vinegar baths to get the casts off—is always reminding her how grateful they should be that "feet can be fixed." And always in his tone there's the unspoken reminder of what he's lived through, of where he comes from and the gravity of his past. Maybe he has a right to that outlook, but she resents his making her feel guilty and trivial about hers.

In the face of her son's deformity, people seem to have withheld their compassion. *Club feet? So and so's daughter has leukemia.* And yet she knows that when they peer at her son's twisted, mangled feet they're relieved it's not *their* child as they tell her to be grateful.

A child's pain is unbearable to withstand, no matter what the affliction. Her boy's anguished screams as the casts come on and off make it difficult to feel grateful. Yes, club feet can be fixed, but she doesn't know if Evan will ever walk normally or run or jump. She doesn't know if his legs will be scarred. She worries he'll be an outcast in school, hobbling around in leg braces like Forrest Gump. She worries he'll remember the physical discomfort of the

casts and the sponge baths and the operations for the rest
of his life. What if he's already emotionally scarred, before
she and Elie even have a chance to get in there and do the
damage themselves?

She made that vow, to love him the best she could. To
give him everything she could. To shelter him from pain for
as long as she could. He's only been in the world for a
matter of months and she's already missed her mark. She
failed him from the very moment of his birth.

"*I* read that Lord Byron had a club foot."

This is meant to cheer the rest of them up. This is how
they console each other at her Parents of Club Foot Babies
support group. There are pictures of famous people who
overcame club feet tacked to the wall. (Kristi Yamaguchi.
Troy Aikman. Dudley Moore. Mia Hamm.) There are
pamphlets scattered on the coffee table, all of them chock-
full of factoids about club feet. (It's the most common birth
defect; it's one of the oldest birth defects; there are
Egyptian mummies with club feet; it occurs more often in
boys than in girls, blah blah blah.) Most of them are here
because it's the only place they can get some genuine
sympathy.

"I keep hoping that maybe this whole thing will give my
son a certain depth he might not otherwise have had." This
from one of the few men in the group, a man called Declan
Gray. He always comes alone. Anne's never seen him here
with his wife, which is unusual. He's quite attractive, with
aqua blue eyes and dark brown hair the color of fresh-
turned soil. He's the one bright spot in an otherwise
abysmal situation.

"Maybe it's where Lord Byron's creativity comes from," he adds optimistically. (That he's heard of Lord Byron at all portends a half-decent intellect. It's not a given with most men.)

"You're saying his creativity comes from his club foot?" one of the other members questions indignantly.

"I'm saying maybe creativity can be enhanced by all the shit that goes along with having a deformity," Declan explains. "Who's to say that suffering early in life and being different can't be an asset down the road? I like to believe it will add dimension to my son's character, maybe even shape who he becomes. I don't know to what degree, but I like to think that way no matter how many people tell me he can be repaired as good as new."

Anne gazes at Declan for a moment. He's well-spoken, earnest, full of quixotic ideals. His theory momentarily uplifts her.

There's a new woman in the circle tonight. She's pale and fair-haired and slight. The rims of her eyes are red and she keeps sniffling into a Kleenex. Typical of a first-timer. "My name is Courtney," she squeaks. She has a high, clear voice, like a drop of water.

"Hi, Courtney." The familiar chorus. "Welcome."

"My . . . my daughter has a club foot," she blurts, as though it's a dirty secret. She flicks her eyes up toward the group and scans the room nervously, trying to gauge their reactions. It's obvious she's ashamed, afraid the others might judge her. Courtney blows her nose again. "I'm so . . . I know this sounds awful," she admits, between nose-blowings. "But I'm just so disappointed. I'm disappointed in *my own daughter*. I almost . . . I mean, when the doctor first told me, my reaction was I . . . I wanted to hide her! I still do. I'm always covering her up, covering up that thing . . . I don't even want my parents to see her, or Jim's parents, or Janet, my sister. Janet's girls are perfect, naturally. And mine has this grotesque ... this ugly . . . I just, I can't let anyone see that foot and so I've been lying to people about it . . . No one can understand why I haven't let anyone see her yet . . ."

Anne gives her a reassuring look. They've all had thoughts like Courtney's, but only in the group are they emboldened enough to voice them aloud.

"I'm sorry," she mumbles. "Thanks for listening."

"Thanks for sharing, Courtney."

Now it's Anne's turn. She draws a breath. "My name is Anne."

"Hello, Anne. Welcome."

"Evan had his casts removed today and there hasn't been any improvement. He has to have the operation."

The woman to her left reaches for her hand.

"I could wait it out," she admits. "We have the option to wait a few months and see if his feet correct themselves. But . . ."

Her voice tapers off. She feels the warmth of tears on her cheeks. "But I just don't want to wait anymore. I want him to be normal."

She lowers her head, ashamed. Someone hands her a fresh tissue. She smiles absently, knowing that at least these people understand how scary it is to send your six-month-old into an operating room where he'll be put to sleep with gas. They understand caudal blocks and vague, semi-optimistic prognoses for the outcome. Most of all, they understand the guilt of being embarrassed by your own child. They never tell her to be grateful that it's only aesthetic or that it can be fixed.

Like Anne, they don't want to settle for anything less than perfection.

Two

Anne stops in front of Mahroum's Coin Shop on Bloor Street and peers through the window at a display of 1878 Morgan silver dollars ensconced in royal blue velvet. She's pleased with herself for being able to identify them, and also for knowing that they're very hot among hobbyists these days. She used to think coin collectors were a bunch of eccentric nerds and social misfits—until she married one. Her theory was essentially correct, but she's developed a measure of respect for them and also for how lucrative a career numismatics can be.

The store is jammed. Anne waves to the security guard—a gigantic, unwieldy guy who's also a bodybuilder in his spare time. He's got thick arms that can't lie flat against his side because of all the bulging muscles, and a neck so broad it looks like his head is sitting directly on his shoulders. He isn't meant to move so much as scare the hell out of potential thieves, and to that end he serves his purpose.

"Busy today," he says, jerking his head toward the counter. Anne knows right away that Elie won't have time to go out for lunch.

She loved the coin shop from the very first time she set foot inside. It makes her feel safe, the way a library feels safe. The world happens outside of it. Time, reality, club feet, all that stuff cannot penetrate its mahogany-paneled walls—

walls that are lined with bronze plaques, busts of American presidents, framed awards from the Numismatic Literary Guild and Professional Numismatics Guild, and mounted displays of paper money from the nineteenth century.

She always feels as though she's entering a Merchant-Ivory film, half expecting to find Judi Dench and a pipe-smoking, Edwardian upper-classman perusing the books above the old brocade sofa. Each and every book is a leather-bound heirloom—*U.S. Silver Dollar Encyclopedia, California Gold Country, Bust Half Fever* . . . There are hundreds of them, all lovingly collected over the years by Elie. Everywhere you look there are coins and treasures and historical relics.

In the middle of the store a long glass display case holds endless coins floating in ripples of red velvet. Behind the counter the wall is lined from ceiling to floor with metal card-catalog drawers labeled in calligraphy: *Indian cents, Confederate, Halves, Quarters 1804–1907, Franklin/Kennedy rolls* and on and on. Rachmaninoff's *Piano Concerto No. 3* drowns out the bickering and bartering of the collectors as they shove each other aside to get a better look through their magnifying loupes. This is her husband's world.

She manages to squeeze in between two old guys and grab the attention of one of Elie's employees, an exhausted-looking kid in his mid-twenties whose name she can't remember. "Where's Elie?" she asks him.

The kid looks up from a tattered red volume the size of a phone book. "Hi, Mrs. Mahroum. Try his office or up in the appraisal room."

She finds Elie in his office, a small, chaotic space that reeks of cigarette smoke and chicken shwarma. Papers and coins everywhere. Catalogs and magazines piled on the floor. A half-smoked cigarette burning in the ashtray. He's on the phone. "The show's tomorrow night at the Four Seasons," he says into the receiver. "You can view today until five."

He motions for her to sit. She has to scoop a pile of invoices off the only spare chair.

"We're featuring the King of Canadian Coins," he goes on. "And the 1936 one-cent dot."

His other line rings, and without missing a beat he grabs it. "Mahroum's," he says. "Until five."

She observes him grimly while she waits. He's wearing his hair in a ponytail, slicked back with that wax stick he makes her buy for him at Trade Secrets. He's left the top three buttons of his black Versace shirt open, which she thinks makes him look like some kind of Lebanese pimp. He reaches for his cigarette just as he sees her lunging to stamp it out.

"I guess you can't leave," she says when he's finally off the phone.

"We're mobbed—"

"I thought I'd surprise you. I wasn't feeling very focused at the studio."

"I'm just going to order in a shwarma."

"Elie, your *hair*. Ponytails on men went out with grunge."

"So you keep telling me."

Anne had to explain "grunge" to him. He had no clue what it was; he was about a decade and a half too old. At first she was startled by his pop-culture ignorance, but eventually she came to find his maturity and Middle Eastern background quite compelling. She was in her early twenties during the grunge era and had naturally succumbed to the whole thing—the plaid flannel shirts, the combat boots, Nirvana. She even had a brief relationship with a guy who looked like Eddie Vedder.

Elie, on the other hand, was in his thirties at the time. He was way past all that, busy contending with grown-up affairs. When they met just over five years ago they had very little in common except a strong physical attraction that bordered on compulsion. He showed up at her studio one day intrigued by her coin table, which she'd put in the window.

Anne is a table artist. She refurbishes old tables—coffee tables, kitchen tables, bedside tables—painting them in wild colors and gluing things to their surfaces. She'll use anything—photographs, newspaper and magazine clippings, her own drawings, wrapping paper. Coins. Whatever. Sometimes she makes mosaics out of buttons, broken plates, stones and jewelry. Once she wrapped a table in fur. The first table she ever sold was painted moss green and had dozens of dried flowers pressed beneath a glass top. She painted the table legs to look like stems and sold it for fifteen hundred bucks. She's got her own studio just off Queen Street, which has expanded to include a forge and a modest collection of blacksmithing tools.

A few years ago she took a thirty-week blacksmithing course at Algonquin College. She'd been a longtime admirer of Albert Paley, so when she started getting a bit bored with decorating conventional tables, hand-forging felt like a logical and inspired direction to take her art. She became renowned in school for her funky metal tables, crooked and misshapen but divinely imperfect. She ended up selling a few and convincing Elie to buy her her own equipment.

She fell in love with hand-forging the very first time she smashed hot metal with a hammer and it actually changed shape. She felt so powerful. Metal is such a cold, sterile thing, but in her hands it came to life; it heated up and became malleable and she had that power. That's what she loves most about it, the feeling of being able to conquer steel with brute force and transform it into art. Everything about it—the smell of the hot metal as it fuses together, the heat, the sparks, the deafening noise—makes her flesh tingle.

She also loves that there are no hard-and-fast rules. The inherent beauty of hand-forged metalwork is that it's asymmetrical, dented, chaotic. Each piece is as unique as a fingerprint, which gives her total creative freedom. She rarely bothers to hide welds—not only exposing the flaws in her forging, but celebrating them.

Knowing how to hand-forge has added a new dimension to her career. She holds a show for the public four times a year, but mostly her tables are commissioned by specialty retail stores and decorators. Elie says her creativity is like a wild vine, morphing and meandering, growing in all different directions. Creatively, she is insatiable. At least she used to be, before she had Evan. She remembers how the inspiration used to just flow through her like a river rapid. Not so much anymore.

These days it comes in intermittent spurts. She hasn't touched her welding equipment since her first trimester. She did make one collage table—*Ode to Motherhood*. She glued some mementos to it: Evan's hospital bracelet, his birth record, his first baby blue skull cap, a few pictures of them in the hospital after he was born. Most women use scrapbooks. Anne made a table. (She didn't include anything to do with his club feet. When Evan is much older, maybe they won't even remember he had club feet. Who says art can't be used to rewrite history?)

*T*he day she met Elie he pounded on the door of her studio. Her blond hair was in braids and she was wearing her favorite patched denim skirt from Pre-Loved with a new pair of platform boots that added an extra few inches to her height.

"Are you Anne?" he asked her after she'd let him in. He was breathless and excited. "Are you Anne of Green Tables? Is this your store?"

"It's a studio. I only open to the public four times a year."

"The coffee table in the window . . . the one with the mosaic of coins . . . I'd like to buy it. I'm a numismatist."

"A what?"

"A numismatist. I have a coin shop. I deal in high-grade coins."

There was a soft trace of an accent, though it was unidentifiable. "You're a coin collector?"

"Coins are my passion," he said. "I study them and write about them . . ."

He had dark skin. She thought he was attractive despite his odd interest in "high-grade" coins. (Whatever that meant.) He was wearing all black—a black leather jacket, black jeans, a black turtleneck. His eyes were black too, with exquisitely long lashes. He was wearing cologne, which she thought was sort of classy. He was a man and she was used to boys.

"It's two thousand dollars," she told him. She was being greedy. She didn't want to sell it. It was her first real masterpiece.

"I'll give you eighteen hundred," he countered.

She was living on her own at the time, in a shitbox at Bathurst and St. Clair. She was carrying two rents, for the apartment and the studio. She couldn't really afford *not* to sell him the table. "Do you know how long it took to glue all the coins on?" she said. "I mean, even the legs are covered."

He smiled. A beautiful smile. His teeth were white and perfect. They stunned her. "All right," he said. She couldn't believe it. She figured he had to be rich. Rich enough to drop two grand on a kitschy coffee table. Artistically it may have been a masterpiece, but it was still a piece of kitsch.

She was starting to feel self-conscious around him. It was the cologne. It was the money. He had an exotic quality that was sexy. She thought he was Sicilian. There was something dark and sophisticated about him and she was drawn to it, probably because she thought of herself as the exact opposite—conventional and fair and tediously unmysterious. She had a stigma about her appearance. Back then, she thought she looked like her name sounded. Anne. Bland. Blah.

She distinguished herself in her twenties with the usual trappings—body art, bleached dreadlocks, piercings. She got a tattoo of an ancient rune on her shoulder blade, and then another one (a dragonfly) on her ankle, all repercussions of the grunge era. She felt they gave her a necessary edge, but by the time she met Elie they were something of a cliché.

Now that she's in her thirties, married and presumably settled, she's made some peace with how she looks. Overall, the sum of her parts is fairly attractive. Her features manage to rally together and rise above a certain level of mediocrity, elevating her into a much higher bracket. In her mind, her beauty happens more by default. There's nothing too hideous or offensive or out of proportion, and by accentuating her strong points—excellent blond hair and a decent body—she can occasionally achieve moments of greatness.

"If you want," she told Elie that day, "you can write me a check for the table." So he did. It was that simple.

When he came to pick up the table the next morning, he asked her out. Usually she wasn't the kind of woman who got asked out like that, by strangers. The majority of her previous involvements had been painstakingly cultivated out of friendships. And yet when he asked her to dinner it was natural, almost predictable. She said yes with uncharacteristic poise, as though she were used to such invitations. Looking back now, she figures it must happen that way when you meet the person you're going to marry. You must just know, somewhere inside your body, in your cells.

They went to a French restaurant off Dupont. They ordered beef bourguignon and a bottle of red wine. He offered her a cigarette, which she took, even though she'd quit years before.

"Are you Italian?" she asked him.

"Lebanese."

"Oh. I thought . . . I didn't realize you were Arab."

"I'm not. I'm a Maronite Christian."

"Oh."

She didn't want to let on that she had no idea what a Maronite was, so she said "My mother went to Morocco a few years ago."

"Lebanon is in the Middle East," he corrected.

"Oh, I thought Morocco was too. Isn't it?" She could feel her face heating up. She couldn't believe she'd already exposed him to her ignorance.

"Morocco's in Africa," he explained. "But people often get mixed up because of the Arab presence." He was being judicious. "And also they both have a strong French influence. Before the war, Beirut was known as the Paris of the Middle East."

"My mother said it was the best *pain au chocolat* she ever ate," Anne told him moronically. "In Morocco, I mean."

He laughed. She felt like she was drowning in her own inadequacy, bobbing and gasping for air, but his gaze never wavered.

The beef bourguignon arrived and it smelled of red wine and bacon; it was a deep reddish brown, rich and heavy. Elie dipped his bread into it. When he put the soaking bread to his lips he closed his eyes, savoring the taste. He didn't open his eyes again until he took a cleansing sip of wine.

Anne was intrigued by him. His dark wavy hair was tucked behind his ears. It was long enough to cover the nape of his neck, and when he moved his head a certain way, strands of it would fall over his eyes. Up close, his eyes looked too old for the rest of his face. There was an intensity about him—he spoke softly and seriously—but when he smiled all his features came to life. With his eyes closed and his mouth full, his expression melted in rapture. He had a brooding, moody beauty that frightened her even as it reeled her in.

"When did you leave Beirut?" she asked him.

"In eighty-two," he said. "After Israel invaded Lebanon. There were so many bloody armies by then I don't think *they* could even keep track of who to fight anymore. Israelis, Syrians, Muslims, Maronites, PLO, Phalangists . . . it became absurd. I decided to leave the day I had to drive my car ten blocks out of the way to avoid a traffic mess where a car bomb had exploded."

"No one could blame you for being scared, given the situation—"

"You miss the point," he said. "I *wasn't* scared. I was inconvenienced. I thought, Oh no, another car bomb and I'm late for work. I was twenty-two and totally blasé about it all. That's when I became very disturbed about the situation in Beirut. So I left. I traveled in Europe and then settled here. I've only been back once, right after my brother disappeared—"

"Your brother disappeared?"

"My younger brother Ziad. We think he was kidnapped. He never . . . he's probably dead. It's been over a decade."

All that before dessert had even arrived. She was reeling. His straightforwardness, that willingness to expose himself without pretense, fascinated her. And yet there was something impenetrable about Elie that she thought she could scour and probe. She conjured a past full of painful mysteries that needed coaxing, raw wounds that needed tending. He was more complex a man than she normally would have chosen, although she knew from previous experience that a bright, simple exterior did not guarantee against hidden dangers.

*L*ately, the things about Elie that she was first attracted to are what irritate her most. His slicked hair, his dark clothes, his cologne smell. His dark side most of all. She still has moments of lust toward him, sharp and urgent, like hunger pangs. But when she occasionally fantasizes about other men—the UPS guy, for instance—they're usually the complete opposite of Elie: younger, rougher, with army buzz cuts and possibly a cross around the neck. The daydreaming is all innocent, of course, so why not let her imagination stray?

The constraints and familiarities of marriage, the disruption of their leisure time since the baby, and the sheer passing of years have dulled the sharp edge of their relationship. She knows that the progression from sexual tension to plain old tension is normal in a marriage, so she doesn't worry much about it. She loves Elie, the way a wife is supposed to love a husband—consistently and enduringly. They may not be frenetic with passion every day, but they're solid.

"Why don't you cut it?" she suggests. "There's a salon up the street on Bay."

"Do you want money for lunch?" he asks, ignoring her.

"He's Lebanese, you know."

"Who?"

"Jad."

"Who the hell is Jad?"

"The hairdresser."

Elie responds with an exasperated look. "Why don't you go to Sassafraz?" he suggests impatiently.

"Not alone. There's always celebrities there."

"Well, I can't go with you."

For just a split second it occurs to her that he could be having an affair. Just the way he's shooing her out the door . . . She wonders about him sometimes—if he's the type. She wonders if he's already had one, or even a handful. Sometimes she even considers the possibility that he's a serial adulterer, like those men who cheat for decades without their wives ever knowing. Or worse, like the ones

who've got wives stashed all over the place. Yet she can see
with her own eyes that he's busy, and there *is* an auction.
And just like that she can forget about her misgivings.

A man thrusts his head into the office and says "One last
chance, Elie. I've had it appraised before. It's worth one-
twenty."

Elie sighs. "Bill, it's a low-grade colonial that will probably sit in my inventory forever," he says impatiently. "Like
I said, I'll give you sixty-five."

"Don't hustle a hustler, Mahroum."

"Sixty-five."

Bill shakes his head. "I'll be back," he says, smiling. He
disappears.

"What the hell am I going to do with a low-grade colonial?" Elie mutters.

"So I'm on my own this weekend?" she says.

"The show's running till Sunday, love."

"The weekends are so tough without you . . ." Not that
Elie helps much with the casts or the sponge baths or the
late nights, but at least he cooks and keeps her company.

"We're featuring some fantastic coins," he says excitedly, shoving the open catalog at her. He points to one of
the pages. "The 1921 fifty-cent piece, the King of Canadian
Coins. It's got a $150,000 pre-sale estimate. And here . . .
over here, see? The one-cent dot. See that dot right there?
It was to note the emergency transition between King
George V and Edward VIII. We're estimating a bid of
$250,000."

Her head quickly discards all the extraneous historical
information and she does the math. Two-fifty plus one-
fifty. Fifteen percent from the buyer. Not bad for a couple
of coins.

"I guess I'll head back to the studio," she decides.

"I'm sorry, love."

She leans across his desk and they kiss. She still thinks he has lovely lips. They always feel nice, even when she's in a bad mood.

"Say hi to your mother," he says. And then the phone rings again and he waves her out.

Three

*H*er mother's name is hand-painted on the mailbox in front of her house. JEAN BIFFIN, 193 MANOR ROAD. She ordered the mailbox from the Great Canadian Bird Company, a quaint country store that sells those fancy, old-fashioned address plaques that are so popular with what Elie refers to as the North Toronto Bourgeoisie: 124 Glen Forest Road or the Chudleighs' written in charming white script on black resin.

Anne grabs her mother's mail and heads up the front walk toward the house where she grew up—a three-bedroom, postwar semi just off Mount Pleasant Road. When Anne was living here there was no hand-painted mailbox, no Adirondack chair on the porch, no lovingly tended garden on the front lawn. Her mother never had time for such hobbies or decorative extravagances.

In 1979, three years after they'd left her father out West, Anne's mother got her Legal Secretary diploma at Seneca College and started working full-time at Keilty Perlmutter Solway & Stein, LLP, a big firm in First Canadian Place. For more than twenty years Jean devoted her life to Sheldon Solway and real estate law, often working up to twelve hours a day, and then for a time going to night school at the Law Clerks Institute of Ontario because Sheldon thought it would be a good idea. She used to say that Sheldon was the only husband she needed. They had a good rapport;

she suffered his moods and his self-importance and he thought her a loyal, hardworking lesbian with a precocious daughter.

Needless to say, she wasn't around much to take care of Anne. She had help from their next-door neighbor, Mrs. Roberts. Mrs. Roberts was the babysitter. On Sundays Jean would prepare Anne's suppers for the week, storing them in Tupperware and labeling them in black marker— Monday, Tuesday, Wednesday, Thursday. Anne was five and that's how she first learned to read, by the days of the week on those containers. It was Mrs. Roberts's job to heat them up for her. On Fridays, they ordered pizza.

Whenever she asked her mother why they'd left Harmony, her mother would say, "So you could have a better life."

"Better than what?"

"Better than mine."

*H*er mother is a licensed massage therapist now. She retired from her job at the firm and went to Morocco in search of some kind of meaning to her life. Upon her return she took a massage therapy course and then opened up shop in her living room. Massage, she says, is a tactile art. It necessitates human connection and is therefore a nobler, more fulfilling calling than her previous profession. As far as Anne knows, the hand-painted mailbox and the pretty garden are also part of this spiritual journey-slash-midlife crisis. Jean reads a lot now in her chair on the porch, she bakes, she babysits; she does all the things she never had time for when she was trying to give Anne a better life. Lucky for Evan, she is a doting, available grandmother.

Anne lets herself in and calls out to her mother. The house smells like warm cake. She passes the living room, where a massage table is set up in the middle of the Persian rug.

"In here!" Jean answers.

She can hear Evan squawking down the hall.

"You baked again," Anne remarks, joining her mother in the kitchen.

She drops the mail onto a heap of other papers and bills collecting on the ledge of the pine buffet. The kitchen is always the messiest room in the house, but it has an absent-minded, affable feeling that encourages long, pleasant hours spent at the pine table. There's no discernible style to it—it's a blend of Shaker, English country and garage sale—and yet it's a room where life is lived. It's large and round, workmanlike and full of vigor. Her mother spends so much time in here that Anne thinks it's beginning to take on aspects of her appearance and personality, the way dogs can start to resemble their owners.

Jean is sitting at the table, reading. The way she looks these days troubles Anne. She was never a beautiful woman, but when she was younger and slimmer and well put together her haughty purposefulness could fool you into thinking she was attractive. Now she couldn't care less about how she presents herself to the world. It's not just modest indifference either, it's outright rebellion—against aging, against society, probably even against men. She's given up. She wears rumpled, unlaundered clothes, usually the jalapa she bought in Casablanca years ago. (Elie calls it the Moroccan muumuu.) It's fraying and snug and it still jars Anne to see her mother in it day after day. She also wears her gray hair in a blunt bob cut, a style that's too youthful for gray hair and too angular for her round face, making her look like an oversized, aging flapper. And the large plastic reading glasses from the drugstore don't help either.

Little about Jean Biffin resembles the proud woman who used to leave their house each morning wearing tweed blazers with big shoulder pads and dress pants from the department store.

Evan is in his swing, eating one of the plastic Link-a-doos that dangle from the overhead bar. Anne goes over to him and unfastens the strap around his middle. "Hi, little man."

He smiles up at her adoringly and she folds him into her arms. Oh, that toothless smile. It never fails to melt her insides.

"I made you that beet cake you like," her mother says. Anne notices the cake on the table next to her.

"Listen to this," Jean says. "I want to read you your name analysis." She flashes the cover at Anne—*The Kabalarian Philosophy*. "'Your first name of Anne has given you a rather quiet, reserved, serious nature—'"

"Since when are you into the Kabala?"

"Just listen. It's fascinating. 'You do not express yourself spontaneously when conversing with others, hence other people may often regard you as being aloof, and even unfriendly.' That's true, Anne." She looks up at her as though waiting for some confirmation. When none is forthcoming, she continues.

"'The name Anne has caused you to live much within yourself. You are rather easily hurt or offended. At such times you can withdraw into a mood, and may not even speak to others.'" She looks up again, this time with a satisfied expression. "It's as if it was written about you."

"*You* named me."

" 'Worry and mental depression could be problems in your life,' " she reads on. " 'Physically, any weaknesses in your health would center in the heart, lungs or bronchial organs.' " She slaps the book shut and wags her finger at Anne. "Tell that to your husband."

"He doesn't smoke in the house anymore."

"I hope not. Because they say it causes SIDS, eh? Smoking in the house with a baby."

"Did Evan sleep?"

"He dozed in the swing for about fifteen minutes."

Anne can feel her entire body clench, but she tries to contain her exasperation. She knows it's inappropriate to berate the person who is babysitting your child free of charge, but she's told her mother at least two hundred times that when Evan misses his morning nap it's the precursor to another sleepless night for all of them. "Couldn't you get him to go longer than fifteen minutes?" she asks, keeping her voice light and neutral while gritting the enamel off her teeth.

"I tried to put him in the crib," Jean says. "But he went bananas."

"You can't just give up or he'll never learn."

"Anne, I'm not going to Ferber him, if that's what you want me to do." She gets up from the table and shuffles over to the pantry. There is something so grievous about her listlessness and her aura of defeat. It makes Anne pity her, and she would hate that if she knew.

"I never let you cry it out and you learned to sleep," Jean reminds Anne.

"It's just that when he misses his morning nap he gets all screwed up and doesn't sleep well at night." On cue, Evan lets out a noise.

"That's because he needs food." She pulls a jar of baby food from the pantry. "I bought this for him," she says. "Organic sweet potatoes."

"You know we don't feed him solids yet. Not till he's six months old."

She rolls her eyes. "That's in two weeks."

"Then that's when you can give him sweet potatoes."

"You were eating steak at five months!" she boasts.

"Yes, I know. And you hand-washed my cloth diapers every day. Times have changed."

"If you'd rather a nanny," she says, in her grating martyr voice, "you could get a stranger to move in with you. God knows Elie can afford it, and you've certainly got the space in your mansion."

Although the great sacrifices Jean made in her life were so that Anne could have a better one, she still begrudges Anne's affluent lifestyle and her big house on Dawlish Avenue with its view of the ravine and Lawrence Park. Anne's privileged life seems to goad her because it's provided for by her husband and she didn't earn it the way Jean had to earn hers. That Anne is dependent on a man seems to negate the fact that she's attained the very life Jean has supposedly always sought for her. The fact is, despite brief flurries of notoriety within the decorating community, her table art could never have supported her as lavishly as Elie does.

To understand her mother's disappointment you'd have to know where she comes from and what she left behind. She was born in Harmony, British Columbia, a speck of a town in the Creston Valley of the Kootenays. It's tucked away at the bottom of the Skimmerhorn Mountains, just a few kilometers north of the Idaho border. It's known as the

Valley of the Swans, which, Jean says, makes it sound a lot more romantic than it really was.

She was raised on a farm and got married in her teens, like most of the women in her community. It was a place where women had no options, which is why they left. She didn't want that sort of life for Anne—a husband at sixteen, working on the farm, no proper education. Secretly, to Anne it always sounded like a quiet, simple way of life that filled her with inexplicable longing.

Anne was also born in the Creston Valley, in a farmhouse that bordered an apple and cherry orchard. She's got gauzy memories of that time. Their house was one of four long bungalows on the property. It had a kitchen with lima bean–colored walls. It was always full of people—men, women, children—all coming and going. It was sort of a commune, one of those hippie arrangements from the seventies. There were bunches of families in each of the houses. They all wore homemade clothes that resembled the costumes they wear at Upper Canada Village. Anne shared a bed with a pile of kids whose names she can no longer recollect. One of the older girls who slept beside her got her period in the bed. Anne remembers that. She also remembers three swing sets in the yard and a blue pickup truck that was always parked on their gravel road. Yet she finds it hard to distinguish between her own memories and the facts her mother has related to her over the years.

Anne's father owned a fruit stand where all the women worked selling apples and cherries from their orchard. Jean used to drive them there every morning in the pickup truck. Anne still remembers the way her mother looked sitting in the driver's seat, with her long brown hair tightly braided, her suntanned face and the old-fashioned dresses she wore, like floral potato sacks.

After they moved to Toronto it occurred to Anne that *that* mother—the one who picked fruit for a living and passed her days laughing and chatting with other women and who was a dutiful wife—was utterly incongruous with the fierce, independent working woman she became.

These days, Anne often thinks the very same thing—that her mother is nothing like her former workaholic self of even a few years ago. Jean has a way of shedding lives the way reptiles shed their skin. It's called molting; it's a cyclical thing. Anne knows this from Natural Biology. When it's ready the skin just sloughs off, sometimes in large patches or sometimes the whole skin at once. With her mother, it's the whole skin at once.

Since Anne was only five when they left, the precarious memories she has come to her in clots. She barely knew her father, so there was nothing much about him to miss after they left. So many people were living in their house that she hardly felt wrenched away from him any more than she did from the others. She didn't even have a substantial impression of him, let alone an enduring connection. It's only since Evan was born that she finds herself wondering about him.

She's always assumed that her father cheated on her mother with one of the commune women, which would explain the suddenness of their departure. It also explains why Jean left everything behind; why there isn't even a photograph of him in their possession. And why Jean never dated another man again. It seems to Anne there had to have been a betrayal; how else would you account for the bitterness that has hardened inside her mother like shellac?

"I don't want a nanny," Anne reassures her mother. "Evan adores you."

"And I adore him," she says, kissing his nose. "Granny-Bananny adores her little boy."

Evan has a way of exposing Jean's fissures of warmth and vulnerability that instantly softens Anne toward her.

"I massaged his legs," she says. "He loves when I massage him."

Anne bounces Evan in her arms. "Did Granny give you a nice massage?" she coos.

He gurgles, sputters some gibberish.

Anne starts sliding his unwieldy feet into his snowsuit. After some difficulty she gives up, deciding to put his arms in the jacket and leave the bottom hanging behind him like a cape. Watching her struggle, Jean lets out a sigh. "Those fucked-up feet," she laments.

"I hate when you say that."

"Sins of the father."

"You think this is Elie's fault?" she cries. "Because no one on his side ever had club feet—"

"Not Elie. *Your* father."

"So the theory is that Evan is paying for my father's sins?" Anne laughs out loud at her mother's preposterous views on retribution, which are as twisted as her boy's feet. "It's a birth defect, Mom. It's no one's fault."

The doorbell rings and Jean looks at her watch. "That's my four o'clock," she says, rushing out of the kitchen. Anne follows her down the hallway and stops at the living room to load Evan into his car seat.

Jean answers the door and then returns with a short, middle-aged man in tow. Anne takes one look at him— balding and stocky and flushed from climbing the three stairs out front—and can't understand how her mother can touch his bare flesh with her hands, let alone knead his sweaty back (and others') for a living. It's no better than being a dentist and spending your life inside the decaying, plaque-filled mouths of strangers.

"Anne, this is Ken Schlittman. Ken, this is my daughter, Anne. She's just leaving."

Ken Schlittman takes off his gloves and they shake hands. "And who's this little guy?" he asks, touching the tip of Evan's nose.

"This is my son, Evan."

She watches his eyes drop down to Evan's casts and waits for the inevitable. "Was he in an accident?" he asks.

Then the moment she dreads most. "He's got bilateral club feet."

To which Ken responds with a benign, helpless frown. "Well, it's cold out there," he says, after a sufficiently awkward silence. "Bundle him up good."

"I'll see you later," Anne says, shoving her forearm under the handle of the car seat. And then to Ken Schlittman: "Enjoy your massage."

Jean kisses Evan's cheek and hands Anne his diaper bag.

*H*er car doesn't start. She turns around to check on Evan. He's gazing out the window, content and unbothered. She gets out of the car and unfastens him. Back to her mother's to call CAA and wait.

Ken is splattered on the massage table, half hidden under a towel. His back is a blanket of dark fur. Anne tries not to look.

"I'm sorry . . ." she mutters, passing by the living room.

"What's the matter?" her mother asks, sounding irritated. "Why're you back?"

"My car won't start. I have to wait for the CAA. I can wait in the kitchen . . ."

"Don't be silly," Ken says. "I don't mind if you keep us company."

Anne calls the CAA and they tell her it will be forty-five minutes to an hour. Evan is already getting fidgety and uncomfortable in his snowsuit. She unwraps him, settles him on his tummy inside his playpen and sits down on the couch to wait.

"Patchouli or rosewater?" Jean asks Ken.

"Rosewater," he says. She squirts the scented oil onto his back and starts rubbing.

"You're very tense today," she remarks. "Your back is like concrete."

He takes a deep breath and shakes out his limbs beneath her open palms. "I'm under a lot of stress these days," he confesses. "My sales are down. Way down."

"What do you sell?" Anne asks cordially.

"Men's clothes."

"Ken's been working at Meltzer's since 1968," Jean explains.

"The Short Man's World of Fashion," he adds. "We're Canada's premier shopping destination for men under five eight." He lets out a long, mournful sigh, and then: "But it's not the same anymore. There's more competition now from the younger salesmen. I'm up against these twenty-something bullies with their whole lives ahead of them. Who wants to buy clothes from an old schmuck like me anyway?"

"Consumers want experience," Jean assures him. "Don't knock experience, Ken."

"The other thing is," he goes on, "Jennifer's show got the ax this week."

"*Clarence & Co.* was canceled?" Jean cries. Then to Anne: "Ken's daughter is a TV producer."

"*Mr. Dressup*'s been on for fifty goddamn years," he rants. "You'd think CBC could have given *Clarence* a second season."

"Relax, relax. Anne, read Ken his Kabalarian name analysis."

Anne goes into the kitchen and obligingly grabs the book. As she's reaching for it she happens to glance down at the pile of mail she'd brought in earlier. She hadn't paid any attention to it before, but now the letter on the top catches her eye. The return address is from Polly Greer in Edmonton. She immediately recognizes the name.

"Mom," she says, rushing back to the living room. "Did you see this letter?" She shoves it under Jean's nose. "It's from Polly Greer. That's your maiden name—"

"I know it's my maiden name, Miss Marple."

"Is she one of your sisters? Do you have a sister in Edmonton?"

Jean sighs. "I don't know, Anne."

"You don't know if you have a sister?" Ken remarks, baffled.

"I don't know if she's living in Edmonton," Jean says impatiently. "I haven't spoken to any of them in almost three decades."

"Have you heard from her before this?" Anne presses. "Is this the first letter?"

"I was cut off when I left Harmony," Jean says tersely. "We're dead to each other."

It's typical of her to be so evasive and closed. Anne knows better than to push. She's always intuited that she's supposed to let these comments pass without probing or questioning. She is never to open up or pick at Jean's old wounds, an understanding that has been implicit between them since the day they left Harmony. This pact of theirs has served them both; up until recently it was essential to the maintenance of their relationship. Anne has never wanted to be exposed to the side of her mother that contains all her hurt and vulnerability and rage from the past. She's preferred her to be stoic and impassive; a warrior, not a victim. Doesn't everybody want a mother who's ordinary and uncomplicated? Jean seemed to want this too.

But now Anne's interest is piqued. From the moment she first peered into her newborn son's face, that vault of intrigue surrounding her own past got pried open, which she thinks is a natural, healthy evolution for a new parent. After Evan was born there were many questions about heredity. Doctors wanted to know if club feet had occurred on either her mother or father's side before. She couldn't answer anything about her father's side. It got her thinking; it lit a few embers of curiosity inside her.

Motherhood has suddenly engaged her in her own history and, by virtue of their inexorable connection, her mother's too. Now she wants to know more about who she is, about her mother's family tree, about her past. Most of all she wonders about this man who is or was her father, a man she hasn't seen in almost thirty years; a man whose blood runs through her son's veins and whose absence in her life feels like a tumor, a kind of dense, dark mass that takes up space inside her but is filled with nothing.

Do Evan's green eyes come from him? Or his club feet, which are supposed to be hereditary?

Her curiosity seems to have gained momentum as Evan grows and changes, demonstrating undeniable fragments of them all—Anne's smile, Elie's eyebrows, her mother's upper lip. What else about him belongs to the strangers out West who are his family by blood?

She glances over at her mother and the expression in Jean's eyes confirms she'll get nowhere today. She looks grumpy and remote. Ken is also quiet as Jean continues to massage him, looking visibly upset.

Unable to let it go, Anne waits an acceptable amount of time before pouncing again.

"Why do you think she's writing you now?" she finally asks.

"I don't know, Anne. Let's talk about it another time when I'm not working. Read Ken his name analysis, would you?"

Relenting momentarily, Anne opens the book to his name and reads the passage. "'Kenneth, Kenny, Ken. There is a seriousness to your nature which could cause you to worry over your responsibilities, especially when confronted with change and uncertainty. You are overly fond of heavy foods such as meat, potatoes, breads and pastries and could suffer with stomach and intestinal disorders, constipation or boils.'"

"I can see your eczema is flaring up again," her mother warns. "That's from stress."

Ken cranes his neck around to look at Anne. "Have you ever seen *Clarence & Co.*, Anne?"

"I haven't, no. I don't watch much TV . . ." (A fib.)

"It's a good show," he says proudly. "A good puppet show."

Flakes from his back are landing on the carpet like shredded coconut. Anne looks away.

"Your mother tells me your husband is a coin collector," he remarks.

"Yes, Elie's a numismatist. He's got a shop on Bloor."

"I'm a collector myself. I've been collecting Canadian coins for thirty years. I have no idea what they're worth though. It's more a labor of love."

Anne reaches into her purse and pulls out one of Elie's business cards. "Maybe Elie could appraise it for you," she offers, setting the card down beside him on the massage table.

"No need," he says. "I'll never sell it. I'll let my daughter do what she wants with it after I'm dead. It's all going to be hers."

His devotion reminds Anne again that she's severed from her own father, something that makes her chest constrict with resentment and envy toward Ken Schlittman's daughter.

As she watches her mother's hands work their way across his back, a plan begins to crystallize in her head, grabbing hold of her in a way that feels as irrevocable as it is sudden. One day soon, when Evan's feet have healed and he's restored to his natural, divine perfection, she's going to take him out West to meet his grandfather. She's also going to look up her mother's family and get to know them. Jean wants her to forget about this letter from her aunt Polly, but she doesn't want to keep playing this game. She's got a son now. Denial and passivity just won't do anymore.

These people may be dead to her mother, but for Anne they've only just begun to come alive.

Four

*E*lie is in one of his moods. The auction didn't go as well as he'd hoped and his prized King of Canadian Coins went for only seventy-seven thousand. Now he's shut away in his office, sulking. She can smell cigarettes, too. He thinks he can open the window and she won't notice.

She saunters in and he looks up from his desk. "You've been smoking," she accuses.

The room is blurred by a haze of gray smoke. This is Elie's sanctuary, with its floor-to-ceiling bookcases built of oak and all his dearest possessions in the world. The bookcase is neatly lined with his treasured literary and numismatic books. He keeps it polished and gleaming like she imagines the Library of Congress would be. He's made some room in the bottom left corner for her books—*The Diary of Frida Kahlo, Albert Paley's Man of Steel, The Art of Blacksmithing, Between Anvil and Forge, The Book of Fire*. She's never been an avid reader of literature, but she is fiercely protective of her collection of art books, which have inspired and influenced her over the years.

Notwithstanding her slim space in the bookcase, the room is all Elie in the same way the coin shop is Elie, filled with his style, his scent, his breath and his life. There's a tufted brown leather club chair and ottoman by the fireplace and a massive oak desk in the center of the room, which he bought at a flea market in France. The dark wood floors are mostly covered by the heirloom Persian rugs that belonged to his family, each one a work of art, intricately woven in jewel tones of navy blue and crimson. They're worn out just the right amount—like everything else in the room—revealing their status and longevity and worth.

"The window's open," he says grumpily.

"It still smells. You promised, for Evan."

"Don't start, Anne." He shuffles some papers. She can see he's going over the numbers from the auction. He looks tense and somber, his forehead divided in two by a vertical slash of bulging blue vein.

She could understand it if their entire income depended on his coin business, but Elie is independently wealthy. Most of his money comes from his family's import business in Lebanon. Numismatics is, as Ken Schlittman put it, a labor of love. Yet every time he overestimates the pre-sale value of a coin, or an auction doesn't meet his expectations, he takes it as a great personal failure. She supposes it's a somewhat admirable quality, how hard he is on himself. That he's opted for personal challenge rather than just living off his parents' fortune speaks to a certain measure of integrity and intrinsic motivation, both of which have fueled his pursuit of success over the years. However, it's a success that carries with it the burden of his unpredictable moods.

She can't say she didn't know Elie was the brooding type before she married him, but in that stage of their romance she preferred to interpret his sullenness as depth, unpredictability, pensiveness. She didn't have to pretend to be peppy and easygoing with him the way she'd had to with previous boyfriends. With Elie she could be herself right away. From the moment they met they revealed their most damaged selves to each other and were irrevocably connected. Their love grew out of their freely shared wounds. At least that's how she romanticized it back then, during the more forgiving days of their relationship.

Their official courtship ended on their second date, when she slept with him. She had no rigid morals about such things; no random number of dates that made it acceptable or respectable. She just slept with him because she wanted to and because she was there, at his place.

He lived in an ultra-cool converted loft on Queen's Quay. He'd had it professionally decorated in tones of deep cocoa and charcoal gray, with concrete floors and exposed brick walls and skylights overhead through which blinding beams of white sunlight flooded in at all times of the day. The place was dominated by a south-facing wall of glass that overlooked Lake Ontario and a marina down below that could just as easily have been in Santa Barbara or Maine.

He had some art in his loft, mostly paintings of Lebanon. She thought they were quite lovely in a childlike way, and she asked him about them.

"That's French Avenue on the Beirut seashore," he explained. He was smoking and he pointed his cigarette at it.

"It looks like the French Riviera," she remarked.

"Doesn't it? And that one is Beirut Harbor," he went on. "You can see the snow-covered Al Arz mountain in the background there, and the Shouf mountains over there."

"Who painted these?"

"I did," he said, without a trace of boastfulness or pride. She's absolutely certain he wouldn't have even mentioned it if she hadn't asked. She knew then that she was already in love with him. Soon after, she moved in with him. It wasn't a formal, grandiose arrangement—she didn't come with any furniture or personal effects—but she slept there almost every night until they were married.

*E*arly in their relationship, he took her to Paris. He was attracted to all things French, probably because they recalled Beirut. They stayed at the Madison Hotel in St. Germain des Prés. They had a tiny room on the top floor, with sloped ceilings and dormer windows. It was overdone in bloodred toile de Jouy—the wallpaper, the bedding, the drapes, the upholstered headboard. All of it was in the same gaudy, quintessentially French fabric, but it was charming.

They went from café to café, lingering over carafes of wine or *café crèmes*. Elie smoked Gitanes and gazed at her through dense clouds of smoke; his eyes were black and sultry and inevitably they led them back to the red toile room up in the attic. They kept meaning to visit the Louvre and the Musée d'Orsay, but each day they'd put it off until the next day and instead they'd laze around the room, slipping out for either a coffee or some wine and then a rich, filling meal late in the evening. The next morning they'd wake up and remind each other that they still hadn't visited their museums, and they'd giggle like two kids playing hooky from school and skip them again to make love all day. They kept the room dark. They barely came up for air—Elie only to light cigarettes and Anne to pee. They ate croissants in bed for breakfast every morning.

Finally, on the last day, they ran frantically from one museum to another, trying to cram them in, guiltily and giddily. She almost let him talk her into staying in the room—that's how drugged she was with lust. But she knew that later on, especially if their passion ever cooled, she would regret not having seen the Musée d'Orsay or the Louvre.

On that last night, over veal Marengo at Le Petit St-Benoit, Elie said, "Why don't we get married?"

"In Paris?"

"When we get back to Toronto."

She thought it over for all of five seconds. "Okay," she said, without a single reservation. There were ample criteria to recommend him. He was intellectual, wealthy, educated, generous, passionate, witty and well-groomed. To boot, he had substance, he was an appreciator of luxury, he trusted few people, he never acted like a buffoon or made an ass of himself, he had a complicated past that made him interesting and mysterious and worth probing, he had good taste across the board—in food, clothes, decorators—and, like Anne, he wasn't fond of socializing. He could be selfish and moody, but then, who doesn't have flaws? In reviewing his credentials, she found him to be perfect for her.

She'd had only one other serious relationship before and it was with her Beaver Studies professor at Western. The course was actually called Natural Biology for Non-Biology Majors and it was a nice break from all her art history courses. It was a popular elective because it was an easy credit and because Hamish—the professor—was a legend on campus. He wore overalls to class with mud-stained Kodiak boots, a red-and-black checkered lumber jacket and a fishing cap.

He looked more like a hillbilly than a professor, but when he spoke about beaver shit or passed the bone of a moose's penis around the room you never witnessed a more genuine passion. He was spiritual and earthy, with a notoriously reverential devotion to nature. He got excited about things like bird-calling and howling at wolves. He did all his own photography and had three nature books to his credit. Anne used to tease him that when he was walking outside bunny rabbits and chipmunks would gather at his feet and birds would land on his shoulder. He was endearingly uncomplicated, so she thought.

She had a crush on him all semester of her second year, but they eventually fell in love at one of his nature seminars in Algonquin Park. She had gone along posing as a nature geek just to get closer to him. On one of many wet, swampy walks he pointed to a tree and exclaimed, "Look, a southern wood thrush!" She glanced up and the bird was staring unflinchingly back at Hamish. The way Hamish was looking at it, that wood thrush must have felt like the most beautiful creature in the forest. Later that night, when he gazed at Anne by the camp fire, he made her feel the same way.

They dated for two years. She thought she'd marry him. Her mother approved wholeheartedly; in fact, she treasured Hamish. He had a special way with all living creatures more vulnerable than he—animals, plants, flowers and women.

They stayed happily together until Anne found out he'd cheated on her with another one of his students, and then another one after that. And finally, after the third betrayal (and after she'd learned of dozens more), she dejectedly left him. She got her art history degree but lost her first love.

Anne has enough wisdom and perspective now to realize it was her own foolishness—the dumbness and naïveté of youth—that allowed her to fall for a womanizing professor. She never did see the writing on the wall.

In the scarring aftermath of Hamish, what she liked so much about Elie was that he was artsy and wary and somewhat glum where Hamish had been outdoorsy and open and buoyant. Elie was also honest and upfront about his complexities where Hamish had been deceitful and cunning in portraying himself as an uncomplicated man.

*A*nne goes over to Elie now and lays her hand on his shoulder. "I'm starving," she says. "I've been looking forward to your lamb all day."

He looks up at her, as though noticing her for the first time.

"Evan and I went to Pusateri's," she tells him. "I bought kebabs."

He rests his cheek on her knuckles. His beard—a new thing he's trying—tickles her skin. "Is Evan asleep?" he asks.

"Mm. Let's have a nice dinner. I missed having you here this weekend."

He pulls her down on his lap. "I had a pretty shitty weekend myself," he says. "At the last minute the Furstenbergs put a reserve on their 1904 Newfoundland fifty-cent coin. No one matched the required minimum bid."

"What was it?"

"Eight grand. It would have been a nice sale."

"There'll be others," she assures him. "I bought fresh mint."

She notices he's got his mahogany coin box out of its usually locked drawer. She reaches across his desk and opens it. "What're you doing with these?" she asks him.

"I've been thinking about selling them," he says matter-of-factly.

To know Elie is to know he would sooner sell his own child than part with his personal collection of coins, which is why she practically falls off his lap in shock. "You're *what*?"

"I'll never complete it. So what's the point?"

"But you're just missing the one coin," she reminds him. "You can't give up now."

"It's a conflict of interest anyway."

She remembers the first time he introduced her to his personal collection. They were at his loft and he very ceremoniously pulled out the mahogany presentation box. She was expecting to see hundreds of coins in there. There were precisely three, each one sealed in an airtight plastic coin holder. There was a fourth slab in the royal blue velvet interior, but it was empty.

"That's it?" she cried, unimpressed. "Three coins?" She couldn't believe this was the collection he'd been building for almost fifteen years.

He smiled proudly. "If I ever get my hands on the fourth coin in the set, this little box will be worth more than a million dollars."

"For *four* coins?"

He handed her one and she stared at it in awe. It was a British Columbia ten-dollar silver coin.

"They were minted in 1862, during the B.C. gold rush," he explained. "The complete set includes the ten- and twenty-dollar silver coins and the ten- and twenty-dollar gold coins. So far, there's no known complete set."

She gazed down into the box. "You're missing the ten-dollar gold coin."

"The rarest of the four. There are only three of them in existence. One is in the B.C. Archives and the other is in London's British Museum. That leaves one."

"What are your chances of ever getting your hands on it?"

"Who knows? But that's the thrill of collecting," he told her. "It's all about the hunt."

"Then why don't you have more than this?" she asked him.

"When I decided to open the shop and start dealing professionally, I sold off most of my own collection."

"Why?"

"I'm a dealer first. If I was always on the hunt for my own private collection, I'd have no business. It's a conflict of interest."

He took the silver coin from her hand and gently laid it back in the mahogany box. "But I couldn't part with these," he said. "One day, that elusive fourth coin will fall into my hands."

That was when she told him she was from B.C., suggesting in a manner that seems so young and silly to her now that the missing pieces in his life—his coin, his soul mate—had originated in the same place.

"You're just in a bad space," she soothes now. "You don't really want to sell these." She strokes his hair. The wax in it makes her hand sticky.

"I could make a lot of money off them."

"We don't need the money. Just sit tight. You've waited this long."

He looks so melancholy and hopeless. Maybe it also has to do with his fear about Evan's operation. Whatever it is, he leaves Anne out of it; leaves her to draw her own conclusions.

"Let's eat," she says. "I've been dreaming about your lamb all day. We could barbecue . . ."

He gets up and puts his coins back in the drawer. Then he closes the fireplace doors and they go downstairs.

Elie designed the kitchen himself. He put in a wood-burning brick oven and a lava-stone barbecue and a glassed-in alcove where they eat. The focus of the room is the twelve-foot oak table with carved cabriole legs that faces onto the backyard. The view is breathtaking, especially in winter, when the tree branches are bare and haunting, reaching out to them like ancient, bony arms. He had the floor tiles replaced with wide planks of warm, golden-brown walnut and he hung a massive iron chandelier smack in the center of the room, above a stainless steel island where he does most of the cooking. They've lived in the house for three years and Anne still finds it surreal every time she sets foot in here.

Luxury is a requirement for Elie. There had to be a fireplace in every room, six-hundred-thread-count sheets on the beds, an espresso machine imported from Italy. That's Elie.

Some days it still shocks her, the idea of *her* living in this place. Occasionally she feels like a fraud. She wonders if the people in her wealthy North Toronto neighborhood, who've probably made assumptions about her life based on brief glimpses when she's returning home with the groceries or planting her garden in spring, would ever suspect that she's really this odd girl from Harmony, B.C., a table artist and blacksmith and the mother of a son with club feet.

"I've been thinking about taking Evan out west," she mentions while she's chopping up the mint.

"What's out west?"

"Mountains. Trees. My father."

Elie looks up from his bowl of marinade. "Your father?"

"I do have one, you know."

"You've never mentioned him before. I mean, not in a way that ever suggested you wanted to see him again."

"I never did."

"And now?"

"Now I have Evan. I want him to meet his grandfather, his aunts and uncles, his cousins. My mother's sister sent her a letter today. They haven't spoken since we left—"

Elie doesn't say anything. That's how he is. His silence is always a comment.

"Anyway, it got me thinking about them all. I don't think it's such a big deal."

"How do you know your father's still there?"

"People who live in Harmony don't leave."

"*You* did."

"That's different. My mother was rebelling against something."

She dumps the cutting board in the sink and rinses it with hot water. "The men don't leave anyway," she corrects.

"It's almost thirty years. That's a long time," Elie remarks, soaking the lamb kebabs in the marinade.

"Let's talk about it when Evan's feet are healed."

"That might take years."

"That's optimistic," she snips.

Elie goes over to the barbecue and turns it on. He swishes the kebabs around in the marinade one more time before laying them on the grill. "Pass me the mint."

"Maybe part of me does want my father to know what he's lost," she defends, handing him the mint. "So what? You know, he never once tried to contact me after we left. He just let me go . . ."

"Exactly. He let *you* go," Elie points out. "Not Evan."

"But Evan is part of me. And when his feet are fixed—"

"He doesn't have a broken carburetor, Anne."

"You know what I mean. I just want to show him what I've accomplished in my life—"

"So send him one of your tables," he says, dumping the empty bowl in the sink before turning to face her. "I don't care if you take Evan out West to see his grandfather. It's your intention that troubles me."

"What exactly does that mean?"

"It feels like you're after some kind of redemption."

The lamb is sizzling on the grill and oil is splattering everywhere. The smell of mint and browning meat fills the kitchen. Elie is right. This *is* about redemption. She's just not sure if it's her own she's after or her father's.

"What about your brother?" she asks. "Don't you ever want to go back to Beirut and look for him?"

"Ziad is dead," he says. "I'd be a fool not to think so."

"But you don't know for sure."

"I suppose I don't. And yet I choose to accept that he's gone and that gives me peace. I never wanted to live my life hanging on to shreds of hope. That would have been desperate and obsessive. It could have ruined my life."

"Yet, what *if*—"

He grabs hold of both her shoulders and turns her toward him. "I don't play those games," he says. "I've got all I need right now, at this moment. No one, not even my brother, could make my life any more complete."

"What about your B.C. ten-dollar gold coin?" she reminds him triumphantly.

A slow smile spreads across his lips. "It's not the same," he says weakly.

"Isn't it? I mean, acquiring it would bring closure, wouldn't it? And a certain amount of fulfillment. And victory. And *redemption*."

"My collecting coins and your searching for the father who abandoned you is hardly the same thing."

"I think it *is* similar," she argues. "We're doing it for the same reason."

"Why?"

"Why does anyone chase after something that's virtually unattainable?"

I remember we used to have these picnics by the lake," she remarks offhandedly. They're finishing off a bottle of wine. There's a light snowfall outside—the first of the season—and she's a little drunk. There's a feeling inside her that closely resembles happiness; an awareness of this being a flawless moment. It's not one thing or another, but all of it together: the wine, the snow, the lamb in her belly, her husband, Schubert on the stereo, her boy asleep upstairs, her hopes and plans for the future.

Elie is gazing contentedly out the picture window that he designed. She wonders if he feels the way she does, sitting here like this. "Who?" he asks. "Who had picnics by the lake?"

"My mother and I, and some of the other women and kids who lived with us. In the springtime the whole valley would get inundated with tundra swans. We used to feed them. There were so many . . ."

"Children or swans?"

"Both."

"What about your father?"

"I can't get a sense of him," she admits. "His name was Tobias. My mother called him Toby. He had a beard. He was tall. At least he seemed tall to me. He wore suspenders."

Elie reaches across the table and starts circling her knuckles with his fingertip. "Why all this now?" he asks her.

"What?"

"This nostalgia."

"I guess because I'm a mother now. I look at Evan and he makes me want to know more about who I am and where I come from. He makes me wish I had more of a connection to my roots. What can I pass on to him if I've got nothing? There's a gaping hole in my family tree."

Elie refills her wine. "Does that really matter as long as he's got two parents who love him?"

"I guess it matters to me."

Five

*T*he Hospital for Sick Childrens' surgery department is as well-designed and pleasant as it can be under the circumstances, but all the flowers, paintings and ambient lighting in the world don't make sending your baby into surgery any easier.

Anne and Elie took the pre-admission tour last week so they know the drill. The admitting room is bright red with furniture that looks like it's from Ikea. The secretary is sitting at the front desk. She greets them warmly. A big smile, tickling Evan's chin, handing them papers to sign before they hand over their son. They sit on a couch while the nurse checks Evan's blood pressure and changes him into blue hospital pajamas. Anne can hear him wailing from the other room and it makes her cry. Does he think she's abandoned him? She wonders miserably if six months is old enough to start building resentment toward your parents.

They're taken into the pre-op room, which is sunshine yellow and full of toys. Evan wants no part of them. He knows this is no ordinary playroom; that whenever his parents bring him to this place he will be handled by strangers in white coats who make him suffer. The wooden horse and the Fisher-Price farm don't fool him. He's screaming and squirming in Anne's lap. Her heart is racing. She keeps looking at the two big doors to her right, the ones that lead into the operating room. Suddenly Dr. Hotz and the anesthetist burst through them and she knows they're coming for her baby.

She gets a plummeting sensation from her collarbone down to her abdomen. Evan's face is purplish red. He is inconsolable.

"I'm going to put Evan to sleep with gas," the anesthetist is saying. "And then a breathing tube will be put down his throat and we'll start an IV—"

She can hear the doctor's reassurances as he takes Evan from her arms, but his words pass through her. She wants to tell him to be careful, but nothing comes out of her mouth. She smothers Evan's warm, damp cheeks with kisses. Elie does the same. And then their baby is taken from them.

They know from the pre-admission tour that they're supposed to wait in the parents' waiting room for the next two and a half hours. It's a relatively calming room, full of amber lighting and plants and artwork on the walls, with a maze of couches where other tense, anxious parents are trying to pass the time without going crazy. The usual outdated magazines are provided—*Newsweek, People, Time.* As though any of those could keep her mind off Evan's operation.

She tries not to look at the other parents. The fear and tension she sees carved into their faces just exacerbate hers. She keeps her head low, her eyes glued to her watch. It's nine thirty-three. She didn't even bring a book, knowing she wouldn't be able to concentrate.

Elie's brought a pile of magazines from home—*The Numismatic News, The Numismatist, Numismatica!*

Men are like that. They can escape.

"Do you think this will work?" she asks Elie.

"What?"

"The operation. I mean, do you really think they can correct his feet?"

"Of course."

"I don't want him to be a misfit."

"He won't be a misfit."

"I went on the Internet last night and there was a picture of this nine-year-old boy who'd had the same operation as Evan when he was a baby. His calves were underdeveloped and he was bow-legged and pigeon-toed. The kids in his class teased him because he ran funny."

"Anne, why do you do this to yourself?"

"I was doing research."

"Haven't you read plenty of stories about kids who turned out just fine and were perfectly normal after the surgery?"

"But maybe Evan won't be."

Elie sighs. "Let's just wait and see," he says wearily.

Nine forty-seven.

*I*t took her sixteen months to get pregnant with Evan. Around the eighth or ninth month she started bargaining with the fertility gods. *Let me get pregnant and I'll be the best damn mother in the world; give me a child and I'll never let him suffer.* Obviously her pleas were too lofty, arrogant. Yet throughout her pregnancy she believed vehemently that she would yield that sort of power—the power to shield Evan from humiliation, alienation, torment. She naively thought she could at least fill him up with enough love and self-esteem and confidence to see him through life relatively unscathed. Her plan had not allowed for any sort of physical deformity. She never would have foreseen something like club feet.

Elie gets irritated with her for obsessing over it, but she just wants her son to have a fair shot. She wants him to get out of the gate alongside the rest of the pack, walking and running with two straight feet.

"Holy shit," Elie gasps.

"What?"

"The 1913 Liberty Head nickel just sold for *four million dollars*."

"How can you concentrate on that?" she asks irritably.

It's nine fifty-three.

She roams the corridors, the private waiting rooms, the kitchen. She wanders out to the balcony and peers down at the hospital's atrium. It looks like a big modern shopping mall. They work hard at making you forget why you're here.

"Anne?"

She turns and there's Sharon. They embrace.

"You didn't have to drive in from Peterborough," Anne says, pulling away.

"I knew you'd say that."

She hasn't seen Sharon in at least two years. They've been friends since elementary school. They met in fourth grade and have kept up all these years. The relationship amounts to a cursory phone call every few months and a card at Christmas, but there's a bond between them that neither has been able to relinquish. Their friendship still has a faint pulse, which is better than nothing.

"You look good," Anne tells her. Sharon is still heavy, but her height offsets the extra weight and she pulls it off. Her legs are long, which helps. "You're a redhead now."

"Bruce likes it," Sharon says modestly, fluffing it.

She takes Anne's hand and they continue strolling along the corridor. "Is your mother here?" she asks.

"I told her not to come. I figured if she wasn't here it would minimize the gravity."

"You don't have to do this alone," Sharon assures her.

"I have a support group."

"That's not what I mean."

Anne knows she means friends. Other women. A girls' night out to get her mind off things. "I just haven't been up to it," she confesses. "I haven't felt like doing anything or seeing anyone since I had Evan."

"That's your hormones," Sharon chirps. "I had the same thing with Emma and then it was really bad after the twins."

"It's the club feet, Sharon. It's his *feet*."

Sharon stops walking and turns to Anne with a stern look. "You should be grateful it's just his feet," she says firmly. "It could be a lot worse. There's a woman on my street whose daughter has—"

Anne tunes her out. This is precisely why she hasn't felt like seeing anyone. Sharon has three healthy children with all their limbs intact. How could she possibly understand? She shouldn't have called to tell her about Evan's operation. Now she has to act chipper and brave today. She has to be defensive.

They wander back into the waiting room, making small talk to pass the time. Sharon tells Anne she's had a short story published in the *Peterborough Review* and that now she's working on a collection of poetry. Emma has just learned to read but she thinks the twins have A.D.D. Bruce has a hernia.

"I read about you in *Style at Home*," she goes on. "Your tables are really hot. You're in all the magazines."

Anne smiles distractedly, feeling mildly grateful and mildly irritated by Sharon's incessant chatter.

Finally, at about noon, a volunteer comes out to tell them the surgery is over and that the doctor will be out shortly.

"Is he okay?" (What she means is, *Is he alive?*)

"The doctor will explain everything to you."

And then Dr. Hotz is there, beaming at them. "It went beautifully," he says. "Better than expected. I was able to correct the foot with a heel cord release."

"How soon can we see him?"

"In a few minutes. He's being transferred to a private room. You can go in and wait for him there." She wants to collapse with relief. She leans against Elie for support. Sharon is squeezing her hand and Anne is glad she's there.

"Evan's going to be very groggy and cranky," Dr. Hotz says. "He may have a fever. I gave him a caudal block for the pain and I've split his cast to allow for swelling—"

Anne isn't listening. All she can think about is getting to Evan's room and hugging her baby.

"I'll be back in the morning to check on him and hopefully to release him," Dr. Hotz says.

"Thank you." *Thank you thank you thank you.*

Sharon hugs her. "I'm going to head back," she says. "I've got a thing at my church . . ."

Anne remembers now why she hasn't been able to let her go. She's a good person. She isn't catty or vindictive; there's never an agenda. They have nothing in common except for their long history, but her loyalty is uplifting. Anne has always had trouble trusting other women—it's the competitiveness that puts her off—but there's nothing like the friendship of a good woman who has nothing to prove.

Anne watches her leave, knowing it will be months before they speak again and possibly years before they see each other but reassured by the fact that she's one of those people in her life who'll always be there.

The volunteer comes back and takes them to a private room to wait for Evan. There's a TV, which will help them pass the night, and a green couch where she'll be able to sleep. She calls her mother to tell her it's over and Jean promises to be there within the hour. Then the nurse comes in with her groggy baby slumped over her shoulder.

"You might want to hold him for a while," she says. "Whenever we lay him down, he cries."

She hands him to Anne and he's never felt so good in her arms. His lids are droopy but he's fighting to stay awake. He keeps rubbing his eyes and burying his face in his fists. He's warm, radiating heat. She sits down with him and presses her cheek against the top of his head. His soft milkweed hair tickles her nostrils. Elie sits down beside them and takes Evan's tiny hand in his. "Hey, Stinker," he says.

The night is long and harrowing. The nurse gives Evan Tylenol with codeine every four hours, but he's in terrible pain. Elie and Anne take turns walking with him up and down the hall and then they sit with him in front of the TV. The noise briefly distracts him, but not for long. She rocks him while singing "Tiny Dancer." He loves Elton John. Elie falls asleep instead.

The sound of Evan whimpering in her arms causes something physical inside her, like a clamp tightening around her heart. She doesn't know how much more of his pain she can handle.

Six

*D*eclan Gray arrives late to the meeting and noisily drags his chair into the circle. He inserts it next to Anne's, disrupting her train of thought just as she's about to speak. She turns to scowl at him, but his gorgeousness catches her off guard. Her indignation melts away and it's as though the church basement is suddenly infused with life. Nothing comes out of her mouth.

The rest of them in the circle are watching her expectantly. She struggles to refocus. "Evan had his operation," she stammers, pulling herself back to the group. "It was tough, but the past week has been even worse—"

This is why Anne keeps coming back to the meeting—to unload her grievances in a place where, for the most part, people will listen to her. Compassion is like a panacea for her pain. It washes over her and soothes.

Which is not to say that everyone in the circle is compassionate. She's become an expert at picking out the ones who aren't listening. There's a look people in support groups get when they're pretending to listen but their thoughts are really elsewhere. She calls it the glazed-ham look.

"It's been absolute hell," she continues. "He's not eating or sleeping. He'll sleep for an hour at most and then he's restless and fussy all through the night. I'm completely sleep-deprived. And we have to start all over again next week when they operate on the other foot—"

Her voice breaks. She sobs into the sleeve of her sweater, unable to remember the last restful sleep she had. She's hovering between delirium and hopelessness. "I want this all to be over," she confesses. "I want to sleep. Just want to sleep through the night—"

She sees the others nodding. A hand comes out of nowhere and wraps itself around hers. Her head feels so heavy.

"Thanks for listening," she manages.

"Thanks for sharing, Anne."

After an appropriate pause, the new woman, Courtney, clears her throat and says her name. She's wearing a cream-colored turtleneck and cream wool pants tonight, and with her fair hair and pale skin she reminds Anne of a vanilla wafer. "Angelica's doctor says the casting is working," she informs the group. "I guess because her club foot isn't so severe and it's also unilateral, the doctor doesn't think she'll need surgery . . ." Her voice is apologetic as she bats her eyes in Anne's direction. "It's such a relief . . ."

Vanilla Wafer's good fortune engulfs Anne with anxiety. That's the problem with these support groups. When someone who's supposed to be commiserating with you suddenly drops a good news bombshell into the circle it's like a thundershower at a picnic. It completely douses the mood; it also shatters the solidarity.

As far as Anne is concerned, sharing good news at a support group is tantamount to gloating. It rarely brings her hope; if anything, it arouses panic. She *wants* to be happy for others—she really does—but her own fears about Evan make her more frugal than she'd like to be.

They make her heart clench and tighten in a way that fills her with remorse.

At the break Anne slips outside to get some air, hoping it will keep her awake through the rest of the meeting. (She swears she did not see Declan Gray go outside first, nor did she follow him out.)

He lights a cigarette. "Are you a smoker too?" he asks her.

"No. Just trying to stay awake." She shoves her freezing hands inside her pockets and sways from side to side to keep warm.

He exhales a cloud of smoke which, mixed with his frozen breath, hovers thickly in front of his mouth and obscures part of his face.

"Aren't you cold?" she asks him. He's got on a charcoal-gray wool turtleneck with the sleeves pushed up. That's how she notices his forearms, which are her weakness. She loves the way a man's veins snake from wrist to elbow, bulging when they're lifting something heavy. She loves the golden hair of a male forearm and even better if it's suntanned. And she loves its width, the way it promises strength. Forearms are for holding other men in headlocks during a bar fight. Sexy.

She'd put him in his early thirties. He's got long lashes and about three days' growth of beard. He's also got short, spiky dark hair, not quite a crew-cut—not as square—but pretty close to the army style she's always liked.

"You get used to the cold when you're a smoker," he says. "Besides, it's too hot in there."

"I wish they'd find another venue for these support

groups," she complains. "Why are they always in church basements?"

He laughs. A look passes between them—a giddy, awkward look that signifies a budding flirtation. Her heart does a high-dive inside her chest. The physical attraction inundates her body like a flash flood, suddenly turning her benign attraction into something more substantial and consuming.

Her last "innocent flirtation"—(as she refers to them)—was with the UPS delivery guy at her studio. He reeked of cigarettes and had chewed black fingernails, but what a set of forearms, especially when he hoisted her tables onto his dolly.

Declan flicks an ash and she notices a tattoo on his inner forearm. *Creideamh,* in block letters. It's not recent either; she can tell by the way the ink has faded and turned blue. *Early nineties,* she thinks. They all did it.

"Your husband never comes with you," he remarks.

"He hates support groups. He's not the type."

"Meaning?"

"He's not the type of guy who will ever ask for help. He hates to be vulnerable, especially in public. He thinks it's weak."

"Does he think you're weak?"

"Yes."

He takes a drag of his cigarette and then flicks the ash again.

"What's Creideamh?" she asks, pointing to his tattoo.

"It's embarrassing," he says. And then, after a pause, "I guess Margaret must think *I'm* weak."

"Margaret's your wife?"

He nods. "Obviously, she doesn't come here either," he tells her. "She doesn't need it though."

"Why not?" Anne asks, curious.

"Margaret's a saint. She hardly thinks of Sean's club feet as a challenge. She *handles* it, you know what I mean? Like it's a breeze for her. The castings, the soakings, the pressure to put him through surgery. She never complains. She's all, 'We're lucky it's not Down's syndrome.' You know? Like that."

"I wish *I* was handling it better," she admits, remembering her whiny outburst back in the circle. (She must remember next time to make her sharing less honest and more noble.)

"Margaret's a hero," he says. "But sometimes I wish she'd just . . . I don't know . . . cry or something. Or get angry. Or feel sorry for herself. Then *I* wouldn't feel so bad."

He cuts Anne another look and then casts his eyes down at the ground. He has a sublime face. Lips you want to smear your mouth against, haunted eyes, like cloudy pools of mischief or pain, or both.

"I was no great athlete," he confides. "But a boy should do sports. I look at Sean sometimes and I think of that scene in *Forrest Gump*. You know, the one where he's running—"

"In those goddamn leg braces!"

They're both laughing again and for the moment her mood feels lighter, more hopeful. Her exhaustion, Evan's looming operation, the church basement—none of it feels as bleak as it did before she stood here laughing with him.

"Run, Forrest, run!" he says.

When their laughter peters out he stubs his cigarette under the heel of his black boot. He shivers and pulls his sleeves down. He smiles at her, which sends a shiver from the base of her spine directly into her skull, and then he turns and goes back inside.

Seven

"So what was in that letter from your sister?" she asks her mother.

Jean looks up with a blank expression.

"I meant to ask you about it before Evan had his operation, and then I forgot."

"Can I at least order first?" Jean says, sounding put out. She calls the waitress over and a busty girl with rosy cheeks and big blue eyes makes her way through the lunch crowd to their booth at the back.

They're at the Sweet Gallery on Mount Pleasant, a favorite of Jean's. She claims she comes for the home-made Hungarian goulash, but she's never left without a box of pastries. The lunch crowd here consists mainly of people in their eighties and nineties, partly because it's reasonably priced, home-cooked food, but also because it's situated across the street from a senior citizens' home.

Jean orders a goulash soup, an omelette and a mille-feuille. "And bring me a cup of coffee, Anna. Please."

Anne orders a tuna sandwich on rye.

"I wish I'd named you Anna instead of Anne," Jean remarks, gazing at the back of the waitress. "It has more flair." She spreads her paper napkin across her lap. She's wearing a black Roots sweatsuit. "Who's looking after Evan today?"

"He's at home with his father," Anne says. "Elie always has him Sunday."

"He didn't last Sunday. I called and got the babysitter—"

"Elie had an auction last weekend. I told you."

She yawns, sips her water. Finally, she says, "The letter was just to tell me she's left."

"Left Harmony?"

"Apparently."

"Why?"

"I guess for the same reason I did."

"I mean why *now*?"

"How should I know?"

"Didn't she say in the letter?"

"Not really."

"Stop being so damn cryptic," Anne snaps.

"I'm not being cryptic, Anne. You're looking for drama where there is none."

"Did she live with us?" she asks, increasingly frustrated. "In one of the houses on our orchard?"

"No."

"She must be pretty old. Isn't it a bit late for her to start a new life in Edmonton?"

"It's never too late to make a new beginning," Jean says hotly. "Besides, she's younger than me by a couple of years."

"Why does she want you to know she's left? You haven't spoken in years."

The food arrives just before she answers and they suspend their conversation so that Jean can take a few gulps of her goulash soup. Anne watches her mother eat; she has no interest in her sandwich.

"I don't know," she resumes. "I guess she got to the same place I'd got to and wanted me to know it."

"Does she want to see you?"

"She didn't mention anything like that."

"Do you want to see her?" Anne asks, leaning forward. Her question is more of a plea for Jean to say something substantial.

"I haven't thought about it," she says.

"I don't believe you."

"She reminds me of a life I've worked very hard to forget."

"What was so bad about it? I don't remember it being so bad."

"That's because I got you out in time."

"I know you got married young, but I could have made a different choice with my life. Was it really that bad for women?"

She smiles obliquely. She finishes her soup and then starts on the omelette.

"Was it a cult?" Anne asks her. "Is that it?"

Jean laughs dismissively.

"Didn't we leave because my father cheated on you with one of the commune women?"

Jean lets out a noise—either a laugh or a choke, Anne isn't sure. She looks up from her omelette. Her expression is pure bafflement. "Where'd you get that?" she wants to know.

"From my head. I deduced it."

"You deduced wrong."

"I think he must have pissed you off or hurt you or something."

Jean continues to eat her omelette. With a mouthful of egg, she says, "We never talk about this."

"You had to figure that eventually I'd want to know. Or need to know."

"You *do* know everything," she says. "We left Harmony so that I could give you a better life than what lay ahead for you in that backward community. That's all there is to it."

"That's all?"

"I wanted you to have an education and a career and to choose your own . . ."

Her voice trails off. She wipes her mouth with her napkin. She seems suddenly flustered.

"Choose my own what?"

"Path."

"That's not what you were going to say."

"Path," she says again.

Anne studies her mother's expression carefully, searching for cracks in her cool, noncommittal facade. Beneath her surface is an undercurrent of panic. Anne can feel it vibrating between them.

"Does Polly have children?" she asks.

"She was pregnant with her first when we left."

"Can I read her letter?"

"I threw it away already. Anne, I don't want anything to do with that place or those people—"

"Those people are your family. Polly's not even there anymore. She seems to be reaching out . . ."

"She *is* still there, up here." She touches her head. "In my memory, she'll always be there. *It's* still there, too, unchanged. It's exactly as it always was."

The waitress brings Jean's pastry to the table and refills her coffee. "Do you want an extra fork?" she asks Anne.

She shakes her head and says thank you. The waitress smiles. She's flushed and slightly out of breath from the lunch rush.

Jean presses her fork down into the mille-feuille. The yellow custard squirts out the sides as she saws through the layers of pastry. She leans into the table and shovels a piece into her mouth. A flake sticks to her cheek. Looking at her with that pastry flake on her face makes Anne regret bullying her into talking about her past. It makes Anne feel sorry for her, which almost never happens. She's only ever felt sorry for her maybe a handful of times in her whole life.

Once when she was about fourteen she came downstairs in the middle of the night and there was her mother sitting at the kitchen table with her head buried in her hands. She was sobbing. Anne was startled. She stood in the doorway watching her, not knowing what to do. She'd never seen her mother cry before. Jean wasn't that type of mother— she hated to expose Anne to her pain. Even back then Anne understood that and honored her by withholding pity.

When Jean finally realized that Anne was standing behind her she turned to face her. Her bright blue mascara had run down either side of her face in two straight lines. "I'm lonely," she blurted, which surprised Anne even more. "And I'm tired and stressed and overworked—"

"Did something happen today?"

Usually when she was upset it meant something bad had happened at work. Either Sheldon had berated her for something or she'd been overlooked for her work on some task. She seldom got the credit she deserved.

"No," she said. "Nothing happened today. It's just hard."

"What is?"

"This life." She looked at Anne then, as though she wasn't sure of something, and said, "Maybe we had it easier back home."

Back home meant Harmony. It was years and years before she stopped referring to it as home. "Then why did we leave?" Anne asked her, knowing she'd get the standard answer.

Jean said, "So you could have choices."

Her voice sounded weary and forlorn. The bright blue streaks of mascara were distracting and Anne couldn't help feeling sorry for her. "Do you want to go back?" she asked her mother. She was only fourteen and didn't have that much vested in Toronto.

"We can't go back," Jean said. There was something ominous in the way she said it. "We can never go back."

Eight

Anne wakes up disoriented, gripped with panic. She squints at the alarm clock and then checks to make sure the baby monitor is on. Three thirty in the morning and not a sound from Evan's room since she put him down at eight. She flings her legs out from under the duvet and, unable to locate her robe in the dark, stumbles naked down the hall to Evan's room. Her heart is pounding in her throat as she rushes to his crib. She's not even sure what she's going to find but she's filled with dread and guilt. He hasn't slept this long since the operation.

She peers into the crib and there he is, flat on his back with his two casts spread-eagle and his arms flung out on either side of him. His little face is turned to the side and buried in the floppy ear of his stuffed doggie. She gently lays her hand on his tummy to check for breathing. And there it is: the soothing rise and fall of his rib cage beneath her palm. Her whole body sags with relief. Normally she'd lean over the rail and kiss him, but she doesn't dare wake him from his longest night's sleep in weeks. Instead, she tiptoes quietly out of the room, easing the door closed behind her.

She heads back to the bedroom, dying to crawl under the covers and return to what had been a very deep sleep. Elie's body is warm and she curls up against him, pressing her face into his back. She waits. She snuggles in closer, eagerly anticipating unconsciousness. She waits some more. Thoughts weave in and out her brain. She tries to discard them before they seize hold of her, but it's no use. The more she tries to sleep, the less attainable it is.

Thoughts keep coming, one after another, each one waking her just a little more, carrying her further and further away from her dreams. *There were too many onions in Elie's osso buco tonight.* She rolls over onto her other side. Then onto her back. *Evan's been sucking on his doggie's ear so long it's starting to stink. She'll have to wash it.* Flat on her stomach. Squirming, tossing, all to no avail. *She has to do a load of laundry anyway or her best-fitting jeans won't be ready for the support group meeting tomorrow night. She'll wash them with Evan's dog. When Declan sees her in those jeans* . . . She checks the clock and then turns it away from her. She burps, which leaves an onion taste in her mouth. *She didn't call her mother back this afternoon. She did it on purpose. She's irritated with her for being so vague and dismissive about the letter from Polly. Jean lives in denial and she expects Anne to live there with her. Most of Anne's past is really just her mother's version of it anyway—*

Everything Anne knows about how they left Harmony was told to her by her mother. She knows that one of the women in town drove them to Spokane, Washington, in a pickup truck, and that from there they took a train to Chicago, then another train to Buffalo, and finally another one to Toronto. Jean says the whole trip took nearly three days. It was 1979 and Jean had brought lots of cherries and dozens of peanut butter and apple sandwiches, which were wrapped in wax paper. Maybe Anne doesn't remember any of that and just thinks she does because it's become part of their folklore; the mythical peanut butter and apple sandwiches in wax paper.

She does remember the exact moment they came out of Union Station and stepped onto Front Street in downtown Toronto. It was April and raining. She remembers looking up and gasping. She'd never seen a skyscraper before. She remembers the way they towered above her, gray and erect. She remembers all the fancy-dressed people coming and going, in and out of the buildings, zigzagging across the street. They moved with such purpose, with their heads down, never looking at anyone else. Everyone seemed to be in a rush. No one smiled or said hello. Not like in Harmony, where they all knew each other.

Her overall impression of Toronto was that it was a gray place—the concrete buildings, the trench coats people wore, the slick roads, the sky. Harmony had been green and lush.

There was a hot dog vendor on the sidewalk in front of the train station and people were lining up in the rain to buy hot dogs. Across the street from where they stood there was a hotel. It was like a castle. Anne was just learning to read and she read the word *Royal* above the front entrance. Her mother said, "Royal York Hotel." It was also gray.

Big shiny cars splattered water at them as they sped past. Taxicabs lined the road by the station. All of this was new to her, horrifying and incredible. Nothing was familiar or safe. What about grass? Where was the grass? And where was her mother going to find a job picking apples, which, she knew, was just about the only thing her mother knew how to do?

Jean was holding her hand on the sidewalk. Anne looked up at her mother for reassurance. Up until then she hadn't been paying much attention to her mother's reaction; she'd been too consumed with her observations, too lost and overwhelmed with her own childish concerns. She felt like crying, but when she noticed the look on her mother's face she made an effort to act brave. Jean was also taking in their surroundings, her eyes darting all over the place. She was trying not to show her panic, but Anne wasn't fooled. She was only five, but she knew intuitively that her mother was as petrified and disoriented as she was. Jean was a grown woman—thirty-one years old—and had never left her small town. All this was new to her too, and she also had Anne to take care of.

It was damp and Anne was sleepy. "Where are we going?" she asked her mother. She wanted to go home, back to Harmony where it was peaceful and familiar; back to the bed she'd shared with girls whose names were still in her head at the time.

She'll never forget what her mother did then. She bought them each a hot dog and loaded them up with mustard and sauerkraut, trying to make them as filling and substantial as possible. Then she went over to a phone booth and ripped out a handful of pages from the Yellow Pages. The torn pages contained all the information they needed to find a hotel. She also bought a map of the city and a newspaper. They went back inside the train station to get out of the rain and while Anne dozed beside her on a bench she must have found a hostel, located it on her map of Toronto and charted their course, because when Anne woke up her mother knew exactly where they had to go. It was a short walk and she'd already called ahead to find out the price and make sure there was room. She led them there confidently, without getting lost. Anne was starting to feel much better about things.

Their first home in Toronto was in an ugly 1960s apartment building downtown. The facade was turquoise, like Crest toothpaste. They had to take an elevator to their apartment on the sixth floor, which, having never ridden in an elevator before, frightened Anne to tears. Their windows faced the back alley, which was always full of garbage and cats. Her mother complained that the street was overrun with prostitutes at night. She said they crawled out of the woodwork after dark.

At first she paid the rent with the fruit-stand money she'd secretly been stashing away for two years. (Anne later figured out that's how long she'd been plotting their escape from Harmony.) Then she got two jobs. She did phone sales at night, which allowed her to stay home with Anne. During the day, while Anne was in school, she waitressed at the Coffee Mill in Yorkville. It was a cozy sandwich place owned by a Hungarian couple. She kept her job there until she was hired full-time at Keilty Perlmutter Solway & Stein.

By the time Anne was in second grade her mother had saved enough money to pay for her secretary school and a new place for them to live, in the home she now owns. At first she rented it for a reasonable amount, but when it came up for sale years later, she bought it.

The most startling thing about their new life in Toronto wasn't Jean's resourcefulness or courage or unwavering resolve in establishing it, but how lonely it was. There they were in this giant, overcrowded city but they were virtually alone. Anne remembers asking her on that first day who they were going to live with.

Her answer surprised Anne. "Just us," she said.

Their new living arrangement couldn't have been more different from the one they'd left back home. Their old life had managed somehow to be much smaller and much fuller at the same time. Anne could hardly remember a lonely moment in their farmhouse in Harmony. Never did you walk into an empty room or have to eat supper by yourself. It was always warm and noisy and busy—women cooking, children playing, music coming from somewhere inside the house.

Her mother didn't cultivate relationships with anyone in Toronto—not with other women and certainly not with men. She made no friends, took no lovers, went on no dates. It was just the two of them, and most of the time Jean wasn't even there. Anne spent a lot of time with Mrs. Roberts, the next-door neighbor who babysat her. She was nice enough, but she used to sit in front of the TV almost the entire day. Anne remembers watching her from the hallway when *The Price Is Right* was on. She'd yell at the TV, "Bid lower! Bid lower, you moron!" Like that. Anne thought it was hilarious, but Mrs. Roberts wasn't much of a playmate.

Her mother assures her she wasn't a lonely kid. "You were perfectly happy alone," Jean likes to say. "You preferred it."

Anne still doesn't know if Jean was shielding *her* from people, or protecting herself. Either way, when it came time for socializing in school, Anne was shy and self-conscious. She struggled to blend in.

Her only friend was Sharon. Sharon was plain and not very popular back then, but she was easy to be with and Anne didn't have to extend herself too much. Sharon didn't frighten Anne the way other girls did. In fact, she liked Anne in spite of her shyness and her bad consignment-shop clothes. Sharon was considered an outcast because she was fat. She also wore Wallabees. Her last name was Mack and the kids at school used to call her Big Mac. They did terrible things to her. Once they slipped an unwrapped Big Mac on her chair and she inadvertently sat on it. There was special sauce and shredded lettuce on her bum, but she wouldn't leave the classroom to clean herself up.

Anne's mother was fond of Sharon. She seemed relieved that Anne had managed to find the one unpopular friend who wouldn't lead her astray, especially in a big city like Toronto. Jean never said so, but coming from a sheltered place like Harmony, she must have been apprehensive about the type of trouble Anne could get into in a big city. Instead, Sharon and Anne spent most of their time in her room, writing and doodling in their journals. Anne's had Frida Kahlo on the cover. Inside, the pages were brimming with her angst and awkwardness, as well as her burgeoning artistic talent. The most danger she ever got into was when she started experimenting with collage and cut up her mother's special medical encyclopedias.

Anne still wonders if her mother was ever happy after they left Harmony; if she actually liked her job at the law firm, if she missed being surrounded by people, if she wanted a man in her life. If any of that even mattered to her.

She's never said so. She isn't the type. They moved to Toronto and started a new life because it was something that had to be done for Anne's well-being. Jean had a modest mandate for her daughter: she was to get an education and have choices. She was to have an ordinary life.

While other mothers held their daughters to higher aspirations—to shine or to be beautiful or to be astonishing—Jean's ambitions for Anne weren't nearly that extravagant. She just had to blend in and go to school and be relatively normal. Everything her mother did was to that end.

But who the hell knows what's normal? A thirty-one-year-old hermit from the Kootenays? A five-year-old kid with only one friend? It was all left to Anne's interpretation.

*T*he baby monitor suddenly comes to life and Evan's wailing shatters the silence in the bedroom. Elie shifts around but doesn't wake up. Anne climbs back out of bed and hurries to her son. She can tell by his cries that he's in pain. The feet again. The damned club feet.

Nine

"Why did you get us into this?" Elie asks. He's lying on the bed in a towel. The babysitter is already here.

"You're always telling me I should get out more and try to be social—"

"*You*. Not *us*."

"They're very nice. You'll like them."

"You know I hate eating at other people's houses."

She goes over to the bed and yanks the towel off him. "Get dressed," she says. "You've known about this for over a week. We had plenty of time to cancel before tonight and now it's too late."

"I was sure you'd cancel without me having to tell you to," he remarks, sliding off the bed. "You always cancel."

"We're late."

"What if she cooks with garlic powder?"

"You'll live."

He puts on his boxer shorts and pants. "One of the reasons I like being married to you is that you never arrange dinners with other couples. What came over you? And if I have to spend the whole night talking about fucking club feet—"

"Stop already. Their son's been through everything Evan is going through and I thought it would be a good opportunity for us to see how his feet turned out."

"We're going to their house for dinner so you can see the kid's *feet*?"

"What do you want me to tell you, Elie? They invited us for this 'pre-holiday' supper, and I accepted."

"Pre-holiday supper?" he moans.

"That's what she called it."

He shakes his head petulantly. "You could have just gone for a play date with her," he mutters.

He's right. She could have, but part of her wanted to drag Elie into her club foot world. She doesn't nag him anymore about coming to the support group meetings with her, but she can still try to inflict it on him just a little bit.

"How does this look?" she asks.

"Aren't leather pants a bit much for sitting around someone's living room discussing club feet?"

"Maybe they'll be an interesting couple. Maybe we'll really connect with them."

"Now we have to 'connect' with them? Aren't you aiming a little high?"

"I'm just trying to keep an open mind."

"Since when?" he snubs, reluctantly putting on his clothes.

"Do I look good?" she asks him again. She knows it's just supper in the neighborhood, but she rarely gets out. The opportunity to put on leather pants and mascara doesn't present itself very often these days.

"Of course you look good," he says.

"If you weren't married to me, would you think I was attractive?"

"Would I know your personality?"

She has to laugh; he's witty, even if it is at her expense. "Could you at least try to be less morose and biting tonight? Please?"

"That's like asking me to be less Lebanese. It's who I am."

She turns away from the mirror and inspects his outfit. It's impeccable—a crisp white shirt, untucked, with just the right amount of buttons open; loose black gabardine pants; shiny Hugo Boss boots. His hair is wet and long. He hasn't put any greasy products in it yet and it looks pretty good. She can even live with the beard. She thinks he'll make a nice impression on Tami.

"Is she good looking?" he asks.

"Who?"

"The wife."

"I don't think you'll think so."

"Is the husband attractive?"

"Darren? No. God, no. He's average. Anyway, it's not a swinging party. Does it matter if they're attractive?"

"It usually does to you."

"What's that supposed to mean?"

"I've observed you at social gatherings," he says matter-of-factly. "You always flirt. You're not comfortable with women, but you're fine as soon as you pick a new intrigue."

"A new intrigue?" she scoffs, looking away guiltily. "You make me sound like a Desperate Housewife."

Elie kisses her on the mouth. She shoves him off.

"I know it's harmless," he laughs. "It's just what you do."

*D*ownstairs, the babysitter is waiting for them in the kitchen. Her name is Nadine and she lives three doors down. She's a bookish girl of about sixteen, thin with no breasts. She has bright, clear brown eyes and some pimples on her forehead. She hasn't blossomed yet, so Anne figures she doesn't have boyfriends. There was a flyer advertising her babysitting services taped to the telephone pole in front of their house. *I am trustworthy and love children. I'm trained in first aid and have lots of experience.*

Anne's given her a tour of the essentials—the junk food pantry, the phone, the TV remote controls—and explained to her about Evan's feet. In case of any bloodcurdling wailing, she is to call Anne's cell phone immediately.

"Don't worry, Mrs. Mahroum," Nadine says. "I've babysat special-needs children before."

"Special needs?" Anne echoes, wounded. "Evan isn't a special-needs child. It's just club feet."

"I didn't mean—"

Anne shakes her head. "It's okay," she says. But she feels bruised wondering if that's how people perceive her baby.

*D*arren and Tami live a few blocks away. Their house is on Chatsworth Avenue, on the west side of Yonge (Elie and Anne are on the east side, in the coveted heart of Lawrence Park). Theirs is one of those cookie-cutter North Toronto houses built at the beginning of the century, with the red-brick exterior and the bay window; a house you'd call "charming" or "quaint," situated on a sliver of land.

They've got a wreath up on the front door already, surrounding a knocker shaped like a cross. Elie looks nervously at Anne. She grabs the cross and bangs.

There are awkward introductions in the vestibule. "This is my husband, Elie," Anne says, already regretting that she got them into this.

"Ely?"

"El*ee.*"

"Elie. How do you spell that?"

"E-l-i-e. It's Lebanese."

Tami and Darren smile encouragingly, as though to say "It's okay to be Middle Eastern!" But Anne can tell Elie's guard is already up.

They're given a tour of the humble home. It's exactly what Anne imagined for them: scuffed wood floors, taupe walls, a small fireplace in the living room, an unrenovated kitchen, three small bedrooms upstairs, no landing, one bathroom. It's a typical shabbily charming Toronto home. There are toys everywhere—lining the hallway, stacked in the dining room, the fancy living room, the kitchen—an open declaration that the house belongs to their son.

Anne worries that Elie will find them bland. Mild cheddar, he'll call them. Tami's dirty blond hair is cut short and practical, lacking any discernible style. She's got a pug nose and a warm, toothy smile. Darren is one of those Eddie Bauer chino-wearing guys who probably puts on a treasured Maple Leafs jersey during the playoffs. He's got a doughy, shapeless face and some thinning brown hair that seems to be clinging for dear life to his scalp. Like their house, they could both use a renovation—a little firming up, more style, sexier clothes. They're sensible and utilitarian, the type of people for whom having children initiates a sudden apathy toward the fundamentals of style and fashion, and probably a mandatory resignation to asexuality.

"Parker just went down," Tami whispers as they reach the top of the stairs. "There's a good chance he's still awake."

Anne peers inside the dark nursery, but it looks as though Little Parker—whom Anne has heard so much about in the support group meetings and whose feet she was dying to inspect tonight—is fast asleep, curled on his side in his crib.

"I'm sorry," Tami says. "But take a look under the blanket."

Anne creeps closer and lifts the soft chenille blanket off his legs, trying to get a decent look at his feet, hoping to see how they've turned out after two years of casting, operations and braces. It's too dark though and she can't see a thing.

She can hear Elie and Darren making small talk out in the hall. They're discussing how old the house is (a hundred years), the electrical wiring (recently redone at a prohibitive cost) and the storage space (limited), and already Anne is dreading what Elie will have to say about all this later on when they're back home. Especially since she didn't even get to see Parker's feet.

Tami takes Anne on a small tour of the rest of the upstairs—their bedroom and the bathroom. The only thing Anne notices in their room, aside from a massive chestnut-stained four-poster bed, is a Rogers video cassette of *The Klumps* on the matching chestnut dresser. "Very cozy," Anne says politely.

"Tami wanted to be in this neighborhood," Darren is saying to Elie when the women join them. "You have to sacrifice something to own a house here. It's a trade-off, right? But it's worth it for the community and the schools. We're around the corner from Robertson."

"Who?" Elie asks.

"John Ross Robertson," Darren says, startled. "It's one of the best public schools in the city. You live in the area, don't you?"

"On Dawlish. But Evan is only six months old," Elie says tightly. "We haven't enrolled him anywhere yet."

Anne glares at him. She doesn't want his bad attitude to expose them as misfits. For one night, she just wants to blend into the community! And yet a voice in her head is already screaming, *We don't belong! We don't belong!* Not even with other club foot parents.

"We moved here partly to be closer to Robertson," Tami says, and when Anne responds with a blank expression, a shadow of recrimination darkens Tami's eyes. "I mean, it's so convenient, right? Parker will be able to walk there," she goes on. "We won't have to worry about car-pooling."

Anne's worst fear by the time they sit down in the dining room is that Tami and Darren will say grace before dinner, or worse, make Elie say grace. If they thank the Good Lord for their blessings, Elie may flee. He's phobic about people who refer to God as the "Good Lord."

Darren puts on *The Greatest Power Ballads of the 80s & 90s*. "This is a great CD," he gushes. "Remember necking to 'Love Hurts' by Nazareth?"

"I don't think we had Nazareth in Lebanon," Elie responds helplessly.

Dinner is a great big bubbling lasagna. "I forgot to ask if you were vegetarians," Tami says apologetically, setting down the casserole dish. "So I made it half with meat and half with ricotta and vegetables. I put a sprig of basil on the vegetarian side."

Darren opens a bottle of red wine. No one says grace but they do make a toast to their "beautiful sons." The lasagna is delicious, made with real garlic. Anne's mood starts to lift as Elie offers up his plate for a second helping. And Tami's probably made something deliciously fattening for dessert. Old-fashioned triple-layer chocolate cake or strawberry-rhubarb pie.

"So did you have to pump before you came here?" Tami asks Anne. "You're still breast-feeding, right?"

"Um, no, I couldn't."

"Couldn't?"

"It didn't work. I didn't have enough milk."

Tami looks surprised. "What a shame," she says. "I breast-fed Parker right up till his second birthday."

"His *second* birthday?" Anne gasps, trying to suppress feelings of inferiority and unworthiness.

Darren pipes in, "Hon, does Anne know about the Lawrence Village Neighborhood Center?"

"We haven't talked about it," Tami says. "Anne, you must know about their programs?"

"I don't really . . . I mean, we haven't . . . with all Evan's medical stuff, we haven't really had time to think about social programs."

"I understand," Tami says, her tone steeped in compassion. "But you know, I found some of those classes to be a wonderful distraction. Parker does their music class and their reading class. We also did Fit-Mom classes and body movement . . . he loved them all. Frankly it was a relief to forget about his feet for an hour every day."

Anne smiles wanly and imagines herself sitting in a circle with a bunch of other moms, singing songs and clapping hands and doing "body movements." The idea of it fills her with dread and she wonders if this is what's expected of mothers nowadays.

"I'll look into it," she promises vaguely.

Tami and Darren smile at each other, pleased with themselves. "So what do you do, Elie?" Darren asks.

"I'm a numismatist."

Confused looks from both of them.

"Coins," Elie explains. "I deal in high-grade coins."

Anne can see it's on the tip of Darren's tongue to say, "That's a real job?" Most people react that way.

"He has a store on Bloor," she adds.

"That's fascinating. Coins . . . eh?"

"Mm." Elie looks bored.

"What do you do?" Anne asks Darren, knowing Elie won't.

"I'm a software engineer."

"At an accounting firm," Tami adds, as though that might somehow elevate him.

"Tami tells me you're an artist, Anne."

"Yes. I refurbish tables. And recently I started welding . . ."

"That is so cool," Tami interjects. "Eh, Darren? Just like *Flashdance*, remember? I wish I had an outlet like that. I'd love to see your work, Anne. Do you have a studio?"

"On Queen, near Spadina."

"Oh, you're right near the Pottery Barn. I *love* that store. I bought these plates there. And the funky lamp in the living room."

"I don't think there's a Pottery Barn down there—"

"And our sushi set!" Darren adds proudly. "We got our sushi set there, too."

"So when is Evan's second operation?" Tami asks.

"The beginning of January."

"Good luck," she says. "Parker's second operation was worse than the first one because the doctor decided not to give him a caudal block. It was a fiasco. He was screaming and screaming. It was gut-wrenching. The doctors had to give him morphine. Remember, Darren?"

"Just make sure Evan gets a caudal block or you'll live to regret it," Darren says. "Trust us."

"What about the swelling?" Anne asks. "Evan's swelling hasn't gone down since the first operation."

"Are you keeping his leg propped up? It's supposed to stay raised above his heart as much as possible."

"I am. Trying anyway."

"Your doctor will tell you what's going on when he changes the first cast. Parker was the same. He had all these sores from the cast rubbing the wrong way."

"How's Parker now?" Elie asks, and Anne is inspired by his sudden interest in joining the conversation. "What do we have to look forward to when Evan is two?"

"He's still in the AFOs. Those are the orthopedic braces. Parker hated them at first, but he was walking within a few days after he got them. And no more soaking casts off!"

Elie smiles as though this is good news for him, but he's never soaked a single cast in six months. He doesn't mention that though and neither does Anne. Tami and Darren would think they were archaic. They would make judgments. Surely Darren must have soaked his fair share of casts.

"Parker still wears his AFOs for the tibia torsion," she goes on. "But the main thing is he's walking. His feet still turn in and he refuses to walk without the brace, but, hey, he's *walking*."

Anne's heart plunges. Walking with leg braces at two years old is not a significant enough achievement to inspire optimism. She's hoping for much more than that. She's banking on Normal.

After the lasagna Tami brings out a hot, bubbling apple crisp. Everything about Tami bubbles. Darren gets up to change the CD. "Put something mellow on!" Tami calls out. "What about the Williams-Sonoma dinner classics?" She scoops a healthy pile of apple crisp onto Anne's plate and adds, "They make wonderful CDs for entertaining."

Then Darren comes back and says, "After dessert, we'll show you Parker's progress on the computer."

"On the computer?"

"We used our digital camera to catalog every step of his progress, from birth to his second birthday. Every casting, every operation. The day he crawled, the day he walked. It's all there. Tami wrote little updates for every picture, so you'll have an excellent idea of what to expect with Evan."

Elie looks at Anne beseechingly, like he's just been sentenced to a lethal injection. Anne smiles at him encouragingly.

*E*lie seethes quietly on the way home.

"It wasn't so bad," she says, turning on the radio for levity.

He glares at her, silent.

"Supper was good, wasn't it? She used real garlic in the lasagna. And that apple crumble—"

"They were so goddamn un-extraordinary," he mutters.

"I'm sure they're thinking 'A table artist and a Lebanese coin collector . . . ?' Anyway, I think they're nice."

"Nice," he snorts. And then: "'What a fate—to grow rotund and unseemly, to lose self-love, to think only in terms of milk, oatmeal, nurses, diapers . . .'"

"What's that from?"

"*The Beautiful and Damned,*" he says. "Fitzgerald."

Elie majored in literature at Oxford University. He knew after graduation that he'd be going back to Beirut to work for the family business, so he was able to study something languid and impractical. His education was an intimate, leisurely affair, during which he memorized—and can still recount by heart—the entirety of Chaucer's "Wife of Bath's Tale" in Old English and the translated version, as well as *Hamlet* and *Macbeth*. To this day he's able to quote the most apropos literary gems off the top of his head, dropping them quite naturally into conversations without coming off as pretentious or self-important. He's always urging Anne to read the classics, but she finds all the references to thirty-year-old women as middle-aged spinsters far too depressing. She still prefers an art textbook.

"Well, I feel good about tonight," Anne declares. "Frankly, Parker's feet look pretty good now. They're not quite perfect, but they're pretty good. At least in those pictures."

"In which of the two thousand we were subjected to?" he mutters.

They stop at a red light and Anne glances over into the car beside theirs, observing a grim, elderly couple who look like they haven't exchanged a single word in decades. They're both frowning, their mouths falling in identical arcs, with deep lines leading from the corner of their lips to their chins. They look to be about in their eighties, with their glum profiles and their conjoined bitterness beaming through the windshield out at the world. They seem so far apart, as though they've already said everything there is to say to each other and now it's just more practical to be silent and miserable, and to leave each other alone. There's probably not an idea or a joke that hasn't already passed between them. Nothing left to laugh at, which scares her.

"Did you see the way they looked at me when you told them I was Lebanese?" Elie barks. "Like they thought I was going to declare Jihad in their living room."

"That is so ridiculous. It's all in your head, Elie. You're paranoid."

"I don't want to be part of a 'community,'" he gripes. "What the hell is that about anyway? The 'community'?"

"That's how people talk here."

"We don't talk that way."

"That's because we don't belong."

"Inshallah."

He turns the car into their driveway, brings it to a stop and pulls the key out of the ignition.

"You know, with the shoes over the AFOs, you can hardly tell there's a problem," Anne says optimistically. "And I don't think Evan's feet are as severe as Parker's were. Tami says Parker wasn't crawling around much in his first year, whereas Evan never sits still. So I think Evan will be better off. I mean, who knows? Maybe the next operation will correct the problem once and for all."

Elie sighs, slumping back in his seat. "Anne," he says softly, "I don't know how you can come out of there so cheerful. Gauging from those interminable pictures, the kid's feet look no better now than they did two years ago."

"Of course they do. Besides, Evan's aren't nearly as bad—"

"Stop lying to yourself. Evan's are *exactly—the—same*. He's still got years ahead of him of casts and operations. And even then there's no guarantee."

"No guarantee of what?" she cries, panic rising up in her chest.

"No guarantee of him looking normal. Or perfect. Or whatever the hell it is you want from him."

"*For* him!" she corrects.

"No," Elie says. "From him."

Ten

She takes the thermometer out of Evan's mouth and sets it down on the change table. His temperature is a hundred and three. He's screaming. He's already had his Tylenol with codeine and she's bathed him with a cool cloth, so there's nothing else she can do. As usual, she's utterly helpless.

He had his second operation right after New Year's. Despite the caudal block they gave him he had to stay in the hospital for three days with agonizing muscle spasms that seemed impervious to the morphine IV. Dr. Hotz told them there are also some sores on Evan's left foot from the first operation, which he discovered when he was changing the cast. They have to go back next week to make sure the sores aren't getting worse and to have his casts changed again. The swelling in his left foot hasn't gone down either and they have to monitor that closely, in case it disrupts the blood flow and cuts off oxygen to his foot.

This is her son's lot for the next three months, until the casts are removed for good in the spring. They still have no guarantees as to how his feet will turn out at the end of all this. What she'd really like to do is saw off one of his casts and see if the surgeries have made any difference at all—just some reassurance that his feet are straighter, that his pain hasn't been for nothing.

Evan continues to scream, his little fists beating her chest. She walks him in circles around the nursery, bouncing him gently in front of the window, hoping the occasional truck zooming past might distract him. Nothing is working and she's starting to get frustrated.

She thinks about all the other mothers out there, proudly showing off their healthy babies, and it infuriates her. She knows it could be worse—leukemia, Down syndrome, yes, all those—but does a potentially worst-case scenario automatically negate what they've been suffering since the day Evan was born?

His screams get louder. Evan writhes in her arms, trying to escape. His face is dark purple. She tries lying him back down in his crib but it only exacerbates the situation.

Elie comes in then with his suitcase and says gravely, "How is he?"

She looks up at him with disgust. "Can't you hear him screaming? How do you think he is?"

"My limo's here, Anne. You know I have to go. This thing's been booked for months."

"You don't *have* to."

"I'm not going to get into it with you again. I'm too tired—"

"*You're* too tired?"

He sighs. They were up all last night fighting about this. He's going to New York for a conference at the American Numismatic Society—"The Heritage of Iran: Dinars, Drahms and Coppers of the Early Muslim Period." At least that's what he *says* he's going to do. For all she knows, he's going to meet a lover at the St. Regis.

"I'll call you when I get there," he promises, acting as

though she's given him her blessing. "I left the number of the hotel in the kitchen."

Anne blinks back tears, not wanting to give him the satisfaction. But she's disappointed. She thought he'd change his mind. She was sure Evan's screams all morning would persuade him to reconsider, which shows how little she knows her own husband. "How can you just walk out on us like this?" she asks plaintively.

"I'll keep my cell on," he says graciously, as though it were some noble compromise.

"Are you meeting a woman?" she asks out of the blue. "Is that it?"

"That's not fair," Elie says.

"Why else would you leave us now? Not for some bull-shit conference—"

"He had the operation almost a week ago."

"But listen to him!" she cries, shaking her head in disbelief. His selfish rationalizations astound her. "Look at him! Your son is in excruciating pain, Elie. Yet off you go to New York for God knows what reason, or should I say God knows who . . ."

"I'm going for a fucking lecture," he says wearily.

"Right."

"What can I do here?" he asks impatiently.

She wouldn't even know where to begin. She's too drained. He shouldn't need her to tell him. He should know. As a father, he should know.

"Just go then."

He kisses Evan on the forehead, evidently not noticing how hot it is (or else choosing to ignore it). "Be strong, Stinker," he says brightly, which makes Anne want to punch him in the face.

When he leans in to kiss her, she shoves him away.

"I'll call you when I get there."

She watches him leave, stunned. Right up till the last second, she thought maybe he'd relent. He's been known to display sporadic bouts of selflessness. There was the one time a couple of years ago when he surprised her with a trip to New Jersey to see the Jonathon Talbot "Patrin" exhibition. Elie abhors collage almost as much as he abhors New Jersey, so for him the trip was an unparalleled marital sacrifice, completely out of his comfort zone. Although Anne was thrilled, the gesture opened up a small window of expectation that has yet to be replicated.

She hears him thumping down the stairs, not a care in his head for her or for Evan. All he's probably thinking about right now is the martini he's going to have at the King Cole Bar.

She retrieves the cherry Tylenol from the bathroom, and even though its pain-relieving effects are useless on Evan the sticky red sweetness appeases him for a few seconds. She droops tiredly over the rail of the crib and strokes his hair. For some reason she's thinking about that Jonathon Talbot exhibition Elie took her to. It was called "One Hundred Patrin," which is the Romany word for the signs Gypsies leave behind to tell other wanderers where they've gone. In his artist statement Talbot wrote that his collages were his patrin.

Anne's patrin are her tables. They are the markers that will tell her story after she's gone. But so will Evan—the man he becomes, the life he leads. Unlike her own father, who passed along no information and no clues about himself, Anne feels strongly that in creating this child she has created her legacy. That's why she has to make sure she gives him a good life, the best. It's why she has to get these club feet fixed before they cause lasting damage.

Evan clasps his doggie and rubs its ear into his nose. Then he rubs his eyes, a hopeful sign that sleep might be close. What she would do with an hour to herself! A nap, a bath, some art . . . She hasn't worked on a table since before the holidays. Her creative well is dry; everything she's got these days goes to Evan.

Elie has offered many times to hire a nanny. Obviously money isn't the issue; she's just never wrapped her head around the idea of a stranger taking care of her son while she's, say, upstairs lounging in a bath. She's hung on to this notion of the perfect mother who doesn't need any help, even though it certainly would have alleviated some of her burden. Especially since Elie is virtually useless. He's supposed to look after Evan for a few hours every Sunday, giving her some time to herself, but that's only if there isn't a weekend auction or a trip or something else more important to him than their son.

His views on child-rearing are pretty culturally traditional. He rarely changes diapers or, in their case, casts. He doesn't wake up in the night when Evan cries. He doesn't sterilize the bottles or prepare the formula. He doesn't even know Evan's schedule, which except for the surgeries hasn't varied in almost seven months. It's just not Elie's way.

She shouldn't complain. He pays for a cleaning lady and he cooks, although it must be noted that neither of those gestures is necessarily to lighten *her* load. He pays for Marta because they both like a meticulous house, and he cooks because he enjoys it. Over the years she's learned that a good majority of Elie's generosity is transparently self-seeking.

*E*van eventually dozes off in his crib, leaving Anne to figure out what she wants to do with the next (if she's lucky) half an hour or (if she's really lucky) hour to herself. A bath is risky. If Evan wakes up she'll have to get out of the tub and drip down the hallway, naked and freezing, to tend to him. A nap isn't worth it either. What's a half hour of sleep when you haven't slept in 144 hours?

She goes into the den and flops onto her oversized down-filled couch. This room is her sanctuary, filled with her framed early collages on the walls, photographs of Evan, her very first hand-forged side table with the double-flared scroll feet she's so proud of, her flat-screen TV and DVD collection—which consists of every Woody Allen film between 1977 and 1997 (ending with *Deconstructing Harry*) and all six seasons of *Sex and the City*.

She's got an *In Style* magazine from last month that she still hasn't gotten around to reading. She picks it up, starts to flip through it, and then, just like that, Evan starts screaming again.

Grappling with feelings of selfishness and guilt, she ignores him and calls her mother. She knows Jean isn't the ideal person to call for sympathy—she's not someone who doles out pity or kind, consoling words—but she's practical and reasonable, and that will have to do for now.

"Evan's got a fever of a hundred and three," Anne blurts, returning to the nursery where Evan is snotty and choking. She lifts him out of the crib, cradling the phone in her shoulder. "Dr. Hotz said he'd probably have a fever for a few days, but it's been nearly a week now—"

"I can't hear you very well."

"He won't stop screaming," she vents, juggling Evan and the portable phone. "He's in terrible pain, Mom. I'm scared. I don't know what to do—" Her voice breaks.

"Calm down."

"I can't do this anymore!" she cries wildly. "For all I know, he's teething too—"

"Don't be melodramatic. Where's Elie?"

"He just left for New York," she answers, ashamed.

"What?"

She repeats it louder this time, bellowing over Evan's screams: "He's gone away on business. He's going to New York!"

"It figures."

"Meaning?"

"He's a typical Middle Eastern man," she remarks. "It's the Muslim culture."

"Elie isn't Muslim. I've told you a million times. He's a Maronite."

"A marionette?"

"You heard me," Anne says irritably, thinking her mother must do this on purpose to goad her. She collapses on the baby blue chenille glider in the corner of the room. Evan is, unbelievably, still screaming.

"Why don't you bring him here," her mother suggests. "You can leave him with me and have a break for a while."

"That means I'll have to get him into his snowsuit and then squeeze him and his goddamn fiberglass casts into the car seat and drive over there with him screaming—"

"I hate coming there," she says. "Your house is too big and neat."

"I know."

She sighs, relenting. "I'll be there in half an hour."

Anne puts down the phone. For some reason, her mother's generosity triggers an onslaught of tears, leaving her tired and droopy and melancholy, but relieved of some of the week's tension. Evan's whimpering begins to taper off and they rock together in merciful silence. She wipes her nose with his burpy.

She notices him gazing intently at the floor, where slashes of sunlight have come in through the shutters and cast a pattern of distorted horizontal lines on the hardwood. She rubs his small back and glances around the nursery, remembering with nostalgia what it was like when she and Elie were decorating it. She was eight months pregnant. She knew she was having a boy so she went out and got dozens of blue paint chips. She agonized over the perfect shade for weeks. Their painter thought she was nuts. "Just a perfectionist," Elie told him.

Finally she settled on Windmill Wings, the perfect blue. They put white California shutters in the windows, had the hardwood floors restained a warm walnut brown, and ordered custom-made crib linens from a fancy French boutique in Yorkville. She found a crystal chandelier with light blue embroidered sconces and had the name *EVAN* monogrammed in baby blue on a white lace cushion.

Most of her naive pregnant fantasies involved dressing her baby in impossibly cute Baby Gap sleepers, rocking him in the glider and singing lullabies while he slept peacefully in her arms. Motherhood was going to be her salvation. And while there have been a few enchanting moments, the majority of their time together has revolved, in some way or another, around his deformed feet.

She reaches for the bottle that's been warming on the night table next to the glider, figuring he may as well have some lunch while he's calm. She sprawls him across her lap with his right cast raised above his chest and he accepts the bottle without much fuss, gulping hungrily for a few seconds, swallowing two or three ounces without coming up for breath.

She used to worry that not being able to breast-feed him was just another black X in the "ways to damage your child" check box. She had to stop nursing after two weeks because she couldn't produce enough milk. Her lactation specialist encouraged her to keep at it, but it was way too hard. Anne was certain she had some kind of hormonal disorder, but the specialist didn't buy it. She conceded that Anne probably did have a low milk supply, but only because she hadn't gotten breast-feeding right from the beginning. She led Anne to believe that it was *her* fault, that her breasts had dried up due to her incompetence and lack of resolve. The fact is, Evan wasn't gaining weight and their pediatrician had ordered her to switch to formula.

When she had to give it up she fretted about bonding with Evan and felt like a failure. That all seems ridiculous to her now. She can't imagine that he knows the difference. If anything is going to scar him for life, it's his club feet, not a can of Similac.

He pushes the bottle away from his lips and twists his upper body around in her arms. She can tell he wants to stand up on her lap. It's what normal babies do at seven months.

All of a sudden he looks up into her face with those big green eyes and proclaims for the first time, "Mamamama."

Her spirits soar and she embraces him proudly. And then right away there's a slight puncture in her jubilation and she finds herself thinking that this moment would be perfect *if only* . . .

His club feet ruin everything. She still wants to take him out West and show him off to her estranged father and relatives. He is her one great accomplishment, the singular momentous achievement of her life, and yet his club feet are an embarrassment. She hates that she feels this way, but they just won't make the proper kind of impression. They never do.

Eleven

A loud knock on the door startles her and she looks up from a pile of shattered glass. She decides to ignore it since the studio is closed and her hours are clearly indicated in the window.

It's the first time in weeks she's been able to work on one of her tables. When her mother showed up yesterday to take Evan off her hands she was thoughtful enough to have brought an overnight bag with her. Jean wound up sleeping in the guest room and taking care of Evan whenever he fussed.

Anne slept through the night and woke up refreshed. She was thrilled to discover that her mother had taken Evan out for a morning walk. Her note said: *Gone for a walk. Back in an hour. Evan feeling much better! Please tape* The View.

Anne had a twenty-minute shower, sipped a cappuccino and didn't worry about Evan the entire time. When they returned Jean offered to stay for the rest of the day in case Anne wanted to get some work done at the studio. Since she happened to be feeling somewhat creatively inspired, she took her mother up on the offer.

The idea for a new table came to her yesterday when she dropped her glass of grapefruit juice on the kitchen floor. As she stooped to pick up the shards of glass, she decided to save them and use them on a table. She's going to splatter it with white paint and call it *Crying Over Spilt Milk*. Maybe it's lame. She doesn't know. She can't tell the difference anymore between creative brilliance and desperation.

It happens all the time that she gets an idea, something she thinks is absurd or funny but utterly unmarketable— like her *Scales of Justice* table, which tipped every time you put something on one side of it—and then some rich Toronto lofter snatches it up at Urban Mode. Her success has dulled her ability to differentiate between the sublime and the ridiculous. Her best inside jokes have been received as masterpieces. Either she's a great visionary with a Midas touch or Torontonians will buy just about anything. Her *Literary Masterpiece* table, for instance, which was covered in book jackets, sold instantly to a local prize-winning author (and was later featured on an episode of *Designer Guys*). Even her *Seesaw* table, which for obvious reasons was totally impractical, sold to one of those elite interior designers on Davenport.

She never used to think about a table's potential market value, who it might appeal to or how much she could get for it. Now such thoughts are inevitable. Who will want a table made of broken glass and simulated milk? *Someone.* There's always someone.

She dumps a pile of shattered glass onto her work space, grateful for this time to herself. She hasn't got the energy or strength to turn on her forge and handle the metal, but it's a relief to be doing *any*thing creative with her hands. The appealing thing about decoupage is that it's a thoroughly mindless task. She's essentially gluing tiny bits of things to something else, but it's wonderfully therapeutic. It requires nothing more of her than was required in kindergarten— her hands, a creative spirit and a gallon of glue. She can't imagine a better release from the stress of Evan's operation than her art.

As she glues her bits of things, the world begins to recede—the echo of Evan's screams, her fears and worries about his feet, even her resentment toward Elie. They haven't spoken since he left on Thursday and she's determined not to relent until he gets back from New York tomorrow. He called again this morning and she ignored it. Let him worry. Let him stew. Let him think the worst. She doesn't even care if he—

The intruder thumps on the door again. Anne wipes her sticky hands on her apron and marches over to the front door to peer angrily through the glass. There's a guy standing there in a black leather jacket and a black toque. He's looking down and she can't see his face. "I'm closed!" she yells through the door.

He lifts up his head and looks right at her. A weird little sound comes out of her mouth—a gasp that dies on her lips. He mouths the words, "Can I come in?"

It's him. *Him.* Her heart is pounding. She unlocks the door with slightly trembly fingers.

"Hi," he says.

"Hi."

"I know you're closed, but I could see you working in there."

"Don't worry about it—"

"Declan," he says. "From the support group."

"I know."

"How've you been?"

"Okay, I guess. My son had his second operation right after the holidays."

"How's he doing?"

"He's a fighter," she says. "But I wish it was over. I can't stand to watch him suffer . . ."

"It makes you feel helpless, doesn't it?"

Tears spring to her eyes. "So helpless . . ."

"How are his feet?"

"He's got his first cast change this week, but they'll probably be too swollen to tell. We'll have to wait till next month."

"That's rough." He pulls his toque off and stuffs it into his pocket. "I guess that's why we haven't seen you at the last couple of meetings."

"I was at the one right before Christmas," she mentions. "But I don't think you were there." (That was the night she wore her fabulous "hot mom" jeans and he didn't show up. She had to sit there in the circle with the jeans digging into her abdomen and cutting off her circulation.)

"Right. We were in Cuba," he says, straining for conversation. "We left that Monday night."

Not knowing how to respond, Anne nods awkwardly. It seems about all they have in common—other than sucking at small talk—is that their sons have club feet. Out of the context of the support group, they're complete strangers.

"So you're Anne of Green Tables," he says, looking around her studio. "There was a write-up about you in one of those decorating magazines. I recognized your picture."

"You read those?"

"My wife's into decorating. I just flip through the magazines on the—"

He flushes. They both chuckle. He looks like an Irish Spring commercial with his cable-knit sweater and his flushed cheeks.

"The table in that article—" he says.

"The mosaic coffee table?"

"It's very cool," he tells her. "Margaret just redecorated our den. Our anniversary is coming up, so I thought . . ."

Her spirits deflate. She thought maybe he'd dropped by just to see her. It would have been flattering. A boost to her ego.

"I think Margaret will love it," he's saying. "She's got great taste and she appreciates art."

Anne smiles wanly. She tells him the price and he flinches.

"Can I get a club foot discount?" he asks.

Because it's for Margaret, she's feeling rather ungenerous. "You can pay cash and save the tax," she offers.

He mulls it over. "Can I see it?"

She leads him to the back of her studio, where the mosaic-tiled table—one of her more conventional and uninspired pieces—is stashed with some other duds and all the tables she's deemed substandard but hasn't had the heart to throw away.

"Is that a coffin?" he asks, pointing to her *Decapitated Doll Heads* table.

"It was for a Halloween display window," she explains, embarrassed by the shallow box she designed to look like a coffin. Inside it's crammed with creepy doll heads staring up through the glass. "It's pretty morbid, I know. It was just a joke, but I can't seem to part with it."

"You weld too?" he comments, noticing her propane oven, her anvil and hammers.

"I hand-forge," she explains. "I took a course, but I sort of abandoned it after I had Evan . . . It's very physical work and I just don't have the energy these days."

He looks impressed with a table she made for a model suite, one of her early metal pieces. It was pretty simple— a glass top sitting on cricket's legs.

"There's yours," she says. "See it back there?"

She attempts to drag it out but Declan stops her. "Let me," he says, taking off his jacket and pushing up his sleeves. Her eyes slide directly down to his forearms, lingering there for a moment. She can't help it. She notices when he bends forward that he's wearing a gold cross under his sweater, which somehow manages to blur the line between cheesy and hot.

He pulls out the mosaic table and examines it, running his hand over the surface, inspecting the legs. Then he does something that surprises her. He pulls out a paint chip and holds it next to the table. "Margaret saves all the paint chips," he explains sheepishly. "Look. The aqua in this tile is a perfect match with our den."

Anne forces another smile. Aqua like his eyes.

In the end, he's just like her. A yuppie. He carries a paint chip in his back pocket, he's able to drop two grand on a kitschy table, and his den is aqua. The smoking and cynicism and *Creideamh* tattoo are all red herrings. They almost threw her off.

While he's getting his car, she removes her apron. There's an antique Venetian mirror in the bathroom that she uses to sneak on some blush and lip gloss. She may yet have a few minutes with him to make an impression. These physical attractions have a way of overwhelming her logic. Her composure seems to just fall away like meat off a bone, leaving in its place a messy tangle of lust and longing. She loves the thrill of a flirtation. She knows when to stop, which is how she justifies it. She's never cheated on Elie.

She believes she never would. It's a game, the way collecting coins is Elie's game. The key is that both their pursuits are unattainable.

When Declan returns, smelling like he's had a cigarette in the time it took to get his car, she feels more like a nervous fourteen-year-old than a wife and mother.

She notices he's parked his Pathfinder on the curb in front of her studio. The hazard lights are blinking. He goes over to his table and lifts it easily over his shoulder. She watches him load it into his trunk, wishing he wouldn't leave just yet but consoling herself with the fact that she'll see him on Monday at the support group meeting. Just the possibility of their next encounter begins to lull her. Seduction is a powerful drug.

She can feel her attraction escalating. Elie referred to it as an "intrigue," which is surprisingly accurate. It captures the essence of what she loves about it—the rush, the exploration, the challenge.

"I'll see you Monday," Declan says, lingering in the doorway. He hesitates a moment—she thinks she's got him too, the way women intuit these things—and then he puts his toque on and heads out to his car.

After he's gone, she second-guesses herself. Is she hallucinating his side of the attraction? She flip-flops back and forth, ultimately deciding, based on that last look he gave her, that there *is* something between them, perhaps just a seed, but something that definitely has the potential to grow.

Twelve

Anne and Elie have stopped at the coin shop so that Elie can make sure everything has run smoothly while he was away. Later, they have to take Evan to the hospital for his first cast change. Dr. Hotz made a point of telling them not to get their hopes up. They probably won't be able to tell if his feet are straight yet, not with all the swelling, but Anne is hoping for even a small sign of encouragement, if not a miracle.

"What's this?" Elie asks.

The customer blinks a few times in an agitated way, like a tic. His head is shaped like a lightbulb. He's wearing thick glasses and the lapels of his coat are dusted with dandruff. He hands the coin over to Elie. "It's an 1842 D-mint Dahlonega gold quarter eagle," he says. "Part of the Georgia gold collection. Very sought after."

Elie calls over his apprentice, Dirk, and together they inspect the quarter eagle, turning it over and examining the obverse.

The night he returned from New York he was sheepish and obviously expecting a fight. He was baffled to discover that she'd completely cooled down. "You're not mad anymore?" he asked her over Chinese takeout.

"No."

For a moment he seemed disoriented, but then he seized the opportunity to bore her with the details of his trip.

"The conference was fascinating," he said, reaching for the sesame beef. "Especially the workshop."

She was pretending to listen. Living in a separate fantasy world requires very little more than a knack for pretending—pretending to be interested in what your husband is saying while you're actually daydreaming about someone else; pretending to be attentive when all you can think about is when you'll see the other guy again.

Really all she wanted to do was shut down and crawl inside her head and stay there, lost in fantasy. She didn't want to be in the same room as Elie. She wanted to be in her head with Declan.

"Which workshop?" she asked him absently.

"The one I just told you about. Where we were shown how to read the Pahlavi legends on early Muslim coins?"

"Right."

"There are so many interpretations . . ."

(She felt empty, sitting there with him.)

". . . each one is a document representing the social, political and economic life of early Medieval Iran. And after the workshop, we had a roundtable discussion about the Sasanian monetary systems . . ."

On he went. All she kept thinking about was Declan. She was silently running his name over her tongue. Declan Declan Declan. Thinking about his gold chain, his arms, the way he'd hesitated in her doorway. Maybe the table for Margaret was a ruse. Maybe he really came to see *her*.

"I know it was a tough weekend for you," Elie said. "But this conference was a once in a lifetime opportunity and it really means a lot to me that you're not giving me a hard time. I'm glad you're over it."

She smiled blandly. Elie leaned over and kissed her cheek. His lips left a smudge of peanut sauce. "That's it for traveling until the auction in Calgary," he promised. "I'm all yours till then."

*E*lie hands the quarter eagle over to Dirk. "Back in the mid-nineteenth century," he explains to his apprentice, "Dahlonega was a gold-mining town, one of the first places in America where native gold was ever found. A mint was set up there. The surviving coins, all of which bear a distinctive 'D' mint mark—see this here?—are evidence of a noteworthy historical era."

"You can see it's well-struck," the customer pipes in eagerly. "With uncommonly sharp details."

Elie puts the coin under his loupe. Evan is wiggling in Anne's arms, trying to grab the coin. Given the chance, he'd probably hurl it across the room the way he does lately with those vile Healthy Time teething cookies she tries to feed him.

She touches Elie's shoulder and gives him a look. *Hurry up*. He barely acknowledges her; barely sees her. He goes back to his loupe. "Its grade is About Uncirculated," he says.

"It's free of any trace of wear whatsoever, and extremely fine," the customer adds. "No traces of rubbing or bag marks to interfere with the details. What do you think I could I get for it?"

Elie shrugs coolly. "Maybe six or seven."

"You're telling me that if you auctioned this coin you'd only pull six or seven grand?"

"I'm telling you that if *I* bought it from you right now, that's what it would be worth to *me*. I generally don't auction off individual coins unless they can earn me a substantial amount of money. I also don't carry much Americana, so on its own you haven't got much here."

"It's got to be worth more than what you're offering!" the guy says desperately, pushing his glasses into his face. Anne imagines for him a hovel of an apartment with no heat, a barren fridge, a car whose engine won't run, or a debt so gigantic it could cost him his life, and all he's got to bail him out is this little coin. Then there's her husband— cool, indifferent, smug.

Elie always claims that his passion for coins is about the thrill of the hunt, but she thinks it's more about control.

Evan continues to squirm wildly in her arms. She transfers him over to her other hip and glares at Elie. He ignores them both.

"I'll be honest with you," Elie says to the man. "I'm not a big Americana enthusiast. If this were an 1855 quarter eagle, *that* would be something else. But it's only an 1842—"

"*Only* an 1842!"

"I'll cut you a check for six and half right now. Otherwise we're wasting each other's time."

The poor guy mops his forehead with a rumpled handkerchief. Any decent collector who wasn't in deep financial trouble would have walked out by now.

She can see the smile in Elie's dark eyes. He knows victory is at hand. He stands up and takes Evan from Anne, as though Evan is a prop.

The man sighs dejectedly. "Okay," he mutters, his voice sounding heavy with remorse and relief. Anne feels so sorry for him she has to look away.

A part of her loathes Elie for his smugness, his glee over the man's defeat. She wanders off while they complete the transaction.

When the man is finally gone Elie comes over to her, beaming. "This coin is worth double what I paid!" he gloats. "I can get at least fourteen or fifteen at auction. It certainly won't go lower than twelve."

He holds the coin in his hand, tenderly admiring it. "The grade is fucking startling," he murmurs. "There's only about ten in existence in this high a range. It's the third rarest of all the high-grade quarter eagles. Check out this orangey-gold color and the splashes of gold on the obverse."

"Elie, we have to get to the hospital," she says, peeved.

"I think at one point it sold for almost fifteen thousand bucks," he boasts, still on about the coin. "That guy was a fucking moron."

He notices her scowl and says, "It's just business, Anne."

"I didn't say anything."

At the hospital they fill in the usual paperwork and then Evan is whisked away by one of the nurses. Dr. Hotz emerges just over an hour later, removing his bifocals as he approaches. He rests his clipboard against his chest. "The nurse will bring Evan out in a few minutes," he tells them. "We put him to sleep, so he's still pretty groggy."

"How are his feet?" Anne asks impatiently.

"They're healing nicely. The sores aren't infected."

"Are they straight?"

"They're still too swollen to tell, but there's no reason not to be optimistic, right?"

"Right." Through clenched teeth.

His smile is bright and placating. His teeth are all veneers; they look fake. "We'll know more in a month when we take out the pins and change the casts again," he says. "Try to stay positive until then."

He winks at her and then retreats down the corridor.

She sulks on the way home, the weather outside reflecting her bleak mood. The city looks underexposed, all shades of dull gray with no contrast or definition. The streets are lined with slush and dirty snowbanks. Everything is ugly. "I hate January," she mutters sullenly.

"They're calling for more snow."

"Why couldn't Dr. Hotz have given us even a hint that the operation worked?"

"You knew it would be too early to tell," Elie reminds her.

"I thought he'd at least be able to report *some* improvement."

"Just be patient."

"I'm sick of being patient," she flares. "I want my son to have a normal life already. Okay? I want him to be normal. There. I've said it. That's what you want me to say, right?"

Elie sighs and she feels the usual jab of guilt. She turns around to check on Evan. His eyes are closed and he's sucking contentedly on his pacifier. Not that he would understand her anyway, but all the better if he's asleep.

"It's not like I don't love him no matter what," she defends.

Elie doesn't respond. His eyes are fixed straight ahead.

"Because I do. I love him exactly the way he is. I just want to put this behind us, for *Evan's* sake—"

She stops speaking abruptly and looks away, horrified by the words coming out of her mouth. It's the shame of her own vanity that prevents her from admitting out loud that this is *her* problem, not Evan's. She can see she's already burdened him with the full weight of her expectations.

The truth is, Evan is lovable and sweetly imperfect. And even though she feels in some way that he's failed her, she knows that ultimately the failure is her own.

Thirteen

Sunday. Elie's day with Evan. Anne manages to escape the house by ten and be on her way downtown for some glorious time by herself. Driving down Mount Pleasant, she contemplates what she misses most about her life before motherhood. She would have thought she'd miss things like traveling and dining in fancy restaurants and sleeping in till noon. And she does, but not as much as the simpler things. Aimless, lingering walks. A spur of the moment dim sum in Kensington Market. *Silence.* She also misses being a separate entity, a woman unto herself and not merely an extension of her baby. She doesn't want to only ever be two arms attached to a stroller.

At the studio she finishes gluing the last shards of glass to her *Spilt Milk* table. Despite her earlier doubts, the table is beautiful. She used different colors of glass to create a pattern of tears on the surface, and long glass cylinders for the legs. All that's left to do now is sand it down to smooth the edges and then shellac it.

When she starts to feel hungry at around noon, she wipes the glue off her hands and goes into the bathroom to touch up her lipstick. On her way out she stops for a moment and crouches down in front of her forge. She brushes some dust off the top. It's ice cold.

If only inspiration were as abundant and accessible these days as her self-doubt. She has this idea for a new collection of hand-forged tables, something she could show at a spring vernissage. She had a teacher at Algonquin who made life-size metal busts with angel wings on the back. What was so astounding was the way he used sheet metal to create skin over bones. She loved the concept of wrapping metal over metal, layering it to create something fluid and organic. Her idea is to do something similar; a series of metalwork tables incorporating body parts. She imagines a curvy, muscular arm with an open palm holding up a glass tabletop, the way a waiter holds a tray. Two nude, crossed legs as a table base, or a torso with arms extended, reaching up and holding the tabletop in place.

She might call the collection *Limbs*. It would be dark and gothic, heavy. The challenge would be in sculpting the metal to look as though it were as malleable as clay. It will require painstaking effort and practice to accomplish her vision, but that's what excites her about the project. Doing something brave and unique.

Toronto is still into the minimalist look, anything with chrome and clean lines. But Anne is sick of contemporary furniture. She wants to take a chance and veer in the opposite direction, with pieces that are dramatic, complex, real. Like humans.

She recently read about an avant-garde furniture store that just opened in the west end. Apparently the owner mixes eclectic antiques with contemporary designer pieces like Kartell and Missoni, and he's also got an impressive art gallery on the premises. The moment Anne read about it, she had a feeling it was the perfect retail space to showcase her work. There are two problems. The first is she's got nothing new in her portfolio. The *Limbs* collection is just a spark of an idea. There are still months of work ahead, and so far she hasn't even mustered the energy to turn on her forge.

The other problem is a demoralizing lack of confidence. She's not sure when all this artistic self-doubt began to set in, but she pinpoints it to around the time her hormones started to go awry in the fourth week of pregnancy. She's never been the same since.

At some point she's going to have to focus on her career again. She misses it—and not just creating art either. She misses selling it. She misses schmoozing with clients. She misses being productive. She hates being out of the interior design loop. It's like a vital part of her is dormant, a part that cannot coexist with the part that puts so much energy into tending to her boy.

Being a mother is fulfilling in its own right, but with no other meaningful outlet, it's not *quite* enough. And yet, back when all she had was her career, the reverse was true. She felt as if something significant was missing then too. Without a child her life felt empty, boring. She still thinks there must be a way to have both, in perfect balance, and to be happy. She doesn't want to compromise one or the other, but she doesn't want to settle either.

She grabs an order of steamed octopus balls and strolls through the market feeling something close to peaceful. The sun is blazing and it almost seems like early spring today. It's perfect winter weather—bright and not too cold. She turns onto one of the residential streets where a woman has set up a yard sale in front of her Victorian home. She's wearing a money belt around her ski jacket and is fondly flogging her goods—a decrepit rocking chair, a son's old pair of skis, a box of board games marked $1 each, the requisite used car seat and umbrella stroller (a yard sale favorite), an ancient computer, circa 1985.

"A winter yard sale?" Anne comments.

The woman shrugs. "Why not?"

Anne browses halfheartedly through some of the junk until her eye hones in on a framed collage leaning up against the leg of a battered coffee table.

"It's a Claudine Hellmuth," the woman says, blowing a puff of frozen air about her face.

"I know," Anne responds. "I'm a fan."

"Really?"

"Mm."

The woman hands the collage to Anne. There's a vintage black-and-white photograph of a young man in a sailor's cap, arms folded across his chest. On either side of him, two gold coins. A symbol of balance. Anne recognizes it as the *Two of Coins,* from Hellmuth's 2000 *Tarot Card* series. She flips it over and reads the blurb on the back. *The Querant has some important choices to make in his life. This card warns that when a person makes changes in one area of his life, all other areas are affected.*

"I did a workshop with Hellmuth in Montreal," Anne explains.

"So did I. Not in Montreal . . . I went to her retreat in Arizona . . ."

"Are you an artist?"

The woman blushes. She looks to be in her late forties, a mom. Earthy. "I dabble," she says. "You?"

"I refurbish tables. I do a lot of collage."

"Interesting," she says, standing close to Anne so that

they can admire the *Two of Coins* together. She's got coffee breath, which is probably no more offensive than Anne's octopus breath.

"It was wonderful, wasn't it?" the woman says. "Her workshop?"

Anne nods. She learned a few new techniques—how to scrape and age, how to transfer color and black-and-white copies.

"Why are you selling this?" she asks the woman.

"We're moving to Arizona at the beginning of February, which is why the yard sale is now. My youngest just went off to college this past September, so we thought, why not? We've been vacationing in Arizona for years . . . My husband is a golfer. Besides, he never liked the collage."

"My husband collects coins," Anne reveals.

"Take it then," the woman says. "Five dollars."

"Five dollars?" Anne cries.

"You're doing me a favor."

"It's funny," Anne says, reaching into her purse for a five, "I was just thinking as I turned onto your street . . ."

Her voice trails off. She realizes that what she's about to say is too intimate for a stranger. But what she was thinking about was balance. How to create it in her life. How to sustain it without harming anyone in her family. And then to stumble onto this . . .

She pays the woman and tucks the collage under her arm. "I was just thinking I needed some art for a bare space in my den," she finishes.

The woman smiles. She seems delighted with her five-dollar bill. It's probably the most she thought she'd make for any one thing, even the skis.

"Good luck in Arizona," Anne says, feeling fond of the woman.

"Good luck with your tables!"

Anne heads back toward Kensington, feeling absolutely elated. This is what it used to be like—independence, freedom. She realizes that she's not walking down the sidewalk so much as gliding.

For no reason she can think of, she darts into a tattoo parlor and, a few moments later, finds herself hunched forward with a needle in the small of her back.

*O*n Monday night she decides to go to the club foot support group early and hang out at the coffee shop across the street. She's seen Declan there a few times before the meeting. The possibility that she's stalking him niggles somewhere at the back of her mind, but she counters it with the very plausible rationalization that (a) all she wants is a cup of coffee, and (b) she deserves—no, is *entitled* to— a little flirting now and then, especially after everything she's been through with Evan's feet.

She orders a bowl of coffee and settles into a table by the fireplace. She waits about ten minutes before Declan shows up.

"Hey," he says. "Mind if I join you?"

"Go ahead." (Every piece of her plan falling into place.) "So how did your wife like the table?"

"She loved it," he says. "It looks great in our den. She was very impressed. She couldn't believe the effort I'd made, going out of my way to your studio."

Anne smiles.

"How's your boy?" he asks.

"You know. Same. Yours?"

Declan shrugs. "Same." All of a sudden he leans across the table. "You've got something on your face," he says, grazing her cheek with his fingertips.

"It's probably glue . . ." she mutters, mortified. "It's all over my hands."

She turns her palms up and sure enough there are bits of glue here and there. Declan takes her hands in his and uses his thumbs to rub off the glue. Then he holds her hands there for a moment, looking at her. His hands are warm. A man's skin on her skin. "There," he says.

"I was finishing up a table . . ." she manages, flustered. "I was there all afternoon—"

"Who watches your son?"

"My mother."

"You're lucky," he says, releasing her hands as though it was nothing that he was ever holding them or rubbing them. "It's the ideal situation. My mother-in-law lives in PEI, so Margaret doesn't get out much. She hates leaving Sean with a stranger."

"What about *your* mother?" Anne says, her heart still beating hard from the way he held her hands.

"My mother feels she paid her dues raising my brothers and me. Her policy is she doesn't babysit her grandchildren."

"You're kidding."

"I'm not."

"Anyway, I was telling her about you," he says.

"Your mother?"

"No, Margaret."

Anne is jarred. He's talking about her to his wife? She

wonders, in what context? Is it because she's such a benign and harmless subject, or because she's so compelling?

"She loves the name of your studio," he goes on. "She's from the Maritimes, so she grew up on Anne of Green Gables."

"I'm thinking of changing it."

"Changing it?" he cries. "Why? It's funny. It's Canadian."

"It's funny for a *moment*. It's more of a gimmick. I want to be taken more seriously. I've been thinking of rebranding for my next exhibit. Maybe hiring a PR company . . ."

"Rebranding," he sneers. "That's so corporate. You're an *artist*."

"I'm also a businesswoman."

"When's your next exhibit?"

"That's a good question. As soon as I finish my collection."

"When will that be?"

"As soon as I start it."

He laughs. Has a sip of his steaming coffee. He's gorgeous.

"What do you do?" she asks him.

"I've got a column in the Saturday *Post*."

This automatically places him in a higher echelon of potential lovers than her usual blue-collar fantasy. He is a man she could really fall for.

"What's it about?" she asks, trying not to sound overly impressed.

"Social and cultural issues."

"You must read a lot," she remarks, typecasting him as an intellectual.

"I read a fair bit," he answers. "Why do you ask?"

Elie always says that the mark of intelligence can be measured by a person's reverence and appetite for literature. "You spoke of Lord Byron at a meeting once," she reminds him.

"I did. That's true." He laughs self-consciously. Adorable.

"I wish I had more time for reading," she says. "I used to love snuggling up with a gigantic art book . . . But with Evan's feet—"

"You should do what Marg does," he says. "Every night after she puts Sean down—no matter what time it is—she reads in the tub for one hour. *One solid hour.* She says it's her spiritual regeneration."

Anne forces a smile. Beneath the surface, she is collapsing with jealousy. She gets a sudden vision of Margaret, languishing in one of those old-fashioned claw-foot tubs, her milky limbs spilling over the porcelain ledge; a rosy flush on her Irish cheeks, soft wisps of hair curling around her face. Margaret, who probably discusses cultural and social issues with Declan in passionate, intimate tones; who nobly, gracefully handles her son's club feet.

"I guess we should head over to the meeting," Anne mentions reluctantly.

"Right," he says, sounding disappointed. "The meeting."

They linger there for a moment, neither of them willing to stand up just yet. It's nice. It feels sort of illicit. Or is it all in her head? *Nothing is happening,* she tells herself, trying to stay grounded.

It's just coffee before the support group. She could have been anyone from the group and he would have sat down with her. (Would he have rubbed another person's hands though? Courtney's? Tami's?)

Finally, he says, "Okay, then. Let's go talk club feet."

She fakes another smile. She'd give anything to skip the meeting and go get a drink with him.

*A*fterward, when she's at home getting ready for bed, she tells Elie, "I got a tattoo."

He looks up from his book, *Jude the Obscure,* and says, "You what?"

"I got a tattoo yesterday."

He looks at her strangely.

"What's that look for?" she asks.

"Well, unless you're Maori," he quips, "it's rather absurd that you got another tattoo at this stage of your life."

"This stage? I'm thirty-three."

"Exactly. You're *thirty-three.*"

She lifts her shirt and turns so he can see her tattoo. It's the letter *E* in calligraphy.

"E?" he snorts. "For Elie?"

"For Evan."

"Oh." Indignant. "It *could* be for Elie."

"It was going to be, but if you think it's silly—"

"Of course it's silly, Anne. But it's kind of sexy."

"You think?"

He nods. "You could have at least spelled out my whole name," he gripes. "'E' is hardly an impressive commitment. You could still leave me for an Ed or an Eric."

"Or an Ernie."

"But why?" he asks her. "Why'd you do it?"

She shrugs.

Later, peering at her tattoo in the mirror, she wonders the same thing. The truth is that she was old enough to be the tattooist's mother. It's a recurring thought lately. If she'd had a kid at around twenty or twenty-one she would have a teenager now. Just the possibility of that makes her feel old. When exactly did she start feeling old? She used to only ever feel fat.

Perhaps this is some sort of postpartum identity crisis. Or maybe Declan's got something to do with it. She wonders if it's brazen and cool for a thirty-three-year-old mother to get a new tattoo, or if it's just plain humiliating. She's at an age now where she isn't sure about these things anymore.

Fourteen

"How many other support groups have you been to?" Tami asks, in response to Anne's having divulged something about her former infertility group.

They're sitting in the coffee shop near Anne's house nursing nonfat lattes. It's Monday afternoon and Evan is napping in his stroller beside her. Tami's son, Parker, is at his music class at the Lawrence Village Neighborhood Center. It's unspeakably cold outside, and she has to admit that it's rather pleasant sitting in the upholstered armchair by the fire.

The place is full of their kind: mothers camped out next to their Bugaboo strollers; nursing mothers with their puckered nipples fully exposed; mothers chasing their rambunctious toddlers; loudmouth mothers who don't care if everyone hears their business; stylish mothers in lululemon yoga outfits and Ugg boots; frumpy mothers in baggy, pleated mom-jeans with stretched-out Gap turtlenecks.

It's almost cultish. They've invaded the north end of the city. They've necessitated the installation of change tables and diaper dispensers in the coffee shop bathrooms. But having recently been recruited by Tami, and despite her earlier resistance, Anne is finding it enjoyable to pass the afternoon drinking coffee and talking about the most trivial things—diaper rash, stretch marks, car-seat brands. Here is a group to which she finally, wholly, belongs and from which, by simple virtue of having given birth to Evan, she cannot be ousted.

"The only other one was a Daughters Abandoned by Fathers support group," she tells Tami. "But I haven't been to that one in years."

(At the time, Anne told herself she was quitting because the room was too hot—there were no windows and no ventilation. Then she amended her reason for quitting, blaming it on how screwed up those women were. But the truth was that week after week she'd had to fight tidal waves of pain as she listened to stories of abandoned little girls desperate for scraps of male attention. In the end it was easier never to go back.)

"You find these groups help?" Tami says.

"Yes. I like having people to talk to who understand exactly what I'm going through—whether it's infertility or club feet. It's just easier than with friends who you have to try to convince of your pain and explain your situation to ad nauseam. And there are no . . . obligations."

"I guess you do meet people you have something in common with. Like us, right?"

Anne smiles distractedly, but her thoughts have drifted to Declan Gray. She doesn't mention that one of the pleasant by-products of her current support group is the sudden springing up of a new flirtation. Tami doesn't strike Anne as the type of woman who would *get* that, or seek out a man of her own with whom to flirt. She's probably content with a man like Darren.

"Brooke-Adele! Stop throwing your Cheerios!" Anne turns around just as the woman behind her—a loudmouth mother—is snatching her daughter by the coat sleeve. "Brooke-Adele!" she yells again, causing a scene. "Do you know the meaning of the word *no?*"

Tami finishes her latte and peers into her empty cup, as though the foam at the bottom holds all the answers to her life, like tea leaves. She seems far away. "I asked Parker's doctor if it was normal how underdeveloped his calf muscles are," she says, out of the blue. "It's always the same answer. 'Only time will tell.'" She rolls her eyes. "If I hear that one more time . . ."

"Are you going to the group tonight?" Anne asks, hoping to deflect some of the responsibility of having to console her.

"Maybe I should," she says. "I haven't been in a while."

"I always find sharing at the meetings helpful."

Tami looks up then and smiles wearily. "Do you ever get jealous of other mothers?" she asks Anne.

"All the time."

"I find myself looking at all these women with their perfect babies," she goes on. "They have no idea what it's like for us. It's not fair."

"They just don't get it," Anne agrees, remembering Sharon. "People don't know anything about club feet."

"They don't know how hard it is." Tami dips her finger into the foam and then licks it. "How did you lose all your baby weight so fast?" she asks, perking up.

"The Zone," Anne responds. "And walking with Evan for an hour every day."

Tami grimaces. "I just don't have the motivation," she laments. "I still haven't lost all my weight and I probably won't before I have the next one."

"You're thinking about having another baby?"

She looks at Anne strangely. "Aren't I supposed to?" she says, and Anne detects in her tone the slightest hint of sarcasm. But then it's gone and she adds, "Darren and I always talked about having three." She forces a smile that is totally incongruous with the dim, forlorn expression on her face.

Something about Tami's mood today makes Anne wonder if perhaps there *is* more to her than her perpetually sweet-tempered, generic momness. Perhaps there are soft ripples of dissatisfaction lurking beneath her calm surface after all; a wave of discontent that hasn't broken yet. She's revealed several subtle hints of defiance, but never for very long. She always snatches them back, as though she's afraid to be anything less than the perfect wife and mother, which seems to mean conventional and acquiescent and accommodating. Anne wants to shout at her, "Grow your hair long! Get rid of those high-waisted, tapered jeans and your duck boots! Flirt with a stranger! Find a hobby! Weld something! Let the real Tami out!"

What if she and Anne are kindred spirits? She is, after all, a married woman, and most of them can generally fit into the same mold.

Anne's cell phone rings and she has to dig around in her diaper bag to find it. When she finally gets at it, she checks the call display before answering. "It's my mother," she says. "Do you mind?"

"Go ahead."

"Hi, Mum."

"Ken Schlittman is dead!" her mother blurts.

"Who?"

"My client. The coin collector. Remember? The day your car wouldn't start—"

"Oh my God. He's dead?"

Tami's eyes bulge in horror. "Someone's dead?" she mouths.

Anne holds up a finger for her to wait a minute. Jean is sobbing into the phone, frantic.

"Mum, why are you so . . . I didn't realize you were that close to him."

"Anne, I mean he's dead *here*! At—my—house!" She starts gasping for breath.

"Did you call 911?"

"Yes. But . . . his body . . . it's . . . oh God! I can't . . ."

"Was it a heart attack?"

"I guess so."

"While you were giving him a massage?"

"Stop asking me all these questions!" she shrieks. "I'm standing over a corpse, for Christ's sake!"

"I'll be right over."

Anne tosses the phone back in her bag and stands up. "One of my mother's clients died at her house," she explains to Tami. "She's a masseuse. She thinks he had a heart attack."

"Getting a massage?"

"I know. It seems odd."

"You'd think the massage would have at least staved off the heart attack until he got home . . ."

Anne shakes her head, flustered.

"Do you want me to watch Evan?" Tami proposes.

"Would you?"

"No problem. I'll have Darren pick Parker up from his class."

"I don't want Darren to have to leave work early on my account."

"Anne, don't be ridiculous. Just go."

She reluctantly bends down and kisses Evan's cheek. His skin is flushed and warm from napping so long in his fleece hoodie. She hesitates a moment. Is she crazy to leave him with Tami? They've only known each other since meeting at the support group. She could still drop him off at Elie's, even though it means driving downtown and then back up to her mother's. Jean *is* alone with a corpse, which makes time of the essence—

"He'll be fine, Anne," Tami assures her. "Go."

Anne smiles gratefully and rushes out of the coffee shop, thinking it rather strange that this woman whom she barely knows is willing to put herself out like this to help her. Presumably, it's what friends do for each other, and yet Anne hadn't quite elevated her to that category of people for whom she would put *herself* out.

She bursts into her mother's living room, expecting to find the half-naked body of Ken Schlittman on the massage table, set up as it always is in the middle of the room.

But she finds no massage table, no Ken Schlittman. Just an empty, silent room.

"Mum?"

"Up here!" comes her mother's voice, as confident and collected as Anne's ever heard it.

She races upstairs, taking the steps two at a time. She finds Jean in her bedroom, bent over the prostrate body of Ken Schlittman. He's on the bed, shirtless, staring up at the ceiling fan. Anne's eyes take in the scene faster than her mind can process what she's seeing.

No massage table. No massage oils.

There never was a massage.

Her mother turns to face her. She seems relatively calm, given the situation. She's pale and her hair is knotty and disheveled, but other than that, you wouldn't guess by her appearance that a dead body was in the room with her. She's wearing her Moroccan muumuu and Anne notices that half the buttons are undone.

"What are you doing?" Anne asks.

"Trying to get his pants done up," Jean answers coolly.

"You were—"

"Don't make a big thing," her mother says, her cheeks flushing deeply. Jean sits down on the bed beside Ken's immovable legs and sighs. "He's the first one, you know. The first man I've been with since I left your father."

"Really?"

She looks up solemnly. "And look what happened."

Anne looks over at poor Ken, half expecting to see the rise and fall of his hairy belly. But there's nothing. He's so still. He looks cold too, but that's only because she knows dead bodies are supposed to be cold. She almost wants to reach out and touch him, to know what it feels like, the flesh of a dead man. "This is so . . . I've never seen . . . I mean, he's really *dead*."

"It's surreal," Jean breathes, peering down at him.

"Did you check his pulse or something?"

"Of course I did," Jean snips. "He's dead, Anne. The not breathing is another clue."

"How exactly did it happen?"

Jean looks away. "He just . . . stopped. Everything stopped. He wasn't moving or making any noise. I looked down and . . . I smacked him. But I *knew*. I knew it was God's retribution for the things I've done."

"Mom, this isn't your fault!" Anne reassures her. "He was going to have a heart attack no matter what."

"We don't know he had a heart attack."

"Or a stroke or whatever. He was overweight and stressed from work. It was only a matter of time. The fact that you two . . ." She can't bring herself to utter the words. "Well, it was just bad timing. You can't blame yourself."

"It's God's wrath," Jean murmurs.

"What?"

Anne's heard her mother speak of God only once before this, and that time it also had to do with sex.

"God's wrath," Jean says again, more convincingly.

"You don't believe in God," Anne reminds her.

"I try not to," she says. "But then . . ." She looks over at Ken, then down into her lap. "There's no other possible explanation."

"Of course there is. You're not being rational. You're in shock or something."

"I grew up believing in God."

"You did?"

"Don't you remember?" she asks Anne. "In Harmony? We never missed church on Sunday. Or grace before our meals."

"No. I don't remember."

"Your father was a very religious man. So was my father. It was like that where we lived." She reaches into the drawer of her bedside table and pulls out something that astonishes Anne: an old copy of a bible.

Jean presses it to her chest. "I've had this since I was a little girl."

"I never knew—"

"It isn't easy to just walk away and dismiss all the beliefs you had your whole life," Jean says. "There was a lot of brainwashing while I was growing up."

"But what does that have to do with *this*?" Anne asks, pointing to poor Ken.

"People warned me when I left your father," she says, "that God would punish me and I'd go to hell."

Anne's first reaction is to laugh, but when Jean doesn't join in she begins to wonder if she's serious. Suddenly her mother seems strange and remote to her, ranting about God and retrieving a Bible from her bedside table.

When Anne was eleven her mother had invoked God's wrath in much the same way. It was the first and last time—until today.

There's still so much she doesn't know about her, about who Jean was before they came to Toronto, about what possible circumstance led her to flee Harmony. Anne's consistent choice of ignorance over truth, denial by sheer avoidance, has made it easier for both of them.

"Don't laugh," Jean says. "It was what I feared most when I left your father."

"That you'd go to hell?"

"And that you would too, when all I ever tried to do was get you *out* of hell—"

Suddenly the EMS paramedics are stomping through the house. Anne's mother looks at Ken Schlittman one last time. "Loneliness is a kind of hell," she says thinly.

And then the door is flung wide open.

Fifteen

*T*he last time Anne's mother mentioned God to her in any significant way was when a neighbor of theirs took it upon herself to teach Anne about sex.

The neighbor's name was Norrie. She lived in the second-floor apartment of Mrs. Roberts's semi. She moved in when Anne was about ten—Anne remembers watching her and her boyfriend carry a futon in by themselves—but it was a long time before she saw her again. She knew from Mrs. Roberts that Norrie worked nights and slept all day and generally minded her business.

Their paths crossed the following summer. Anne was on the front porch one morning, sketching in her journal. She was wearing a bathing suit and sneakers and the sun was blazing hot on her bare shoulders. Norrie came outside and squinted up at the sky. She lit a cigarette.

Anne couldn't take her eyes off Norrie. She was really something to look at. Her hair was bleached so much that the ends looked like charred shoelaces. She wore it in a shaggy perm with bangs that fell over a rolled turquoise bandana around her forehead. She had on chalky pink lipstick that Anne admired from her vantage point on the front porch. Every time Norrie caught Anne staring, Anne would quickly drop her eyes down to her journal.

After she finished her cigarette Norrie went over to the street and flicked her butt into it. Then she came over to Anne's front lawn and said, "Don't you have parents?"

Anne looked up at her, too dazzled and befuddled to respond.

"I see you out here by yourself every day," Norrie said. She had a hoarse voice, either from just having woken up or from a lot of smoking. Anne's eyes kept inadvertently drifting down to her breasts. They were enormous; the biggest she'd ever seen. They looked like boxing gloves under her snug T-shirt. Anne was at the age where that sort of thing fascinated her.

"I see you coming home with groceries and stuff," Norrie went on. "You're like a little grown-up."

Anne was flattered to have been noticed. "I'm an orphan," she replied smartly.

Norrie smiled, revealing two pointy fangs on either side of her front teeth. Anne already worshipped her. There was something about Norrie that excited her. She couldn't decide if Norrie was ugly or gorgeous. She was both. She was garish and stunning and tacky and repellent.

"How old are you?" she asked Anne.

"Eleven."

Norrie looked surprised. "I thought you were older," she remarked, and then asked her to guess how old she was. Anne guessed thirty-five. "Twenty-two," Norrie corrected. Anne couldn't tell if she was pleased or offended by that guess. Her expression revealed nothing.

"What's your name?"

"Anne."

"I'm Norrie," she said, talking to Anne as though they were the same age. She didn't have that condescending, babying way of speaking that most grown-ups did. It was thrilling. "Seriously, how come you're always alone?"

"My mother works for a law firm," Anne told her.

"Oh, you're one of those latchkey kids."

"I guess so."

She invited Anne inside her apartment. There were panties and brassieres drying all over the place. Norrie explained that they were too expensive to go in the washer and dryer. She called them "lingerie." She hand-washed her lingerie in her pedestal sink, which impressed Anne.

There was a vanity in her bedroom, piled with compacts and tubes and bottles. She motioned for Anne to come and stand by her and then she looked her up and down. "You need a makeover," she said.

Anne was too excited to be insulted. She offered herself to her entirely.

Norrie proceeded to stuff cotton balls between Anne's toes and paint her nails with frosty pink polish. She did her fingernails too, trimming the cuticles and filing the uneven edges into squares and then applying the same polish. Then she set to work on her face; she smeared beige foundation into her skin, assaulted her with a big powder puff full of something she called "translucent powder," and daubed rouge on her cheekbones with her thumb. "This is to give you the illusion of cheekbones," she told her. "You have a very round face, see?" She took Anne's chin and pointed her face into the mirror. "I've given you some contouring over here. See how your face looks so much thinner?"

Anne nodded.

"There's only so much I can do though," Norrie added.

Anne examined herself in the mirror and had to agree with Norrie. Something had to be done.

"I can help you this summer," Norrie said confidently.

Her earnest undertaking began that morning. She taught Anne about beauty; about how important it was in the world. She felt that Anne was not a natural beauty and that she'd have to work at it, but that it would be worth it. "You're lucky," she said. "Some girls are just totally hopeless."

The way Norrie talked suggested that she considered herself to be one of the lucky ones. She was always so overdone—so much agonizing effort and attention went into her looks—yet the more Anne got to know her and see her up close, the more she realized how sadly unbeautiful Norrie really was. It simply evaded her. Anne wondered if she knew it too, deep down. She just couldn't be made conventionally pretty, despite her pink nails, her fake blond hair, her flowery smell. She was like a bruised fruit. Beyond salvaging.

She could be competitive with Anne, too. One day she'd be rooting for her, encouraging her to blossom into the pretty teenager she knew Anne could become. She believed in her potential, she said. And then without cause or justification she could be just as vindictive and cruel, telling Anne she was hopeless, pointing out a blackhead or commenting on her bum. The more Anne improved, the less enthusiastic Norrie became about the whole project. Anne's success bothered her. It made her want Anne to look the way she'd looked before.

"You look too old for your age," she'd snarl. Or, "That color is a disaster with your pale skin."

One night after Jean got home from work, Anne asked her mother about Norrie's strange behavior. She wanted to know why one day she could be like a loving, supportive big sister, and the next day she could be her worst enemy.

"Girls are like that," Jean said. "It's just the way they are."

"Why?"

"Jealousy," she answered. "We learn it from each other. You'd better get used to it."

In her own blunt way, her mother was right. Girls inevitably learn to stab each other in the back, to compete, to strive for perfection as though there isn't enough of it to go around. It's a rite of passage, as natural to their development as training bras and menstruation.

It never occurred to Anne to wonder why a twenty-two-year-old woman would be so keenly interested in an eleven-year-old girl. They had something in common though: neither of them had a father. Norrie wanted to find hers when she turned twenty-five. That's when she thought she would be ready. In the meantime, she worked as a waitress at a bar called Cheaters, trying to save money and make something of herself so that she could impress him. Anne remembers she was obsessed with the idea of her father being out there somewhere, waiting for her to materialize. Everything she did, all the care that went into her daily beauty regimen and her appearance and her savings account, was all for him.

One afternoon, deep into the summer of Anne's physical metamorphosis, she was in Norrie's room and Norrie was changing in front of her. When she peeled off her dark blue Jordache jeans and got down to her lacy panties, Anne noticed two purple bruises on her inner thighs. Her eyes grew wide, but Norrie didn't seem at all concerned. It was almost as though she wanted Anne to see them.

"What happened?" Anne asked tentatively. She knew enough of Norrie by then to be afraid of what she could answer.

Norrie glanced down at her bruises and shrugged. "Isn't it obvious?"

The room became hot and swirling. Anne knew there was no way to extricate herself from this one. It was like that with Norrie. One step too far and you were trapped. Anne had mistakenly let herself be drawn in, and now she would have to face her taunting humiliation.

"No," she answered, as boldly as she could. Norrie had the hardness about her that day and Anne just wanted to flee. "It's not obvious to me."

Norrie looked at her impatiently. "Sex?" she said, phrasing it as a question to make Anne feel stupid.

Curiosity overtook all Anne's instincts for self-preservation and she lost herself in the moment. "You got those from sex?" she gasped.

"Yup." Norrie went over to her record player and put on the Psychedelic Furs' "Love My Way." "Aaron can be rough," she explained, softening. "Plus he's a pretty big guy."

Then her face brightened and she looked happy and purposeful, the way she'd looked that very first morning when she'd done Anne's makeup. "I've got an idea," she said.

She went to a drawer in her bureau and pulled something out that caused Anne to turn beet red. "What's that?" she asked, knowing precisely what it looked like.

"It's a wooden penis," Norrie said, giggling. "My last roommate worked for Planned Parenthood. She used to give seminars on how to use rubbers. I stole this from her."

"Why?"

"Why not?"

Anne didn't even know what Planned Parenthood was, but she was too terrified to expose any more fissures of ignorance.

"I'm going to give you a lesson as part of your education," Norrie said.

"With that?"

"Well, it's either this or my vibrator."

(Again, right over Anne's head.)

"I don't want to corrupt you," Norrie said sweetly. "But this could come in handy for you real soon."

Anne understood immediately that corrupting her was exactly what Norrie wanted to do.

She grabbed her purse off the floor and pulled from it a small plastic wrapper, which at first Anne thought was something to eat, a candy maybe. "First you put the rubber on," she instructed, and she tore open the wrapper. Then she rolled it onto the wooden penis very slowly and methodically.

What Norrie did next astounded Anne, not only for its inappropriateness but also for its astonishing lack of modesty and inhibition. She couldn't believe how far Norrie was willing to go to shock Anne at the expense of her own morality. To Anne's wild-eyed horror, she took off her panties and demonstrated exactly what you were supposed to do with a hard penis, and she spared no graphic language for the sake of Anne's eleven-year-old innocence.

Anne could feel warm, shameful tears collecting in the corners of her eyes, but she kept squeezing her lids shut to keep the tears from dribbling onto her cheeks. She was caught so off balance that she couldn't even pretend to be unfazed or stoic. She was trapped in the corner of Norrie's soft pink bedroom that smelled of Anaïs Anaïs perfume, and she just watched, mortified, as Norrie performed her ghastly show.

When she was finished, she smiled. Anne remembers her two fangs had never looked so ugly. "Consider yourself one step ahead of all your friends," she said in a self-congratulatory manner, as though she'd done Anne a favor. "Your boyfriends will appreciate your expertise, believe me."

Anne got up and ran from the apartment.

*A*t first she wasn't sure whether or not to tell her mother. She knew she'd get in trouble. She had enough sense to know she would somehow get implicated. If nothing else, it was her fault for hanging around someone as dangerous and mean as Norrie. On the other hand, she knew she could always blame her mother for never being around to supervise her or take an interest in her friends. Jean was a working mother, susceptible to deep bouts of guilt that Anne knew she grappled with daily. If she needed to, Anne knew she could prey on that. After all, Jean had never asked her what type of person Norrie was, or what she did for a living, or why she was so interested in Anne. Frankly, her mother seemed relieved that someone older had taken Anne under her wing, like a babysitter or a substitute mother.

"Something happened today," Anne blurted.

"What?"

She was lying in her bed, watching Johnny Carson. She had a TV in her room to keep her company on nights when her mother had to work late. Jean was sitting on the edge of Anne's bed. It was her routine to come in and kiss her good night when she got home. Anne always waited up for her. She still remembers that her mother was wearing a white blouse with big shoulder pads and a brooch at her neck.

"You'll be mad," she said.

"Then why tell me?"

Anne rolled away from her mother and started to cry. She felt Jean's hand on her back. "Anne, what is it?"

Anne couldn't find the words to describe what she'd seen, what Norrie had done in front of her. She was so ashamed. All that came out of her mouth were sobs muffled by her pillow.

"Please, Anne," her mother said calmly. Then she reached over and turned on the lamp beside the bed. Anne blinked in the sudden brightness. "Just tell me," Jean urged gently. "You'll feel better."

Anne wanted so badly to unload her burden. She wanted it out of her head, out of her body, out of her thoughts. And so she said, "Norrie did sex with a wooden penis in front of me so that I would have expertise because that's what boys like."

Her mother's face went a bluish-white, like skim milk. Even in the dim amber glow of the bedside lamp, Anne could see all the color seeping out of her mother's cheeks. Jean drew a breath. "Norrie did *what*?" she said tightly.

Anne started from the beginning, with the bruises on Norrie's thighs and her explanation of rough sex. Then she told about the wooden penis and Planned Parenthood. "I don't even know what Planned Parenthood is," she confessed. "But I was too afraid to tell her that!"

And then she told all about the rubber and the lace panties coming off and what Norrie had done with that wooden penis. She finished in a sweeping finale of hysteria and waited fearfully for her mother's reaction. Jean just embraced her tightly, enveloping her in her soft white blouse and stroking her back.

"It's okay," she whispered in Anne's ear. "You're safe." She rocked her back and forth in her arms, telling her it wasn't her fault. They swayed like that together for a long time, until Anne began to calm down. Eventually, Jean lay down and Anne fell asleep in her arms, which she couldn't remember ever having done before, even when she was little.

It was a different scene in the morning. Her mother's anger had crystallized overnight and she was in a rage by the time Anne woke up. Her first clue as to the gravity of the matter was that she'd taken the day off work. Jean never took a day off work. "You don't have to stay home," Anne said in a small voice.

"Get dressed," Jean said.

"Why?"

"We're going over to her apartment."

"I don't want to go back there."

"Get dressed," she said again.

They went next door together, before breakfast. Anne skulked behind her mother, hiding in her shadow. Jean knocked on the door calmly and Norrie appeared moments later in a short robe with a towel around her head. She had on no makeup and, stripped bare of all her usual cosmetics and hair accoutrements and gaudy accessories, Anne almost didn't recognize her. For one thing, she looked much younger; no older than a teenager. She looked softer, too. She had some freckles on her nose that the beige foundation usually concealed, and her lips were much thinner without all the gloss and lip liner. She wasn't pretty—she could never be pretty—but she came across as a lot less lurid and menacing.

Anne thought she detected a look of panic come into her eyes when she saw who it was standing in her doorway.

"Norrie?" Jean said.

"Yes," she answered, in rather a polite, demure tone.

"Mind if we come in for a moment?"

"Sure," she said, letting them in. They entered the foyer and Anne continued to cower behind the imposing figure of her mother. Norrie never looked at Anne. She played it as though she'd never seen her before.

"Anne told me what you did to her yesterday," Jean began.

"What I did?" Norrie repeated innocently.

"Yes, with the wooden—"

"Oh, that." She chuckled dismissively.

"Yes, that."

"She asked me to show her."

"I did not!" Anne cried, emerging from behind her mother. "That's a lie!"

"Does Nancy know what goes on up there?" Jean asked, her rage gathering ominously like a slow-building storm. Anne was devastated at the thought of Mrs. Roberts being dragged into this embarrassing situation. What if she never looked at Anne the same again? What if she treated her differently, knowing the dirty things she'd been exposed to?

"Nothing goes on up there," Norrie murmured. Her voice was sounding a bit tremulous.

"Does she know you're a sexual deviant?"

Norrie blinked, startled.

"Does she know the kind of girl you are?" Jean pursued. "Does she know you're a whore?"

Norrie flinched and stumbled back, as though she'd been hit.

"My daughter is eleven years old, *Norrie*." Jean spit out her name like it was bleach burning the inside of her mouth. "What were you thinking?"

"I'm not a sexual deviant—"

"You'll go to hell for this," Jean hissed. "God will see to it. Do you understand that?"

Norrie laughed. "Sure," she said, gaining some confidence.

"How dare you expose my daughter to your perverted sexual practices!"

Anne looked up at her mother then, baffled. Her eyes were black and angry and spit was flying from her lips as she spoke. Strange things were coming out of her mouth; words Anne had never heard before.

"Perverted sexual practices?" Norrie sneered. "Oh please. It was harmless—"

"Masturbating in front of an eleven-year-old child?" Jean screamed. Her rage was good and boiling now. "What you've done is a crime—"

"No, it's not," Norrie muttered defiantly.

"You'd better be moved out by the end of the month or I'll report you to the police for sexually abusing a child."

"She asked me to show her—"

"Be quiet, you whore. I'll be talking to Nancy next. You have until the end of the month to get out or I promise I'll go to the police."

"This is crazy," Norrie argued, but Anne could see she was scared. A limp protest tumbled weakly from her lips. There was nothing behind it, no power or conviction.

"I won't have my daughter exposed to your sexual deviance," Jean repeated. "I've worked too damn hard to protect her to have the likes of you come along and drag her to hell with you!"

She turned then and stormed out of the house. Anne followed her, stunned and frightened. After that, Jean never mentioned God again. Anne figured it was an isolated incident. She thought it was clever of her mother to talk of hell and Satan and deviance in order to scare Norrie away. It must have worked too, because Norrie was gone by the end of the month. Who could blame her?

And yet there was something ferocious about Jean's attack on Norrie that morning. In retrospect, the depth of her anger was disproportionate to the transgression. Norrie had done wrong, no one could dispute that, but she was nothing more than a pitiful screwup with a penchant for bullying little girls.

Who knows what demons Jean was trying to obliterate by ensuring a safer, more expansive life for her daughter? But whatever she was trying to redeem from her past— whatever promise she'd made to herself when she took Anne away from Harmony—Anne suspected that Norrie had almost ruined it by sullying all her promise.

Sixteen

"*N*ow what?" her mother says. They're sitting on the edge of Jean's bed. Ken's body has been removed from the house. It's on its way to the hospital or the morgue, wherever they take corpses first.

"We need to tell his daughter," Anne says practically.

Her mother looks up with wild eyes. "I can't."

Anne puts her arm around Jean's quivering shoulders and gently pulls her close. "I'll do it," she murmurs. "Did she know about you and Ken?"

Jean shrugs. "I don't know what he's told her. I think they were close."

"Was he married?"

"Divorced. His ex-wife left him. She's a real estate agent now. She earns more than he does—*did*. It really bugged him."

"How long were you two . . . ?"

"Just a few months."

"Were you . . . were you in love?"

"With Ken Schlittman?" she cries. "God, no. He wasn't . . . he wasn't 'in love with' material." She sighs nostalgically. "But he was kind."

For the first time, Anne glimpses the full depth of her mother's loneliness. Her heart swells with guilt. How did she miss it?

Jean gets up all of a sudden and starts stripping the bed. "I have to change the sheets," she says urgently. "I can't sleep in these now. Someone's *died* in them." She stops and shakes her head, incredulous. "It's just so hard to believe."

Anne helps her remove the pillowcases and then tosses them on the floor.

"I have no bleach," Jean mutters distractedly. "I should go to the supermarket—"

"I'll get the bleach, Mom. I'll take care of your sheets."

"I'm fine. You should go get Evan. Who's this woman you left him with anyway?"

"She's a friend. Mom, you seem . . ."

"What?"

"You're acting strange."

"A man's just died in my bed. I apologize if my behavior is—"

"No, it's just . . . I wish you would just *cry*. You don't have to be stoic for me."

Jean waves her hand dismissively. "It's not for you," she says, sounding perturbed. "I'm frazzled, but he wasn't worth sobbing over."

Anne nods supportively, knowing her mother is lying. It's obvious she cared for him, and now she's shell-shocked.

"You don't have his daughter's number, do you?"

Jean gives Anne a helpless look. "I know she lives in a condo somewhere."

"Somewhere? Can you narrow that down?"

"I need to open a window in here," Jean mumbles, looking suddenly quite flushed. Her neck is red and splotchy. "I think she lives in a building called the Cotton Candy. I remember Ken mentioning it."

"The Candy Factory?"

"That's it!"

"That's on Queen West."

Anne reaches for the phone and calls information. "Her name is Jennifer," her mother reminds her. Within seconds Anne's got the number.

"Don't do it here," Jean whispers. She's slumped against the window, looking grief-stricken. What if she loved him?

"I'll go downstairs," Anne offers, and then she leaves her mother by herself.

Anne goes into the kitchen, feeling purposeful and bold. She takes a breath and dials. As it's ringing, she remembers that when she met Ken last fall Jennifer's TV show had just been canceled. Now this.

"Hello?"

Anne's heart is racing. She's never had to break the news to anyone that a loved one has died. "Jennifer?"

"Yes."

"My name is Anne Biffin. My mother Jean is a friend of your father's—"

"Yes?" she cuts in. She's got an edge, which unnerves Anne all the more.

"He's actually a client of my mother's. She's a masseuse—"

"And?" Brusquely, impatient.

"Jennifer, your father . . ."

Anne's voice peters out.

"*Yes?*"

"Your father had a heart attack during his massage—"

"Oh my God," she gasps. "Is he okay?"

Her brusqueness has given way to panic. Anne instantly softens toward her and chokes up with compassion.

"He . . . he . . ." She's not sure how to put it. "He passed away."

For a long moment, Jennifer is silent. The receiver gets hot in Anne's hand while she waits for a reaction. Her ear burns. She has no idea what to do or say next.

Finally, Jennifer whimpers, "My father's dead?"

"I'm sorry."

She starts wailing. Anne has to hold the receiver away from her head. It goes on like that for a long time, but she doesn't want to rush her.

"Where is he?" Jennifer sobs.

"I think Sunnybrook."

"You think?"

"Yes."

"I need to call my mom."

"Sure."

"Who are you again?" she asks, sniffling.

"I'm Anne. My mother and your father . . . my mother might have been his girlfriend."

More uncomfortable silence. "I thought you said she was his masseuse."

"That too."

The phone goes dead. Anne hangs up and turns to find her mother standing in the doorway. "How did she take it?" she asks Anne.

"She's pretty devastated."

Jean nods. "I thought so. They were close."

"Why don't you come home with me and spend the night, Mom?"

She shakes her head.

"Elie can make dinner—"

"No. I'm fine. You go."

"I'll wash your linens first."

"I'll do it," she insists. "I'll go get some bleach. The walk will do me good."

Anne relents and starts collecting her things. Jean walks her to her car. Before getting in, Anne kisses her cheek.

"Are you okay?" she asks, feeling guilty about leaving.

"I think so. I just feel like it's my fault. That I caused it to happen."

"Why? How?"

She looks away. "With the things I've done," she confesses.

"That's ridiculous. He had a heart attack—"

"God punishes," she says with conviction. "They were right about that."

*I*n light of the fact that her mother and Ken Schlittman were lovers, Anne decides it's appropriate to go with Jean to sit Shiva.

"What is a Shiva anyway?" she asks Elie, on their way to Ken's apartment on Bathurst.

"It's the Jewish mourning period," he answers. He wasn't very keen on coming, but when Anne mentioned Ken's coin collection he agreed to accompany them, hoping to get a glimpse of it.

"It's up there on the right," Jean says. "Just past Wilson."

Elie finds a parking spot and then Anne unfastens Evan from the car seat. He's wearing a pair of sweatpants today, a slight improvement over his pajamas. A little suit would have been so precious, Anne laments as she lifts him into her arms.

Ken Schlittman's building reminds her of their first apartment in Toronto—it's got that same sixties exterior and neglected lobby. The apartment itself is just as depressing, with windows facing out onto the back alley and scuffed, honey-colored parquet floors. It's a two-bedroom apartment—the second one was his office—with a pink-tiled bathroom, a kitchenette that can barely contain the basic appliances and a balcony that she can see is infested with pigeon shit. She can't help feeling sorry for him; for what a sad life he must have led, selling suits on commission, coming home to this place at night, and Jean as his companion.

At least the apartment is clean. There are still vacuum tracks in the beige carpet in his bedroom and a faint lemony smell of cleaning products. A circle of chairs has been set up in the living room for the immediate family. About twenty people are milling around, conversing intimately with one another, napkins of hors d'oeuvres lining their upturned palms. She wonders about the guests—if they're friends and family, or strangers like herself. She surmises that the majority of them must be only remotely connected. It fits better with her idea of him.

Jean goes directly to the circle and introduces herself to a thirtyish woman with a narrow face and sharp features. The woman is pale and without a speck of makeup, but not unattractive. With her hair pulled back in a severe ponytail and the nondescript black dress she's wearing, she's the picture of mourning.

"Your father was a dear friend," Jean says, sounding formal and unconvincing. "I'm Jean Biffin."

The woman looks up, casting her red-rimmed eyes on Jean. Her lips curl into a frown. There's no mistaking her reaction to Jean's name. Anne can only imagine what's going through her head. *So this is the woman who killed my father.*

"He talked about you all the time," Jean goes on. "He was very proud of you. He was a big fan of *Clarence & Co.*"

Jennifer Schlittman smiles politely. It looks more like a flinch than a smile.

"You were his masseuse?" Jennifer inquires, her tone thick with irony.

"Yes."

It's obvious to everyone that her mother was more than just Ken's masseuse—it was the sexual intercourse that killed him—but that bit of information is left unspoken.

"Thank you for coming," Jennifer utters, with a look of such disdain it makes Anne wonder if she thinks Jean is some kind of prostitute.

Anne leans into the circle and extends her hand. "My mother really *cared* for your father," she emphasizes.

Jennifer returns her handshake with a puzzled look.

"I'm Anne," she clarifies. "I'm the one who called you. And this is my husband, Elie, and my son—"

"Thank you for coming," she repeats in a cold, robotic voice.

An elderly woman seated next to Jennifer stands up and gestures toward one of the bedrooms. "If you're hungry," she says, "there's a buffet table set up in Ken's office." She smiles apologetically and adds, "There wasn't enough room in the living room."

"I could eat," Elie says in a hushed voice, and they all move off toward the buffet.

"Mom, do you want something to nibble on?" Anne asks.

Jean shakes her head distractedly. "I don't think she has a clue who I am," she says, sounding distraught.

"Who?"

"Ken's daughter. He obviously never mentioned me to her."

"You never mentioned *him* to me," Anne reminds her, shifting Evan onto her other hip.

Jean gives Anne an irritated look. "But they were so close."

Anne opens her mouth to retaliate, but Elie takes Anne by the hand and leads her to the table.

"Did you hear that?" Anne mutters indignantly. "*They* were so close. As though *we're* not."

"She's upset."

"She does it on purpose. She's always taking jabs at me."

"It's not about you."

"Isn't it?"

"She cared about him," he says. "You know that, don't you?"

Anne nods, feeling instantly remorseful.

There's a bowl of Pepperidge Farm goldfish crackers on the table, which Evan spots immediately. "Ish! Ish!" he cries, straining to get at them. Anne stuffs a couple in his mouth while Elie serves himself a platter of chopped liver, rye bread and Bundt cake.

They go over to Ken's desk, which is by the window in the corner of the room. It's a safe place to hang out, since no one else is around. Mostly the guests just drift in, grab some food and then quickly escape the cramped office. "Let's just hide out here until my mother's ready to leave," Anne suggests.

Elie nods enthusiastically. She sets Evan down on the

floor to play, noticing a pile of boxes beneath the desk. "El, look at this."

"What?"

"All these boxes." She points to where it says DAD'S COINS in black marker.

Elie's eyes widen. He has that excited look he gets whenever he's around coins. "She's already started packing up his collection," he says, sounding disappointed. He bends down and opens one of them to peek inside. "She hasn't taped them shut yet," he points out, in justification of his snooping.

"Elie, don't open them—"

"Holy shit," he gasps. "There are a lot of coins in here."

Anne peers over Elie's shoulder into the box. Inside there are dozens of the little colored storage boxes she recognizes from Elie's shop. They look like those rectangular boxes that used to hold old movie slides, but they're lined with Mylar coin holders. Each one is a different color—red for one-cent coins, blue for nickels, green for dimes.

Elie pulls out an orange storage box and pops off the lid. "Here's a rare version of a seventy-three Canadian quarter," he observes. Then he pulls out another quarter with a red blob in the center.

"What's that?"

"It's a colored poppy quarter from ninety-four. The mint circulated it to commemorate Remembrance Day. It's one of those novelty coins. I think they put out a red Santa quarter that year, too."

"Put those away," Anne whispers. "You shouldn't be going through his collection."

"You got me to come with you under the pretext that I could see his collection."

"I thought it might be on display, not all packed up."

He continues rifling. "Nothing worth very much so far," he remarks, unimpressed. "Still, I'd love to go through all these boxes . . ."

"You can't. Put that back."

Reluctantly, he closes the box and stands up. "I want to appraise this collection," he says decisively. He's got that gleam in his eyes. "Should I say something to her?"

"Of course not. This is her father's Shiva. His coins are the last thing on her mind."

Nevertheless, when it's time for them to leave Elie ignores her warning and goes over to Jennifer Schlittman. He pulls her aside. Anne watches them speak in hushed voices for a while before sauntering over to listen.

"Whenever you're ready," Elie is saying, "I'd be happy to appraise it."

"I just started going through his things," she says wearily. "I can't think that far ahead right now . . ."

"They might need to be in a safe," Elie advises, attempting to entice her. "They might be worth something."

Her interest is momentarily piqued. He can be a manipulative bastard, but he always gets his way.

"I'll leave you my card," he says, smiling with a masterful blend of sympathy and seduction.

She manages a smile in return. "You think it could be worth something?" she asks.

"Judging by how many boxes I saw, absolutely."

She tucks Elie's card into her pocket and thanks him. Anne can tell that Elie is trying to rein in his exuberance. He's trying to look as blasé as possible, but she can see the greed and impatience all over his face.

Seventeen

She closes her eyes and imagines Declan pushing her down onto *Strawberry Fields*—the table she made with hundreds of assiduously cut-out paper strawberries shellacked to its surface. She conjures the slope of his bare shoulder. His forearm with the *Creideamh* tattoo. *Strawberry Fields* rocking beneath them . . .

"I forgot to take the garbage out," Elie groans.

Anne rolls away from him, embarrassed. She lies there for a while, staring into the darkness, feeling very alone. His warm body doesn't excite her. The sliver of mattress between them feels like a continent.

She drifts back to fantasies of Declan and wonders if that's how cheating would happen. Would it be that effortless? A mutual acquiescence, a tacit agreement to forsake everything to satisfy an overwhelming sexual urge? Then she wonders if he ever thinks of her when he puts his feet up on his aqua mosaic coffee table.

Later, she finds herself flipping to the G section of the phone book, not really intending to call Declan but curious to see if he's in there; to be sure he lives, not just in her head but in reality. Everything about him—the way he looks at her with that curious, mischievous, flirty gleam in his eyes, the way he rubbed glue off her hands that night, the way he sits in the support group meetings with his legs open and his elbows on his knees, his foot bouncing nervously when he shares—all of it is a brilliant distraction from the daily woes of artist's block, marital stagnation and deformed feet.

There are dozens of D. Grays. She could call them all. She has nothing better to do. But she grabs hold of herself. Lust is so consuming and irrational. It would devour her if she let it. She tosses the phone book back in the bottom drawer of Elie's antique secretary and takes herself out of the den.

She quietly pokes her head into the darkened nursery. Evan is sleeping on his side, with his dog firmly clenched in his hand. She pulls the door closed behind her and tiptoes away quickly, before the monitor explodes with his wakening cries. There are days when she loves him so much it blurs into something almost painful, like a kind of gripping, smothering fear; days when she wants to possess him and hold on to those tiny hands that smell of maple teething cookies. Then there are the other days—the selfish, resentful days—when it's her will against his; when there is no acceptance in her heart for his demands; when his crying irritates her, his mealtimes fill her with dread and the mere idea of their daily routine stretched out before her feels like a kind of purgatory she will never escape. She doesn't know if it's like that with all mothers, or just the inferior ones.

She wanders down the hallway into Elie's office and goes directly to his desk. She decides to call Tami.

"You've reached Darren, Tami and Parker!" (Exclamation point!) "We're not here right now, but leave a message and we'll get back to you as soon as possible!" The message ends with Parker babbling nonsense in the background. Anne hangs up without saying anything.

Before she can even set the phone back in its charger, it rings in her hand.

"Hello?"

"I just missed you!" Tami pants. "I was at the gym. I just joined the Dunfield Club. They have day care so I can take Parker—right, Parky?—and I managed seventeen minutes on the stationary bike. It's my belated New Year's resolution to finally lose my baby weight." She pauses to catch her breath, and then, "Anyway, I saw your number on my call display. What's up?"

"Nothing really," Anne responds lackadaisically, not even sure why she called Tami in the first place.

"Did you want to go for coffee?" Tami asks, sounding almost desperate. She occasionally makes Anne feel like the popular girl in high school, like she'll do anything to be her friend or even just to trail after her.

"I'm pretty exhausted," Anne says. "I'm not sleeping much."

"Evan?"

"Actually, no. He's mostly sleeping through the night now. It's me. I'm becoming an insomniac."

"The same thing happened to me. As soon as Parker started sleeping through the night, *I* couldn't fall asleep."

"How long did that last?"

"Until I did acupuncture," she says. "You should try my acupuncturist. He's a miracle worker."

Anne lets Tami give her his name and number. This seems to make Tami happy. She's a person who likes to be of service.

"You have to be open-minded," she warns. "Dr. You does everything—traditional Chinese herbs, chakra acupuncture."

"I don't know anything about that."

"Traditional Chinese acupuncture harmonizes the flow of qi by unblocking your energy channels. Chakra acupuncture expands on that by including the Indian chakra system." She goes on about energy meridians for a while, but after a certain point Anne tunes her out. She's suddenly anxious to go and pour herself a glass of wine, fall onto the couch and daydream about Declan.

"Anyway," Tami chirps, "if you change your mind about coffee, give me a call, 'kay?"

"'Kay."

Hanging up, Anne reflects on how fast they've become like old friends, with that easy, airy casualness of women who know each other too well. It occurs to Anne that she's lonely, just like her mother was lonely at this age, and she doesn't want to wind up like that.

She dials Elie's number at work. "What're you doing?" she asks him.

"Working," he says impatiently. "I'm in the middle of an appraisal—"

"What time are you coming home?"

"I don't know. Seven, seven thirty. What's the matter?"

"Nothing. Does something have to be the matter?"

"Usually, yes."

They hang up without even saying goodbye to each other, not out of anger but out of habit and a mutually agreed upon lack of courtesy. In the beginning, they wouldn't get off the phone without an "I love you, baby." But now they're in the middle of their marriage, which can often feel like that long, boring section of a bloated thousand-page novel.

It's five years ago now since they made their vows. They were married by a petite Asian minister in Jean's backyard. Anne invited Sharon and some of her university friends (whom she immediately fell out of touch with after the wedding) and Elie had a few colleagues from work there. None of his family came from Lebanon. The whole thing was understated and brief, but it was just right for them. It was a happy day. There was nothing traditional or vainglorious about it. She didn't throw a bouquet or have Elie remove her garter belt. There were no schmaltzy speeches or cutting of any three-tiered cake. She had no maid of honor and wore nothing borrowed or blue. There is only a single photograph taken by Anne's mother to mark that moment in their lives, but she can say emphatically that she had no doubts either. No regrets, no moments of wavering or hesitation, not even a question in the back of her mind about the rightness of their union.

There was a peaceful certainty about her wedding day and, in its own humble way, it was quite perfect.

It's not as though her love for Elie has faded over time or that she's begun to desire him any less. She still loves the way he can make a single, crushing point by quoting Fitzgerald off the top of his head. She loves that he was unfazed by living in violent, war-ravaged Beirut but he's terrified of barking dogs. She loves that he has no male friends who spend Sunday afternoons at her house watching football, eating potato chips and guzzling beer. She loves that he hand-paints with watercolors. She loves falling asleep with her feet tucked into the warm, hairy crevice behind his bent knees.

It was that moment when she and Elie got really comfortable together—around the time in her pregnancy when her weight soared past 150 pounds—that the complacency began to set in. The romance took another major blow after Evan was born. Unfortunately, that warm crevice behind Elie's knees is no substitute for the thrill of a new, unfolding seduction. It's a rush every time Anne proves to herself she can conquer a man with nothing more than her body and a lingering, meaningful glance. There's a certain provocative power in extracting the desire of a man, especially if he's unavailable.

Elie cannot supply that same hit of power anymore. She's already conquered him. Instead, they've entered into that numbingly safe time warp that brings great comfort and great boredom in equal parts. Now it's up to the UPS guys and the Declan Grays of the world to keep her buzz going, a realization that fills her with fear and uncertainty. She would love the buzz to come from her marriage, but she suspects that might be a naive notion.

In her more optimistic moments she dismisses her current feelings toward Elie as a typical postpartum phase. (Just like her crush on Declan, her new tattoo, her artist's block and whatever else in her life isn't working that requires a sweepingly efficient excuse.) She still has some hope of rekindling the old lust with Elie, but hope is flimsy and intangible; it comes and goes. Faith, on the other hand, would be a lot more solid.

Dr. You sits behind his desk, glaring at her through thick, dirty glasses. (She doesn't know how his vision could be any worse than it is through all those spots and fingerprints.) He's wearing a black hairpiece that doesn't even pretend to be real hair. It's sitting lopsided on his head, with no part. His office has a mildewy, neglected smell. There's a sign hanging on the wall behind him, written in broken English and advertising an array of peculiar panaceas for just about all of life's most mundane and tragic problems. KANG YUAN ANTI-CANCER TABLET. SLIM 1-2-3 FOR HEALTH BEAUTY & SLIM. ANT POWDER CAPSULE CURE MALE SEXUAL DYSFUNCTION. DAN GUI FOR MENSTUAL CRAMP. BILBERRY EXTRACT IMPROVE BAD BREATH. Her mind keeps returning to thoughts of his needles and the state of their hygiene.

"You have too much yang," he barks.

"You can tell that by looking at me?"

"Can tell everything by looking."

"What do you mean by too much yang?"

"Too much masculine. Need to balance yang with yin. Need more feminine."

"Do you use single-use disposable needles?" she asks him.

He frowns. "No needles yet," he growls. "Start with tea."

He gets up, disappearing into another room. She hears things clanging. Moments later he comes back out holding a mug, which he hands her. "Body system too hot. Not in harmony. Yang is *hot*. Need more cold to balance."

"What's in this?" she asks nervously, peering into her mug of what looks like a murky shit soup.

"Some herbs. And some other herbs."

"I can't drink this," she tells him.

He shrugs.

"I thought I was getting acupuncture."

"Thought wrong."

"Will this help me sleep?"

"Help everything."

She looks at the tea. She thinks she sees a fingernail floating on the surface. Maybe one of Dr. You's grubby nails. She lifts the mug to her nose. Whatever the concoction is, it reeks. She looks helplessly at Dr. You.

"Second chakra blocked," he says.

"What?"

"Tea help unblock second chakra. Help with balance and harmony." He stands up and pats his groin. "Second chakra here. Reproductive organ."

Anne looks down at her second chakra.

"You have fertility problem?" he asks her. "Miscarriage?"

"I had some problems—"

"You have lust for other man, not husband?"

She stares at him, not sure what to say. Her hot red cheeks supply his answer.

He nods emphatically. "Infidelity, infertility, both cause by interference with second chakra."

She closes her eyes and brings the mug of tea to her lips. She drinks it down in one gulp. A horrendous mistake. It slides down her throat like mucus. Some of the herbs cling to her tongue and the roof of her mouth, poisoning her with their bitterness. She gags, trying valiantly to hold it down. She counts to ten, feeling like a contestant on *Fear Factor,* as though she's just swallowed blended rat intestines or something. "Get me water," she gasps.

But before Dr. You can get to his little laboratory back there, Anne lurches forward and throws the tea up all over his desk. The sight of the regurgitated tea makes her heave again and her banana from breakfast lands on his desk in a lumpy grayish-yellow puddle.

"I'm sorry," she murmurs, her eyes watering. "I'll clean it up—"

Dr. You rushes into his laboratory and comes back with a roll of paper towels. He looks away while she mops up the mess. She continues to gag, over and over again, silently cursing Dr. You and his tea. Cursing Tami. "I thought I was getting acupuncture," she tells him plaintively. "I have a weak stomach. I tried to tell you . . ."

Dr. You is watching her with a perplexed look on his face. Her energy system seems to be beyond the scope of his miracle-working capabilities.

"You go," he says blandly. "You go."

She stumbles out of his office and heads straight for the nearest pharmacy to buy a pack of mints.

In bed that night, Elie comments that her breath smells like shit. The remark is pretty innocuous for Elie, but tonight she's feeling downtrodden and wearier than usual. She starts to cry.

"It's not that bad," he retracts guiltily, startled by her sudden fragility. "I mean, it's been worse—"

She blurts out what happened with Dr. You. When she's finished, he stares at her with a blank, pitiless expression— similar to the one Dr. You laid on her after she puked on his desk.

"Why are you looking at me like that?"

"What do you need an acupuncturist for?" he asks her in a bullying tone.

"To help me sleep."

"Why do you always need these crutches—the infertility group, the club foot group, the starving women who go to too many self-help groups group . . ."

"For support. I go for support."

"I don't understand," he says, sounding discouraged. "You're always chasing after some gimmick."

"Dr. You wasn't a gimmick!" she defends.

"Dr. Me?"

"Dr. You, asshole. His name is Dr. You."

Elie falls back against the upholstered headboard and lets out a deep, hearty laugh. Anne has to look away to hide her own smile.

"Hi, Dr. You," Elie taunts. "It's me. You? No, *me*. You're You."

"Fuck you," she says, giggling.

"Yes, fuck You! No more Dr. You for you!"

All of a sudden, Elie takes her hands and pulls her on top of him so that she's sitting on his lower abdomen, straddling him. He puts his hands on her hips and moves her gently forward and back. He moans.

"Elie—"

He closes his eyes and keeps moving her body back and forth, simulating sex. He raises his pelvis and presses his hard-on up against her.

"Stop it," she tells him.

"Why?" He opens his eyes.

"I don't feel like it."

He looks surprised. "You're rebuffing me?" he says.

She tries to laugh off the seriousness with which he's asking the question. "It's not a big deal."

He pushes her off him and she lands in a heap on her side of the bed. "Hey!" she cries indignantly.

"Is there some kind of support group out there for frigid wives?" he asks viciously. (Come to think of it, she once noticed a flyer at one of the churches advertising a support group for "sexual anorexia." But she doesn't dare mention that to Elie.)

"Is it so wrong to want to feel better?" she asks pitifully.

"Better than what?"

"Better than *this*."

He shakes his head disparagingly. "I don't get it," he utters, sounding helpless and betrayed.

"What's not to get, Elie?"

"I just don't understand how someone who has *so much* can still feel so goddamn empty all the time."

Eighteen

She's sitting in a church pew, squinting into the blinding whiteness of the July sun, wishing she was outside. Bored, and with nothing better to think about, she observes how the sunlight has filtered in through the windows and collected in pools of light above the heads of the Sunday worshippers like halos.

Her mother is sitting beside her with an open Bible neatly in her lap. She's wearing a strange, ankle-length gingham pioneer dress. On the other side of her sit two squirming boys, trying miserably to contain their rambunctiousness. The names James and Thomas are in her head, even though she doesn't recognize the boys. They both have blond hair and suntanned faces, but the long-sleeved shirts buttoned at the neck and long pants they're wearing seem strangely out of context considering the blazing summer heat.

She turns slightly, scanning the pews behind her. Then she cranes her neck to the other side of the room, seeking out the face of her father. There he is, in the front row with all the other men.

She stares at him with determination, demanding acknowledgment. Her father is a man who stands out from the rest. He seems to loom larger than the others, standing taller and straighter and broader than they. He has a gloriously thick crown of hair that, depending on the time of day or the type of lighting, can look either reddish-orange like a setting sun or as gold as straw. Same with his beard, though lately flecks of silver have begun to push through like weeds in a garden.

He wears a crisp white shirt, also buttoned at the neck, with black pants. His face has more of a texture than a complexion, with the ruddy, crinkled effect of years of exposure to the sun. He's got a narrow nose with a long, prominent bridge and two slashes for nostrils, but his personality comes through his eyes, the way it does with most people of a certain intimidating character. They're the unreflective, black-blue color of the deepest part of the ocean—that dark, ominous water where ships vanish without a trace. There's no kindness in them either, no warmth or softness. Depending on his mood, they can be withering or slyly clever; a cleverness that belies the simple faith-based life he prophesizes.

"And this town will be lifted into heaven," the preacher is saying, "with the second coming of our Lord, Jesus Christ. And I assure you, friends, that that time will be upon us shortly, despite what the apostates say . . ."

Her father blinks, mesmerized by the sermon. Looking at him in profile, with his silver-flecked beard, his acute, calculating eyes and that large jutting nose, she thinks he resembles a wolf. There's a cold solemnity about his expression that keeps people at a distance, and as he often says, there are plenty of people who need to be kept at a distance. Strangers mostly. He never fails to remind them of it.

He is a man who covets privacy and minds his own business. He is proud and values the hot grueling work that validates his maleness and his rights to the earth. He is intimidating, to be sure, but he treats his family and the members of his community judiciously. She knows this from the women, for whom he is something of an exalted, mythical figure. As he is for her.

She continues to stare in his direction, willing him to notice her. Her gaze is hungry and searching. He must feel the heat or vibration of her burning eyes—whatever it is that pulls him from his religious reverie—because he turns to her at last and their eyes meet across the aisle.

A gust of intolerable anguish sweeps over her like a cold wind. She wants to fling herself over the pews that divide them, claw at his chest and keep him all for herself. She doesn't want to share him anymore, the way she's had to share everything else in her life.

He holds her look for a moment. His expression is stern and pious. The preacher says: "But the people of Harmony will be saved!"

And then her father winks at her, before turning back toward the pulpit.

Long after she wakes up, the dream lingers. The details—though illogical—feel profoundly, poignantly right.

Nineteen

*T*he usual cast of characters is gathered under the garish, fluorescent lights of the church basement, balancing their paper plates of Krispy Kremes on their laps and sipping coffee from Styrofoam cups. There's a sign thumb-tacked to the wall, no doubt forgotten from a previous AA meeting, that says LET GO AND LET GOD, and a peculiar, musty smell of wet wood and cabbage soup, scarcely masked by wafts of percolating coffee. The pipes wail and moan and then clang distractingly like cymbals. The room continues to fill up, plastic folding chairs dragging across the linoleum toward the growing circle. Every time the big wooden doors swing open Anne jerks around to see if it's him.

Anne is wearing her jeans again, determined that he should see her in them. She glances up at the clock, starting to get nervous. She considers that he does this to her deliberately—showing up late, sauntering in long after the last chair has joined the circle. Then she dismisses the notion as preposterously self-centered. (But what if . . . ?)

"Good evening and welcome to our Monday night meeting of Parents of Club Foot Babies. I'm Beth, and I'll be your chairperson for tonight."

"Hi, Beth."

Still no Declan. The disappointment comes in like a tide. Anne's thoughts begin to spiral further and further away from the group. She feels herself retreating into compulsiveness. *Six minutes late. Seven minutes late.* She sees some of the members speaking—the motions of their mouths opening, closing. They could be yawning for all she knows. There is no sound in the room.

All the preparation and adorning—mental and physical—all the building up in her mind, the anticipating: it will all have been for nothing, and it will leave her with nothing to latch onto over the coming week.

Anne keeps nodding her head absently for the benefit of the group. She wears her best glazed-ham look as she pretends to be listening to their tedious rambling. Five more minutes and then she'll leave. She's lost interest in the group anyway. Without Declan, she can hardly force herself to sit here and listen—

The door gives a sudden loud squeak and then trembles shut. She doesn't risk turning to look. *Please let it be him.* There's some shuffling behind her, then a chair is set down opposite her.

Declan.

Their eyes lock. Hers were the first ones he sought. Her body tingles with a fizzy blend of relief and joy. She sits up straighter and listens with renewed focus to the woman sitting beside her, a pregnant woman Anne's never seen before.

"So at my twenty-week ultrasound," she's saying in a soft, flat voice, "the nurse thought there might be a problem with my son's feet. That's when my ob-gyn suggested I have another ultrasound at eight months, to make sure . . ."

She clears her throat and collects herself before finishing. "Turns out my son's going to have two severe club feet. I was hoping to come here tonight and find out what there is to do about it . . ."

She looks at all of them in earnest. Anne knows exactly what she's hoping to hear tonight: confirmation that it's a minor problem, just as her doctor assured her. Poor girl, full of fear and naive expectations, just as Anne was. Anne feels a surge of compassion. This girl is only at the beginning. She has nothing but uncertainty ahead of her.

At the break Declan acknowledges Anne with a cool nod. Then he throws on his navy pea jacket and heads outside. In light of their last encounter at the coffee shop, she thinks a verbal "hello" would have been more appropriate. She follows him out, armed with a neutral opening line—nothing too forward. Nothing that would give away her real motives.

She finds him in the parking lot, huddled under a streetlamp with a cigarette. He's wearing his toque and with his pea jacket he looks like he could be in the navy.

She takes a breath and musters a "Hello."

He looks up. "Hi."

Then nothing. After a few long moments of silence, when it seems as though he has nothing at all to say, she turns helplessly to go back inside.

Just as she reaches the door his voice comes out of the night, lassoing her back. "After the meeting a couple weeks ago, you said you'd be at last week's meeting."

She turns to him. "There was a death," she explains.

"Oh." Sheepishly. "Sorry. Was it family?"

"It was a client of my mother's. It's just—he died in her house and there was a bit of a scene. It happened that Monday."

"I figured your son's operation was a success," he says. "And you wouldn't be back."

"I wish. His feet were too swollen to tell if they're straight. The next cast change is in two weeks."

"More waiting."

She nods, grateful to have club feet between them for lack of anything else to talk about, but wishing one of them had the courage to steer the conversation in a more stimulating direction. "What about your son?" she asks. "I can't remember if he's had the operation—"

"No. Margaret opted to wait," he says tightly. "She didn't want to rush into surgery when Sean was only six months old. She thought it was too young. She figures there's a good chance they'll straighten out on their own. She's an optimist."

"Are they?" Anne asks. "Straightening out?"

"Not a goddamn bit," he says. "And it's been months. I'd have gone for the operation—"

"Don't you have a say?"

"No."

Elie would probably say the same thing about them.

"We're just putting off the inevitable," Declan says.

It's a dark night, and cold. Declan is barely illumined by the small yellow light above him. She wishes they were inside, where it's warm and where she'd see more than just his shadowy outline and could read his expression for clues.

"I feel sorry for that pregnant woman," he says. "Starting this whole fucking journey—"

"At least we're getting to that light at the end of the tunnel."

"Did you know Evan had club feet when you were pregnant?" he asks her.

"No. It wasn't detected." She thinks bitterly about the technician who gave her the ultrasound and missed it.

"We knew," he says. "But what are you going to do, right?"

"There's nothing you can do."

"The doctor said it was a minor problem."

"Which it is, relatively speaking."

"We certainly wouldn't have gotten rid of him," Declan states emphatically. "Not on account of club feet!"

"Of course not." The thought of it is too monstrous, too selfish to even contemplate.

The conversation sags for a moment, and then he says, "Are we still talking about club feet?"

Anne lets out a relieved laugh. "We are."

"We're two seemingly interesting, intelligent people," he observes wryly. "Is there nothing else going on in the world worth discussing?"

"Apparently not."

"Genocide in Africa? Tension in the Middle East?"

"I'd rather stick to club feet."

He looks at her then and it causes her heart to thump wildly and miss beats. It's as though he's contemplating her, mulling over the possibility of her. His eyes twinkle with intrigue, lingering ever so slightly on her face and awakening something raw and hopeful inside her.

Usually her attractions for men are light and buoyant. With Declan it's more like a dense, dizzying mass; it has energy and weight to it and a kind of intangible force that pulls and tugs.

She glances at her watch and motions toward the church. "We should get back," she tells him, hoping he'll invite her for a drink instead. "It's starting up again."

"I don't think I'll stick around," he says.

Her heart plummets. Just when things were escalating.

Watching him head off to his car, she wonders how he manages to look at her that way and still be so indifferent.

Twenty

SickKids hospital again. This time Dr. Hotz is away in Florida and another orthopedist is doing Evan's cast change. Her name is Dr. Turvey and she introduces herself with a firm, self-assured handshake. She's tall and lanky, with something tomboyish about her manner that for some reason Anne finds reassuring. Behind her glasses, her gray eyes are competent and warm. Right away Anne prefers her to Hotz. Perhaps simply by virtue of her being a woman, Anne automatically allots her a certain measure of compassion; or perhaps it's because she has braces on her teeth, which makes her seem more human, instead of those fake veneers that seem to symbolize everything Anne loathes about Dr. Hotz.

"Did you notice how she treated us?" she remarks to Elie as Dr. Turvey disappears with Evan.

"No."

"Like we matter."

He gives her a peculiar look, something between indifference and tolerance.

In the waiting room she flips through an *Elle Decor* and an *Us* magazine, but having slept little the past few nights, she eventually leans her head on Elie's shoulder and dozes. She feels his hand gently tickling the back of her neck, which causes her to shiver with pleasure. "That feels nice," she murmurs.

The next thing she knows Elie is nudging her awake after an undetermined space of time and she feels herself swimming back up to the surface of reality. It's an effort to open her eyes. When she does, Dr. Turvey is standing above them.

"Do you want to see how they look?" she asks. "Before I put on the new casts?"

They follow her wordlessly down the corridor. She finds herself asking God—whom she does not necessarily believe in—for a miracle; a kind of healing that likely exceeds the scope of science and medicine.

Just as she's about to set foot in Evan's room, Elie takes her arm and pulls her back. "Be realistic," he says. "There's still a long way to go, Anne."

"Not necessarily."

He sighs. "Just keep your expectations in check, all right?"

She nods dismissively and pulls away from him. She rushes over to her boy, who is asleep on his back, breathing noisily and steadily. He looks so vulnerable, sprawled out on the table like that. Her heart clenches. She hunches over him and smoothes out the soft dark down on his head and then kisses that tender, fleshy part in the center of his forehead that feels like a ripe peach.

"How do they look?" she asks Dr. Turvey, not quite courageous enough to look for herself.

"The right one is completely straight," she says enthusiastically. Anne's elation is somewhat watered down by the definitive "but" in Dr. Turvey's tone. "But the left one . . ."

"What's wrong with it?"

"It hasn't responded as well to the surgery," she concedes, sounding disappointed.

Elie is inspecting Evan's feet at the opposite end of the table. Anne can tell by his silence that the prognosis isn't good. She goes over for a closer look.

"It's still very early though," Dr. Turvey is saying.

Anne's first reaction is to gasp. She had mentally prepared for the possibility of swelling; even for the possibility that his feet wouldn't be completely straight. But what her woefully misguided predictions had failed to account for was the scarring—two monstrous, purple, L-shaped scars on either foot.

"Those scars . . ." she mutters, unable to conceal her shock.

"But look," Elie says, "the right foot is perfectly straight. It's like it was never a club foot."

"Yes. But—"

"I think that's very hopeful," Elie pursues. "It's better than I was expecting."

"What about the left one?" Anne manages. "Why did one work but not the other?"

"I wouldn't say the left one didn't work," Dr. Turvey says calmly, tempering Anne's rising voice. "It's just a little more stubborn."

"Stubborn?" Anne repeats, her eyes still fixed on Evan's scars. "What does that mean?"

"Maybe he'll need more casting, but just on the left foot."

Anne turns to Elie, crestfallen.

"I'm encouraged by the right foot," he says. "It's as good as new—"

"As good as new?" she cries. "Look at those scars! Those will never heal. He's always going to have them, for the rest of his life—"

"Anne." Elie glances over at Dr. Turvey, embarrassed.

"Dr. Hotz never mentioned about the scarring," she complains. "He never said it would be this bad. In fact, he never said, period."

"You had to know there would be scarring," Dr. Turvey says patiently. "It was a surgery, Mrs. Mahroum."

"Dr. Hotz never said there'd be two giant purple L's on his feet—"

"The healing process can be very different from one child to the next," she explains. "So the extent of the scarring is unpredictable. And Tyler still has another month before the casts come off—"

"Evan!" Anne corrects indignantly, tears springing to her eyes. "His name is Evan."

"Evan," Dr. Turvey says coolly. "I'm sorry. I just had a Tyler—"

Anne crouches over Evan's ruined feet. It's plain to her that the surgery was a failure and that it's left him virtually disfigured.

"There's a wonderful silicone gel—"

"I thought the surgery was a guarantee," she utters weakly, cutting off the doctor.

"It's still too early . . ."

"I'll meet you at the car," Anne tells Elie. "I need some air."

"I still have to put on the new casts—" Dr. Turvey reminds her.

"I'll be at the car."

She kisses Evan before escaping the room, but she can't bring herself to look at his feet. *Poor boy,* she thinks, fast-forwarding to his future.

"You're appallingly selfish!" Elie hurls after her, chasing her down the corridor.

She turns around, astounded that they aren't on the same page; that he isn't her ally in this battle. "Selfish?" she cries, wounded. "Why? Because I want the best possible life for my son?"

"Keep telling yourself that."

"We shouldn't be fighting. We're in this together, Elie."

"No, we're not," he argues. "I don't happen to think Evan's club feet are the end of the world."

"Just because I don't have the sort of impressively traumatic past you've got to compare this to—"

"Impressively traumatic?" he repeats. "I lived through a war, Anne, if that's what you mean by 'impressive.' My brother was kidnapped in the street and presumably murdered. My uncle died in a car bomb. Forgive me if all this"—he gestures with his arms—"doesn't seem so fucking dire to me."

"But it is to me!"

"Yes, well," Elie says, lowering his voice, "that's your problem, isn't it?"

*T*he casts are supposed to be kept clean and dry. She notices there are already stains of pureed squash and turkey and sweet potato on one of them. She sets Evan down on the bed and rubs the stains with a damp cloth and some Comet.

"Loity loity loity," he murmurs.

She wipes away the moisture with a dry towel and then inspects Evan's little toes to ensure they're not swollen or red or foul-smelling. Dr. Turvey told Elie they should be checking them several times a day and that they're supposed to be pink and warm.

Satisfied, Anne slips Elie's old gray and orange wool socks back over the casts and notices Evan rubbing his eyes. She lifts him up and carries him to his nursery, his head lolling groggily about her shoulder.

When he's nestled in his crib she goes to Elie's office and plunks herself in front of his computer. She Googles "club feet" for the millionth time, not sure what she's looking for, but presumably hoping to stumble upon some positive testimonials and happy club feet endings. Eventually, she explores her way into a chat room for parents that she hadn't found before—essentially an online support group.

The first blurb she reads is from someone who goes by the name "Brayden's Mom." The tag line is *4 ½ yr old needs more surgery* . . . She clicks on it with a sense of gloomy foreboding. Elie would tell her to get off the computer now, before she finds evidence to back up all her worst-case scenarios. He would tell her to stop submerging herself in the microcosmic world of club feet.

Our orthopedist recommended another surgery to correct Brayden's right foot, which never healed properly after the first surgery 4 years ago . . .

Her eyes burn as she blinks back tears. She slumps against Elie's office chair and tries to hold back a rising wave of emotion, like trying to keep from vomiting. But a single persistent thought batters open the floodgates of self-pity: *Why her?* Why her and Brayden's mom and Tami and Margaret?

If she could rationalize it, if she could trace it back to something they all did—sleeping with their cousins, overuse of a microwave or cell phone, exposure to pesticides or smoking during pregnancy—it might make it easier to accept. It's the randomness of it that offends her most. The lack of any significant cause or explanation.

She escapes the chat room, feeling suddenly quite angry and bitter. Self-pity is fine, in its own lulling way. But rage is more majestic, more cathartic. She is going to stay angry from now on. She owes it to herself. She's entitled.

Absently, she returns to Google and types Declan's name. A number of search results pop up, all relating to the *National Post*. She clicks on one of the bios about him. *Declan Gray is an award-winning journalist well known for his biting commentary on cultural and social issues. He has received a National Magazine Award for Arts and is a regular contributor to* Toronto Life *magazine.*

She's been buying Declan's paper for the past couple of weeks, following his column. The first one she read was about how Toronto's streetcars are as obsolete and inconvenient as hansom cabs. She actually chuckled out loud a couple of times. The other column put forth his cynical theory that certain scientists have invented global warming, a myth perpetuated by the media. His primary source was *Jurassic Park* author Michael Crichton. Both columns had a smug, audacious tone. They were inconsequential but witty, which still makes not being able to have him painful to her.

He never came back to the meeting. Twice she's gone and sat there waiting for him to show up, waiting to rekindle their flirtations, despite knowing in her gut it was futile. A woman knows.

The last time she saw him she wondered what would happen to all that longing inside her if she were never to see him again. The answer is nothing. Some days it's right up in her throat; she can practically choke on it. Those are the days she can't get her mind to focus on anything it's supposed to focus on.

Other days there's more of a melancholy acceptance within her; a resignation to live with the longing until it fades away. She knows from past experience that it does eventually go, the way grief goes; that desire diffuses over time. It can be a relief too, when the object of her attraction is removed. There's really no other way for these situations to end, since it's never been her intention to have an actual affair.

She turns off the computer, not bothering to read anything more about him, and she leaves the room. Every now and then, she has bits of willingness.

*L*ater, Elie comes home with a gift for Evan—a pair of Baby Gap cargo pants that fit beautifully over his fiberglass casts.

"You can't even tell he's got casts!" Anne exclaims, admiring the adorable camouflage pattern and thinking what an uncharacteristically magnanimous gesture this was for Elie.

"Not much," Elie replies.

"Pants don't usually fit over them," she points out. "Look at him! He looks normal!"

"It's what all the cool babies are wearing anyway," he says sardonically. Anne follows him into the kitchen and he starts rummaging around in the fridge. He pulls out a left-over pork tenderloin and a container of apple sauce.

"Guess who called me today?" he says, dumping the applesauce into a saucepan.

"Who?"

"Jennifer Schlittman."

"For an appraisal?"

Elie nods, looking excited. "I said I'd go to her place and have a look at her father's collection."

"She can't come to you?"

"You saw all those coins. I'm not going to make her schlep all those boxes to my office. It's much easier for me to go there."

"When?"

"She's going away for a couple of weeks. Hopefully as soon as she gets back."

"Her father just died and she's going on holiday?"

"We all have our own way of grieving."

Anne hoists Evan into the air, admiring him in his new pants. "I want to take him out and let him play with other babies," she tells Elie, changing the subject. "Maybe we could join one of those play groups."

Elie looks at her strangely.

"I could go to that music class Tami keeps talking about."

Tami gave her a pamphlet a while ago for the Lawrence Village Neighborhood Center, which she finds crumpled at the bottom of her purse. She glances through it and decides to try the one called Sing-and-Swing on Thursday mornings.

Feeling inspired, she calls Tami to tell her she's going to join up and Tami seems very pleased. She's a champion of these community play groups.

"Oh, Evan will love it," she tells Anne. "Babies love being around other babies. It'll be so good for him."

"I won't have to dance or anything, will I?"

"Of course not. But you'll have to sing."

"I found some pants that fit over Evan's casts."

"That's great. That was always a challenge."

"I should go buy a dozen more of them."

"Listen," Tami says, "I'm having some friends over for dinner. There's about eight of us—"

There have been times in Anne's life where the companionship of a group of women would have been essential. This is not one of them. Evan's club feet induce in her an urge to retreat and hibernate. She quickly starts running through her repertoire of excuses—no babysitter, Elie's away on business, Evan's scars are infected . . .

"We're all mothers," Tami goes on. "And since we all have busy schedules, we get together one night a month for dinner. This month it's at my place. The theme is—"

"The *theme*?"

"The host chooses a theme, so I chose Monopoly."

"You're going to play Monopoly all night?"

"No!" she giggles, and Anne can imagine her blue eyes brightening. "It's a potluck, so you have to pick a property. Let's say you pick Park Place; you could bring caviar and champagne. Or if you choose the Boardwalk, you might bring seafood. I've picked Kentucky Avenue, so I'm going to make fried chicken and cornbread. Get it?"

"What would you bring if you picked the railroad?"

"Well, you wouldn't pick the railroad."

"Oh."

"It's next Friday at seven. Do you think you can make it?"

"Elie has an auction next weekend," Anne blurts, way too exuberantly. "He'll be away. And with it being so soon after the surgeries, I couldn't leave Evan with a sitter."

"That's too bad," Tami says, sounding genuinely disappointed. "We'd love to have you."

"Next month maybe," Anne promises emptily.

Anne tries to get through the music class with an open mind, prodding herself to break free from her shackles of self-consciousness and expose some shameless capacity for silliness. The teacher is a middle-aged hippie with long silver braids who dances around the room with a tambourine, encouraging them to join her in making complete asses of themselves. The rest of them sit in a circle with their babies and sing to them the generic, uninspired songs they've been singing since the day they brought them into the world—"The Wheels on the Bus," "Itsy Bitsy Spider," Barney's theme song.

They're all clapping and bobbing along with their babies. Anne glances down at Evan and is astonished to discover that he's laughing and squealing, having a ball. He's riled up and happy, which riles her up. Inhibition leaves her suddenly and she momentarily forgets about his feet. She forgets he's wearing casts under his father's sweat socks. She forgets that she felt apart from the other women when she first walked in, as though an impenetrable wall divided them.

Next is a Wiggles song. Anne continues to sing along, delighted by her son's joy and a feeling of finally fitting in with all the other mothers. It's what she's always wanted for Evan.

When the class finally ends the women mill around the room, chatting with each other. Not knowing anyone, she busies herself putting Evan in his snowsuit, relieved to have gotten away without his feet being ogled.

"I couldn't help noticing," one of the women says, coming up behind Anne. "Your son's casts—"

Anne turns to face her, feeling her whole body stiffen. She just wanted Evan to blend in.

"Was he in an accident?" the woman asks, smiling down at Evan.

"Yes," Anne lies. "He jumped off his change table and broke both his legs."

She watches as the woman's eyes widen and then just as quickly melt into pools of pity. "Poor thing," she says. "How long does he have to wear the casts?"

Anne lets out a stream of inarticulate murmurings and rushes out.

Twenty-one

*E*arly in the week Anne gets a call on her cell phone from Barry Katz, one of Toronto's most successful interior designers and something of a local celebrity, thanks to his home decor show *Katz at Home* on the HGTV network.

"Functional art," he says, by way of introduction. "We're doing a segment Thursday and we want your tables."

"That sounds great."

"I absolutely *looove* your tables," he gushes. "They're perfect for Thursday's show. Can you be there around eight in the morning with three or four of them?"

Her mind is racing. She's got a couple of hand-forged tables collecting dust at the studio, as well as *Spilt Milk* and her *Ode to Motherhood*. How would she get them there?

"Of course," she says, knowing she can't pass up an opportunity to be on *Katz at Home*. Imagine the publicity. He is *the* design guru in the city. A couple of accolades from him and they'll be beating down her studio door.

"We're featuring some Philippe Starck lamps and Alessi bottle openers," he explains. "That kind of thing. But I'd *looove* to bring you on as a local furniture designer—"

"Artist."

"Even better. That's so cute. Not just tables, they're *art*. But they're functional too. I mean, they're tables, right?"

"Right."

"Perfect. Functional art. It's exactly what we're looking for. So you'll be there at eight on Thursday?"

"Yes."

"It's live, but don't worry. You'll be in the audience. You won't have to speak."

Barry Katz arranges to meet her at her studio before Thursday to have a look at her tables and select the ones he wants to feature. This could be a coup for her career. It's been a while since she's had a mention in any of the important decor magazines. She's fallen off the local radar.

*T*hursday arrives and Elie drives her downtown, loads a couple of her tables into her SUV and straps the third to the roof, and then delivers her to the HGTV studio.

"Thanks, baby."

"I'll be back for you at eleven," he promises. He leans across the seat and kisses her. "I'm proud of you."

He is a good man, she thinks. Out of the blue, he can be so good and devoted and supportive. *I'm lucky,* she thinks. And then it's inside for the taping. Her tables are going to be famous. Her babies are making their TV debut.

Barry Katz chose three tables: *Ode to Motherhood, Sunset in Lagos*—a mosaic of royal blue and yellow Portuguese ceramic tiles—and one of her first metal pieces, a contemporary chrome bedside table with clean lines and hidden welts. He said the ones he chose would show her range as an artist. There were a couple of hand-forged tables she thought were more interesting, but he dismissed them as too gothic and ornate. ("Is this one lopsided?" he asked her. "It's supposed to be," she answered.

"Blacksmithing is imperfect." He nodded and chose the sleek chrome table instead.)

In fact, he loved the simplicity of her chrome side table so much that he commissioned a dozen of them for the model suites he's doing in six new condo developments. Just like that, he cut her a check for the deposit and she was back in business. He said he also needed a few dozen metal display stands for a new retail space he's designing, but she declined. "I'm an artist," she reminded him.

She doesn't mind doing some uninspired chrome tables for him—at least her name will be attached to them at the model suites—but she can't bring herself to make display stands for a store. It's not like she needs the money. It's credibility and acclaim she's looking for now.

"*I looove* this one," Barry exclaims to his sidekick, Marsha, a slender blond TV host whom he stole from another network's morning show. He's standing over Anne's *Ode to Motherhood* table, preening and gesticulating. "First of all, every mother makes a scrapbook of her baby's first year, right?"

"Right," Marsha says. "*I* did!"

"Of course you did. But look at this . . . it's brilliant. She's made her scrapbook into a table! Or she's made a table out of her scrapbook."

The audience oohs and ahhhs.

"What a great idea," Marsha agrees. "So everyone can enjoy it. It's not hidden away in some drawer."

"Exactly. And look here . . . she's even got her son's birth bracelet over here, and his little socks—"

"That is so cute!"

"But it's *functional,* right? I mean, it's a table! It's a coffee table for the den, or it can be in the playroom. It's like having a collage of all your mementos and baby pictures on permanent display."

"And what a great gift idea," Marsha mentions. "For all you husbands out there, you can collect these precious little tokens from your children's first year and call Anne of Green Gables—"

"Anne of Green *Tables,*" Barry corrects.

"Right. Sorry, Anne!" Winking into the audience. "I love that name."

"Isn't it clever? It's so witty."

"And so Canadian."

"Anne has such range," Barry goes on. "Look at this one. It's very contemporary. Nice clean lines. Perfect for a minimalist bedroom in a downtown loft."

"Or even beside the couch!"

"Exactly. And I love it because although it's aesthetically quite simple, remember, it's handmade, which gives it a certain specialness. It doesn't have that mass-produced look to it."

"So she refurbishes tables as well as makes her own?" Marsha quizzes.

"Exactly, Marsha. Anne is actually a blacksmith. I've been to her studio and she's got her own propane oven and she makes these tables herself out of metal, which is so marvelous."

"Like Jennifer Beals in *Flashdance.*"

The audience laughs.

"I think Jennifer was a welder, but tomato, tomahto, right?"

"This one is gorgeous," says Marsha, pointing to the mosaic-tiled coffee table. "It's very ethnic. You'd hardly know it's by the same artist."

"Isn't she absolutely versatile?"

Marsha glances down at her cue card. "The artist is Anne Biffin of Anne of Green Tables," she reads. "I *looove* that name! And her studio is right here in Toronto."

"Right on Queen Street," Barry specifies, and he looks into the audience and beams at Anne.

A few nights later Declan makes an unexpected appearance at the support group. He takes the seat beside Anne and says, "I saw you on TV last week."

Just like that, the familiar desire and attraction clench her throat.

"I wasn't on," she says. "Just a few of my tables were."

"I saw you in the audience. You were in the front row. You had on a black turtleneck."

She feels herself flush. "You were watching *Katz at Home* on a weekday morning?"

"Margaret taped it. She was so excited. You're famous."

Anne shrugs and tries not to look at his face for too long. It's like looking at an eclipse. Dangerous. Besides, she's annoyed with him. All his flirting and leading her on, and then he inevitably disappears. She can't take it anymore. He was just starting to fade from her thoughts, and now here he is again, too stunning and addictive to dismiss.

Someone calls the meeting to attention. Declan leans in very close to her ear and says, "Do you want to grab a coffee or something after this?"

The warmth of his breath on her neck makes her weak. Her heart rallies and soars; the offer unveils a shivering joy inside her.

*T*hey leave their cars in the church parking lot and go around the corner to a cozy Italian restaurant where you can learn Italian over antipasti and get "real" coffee instead of what Declan refers to as "corporate chain coffee."

They're sitting at one of the long wooden tables in the back corner. The restaurant is relatively full, dim and noisy, very warm. Her latte arrives in a milk-shake glass, hot and creamy and divinely bitter. Declan has an espresso.

"Have you got a picture of your son?" Anne asks him.

He reaches into his back pocket and retrieves his wallet. He flips it open and hands it to her. "He was seven months old here," he explains. "That was almost four months ago."

"It goes by fast," she mutters absently, her eyes riveted to the photograph of Margaret, holding the boy.

She looks young, possibly still in her late twenties, with delicate and proportional Anglo-Saxon features. She has an actress's nose—one of those small, perfect, enviable triangles—a flawless complexion, and wavy, honey-colored hair. Her green eyes are flecked with red from the flash, but Anne can tell she's got laughing eyes. She's eloquently beautiful, the way women were beautiful in the thirties and forties, in those black-and-white Hollywood pin-up photos—airbrushed and soft of focus, with cascading hair and skin like silk sheets.

"I should update that picture with a more recent one," Declan says, interrupting Anne's frantic inventory of his wife. "Sean has already changed so much since I took this one—"

Right. The baby. She pulls her eyes away from Margaret's smiling face and gives his son a cursory glance. Naturally, he's a beauty. With parents like Margaret and Declan, he couldn't have strayed too far. He's got those genes.

She hands back the wallet, feeling suddenly unlovely and misshapen, grossly inferior.

"Have you got one of Evan?" he asks her.

It occurs to her she doesn't. "They're all on my husband's computer," she stammers, ashamed. "We use a digital camera. I keep meaning to get some printed and do an album . . ."

"I need a cigarette," he says. "Do you mind?"

"Of course not."

He gets up from the table. "I'll be right back."

She watches him leave, noting how good his ass looks in his jeans. Does Margaret know how lucky she is? What would she think of all this envy Anne has for her? She doesn't even know her.

She calls Elie at home and tells him she's having coffee with one of the women from the group. He doesn't even ask for a name, which reflects either his trust or his indifference. She wonders if lying to him would be this easy if she were off to a motel room with Declan instead of a cup of coffee.

Probably. Then she considers: Is she cheating? Or is cheating singularly defined by sex?

Declan returns. He notices her cell phone on the table. "Everything okay?"

"Fine."

"You don't have to leave?"

"No," she responds, buoyed.

She wants to know everything about him. The more details she collects, the more she can use them to embroider her fantasies. "Where do you live?" she asks him.

"Cabbagetown. You?"

"Lawrence Park."

"Ah."

"What's that supposed to mean?"

"Nothing."

"You've decided something about me already, haven't you?"

"No."

"Of course you have."

"Have you decided something about *me*?" he asks, turning the tables.

She smiles guiltily and presses her finger to the rim of her glass, daubing at the chocolate and foam that have collected there. Her latte is lukewarm now, but still delicious. She licks the chocolate off her finger.

"Tell me," he says. "I can take it."

"All right," she relents. "Let's see. You're upper middle class but won't submit to the suburbs or North Toronto. So your statement about yourself—to prove you still have an edge over all the other yuppies—is to live in a trendy, eclectic downtown neighborhood."

He laughs and she continues in a flirty, teasing tone. "You refer to yourself as a Cabbagetowner and you own a charming Victorian that you're in the process of renovating. You brag about the diversity of your neighborhood, all the pubs and cafés and ethnic restaurants that are within walking distance of your house. And you probably have a social conscience, too."

"Ouch," he says, refuting nothing. "Is it my turn?"

She leans back in her chair. "Go for it."

"Your husband is a millionaire," he begins. "Either a corporate lawyer, a stockbroker or from family money. You've got a full-time nanny, a personal trainer and a cottage on some lake. Your son will go to a private boys' school. You probably give generously to charity but have no social conscience. And I'll bet your toes are perfectly pedicured."

"First of all, my husband is a numismatist," she informs him smugly. "I don't have a nanny or a trainer or even a cottage. My toenails are unpedicured and I have no idea where Evan will go to school."

"A numismatist," he remarks. "That's interesting."

"Is it?"

"Well, I don't know if coins are interesting, but it's interesting you being married to a coin collector."

"Why?"

He shrugs. "It just is."

"You're wondering how we afford a house in Lawrence Park?"

"How do you?"

"Family money," she concedes, and he smiles triumphantly.

The waitress passes their table and Declan orders another espresso. She turns to Anne. The latte is finished. Emboldened, she says, "I'll have a glass of white wine."

She wishes Declan had switched to wine. Then they'd be off in an entirely different direction.

"So what's this mean?" she asks, daring to touch the *Creideamh* tattoo on his inner forearm.

"It's Gaelic," he says. "For 'faith.'" His arm stays outstretched. Her fingertip lingers deliberately. Their eyes are fixed on each other. For a moment, it feels as though they're headed toward a dangerous, unavoidable end.

And then he says, "I probably won't be going back to the support group." Curtailing their flirtation without any warning and smashing the good, lulling feeling she had.

"Oh," she manages, snatching her hand back and trying to conceal the embarrassment that has suddenly overtaken her.

"Nothing is really happening with Sean's feet," he says. "We're just waiting. Besides, Marg thinks it's a waste of time."

She doesn't know what to say. Her mind is calculating, scheming—

"I really only went tonight thinking you might be there," he admits.

Her hopes flourish. "Really?"

Would it matter if it wasn't true? Would it be any less exquisite if he was just some player, dangling lies for sport? She doubts it. He's put it out there now. The lure has been boldly and irrevocably laid out on the table.

"I paid two grand for one of your tables," he reminds her. "For Christ's sake, that wasn't a clue?"

"I don't know," she stammers, making an effort to show some measure of restraint. It's quite likely this means more to her than it does to him. She's usually the weaker one in these kinds of interactions, the one who crosses the furthest over the line, the one more willing to lay herself out like a carpet.

"With some people it's just easier," he says. "Do you know what I mean?"

"I think so."

"Like that couple from the support group. Beth and Gord. I wouldn't know what to say to them if the three of us were stranded on an island. And yet both our kids have club feet."

She thinks of Tami and Darren.

"Sometimes I feel that way with Mar—with my own wife. That it could be easier with her. That maybe it *should* be."

"I understand that."

"Margaret gets along with everyone," he goes on. "She transcends all types. She loves people. She's as social as I am antisocial."

"I'm like you," Anne reveals. "But so is my husband."

"That must be a relief," he says enviously. "Margaret is always trying to get me out."

"That's probably good."

"Probably." But his voice is dejected, weary.

"And yet you're the one who goes to the support group," she points out. "Shouldn't it be the other way around?"

He brings his cup to his lips and takes a sip of espresso. She stares shamelessly at his mouth and has to force her eyes away. "I'm in AA," he divulges.

She lets out a soft gasp. "You are?" It takes her a moment to process the information. "So you're . . . an alcoholic?"

"Most of us in AA are," he jokes.

"So you don't *ever* drink?"

"Not unless I want to start waking up on the curb again."

"Wow. I never would have thought—"

"That's because I'm in recovery," he says. "Anyway, I've gotten fairly comfortable with the support group environment and I needed somewhere to go with all this—"

He pulls his pack of cigarettes out and bounces it on the table, as though just holding the pack might satisfy his urge to smoke.

"This what?" she probes.

"Shame," he answers. "Margaret and I . . . we don't really talk about Sean's problem. She doesn't think it's that big a deal. She doesn't *want* to think it's a big deal. She minimizes the whole thing. But it upsets me, you know? That he can't walk or even crawl yet. I look at him sometimes and I feel so disappointed in him. A father dreams of having a son to do all sorts of stuff with . . . Then comes the guilt and resentment. All the crap I used to drink over. My sponsor thought it would be good for me to find a place where I could share my feelings about Sean's problem with other people who are in the same boat."

"But you said you're going to stop coming to the meeting—"

"Well, you're there and it's a distraction."

She blushes. "So this is it?" she says, alarmed. "We won't see each other again?"

"It's not good for me," he says. "It's dangerous."

She realizes that her wine has sat untouched since the waitress set it down. She gulps it now, hoping to calm some of the wildness inside her.

"I have to go," he says, with a mix of remorse and finality. "I promised Marg I'd be home by—"

She hates how often he drags his wife's name into the conversation. She hates the thought of their intimacy, the promises he must make to her.

He pays for the drinks and Anne follows him outside in what has rapidly degenerated into a tense, uncomfortable silence. They turn off Yonge and head toward the church without uttering a word. A voice in her head is screaming, *Stop him! Stop him!*

He turns to her and says, "Are you cold?"

"A little."

He wraps his arm around her and pulls her close and they walk to his car like that. The feel of him pressed up against her like this fills her with such desperate longing it hurts to breathe. Her feelings for him have transcended anything remotely innocent. *This one is different,* she thinks. And she's suddenly just as frightened about keeping him around as she is about losing him. She wonders where all this longing will go if she never sees him again. They reach the parking lot and he releases her. "Maybe I'll be there next Monday," he says, confused. "I don't know. I doubt it."

No words come to her lips. Nothing. She just stands there, leaving their fate—if one could even elevate it to such maudlin, self-important heights—entirely in his ambivalent hands.

He gets into his car and drives away. Just like that. She stumbles over to her own car and climbs inside, numb.

How do men do it? How do they just leave like that? They seem to possess a callousness (or is it willpower?) that allows them to walk away without any assurances or commitments, with everything unresolved and uncertain. It's just in their genetic makeup not to need the kind of supplicating guarantees that women need.

Twenty-two

*T*he following after-
noon Anne arrives at her mother's house and finds her
upstairs in the spare bedroom, rocking Evan by the window.
The room doubles as a nursery—there's a crib, a change
table and an antique rocking chair that her mother insists is
better than "those stupid new gliders." Anne suspects it's
torture on her mother's back, but Jean resents any new
invention that facilitates the lives of women of Anne's
generation. (Of the baby monitor: "We used our *ears* to
listen for crying"; the electric bottle warmer: "Is boiling
water too time-consuming?"; the ExerSaucer/swing/Kick
& Play: "We used to *hold* our babies once in a while!")

Anne hovers in the doorway a moment, observing them.
It's snowing outside, big white flakes that seem to be
dancing in the air rather than falling. Jean looks so content
and peaceful. The tension and hardness have drained from
her face; there isn't even a shadow. Anne is half tempted to
tiptoe away and leave them undisturbed. But she stays,
watching.

When Jean finally notices Anne she puts her finger to her
lips. She lifts herself out of the rocker with some difficulty
and then deposits Evan gently in his crib. He was in a
grumpy mood this morning when Anne dropped him off,
so she dares not go in and kiss him for fear of waking him
and ruining all her mother's hard work.

Together, they creep down the stairs without saying a word.

"Is the baby monitor on?" Anne asks her mother when they're safely in the messy kitchen.

Jean goes over to the counter, where she's set up the monitor amidst some dirty pots and empty baking pans, and flicks it on, filling the room with static.

"How long did you have to rock him?" Anne wants to know.

"It was about an hour, I guess. Maybe an hour and a half."

"An hour and a half?"

She shrugs modestly. "I'm sure I could have put him down sooner," she admits, "but he's so happy in my arms."

"You rocked him for over an hour in that old wooden rocker?"

"Don't be silly. It's not a big deal."

Anne has judged her mother harshly in the past for more transgressions than she can even recall, yet Jean's remarkable unselfishness, which has, on occasion, reached almost noble proportions, has not gone unnoticed. Anne once saw an episode of *Oprah* about a woman from the projects who had sacrificed her entire life for her children. She worked two full-time jobs around the clock—including at McDonald's—so that her kids could get an education. At one point during the interview she said, "My life is just a stepping-stone. That's how I get through it. It's a stepping-stone for my kids to have a better life."

Anne sobbed through the whole segment. She couldn't stop thinking of her own mother. Of course, they didn't live in the projects and Jean worked as a legal assistant, not at McDonald's, and she was more ill-tempered and critical than this other woman seemed to be. But Anne has recently developed a sense of what it meant for her mother to leave Harmony and make a new life for them here in Toronto.

Jean's life may also have been a stepping-stone. Maybe that's how she saw it anyway—as something given up, sacrificed to ensure something better for her daughter. It put a great amount of pressure on Anne. She felt a sudden heavy weight bearing down on her and she questioned whether or not she'd lived up to her mother's expectations. She thought probably not.

Jean isn't the type to say. Nevertheless, Anne sees that altruistic goodness in her mother revealing itself more and more often lately when she's with Evan; a goodness that is pure of motive, requires not the least bit of acknowledgment or attention, and is utterly without agenda.

"I hate the news," Jean laments, scanning the headlines and then tossing aside the newspaper.

Anne notices it's the Saturday *Post* and reads the teaser for Declan's column on the front page.

Jean lets out a troubled sigh. "To think I wasted the first half of my life on God." She points to the paper, its front page emblazoned with tragedy and misfortune. "A God that would allow all *this* to happen."

"Why do you let it bother you?" Anne asks pragmatically.

"Because I'm energetically connected to the rest of the world. I'm not a self-absorbed person. These things affect me."

"Why don't you try a singles' group?" Anne suggests brightly. "To keep you busy."

Jean gives her a withering look, but doesn't respond.

"You might meet some interesting people. You wouldn't be so lonely."

"People aren't always a cure for loneliness," Jean counters. "Marriage certainly isn't, is it?"

Wounded, Anne sits down at the table and waits for Evan to wake up from his nap. Her mother goes directly to the pantry and emerges with a bag of flour, some chocolate chips and a bottle of vanilla.

"You're going to bake?" Anne says, sounding almost accusatory.

"Oh, Anne," she sighs, and Anne suspects, as she has numerous other times, that her mother doesn't like her very much.

Jean busies herself at the other end of the kitchen, scooping flour into a glass bowl and sifting things and cracking eggs. She hums as she bakes and Anne finds herself quite lulled as she watches her mother. Something about this scene reminds her of a part of her childhood that consists mainly of feelings and intangible senses—a smell here, a sound there—rather than any concrete memories. She wonders if it's possible to miss something you can't even remember, or to feel nostalgic for a figment of your imagination.

Anne almost says to her mother, "We haven't done this in a long time." But then she realizes that perhaps they've *never* done this before. Her memories and dreams, along with the facts her mother has stingily doled out over the years, have all blurred together, hallucinatory and indistinguishable.

Her mother holds the glass bowl under one arm and uses a wooden spoon to whip the dough. Then she drops dollops of it onto a cookie sheet and shoves it into the oven. "Want some?" she asks, holding up the bowl of raw dough. A peace offering.

She brings it to the table and sets it down between them. She hands Anne a spoon, which Anne can't resist.

"God, that's good," she moans, savoring the sweet, creamy batter on her tongue. "You used to bake a lot, didn't you, Mom?"

Jean looks up at her. "Yes. Often. I find it so soothing."

"Did I watch?"

"I'm sure. Everyone was always in that kitchen."

Anne loads her spoon with more dough. "I dreamed about Harmony the other night."

Anne notices a shadow slash across her mother's eyes, sudden as a guillotine dropping. She raises an eyebrow.

"I dreamt we were in a church. The preacher was talking about how the people of Harmony would be saved after the Second Coming."

"That's how the sermons were," Jean says.

"It's strange how I knew that in my dream, but I've never remembered that in real life."

"The mind is very mysterious," Jean says abstractly. "It's full of compartments we don't know about."

They sit there for a while in reflective silence. The smell of baking cookies wafts around them. Suddenly the timer goes off and Jean leaps to her feet to remove the tray and load up another. She returns with a plate of hot cookies and a quart of cold milk.

Anne breaks a cookie open and lets the melted chocolate ooze onto the white porcelain. Her stomach aches from all the dough, but she eats the fresh-baked cookie anyway. Her mother eats one and then another.

"There were two boys in my dream," Anne mentions.

She watches carefully for her mother's reaction, but there isn't one. Her face remains blank, her eyes impassive.

Yet there's something deliberate about her detachment. Anne notices that Jean's body is unnaturally still, as though she's taking great pains not to let out a single breath or make the slightest movement.

"I think their names were Thomas and James," Anne adds, again waiting for some kind of noteworthy reaction.

Jean shakes her head.

"You don't remember?"

"There were plenty of boys around," she answers in a tinny voice that sounds very far away.

"But do you remember those names?"

"Thomas and James?" she says impatiently. "Two generic names like that? I'm sure we had several of each in that house. I certainly can't remember who they belonged to."

"Did my father have a sort of reddish-gold beard?"

"He did."

"Then I remember him!" Anne says triumphantly. "In my dream, I . . . I sort of worshipped him. Was it like that?"

"I wouldn't know how you felt at five," she says dismissively. "Especially about him."

"Was he a powerful man?" Anne presses.

Jean gets up and starts clearing away the plates and glasses. "This'll be good in ice cream," she mutters to herself, about the raw dough. "How do you mean powerful?"

"In the community, I guess. Did people respect him? That was the sense I got from my dream."

"That was quite a dream."

"It was very vivid. It haunted me for days afterward."

Jean dumps the dirty dishes in the sink and turns around to face Anne. "I suppose he was a well-respected man," she

says. "But it was like that with all the men. That's the kind
of place it was. The women deferred."

"I can't picture you like that. Being submissive with a
man."

"I've changed a lot since then," she reflects. "I had to.
Moving here required starting over."

"I know—"

"No, I mean as a person," she corrects, turning back to
the sink. "I had to become a brand-new person, as though
nothing from before had ever counted. Nothing I'd known
or understood was right or could serve me here."

"I guess I'll see for myself when I go."

The spoon Jean has been holding falls into the sink
with a loud clang. She grabs onto the counter ledge as
though to steady herself. "Go where?" she asks, without
looking at Anne.

"Out West," Anne responds. "To Harmony. I'm going
to go, just as soon as Evan is finished with all the surgery
and casting."

"Why?"

This time there's no mistaking the panic in her voice.
She's abandoned her dish washing and returned to the
pine table.

"I want to see my father again," Anne explains defensively. "I want him to meet Evan. And I may look up your
family too while I'm there—"

Jean says nothing. Instead she just looks at Anne for a
long time with a kind of wounded revulsion. Anne wishes
she knew what was going through her mother's head. What
secrets she's got locked up in there. "It's not a betrayal
against you or anything," Anne assures her. "You had to
figure I'd eventually want to go back."

Jean drops down into one of the ladder-back chairs. There's a dish towel in her hand that she keeps wringing. "I thought maybe in your twenties," she says. "You know how people in their twenties are always going off in search of something. Once you passed that stage, I figured you'd never go."

"Which is exactly what you wanted," Anne says sharply. "Well, I'm going. I need to see him."

"What for?"

"Closure."

Jean snickers. "Closure is a myth. There's no such thing."

"Curiosity then. He's my father. I want to see how he's lived and know what's happened to him over the past thirty years."

"Having the answers won't bring you any satisfaction," she states with certainty.

"How do you know?"

Jean smiles without any humor in it.

"You could *tell* me, you know."

"Tell you what?"

"Why you left."

She reaches for Anne's hand and holds it in hers. Her fingers are cold, but the gesture itself brings a measure of warmth.

"You already know all there is to know," she says in a soft, persuasive voice. "It's a very religious community. Hellfire and brimstone and all that. It's backward. The women are subservient. They breed and serve. They're like slaves. They're like nothing. Go if you want. If you think seeing it for yourself will patch up that hole inside you."

Anne almost says, "How do you know about that hole?" But she doesn't want to give her the satisfaction. She pulls her hand away. "What if he's dead?" she asks her mother.

"He's not dead."

"How do you know?" Momentarily excited. "Do you know something?"

"They don't die," Jean says softly. "They live forever there."

"Who?"

"The men. My father, your father. They go on and on."

"Maybe I'll call him first."

"He's got no phone, Anne. He always said that anyone he needed to speak to was under his own roof or down the road or wherever. He didn't need a phone."

"That was then—"

She lets out a laugh; a hard, empty, reverberating sound, devoid of joy. Anne can tell she's angry. Anne has broken their pact. Her sudden urge to go exploring is a threat to the sealed glass coffin in which her mother keeps all her secrets. Jean still thinks she can keep the glass from shattering, but she lives in fear of the possibility.

She rarely speaks of her past. Through denial, she wills it to be other than what it was. She taught Anne how to do the same. Together, they've always played at "normal," hoping to act their way there.

A startling cry suddenly fills the room via the baby monitor and Anne runs upstairs to find Evan wailing in his crib. It's perfect timing, because now she can escape her mother's house and her unspoken recriminations. While she's getting him ready and collecting his things, she can hear her mother downstairs in the kitchen. Pots are clanging, cutlery is being thrown into drawers. Everything is louder than it needs to be.

When she returns to the kitchen she finds Jean bending down in front of the oven, with her head virtually inside it as she inserts another sheet of cookies. Anne's first thought is of Hansel and Gretel, when the witch is peering into the oven and they push her in and escape.

"Thanks for babysitting," Anne hazards.

Jean straightens up and her expression melts at the sight of Evan. She smiles fondly at him, her hostility evaporating at once.

"I forgot to mention," she says. "You'll have to arrange for a sitter the first week of March. I'm going away."

"Away?" This must be her retaliation.

"There's a course in the Berkshires."

"For what?"

"It's a massage therapist thing." Then, reading Anne's mind, she adds, "It's been planned for weeks."

She kisses Evan and he giggles. He adores his grandmother. He knows nothing of her stubbornness, her temper or her irrational fears, and he probably never will. Anne came to truly know her mother's character defects only when she was in her thirties, around the same time she came to appreciate her attributes and the extent of her goodness and courage. She supposes there is a point in people's lives when their mothers become fully fleshed-out human beings; when they're exposed for what they really are—mortals.

Twenty-three

*T*he wind hurls itself at the house, pummeling the windows and smashing its way in through the glass. With each violent gust the entire foundation seems to sway and rock. Anne clasps Evan as though her embrace could save him if the house were blown away. It's February, midway through that most punishing stretch of the year when life isn't so much lived as endured. The temperature has plunged into the negative double digits and Anne wonders why they continue to subject themselves to this year after year.

Elie suggested a last-minute Caribbean vacation, but her first thought was of Evan's predicament and what a pain it would be to travel now—carrying him through airports, hours on an airplane with his legs elevated, sand inside his casts, swimming with the casts. It just isn't feasible.

She feels depressed. Declan hasn't resurfaced either. Gone is that shiver of excitement that might have gotten her through to the warm days of spring. She gave up on the support group meetings after sitting through two more, dressed up and feeling like a foolish clown, with no sign of him. All that's left to look forward to are Evan's casts coming off in a couple of weeks, but even that brings as much apprehension as joy, with the looming potential for more disappointment. She doesn't even have the will to be optimistic anymore. Cynicism feels a lot less dangerous, less cocky.

She secures Evan into his high chair and sits down in front of him. Supper is warm oatmeal, squash, yogurt and puree of pears. He's taken to solids with ease. So far he hasn't turned his nose up at anything she's offered, except bananas, which he flung at her with uncharacteristic anger the other day.

She gives him a spoonful of cereal that he welcomes with the usual delight. "Num-a-num-a-num," he says charmingly.

His green eyes are deep and sparkling. She wonders why he's so happy. After all he's been through, where does that twinkly, unflappable joy come from? Whatever the obstacle—surgery, casting, the frustration of not being able to stand—and whatever the degree of physical pain and suffering, her boy plods on triumphantly, oblivious of his situation. Maybe all babies are this way, with a natural propensity for happiness and resilience. Maybe it just takes longer for their spirits to be crushed by the usual things: parents, humanity, life.

Wait until he feels that first set of diminishing eyes on him, a castigating glance that slices through to his gut; or until he's arbitrarily discriminated against; mocked, ridiculed, humiliated or ostracized. Those are the things she wants to protect him from—the merciless, esteem-smashing judgments of others.

The front door opens and is quickly slammed shut. Elie appears in the kitchen, looking ruddy and battered, but happy. "Hello, family," he says in a surprisingly chipper voice. He kisses Anne on the mouth and then tousles Evan's hair.

"Good day at work?" she asks him.

"In fact, it was."

"On a cold day like this? I'm surprised you had clients."

"Only one," he says mysteriously. "I'll tell you about it over supper."

"This *is* supper," she says, holding up Evan's bowl of oatmeal.

"Not for us," he says. "I made reservations at our French restaurant. That girl from down the street will be here at eight to babysit."

"I can't stand her."

"Well, you don't have to stand her," he rationalizes. "That's the point. You'll be out."

"Why are we going out?" she asks, reluctant to give up her bad mood without just cause.

"To celebrate." He kisses her again, and adds: "And wear something hot."

*E*lie reserved the best table in the restaurant, the one directly in front of the fireplace in the main room. She has to admit, she's glad he dragged her out. It's what she needed but would never have thought to ask for: the blazing fire, the tea-infused ginger martini warming her belly, the elegant music, the softly twinkling tea lights—it's all very uplifting on a grim, chilly February night.

After they order their racks of lamb, Elie requests a bottle of their best champagne.

"That would be a Clos du Mesnil," the waiter says, holding his breath as he points to it on the wine list.

"That's fine," Elie says, not even glancing at the price. The waiter's eyes twinkle with professionally restrained greed.

Anne gives Elie an impatient look. "Okay, what's going on?" she asks him after the waiter has danced off with supplicating promises to return right away with the champagne.

Without another word Elie reaches into the inside pocket of his Armani jacket and pulls out a maroon-colored leather box. He sets it on the table in front of her. Anne considers it for a moment. It's too large for a ring box, but it would do nicely for a necklace or a bracelet. "What's the occasion?" she asks.

"Open it."

Giddily, she reaches for the box and flips it open. It's a coin. She looks up at Elie, not bothering to conceal her disappointment. "A coin," she says tightly. "How thoughtful of you."

He laughs.

Irritated, she snaps the box shut and slides it back to him.

"Anne," he says. "Take another look at it."

She opens it again, reluctantly. It's a gold coin. She looks more closely, this time discovering that it's a ten-dollar coin. The date on it is 1862.

And then she gets it.

"Elie!" she gasps, lifting the coin from the box and holding it in the palm of her hand. "Is this *the* B.C. ten-dollar coin?"

He's beaming, a smile so big it seems to wrap around his head.

"This is the one you were missing?"

He nods emphatically. "Can you fucking believe it?"

"Your collection is complete now!"

"It's worth over a million dollars."

"How did you find it? And when? Tell me everything."

The waiter arrives and pours them each a glass of champagne. They toast to Elie's newly acquired B.C. ten-dollar gold coin.

"Ken Schlittman," he states calmly, finishing off his flute of Clos du Mesnil as though it were ice water and then pouring himself another.

Anne's mouth gapes open. "Ken Schlittman had your coin in his collection?"

"Can you believe it?" Elie crows.

"No—"

"The whole collection is worth about two and a half million."

"Oh my God . . ."

He grabs her hand and kisses her knuckles, one, two, three times. "I have to thank your mother," he gushes. "I owe it all to her. If she hadn't been screwing him—"

"Two point five million," Anne repeats. "But he sold short men's suits for a living!"

"Obviously he had no intention of selling his collection. Ever."

"Do you think he knew how much it was worth?"

"He had to have known."

"But why did he stay at his job? He gave himself a heart attack stressing over his sales and all along he had two and a half million bucks in coins—"

"Intrinsic motivation?" Elie offers. "His daughter's future?"

The appetizers arrive but they barely touch them. Instead Anne reaches for her champagne and then her martini.

"In all my years in the business," Elie is saying, "I've never seen such a complete collection of Canadian coins.

There are about seven hundred in total, some really rare and expensive ones too. He has the 1911 silver dollar, the Emperor of Canadian Coins. There's only two in existence and his is the only one that's privately owned. The other one is in the Currency Museum in Ottawa. It was fucking unbelievable to find it in there!"

"And what's his daughter going to do with the collection?"

"Sell it off, piece by piece."

"Through you?"

"Through me," he responds smugly. He holds up his champagne flute and they toast again. He downs it and refills the glass.

"And you're sure she'll sell you this one?"

"She already has," Elie says, gazing lovingly at his new acquisition. "I told her I was interested in buying it for my own collection. I estimated what I thought it was worth on its own—since she's missing three of the four in the collection—and then I told her to get a second appraisal. She didn't think it was necessary. I wrote her a check on the spot."

The waiter asks them if they're finished with their appetizers. Elie signals him to clear them away, virtually untouched. He orders a bottle of red wine to accompany the lamb.

"What's she like?" Anne asks.

"You've met her."

"I know, but under the circumstances I couldn't make a proper assessment. I thought she had an edge."

"She's a TV producer."

"I know. But is she nice?"

"She's all business," he says, with a look that wonders *what the hell does that matter?* "I'll tell you this: She was astonished when I told her what her daddy's coin collection was worth. I almost had to pick her up off the floor."

"I don't blame her."

"The guy was some kind of eccentric millionaire."

"But remember his crappy apartment? Why would he have stayed there?"

"He preferred to hoard his coins and live a middle-class life, I guess."

"They meant a lot to him, I gather. Is she going to keep any? For sentimental value?"

"I didn't get that impression."

"Cold," Anne mutters. "That's cold."

"Who are you to judge?"

"She's lucky she had a father to leave her such a generous gift."

"Well," Elie says, beaming, "who cares about her? This is the third happiest day of my life."

"Now what?" Anne says, sipping her champagne.

The question seems to knock the wind out of him. That dreamy look vanishes from his eyes; his smile droops. "I don't know," he says, sounding somewhat shell-shocked. "I don't have a fucking clue."

He forces the smile back on his lips and drinks some more. He continues to drink all night, with great gusto. Champagne, wine, scotch. At some point his liquor consumption begins to blur the line between celebration and obliteration.

"I love you, Anne Mahroum," he declares, midway through a glass of eighteen-year-old Lagavulin.

Anne returns the sentiment with a patronizing smile, the only way to respond to a slobbering drunk.

"Are we going to have sex tonight?" he wants to know. "What are my chances?"

"Based on all the booze you've consumed, I don't think your chances are very good."

"I don't want to sound brash," he blares, "but I haven't been laid in—"

"Lower your voice."

Wounded, he slumps back in his chair. "It's lonely without you," he laments.

"I'm here."

"Not really. You haven't been the same—or we haven't been—since Evan."

She reaches for his hand. "That's normal, El," she says soothingly, trying to convince him the way she's been convincing herself all these months. "It's hard for a woman after she has a baby. It takes a while to feel normal again."

"Howlongisawhile?" he asks, in what comes out sounding like one long, unintelligible word.

"You're drunk, baby."

He nods in agreement. "I can't believe I finally got my coin . . ." he manages. But there's a forlorn quality in his voice, as though something has been lost rather than found; as though *he's* lost.

*E*lie flops down on the bed and lies there spread-eagle on his belly. He mutters something into the mattress, but his words are muffled and incomprehensible.

"What did you say, El?"

He lifts up his head. "I miss my brother," he says. "I'd call him if I could."

"I know."

"I can't pretend we were that close," he confesses, drowsily lopping the ends off all his words so it sounds like *I ca preten we were tha clo . . .*

"He was eight years younger than me," he goes on. "Still, when there's big news—when there's something to celebrate—that's when I miss them. Especially Ziad."

She sits down beside him on the edge of the bed. The duvet puffs up around her thighs. "There's nothing wrong with grieving," she tells him. "Even now. It's very healthy."

"I'll join a support group!" he mocks. He rolls onto his back and stares up at the ceiling with glassy black eyes. "They never got over it," he says mournfully.

"When's the last time you spoke to your mother?"

"Christmas. Plus I sent her that photo album of Evan. She never thanked me."

"She's difficult."

"She always was."

Elie has very little to do with his family in Beirut. Aside from his mother, there are some cousins and aunts and uncles scattered about the Middle East, people he feels as indifferent and untethered to as strangers. His father, whom Anne gathers held everyone together, died of a stroke nearly a decade ago, and his mother disowned Elie after he left Beirut. She never forgave him for abandoning her after she'd already lost one son.

He wrote her twice before—once after they were married and once when they found out Anne was pregnant. She never responded.

Anne asked him once how he felt about being disowned by his mother. He shrugged, dismissing it. She asked him if he missed her or ever wanted to go back to Beirut and repair things. "Does it hurt?" Anne wanted to know.

"She was impossible," he answered. "She was an impossible woman."

You would have to be, Anne supposes, to disown your own child.

Only when he's drunk and sentimental does Elie reveal the extent to which the disintegration of his family affects him. On these occasions, right before he passes out, he always utters the same thing: "The war destroyed my family just as surely as if it had killed us all."

*E*van wakes up at six in the morning. Elie is practically in a coma, belting out hard, foul-smelling snores that stink up the room with a nauseating combination of stale booze and morning breath. It's left to Anne to get up and tend to her boy, even though Saturday and Sunday mornings are supposed to be "her time." They go through the usual routine—bottle, oatmeal, puree of some fruit or another—and then diaper change, cast cleaning, foot and toe inspection.

Hours later Elie stumbles into Evan's playroom. His hair is matted and dirty, his eyes puffy and his skin unnaturally pale. "Why didn't you stop me last night?" he grunts.

"I tried."

"How many scotches did I have?"

"Three or four."

He winces. "Where's the Motrin?"

"None left."

Evan lifts up his arms and cries, "Dadadada!"

Elie crouches down and picks him up. "Hi, Stinker." He kisses him all over his face and his bare tummy, eliciting a delighted giggle. "How late did he sleep?"

"It's more like how early. He was up at six."

"Six?" he says, pulling Evan's nose. "Six!"

Evan finds this hilarious.

"I have to go to the studio," Anne mentions casually. "Can you take him until his afternoon nap?"

"I was going to go to work—"

This is parenthood: The eternal bargaining for snatches of time. *You take him for fifteen minutes while I shower; I'll put him down tonight if you let me sleep in tomorrow. I need to make a call, need to pee . . .* On and on.

"I have to go to the studio," Anne says firmly. "I haven't been all week. I've been with Evan every day—"

"All right, all right. No need for a goddamn sermon."

"Loity!" Evan cries, yanking on a chunk of Elie's greasy hair. Elie's face contorts in pain. He lets out a sound that sounds like *Ayyyk!* "That's good for my migraine," he mutters, rubbing his scalp.

"I'm going to shower," Anne tells him, leaving no room for negotiating or haggling. "He's all yours."

She stops at a diner on Queen Street and spends a full hour lingering over bacon and eggs and bottomless coffee. She loves the smell of the place—grease and old-fashioned percolated coffee. She likes the noise, the bustle. She doesn't feel lonely here, even sitting in a booth by herself.

Snippets of conversation waft around her, mingled with clanging plates in the background. "Jenny went out with that guy she met at Reverb. She likes him, but his name's Burt. So that's finished."

Anne chuckles to herself. Downtown is a refreshingly bohemian haven compared to her own neighborhood.

There are very few mommies, no strollers taking up half the space, no squawking babies, no Cheerios littering the floor. Instead, it's girls with pink hair, platform boots and rings pierced into every square inch of their bodies; guys with hangovers and yellow cigarette stains on their fingers. Twenty-somethings who hang out at places with names like Reverb. Anne feels more at home here, among the artists and the misfits, than she does in her own "community."

She notices one of the waiters staring at her and quickly glances away. He's got two piercings the size of bullet holes in his ears and a silver hoop through his bottom lip. Despite the facial desecration and his blue Mohawk, he's very cute. He's lean and chiseled, with a long narrow face. He has a broad chest and hard, round biceps that are barely concealed by the sleeves of his T-shirt. She was never into bad boys the way most girls are in their twenties, but lately she finds herself regretting it.

She wipes her mouth with a napkin, thinking there must be yolk on her lips or something. Why else would he be gawking? This isn't Yonge and Lawrence, where she might be a draw for a yuppie dad at Starbucks.

The waiter gives her a flirty smile that she thinks is intended to reel her in. Is it possible? She's about a decade older than he is; not old enough to be his mother, but certainly old enough to be an aunt.

She looks away again and waits. God, she loves the game. When she returns her gaze, he's still staring at her. She gets that flirting buzz, like from champagne. They go back and forth like that, looking at each other, looking away. Playing. Until finally she can't put off having to leave.

She flags down her waitress, pays her bill and then gets up to leave, aware of Blue Mohawk's eyes still on her. She looks back once and smiles. Their eyes lock. *Thank you,* she's thinking. *I'll be back.*

*B*ecause the weather's been too awful for her to venture out in, she hasn't dropped by the studio in over a week. The mail is piled up on the floor when she gets inside.

Despite Evan's early morning she woke up feeling like her old self, with a burst of creative energy. She leapt out of bed, dying to get downtown, turn on her forge and get to work on that round bar of hot-rolled metal she picked up at the steel yard a few months ago. It's been sitting there, neglected, for far too long.

She dumps all the unopened mail on one of her tables and goes directly over to the forge, feeling giddy and excited, like she used to feel right before lighting up a much anticipated cigarette. She slides the burner out of the burner port enough so that she can see the tip inside the forge. Then she turns on the gas, aiming a propane torch at the burner tip. Blue flames immediately shoot up, so she adjusts the gas until the temperature reaches an even, workable heat.

She puts on her welding jacket and overalls and immediately gets that powerful, superhero feeling she always gets when she's decked out in her protective equipment—the steel-toed boots, the welding mask and the heat-resistant leather from top to bottom. The full gear always makes her feel like she could kick ass.

She turns on her stereo and cranks Damien Rice full blast. Then she goes over to her tools, selects some hammers and sets them next to her anvil. When she first began blacksmithing she used a fifty-five-pound mild-steel anvil, but the rebound from her hammer was so inefficient it took all her energy just to work the steel into a simple hook. So she replaced her first anvil with a brand-new one that weighs 180 pounds, and now when she drops the hammer on its face it bounces up almost as high as from where it was dropped.

She cuts about four feet of the steel and slides it into the hot forge with her tongs. She's going to work on some metal fingers today, which she'll eventually weld to a hand formed from cut-up pieces of sheet metal. The round bar stock she's got is perfect for the fingers. She heats the steel in the propane flame for a few minutes and then pulls it out when it's glowing red hot and easy to pound.

She sets the hot steel on her anvil and uses her ball-peen hammer to form it into a semblance of a finger. She smashes and twists it while it's hot and malleable, and then, when the steel starts to cool and turn gray, she throws it back into the forge and starts all over again.

She's taken a few wheel-throwing pottery courses over the years and, in some ways, blacksmithing is similar to pottery. Although the positions and motions are different— blacksmithing is a much more physical process, much tougher on the body, too—both crafts have to be worked in critical spaces of time. In pottery, the clay is either spinning or still. It has to be worked when it's active. When it loses that energy the work has to stop until it's energized again. With forging, it's all about the heat rather than the motion. The work has to be done while the steel is red hot, which is challenging since it cools in seconds.

It's such an elemental art, requiring careful consideration of heat, air, water and metal. Everything she needs to know about the process is revealed to her in the color of the fire, the color of the steel, the sound of the strike or the resistance against the hammer blow.

She manages to get a reasonable shape of a finger, but she struggles with the finer work—the creases in the skin, the joints. The first few don't have the fluidity of skin she's trying to achieve. She doesn't worry too much about it though. Today's exercise is really just to reacquaint herself with her tools; to get that hunk of cold metal into the oven and start smashing a hammer against it. To that end, she feels exhilarated and satisfied.

Perfection is for a symphony, not hand-forged art. The glory is in her body moving again, the white sparks of metal flying at her, the strength and power of each blow.

After a while her arms begin to wear out and her hands get limp and tired from gripping the hammer. Her left thumb is numb from having to control the metal. Not only is she out of practice, she's out of shape too.

She imagines it's as physically grueling as running a marathon. That's the level of pain and exhaustion she feels at the end of two hours of blacksmithing. With her back and arms aching, she decides to call it quits for the day.

She changes out of her welding gear and turns off the music. She can't wait to get home and slide into a hot bath. She cleans up and turns off the forge, and then just before leaving she hits the voice mail on her speakerphone.

"Hi, Anne."

It's a man's voice. Her first thought is Barry Katz.

"I, uh . . . I've been thinking about you."

And then she recognizes him.

"I know I keep, uh, disappearing, but I'll be at the meeting on Monday. I'd like to see you. I'll definitely be there." There's a long pause and then, "Oh. It's, um, Declan."

She takes a breath and replays the message. She lets out a nervous laugh.

He wants to see her. It's not another one of her fantasies. She replays the message another half dozen times until she can recite it from heart. Each time his words go through her body like liquor, leaving her warm and giddy.

For the first time in her married life, she doesn't trust herself to stop. Declan has proven to be Elie's most formidable opponent yet.

Twenty-four

*T*he two days until she's supposed to see Declan crawl by with excruciating slowness, during which time she finds herself in a constant state of light-headedness and distraction. Attending to the most ordinary tasks requires mental stamina; staying focused on the minutiae of diapers, naps, casts and meals is as much an effort as trying to rein in her excitement and stay grounded.

Some moments she feels like she could explode. Since he left her the message she's been experiencing seizures of elation that come on unexpectedly and require the suppressing of goofy, unwarranted smiles. There have also been moments of deep tenderness and affection toward Elie, which are always accompanied by sobering bouts of guilt.

She's already discovered that being a wife requires only a lackadaisical maintenance. Elie may find her skittish and bemused, but not more than usual and he probably attributes it to her general self-absorption and self-centeredness. Nothing out of the ordinary, as far as he's concerned.

Motherhood is tougher. Evan demands more than a nod here and a placating smile there. He demands her whole heart and the full extent of her attention. She can't float around in a daze while she's on duty. It's like trying to act responsible and composed when you're stumbling around drunk.

She's always thought of herself as a flirter, not an adulterer, deliberately choosing fruitless, unfeasible targets. Not one of them was ever a real threat to Elie. But now Declan is about to erode that line. Her sacred line.

These things have a way of escalating. They either escalate or they die.

How do you compromise between desire and obligation, self-gratification and loyalty? No matter how long she ponders and mulls and bargains and negotiates, it can't be done. She guesses that the enduring dilemma of infidelity is how to have what you want without endangering your marriage, your family and your conscience. Short of having a swinging marriage, you must be completely willing to lose everything.

The word "adulteress" has leapt into her mind several times. She's been thinking about a movie she saw a couple of years ago called *Unfaithful*. Diane Lane plays a married woman who has an affair with a hot French guy. The movie never oversimplifies the affair by trying to explain why it happens; it doesn't suggest that it's because something is wrong with her marriage. Anne thought that was clever. It's what she could relate to the most—that you can love your spouse and not want to leave him and not want to change anything, but simultaneously succumb to an affair. Eventually her husband, the Richard Gere character, kills her lover.

In all the fantasies Anne's had about potential lovers she's never counted on how much time she'd have beforehand to weigh and analyze the implications. In her harmless imaginings the affairs always happened spontaneously, like volcanic eruptions. A violent, passionate kiss; the ripping off of clothes without any warning. Always, they were unplanned and therefore less grievous.

This arrangement to meet Declan is much too premeditated. In a court of law she'd be charged with first-degree cheating. She's had way too much time to strategize and think it through. If she does go to meet him and something happens between them, she won't have any defense to fall back on.

"I thought you dropped the group," Elie remarks, entering the bathroom with Evan in his arms. He catches her staring at herself in the mirror. She turns away guiltily.

"I need one tonight," she says. "I'm nervous about the casts coming off."

(How easy that was! How naturally that glided off her tongue.)

He seems to find it a reasonable explanation. "Should I feed Evan that broccoli soup in the fridge?"

"Yes, good idea."

He leaves the room then, just like that. Evan waves to her on his way out, momentarily piercing her heart with shame. She promptly dismisses the notion that she's somehow cheating on Evan too.

She turns back to the mirror and resumes her assessment. She's settled on black pants, a cream cashmere turtleneck and a fitted, tan corduroy blazer with a dragonfly broach on the lapel. It's not as funky as she usually dresses, but her mood tonight is for something more classic and conservative. (Like Margaret?)

She eventually has to pull herself away from herself or risk missing the meeting. She finds her boys in the kitchen. Elie is feeding Evan his supper; they're both wearing robes and socks (all the more ridiculous on Evan, with his two big fiberglass casts). Normally it would be an unexceptional scene, but tonight the sight of them in their matching robes, connected by a plastic spoon, strikes her as particularly heartwarming. It induces more waves of shame and guilt.

Regardless of his shortcomings, Elie makes a valiant effort at fatherhood. He mixes the cereal wrong, making it too dry and lumpy. He doesn't warm the fruit the way Evan likes. He forgets the yogurt. He gives him a cold bottle. But Evan survives. And after months of trying to get him to do it the right way (or "her" way, as he foolishly calls it) she has started to relinquish her hold over their time together.

"Have fun," Elie says.

"I'm going to a support group," she reminds him, with an edge of defensiveness in her tone.

He turns to look at her. "Say hi to Tracy and Dan for me."

"Tami and Darren," she mutters.

"What time will you be home?"

"Tami and I might have coffee afterward," Anne drops into the conversation, laying the groundwork for a potentially late night. "I'll call after the meeting and let you know."

He nods, perfectly appeased. She's almost disappointed at how anticlimactic it is; how easy the lying and conniving and scheming come. Would she have done this sooner if she'd known there was so little to it?

She clasps Evan's broccoli-spattered cheeks in her hands and kisses each one, tasting the soup on her tongue. "Have fun with Daddy," she says. And then she crouches down in front of his high chair and touches his nose. "Mama loves you."

On her way out she has to fight the urge to turn back. She could go upstairs right now and give Evan his bath as usual, and then get into bed with a magazine or watch TV with Elie, and everything would stay the same. *She* would stay the same. It's not too late to preserve their safe, cozy arrangement, which is solid and warm and reassuringly familiar.

She rushes back into the kitchen and they both look up at her, surprised. She kisses Evan again, knowing that everything will be different when she gets back.

"Okay," she says, gathering her courage. "Bye."

Elie kisses her hand as she brushes past him. She loves him. That's her last thought before leaving.

She sits in the parking lot for a long time, gripping the steering wheel and contemplating the church. The meeting started ten minutes ago. She doesn't even know if he's in there. She couldn't live with the disappointment if he's not.

It feels surreal to be sitting here. Since the first time Declan talked to her their attraction has unfolded so quickly.

It's still not too late to salvage her honor. She could leave right now, even though she knows there's nothing honorable about wanting to flee. It wouldn't only be out of integrity or loyalty. She'd be wanting to preserve his illusion of her—whatever that may be. And she'd be wanting to preserve her illusion of *him,* because the moment they really knew each other the dream would evaporate.

Then what?

She somehow manages to get from her car to the foyer of the church. Once inside, she stands in front of the second set of doors that leads into the support group meeting. It crosses her mind again that if she turns away now she could keep everything intact—not just her family, but her dignity. *She* could be the one to walk away from this, desired and unconquered. Over time, Declan's memory of her might even bloom into something mythical—

The door suddenly swings open and then he's standing in front of her, filling the small space of the foyer. "Anne—" he says, flustered.

"Hi."

"What are you doing?"

"I have no idea."

"I thought you weren't coming," he says. "I was going to leave."

Face-to-face with his impossibly good looks, all her rational musings of the past half hour drain from her head. Lust overrides consequence and there is no more question of leaving. The only option is Declan.

"Let's go somewhere," he says, in a hushed, conspiratorial voice that excites her.

She follows him to his car, feeling as sneaky and rebellious as a teenager. Once they're settled in the front seat he asks her about Evan's feet, predictably grasping for the safety of common ground.

"His casts come off next week."

"Margaret's decided to try Ponseti again," he says wearily.

Dr. Ponseti pioneered the technique of stretching and casting the feet as an alternative to surgery. "Why?" Anne asks, surprised. "If it didn't work the first time—"

"We have a new surgeon," he explains. "He says the only time Ponseti doesn't work is when the orthopedist doesn't know what he's doing. Margaret seems to think that's why Sean's feet didn't straighten out the first time."

Although she's never been fond of Dr. Hotz, Anne finds herself taking up a defensive position. "Our orthopedist is experienced," she asserts. "He's corrected thousands of club feet."

"That doesn't mean he did a good job on any of them," Declan counters. "Our new surgeon says that experience isn't a substitute for a thorough understanding of the deformity. According to him, you're not even supposed to soak the casts off the night before a cast change."

"Why not?" she asks irritably, remembering all the nights she spent soaking those damn casts on Dr. Hotz's instructions.

"Because he says you can lose a lot of correction overnight," he tells her, making it sound infuriatingly logical.

"That's what *he* says. They all say something different."

"Our first orthopedist always had us soak Sean's casts off the night before a change. I wonder how much correction we lost every time we did that. But you're right, most of these doctors don't know a goddamn thing about club feet."

"Isn't Sean too old now to reset his feet without surgery?"

"Our new surgeon doesn't think so."

"He sounds like a real authority."

"Margaret thinks he's a god," Declan returns, matching her sarcasm.

Their conversation is beginning to depress her. In addition to Declan's having mentioned Margaret's name about a half a dozen times already, it's not exactly the stuff of great romance. It certainly isn't what she imagined for this moment.

They sit in silence. The car is still not running and she realizes she's trembling from the cold. She can see her breath and feels considerably more miserable than she did before they got in his car. A conversation doesn't pass between them without Margaret's name coming up over and over again. Either he loves her madly or he despises her or both. Sometimes he utters her name in a halo of intimidated awe. Other times he forces her name out between clenched teeth. His feelings for her seem to be made up of intricate layers of resentment and admiration. Anne envisions Margaret as a ferocious, bullying beauty whom Declan defers to, fears, worships and loathes. She thinks he must be drawn to Anne's mildness, or what he perceives as mildness.

He eventually starts the car. "You're probably wondering about that message I left on your machine," he says, still making no move to leave the parking lot.

"I'm thinking about how we got here."

"Do you mean existentially?" he deadpans.

"I mean here, hiding out in your car."

"You want the chronology?" he asks. "I first noticed you the night you shared about Evan's operation. You had on some jeans—"

"I didn't wear those jeans till later."

"Really? I remember you were in those jeans. Anyway, you just seemed so vulnerable and honest, no bullshit or bravado. I thought it was sexy."

(She wouldn't have picked vulnerable and honest as the most provocative of her qualities.)

"And then I bankrupted myself buying one of your tables . . ."

"You seemed to really like it at the time."

"It sort of looks like a bathroom floor," he admits.

"There are no refunds."

They both laugh.

"Do you mind if I smoke?" he asks.

"Go ahead."

He opens his window a crack and lights up. He turns to face her then, foisting the full intensity of his eyes on her. "I've been thinking about you a lot," he says, lavishing her with a penetrating stare. "I haven't been able to get you out of my head . . ."

Aroused and embarrassed, she has to look away. Vindication comes in a hot, pulsating sensation through her body. She can't help feeling victorious, knowing that as she lay there obsessing over him all this time he was doing the same. It always makes her wonder what unspoken, inexplicable thing it is that draws two people to each other when a million others elicit nothing. Maybe she attributes it more importance than it deserves; maybe physical attraction is more common and meaningless than she likes to think, occurring a thousand times a day between men and women. Maybe it's objective and animalistic, like pheromones or the smell of someone's skin; or maybe on some level people recognize the exact category of their personal attractiveness and are subsequently drawn only to their equals.

Yet occasionally she indulges in a more romantic view of lust. She likes to believe that two souls can instantaneously latch onto each other, causing a physical reaction in the human body. Who's to say "chemistry" isn't an otherworldly connection manifesting itself in the cunning, irrefutable pull of sexual attraction?

"I guess it was pretty reckless," Declan is saying. "Leaving that message for you. Your husband could have picked it up . . ."

"He wouldn't. It's my studio—"

"Anyway, I dropped by a couple of times last week and you weren't there. I guess I started to panic."

The idea of him panicking pleases her, but she doesn't let on.

"I figured I might not see you again," he explains. "I felt like I needed one more shot, to see—"

"What?"

He doesn't finish the sentence. Instead, they're both distracted by the people from the support group emptying out of the church, returning to their cars. A couple of them huddle together in the parking lot, probably still discussing club feet.

Declan and Anne watch them in silence. They watch until the last woman walks past them toward her car, digging around in her purse for her keys. Anne recognizes her. It's Courtney. She happens to look up and notice Anne. Their eyes lock. Then she glances past Anne at Declan. It takes a moment for her to register who he is, but when she does her expression morphs into one of surprise, disdain, judgment; maybe even a hint of envy, though Anne could be projecting.

Anne looks away, feeling exposed.

"Why did you come tonight?" Declan asks after Courtney has driven away.

"Isn't it obvious?"

"For all I know," he says, sounding slightly agitated, "you're here for the meeting." He looks at her expectantly.

"You know why I'm here," she tells him softly.

He shifts his body closer to her on the seat. "Tell me why."

"Will it change anything if you know I'm here for you?"

"It might."

"Would something happen? Would you make a move?"

"Would you let me?"

"If I'm pressed to give an answer in advance," she says, laughing at the inanity of their conversation, "I'd have to say I don't know. If you just made a move, I probably wouldn't stop you. It's all the thinking about it beforehand . . ."

"Why did you come tonight?"

"To see you."

"When did this start?"

"What? My crush?"

"If that's what you want to call it."

"The night you shared about Lord Byron," she admits. "And then when you pushed up your sleeves."

"I wasn't aware women like men who talk about poets."

"I like men who read. Good forearms are a bonus."

"Does your husband read?"

Anne nods, without elaborating.

"You rarely mention him," Declan remarks.

"I guess I don't want you to feel like you're in competition."

He looks at her penitently, as though he's just been caught with his hand in his mother's wallet.

"It can be intimidating," she goes on, deciding to leave it at that.

"I guess I've spoken a lot about Margaret," he admits.

Anne shrugs, pretending not to have noticed.

"Does it intimidate you?" he asks.

"I guess in a way it does. Especially when it comes to how we've handled our sons' club feet."

"How so?"

"You make it sound like she handles it better than I do. I worry you think I've made bad decisions, or that I'm too self-pitying compared to Margaret."

"Maybe *you* think that."

"I guess I do."

"Margaret handles everything," he says edgily. "That's Margaret. Either she's the noblest woman alive or she's in total denial. I still haven't figured it out."

"Are you here to cheat on her?" Anne blurts.

He looks stunned by the question. It takes him a few minutes to recover. Then he tells her he doesn't know.

She sees now that the decision to cheat on a spouse is made at the last possible moment. She thinks there's a kind of denial leading up to infidelity, a lot of self-convincing and minimizing. You can persuade yourself you'll get out in time, that you won't let anything happen. That all the flirting and fantasizing have been harmless.

In the end, it's like a game of chicken. Who will be the first one to leap out of the car, or will they both plunge over the cliff into the unknown?

The next thing she knows his hand is on her face, lightly touching her cheek. He retracts it quickly, as though he's touched a hot element. "Can I do this to her?" he asks himself out loud. He seems genuinely troubled, which comforts Anne. She wouldn't want him to be taking this lightly.

Then he says, "I want this . . ."

This. Does he mean her? Sex? An affair? Perhaps it's all of the above. Whatever he means, he's overthinking it. His eyes are cloudy, his expression tense and strained. His mind seems to be preoccupied with the logistics of things, the where, when and how. The repercussions. The tomorrow. The big lie he will have to tell.

Anne has none of those things in her mind. She's zoomed in on the moment. She wants to kiss him. That's all that's in her head. Her eyes return again and again to his lips. How would they feel on hers? How does he kiss? Light and fleeting, like his hand on her cheek, or brusque and devouring? (Both have their appeal.) Beyond those concerns, everything else is a blur. She hasn't got an agenda or a plan; she seems to be floating in a consequence-free orbit.

He's not more witty or intelligent or handsome than Elie, yet her heart is pounding and she's certain she has never wanted anything this much in her entire life. She's vibrating with it. (Was it ever like this with Elie? She can't remember.)

"What's going through your head?" he asks her.

"Nothing," she answers, flushing. Which is the truth. Everything is going through her body.

"Then what are you feeling?" he presses.

"Fear. Guilt." (She leaves out desire, not wanting to reveal too much of her hand.)

"Me too," he says, fixing her with a purposeful gaze. She can tell by the yearning and determination in his face that he is about to kiss her. And then his lips touch hers for not more than a second. It's enough of a kiss to make forgetting him impossible, but not nearly enough to satisfy her and barely enough to qualify as an act of infidelity.

"Do you realize we're still in the parking lot?" he says, laughing nervously. "Is there anywhere you want to go?"

"I'd like a drink."

"So would I," he says. "But I'm an alcoholic, remember? It's probably not a good idea."

"God, I—I wasn't even thinking. I'm sorry. I just . . ."

"Don't worry about it," he assures her. "Believe me, if I still drank, we'd be in a motel already."

The remark makes her wish he did still drink. It would be a hell of a lot easier. Doing this sober is tantamount to having her teeth drilled without Novocain.

"What were you like?" she asks him. "When you were drinking?" She's tried to imagine him as a drunk, but she can't get a picture in her mind. She can't see him passed out on a sidewalk, as he once described, or stumbling home to Margaret hammered. Yet for some reason the whole idea of his being an alcoholic turns her on. It's the wildness he must have had in him back then; the recklessness.

"It wasn't pretty," he responds, chuckling. "I was a fucking disaster. There were all these things I wanted to do . . . like it would be a gorgeous day and I'd stop at the pub for a beer, thinking I'd go outside and spend the day doing something meaningful or useful. And then it would be dark and I'd still be sitting in that pub, and there'd be nothing else to do but stop for beer on my way home and buy another case to last me the night. It was like that day after day. I never got anything done. I just drank."

She's shaking her head. "I can't picture you . . ."

"My sponsor didn't want me to come here tonight," he says, staring absently through the windshield.

"Your sponsor?"

"I've got a sponsor in AA," he explains. "He's kind of like a mentor who guides me through recovery."

"And he knows about—" she almost says "us," but instead she says, *"This?"*

"He knows everything about me. All my deep dark secrets."

"I can't imagine anyone knowing everything about me."

"I guess that's the point of the program," he says. "Holding on to secrets and resentments is what gets us into trouble. The Big Book says those are the luxuries of normal men."

"What big book?" she asks, confused. "The Bible?"

"*Our* bible, the AA big book."

"I've always been curious about twelve-step programs," she tells him. "But I've never had an addiction to warrant going."

"Everyone should be in one," he says. "My sponsor has thirty-seven years of sobriety and he's the best man I know."

She's got a plunging feeling that by bringing up his sponsor and talking so much about AA, he's having second thoughts about being here with her. It certainly doesn't bode well for an affair.

Declan continues to stare out the windshield, lost in thought. She can tell he's trying to make a decision, to answer something for himself. He's obviously struggling with some kind of profound moral dilemma, which seems less to do with Margaret than with his revered sponsor.

"Do I need to be here?" she asks him, feeling suddenly impatient and extraneous.

"What do you mean?"

"You seem to be trying to figure something out that doesn't really require my being here."

"You want the truth?" he asks, shooting her a quick look out of the corner of his eye and then looking away again.

"Probably not," she says, discouraged.

"I'm sitting here trying to decide if I should just fuck the whole thing and drive to a bar with you right now and let whatever happens happen."

"Fuck what whole thing?"

"My sobriety. Six years next month."

"What does being with me have to do with your sobriety?"

Declan sighs, a deep, sad sound that seems to emanate from the very core of him. "It's an addict thing," he says. "It's all or nothing. If I'm going to be unfaithful and ruin all the hard work I've put into my marriage and into being a good man, I may as well take a drink and throw everything away in one shot and enjoy the ride."

"So I'm an excuse to drink."

"Or drinking would be an excuse to have you," he clarifies. "Either way works. That's why we're still sitting here in the parking lot. I want to go to a bar. I mean, part of me does. Another part of me is fighting it. AA has given me a fucking conscience."

"It doesn't sound like this is what you want," she observes, crushed. "You can't even look at me."

"I know. Because if I do, I'll want to kiss you again. And then . . ."

"It's all over."

He nods.

"Why don't we go for coffee—" she suggests, sensing that he's slipping away. He's talking himself out of it, she can tell. She's losing him.

"You don't understand," he flares. "I don't want to go for coffee with you and have an interesting conversation and find myself attracted to you and consequently more tormented. Either we're going to get loaded and go to bed and have a wild time or we're going to part ways. We're not going to have coffee together."

"This is about your drinking," she concludes. "It has nothing to do with me."

He can't even refute the accusation. He just sits there, slumped dejectedly in his seat, probably longing for a drink. All her fantasies about necking drowsily in the front seat of his car begin to recede and float away.

"I'll have to make amends to Margaret," he mutters.

"What?"

"If something happens between you and me, I'll have to tell Lloyd and eventually I'll have to come clean with Margaret."

She smiles at him through her humiliation. "I understand."

"I've got to call my sponsor," he says, sounding desperate all of a sudden. "This disease is so insidious. I didn't realize how far I'd slipped, but you're right. I want a drink more than . . ."

She reaches for the door, her ego unable to withstand another degrading blow from his lips.

"I'm sorry," he says woefully.

She climbs out of his car, wondering if she could have been more overt, more irresistible. She is full of regret and self-recrimination. He was so close, and yet she let him slip out of her grasp. She should have insisted he take her somewhere, at least to get him away from that parking lot.

Instead she sat there placidly and gave him all the time he needed to talk himself out of it.

Certain things make sense to her now, like the message he left on her machine. It *was* reckless. He probably called in a moment of craving a drink and another woman and whatever else he could reach for that might blot out his pain and sabotage his sobriety and help him recapture his old life. She can see how he might occasionally miss the freedom of having nothing to lose, no expectations to meet. Margaret must set a very high standard.

In some strange way, Anne can understand his craving to drink and why he'd want to blot out reality. Isn't that why she wants *him*?

It's just her luck to fall for a recovered alcoholic, that rare type of guy with a conscience. She brushes the tears off her face and wonders if he'll regret passing her up. Maybe he won't be able to forget her so easily. Maybe he'll show up at her studio again, pleading for another chance. There's always the possibility.

Elie is asleep when she gets home. She creeps into the room, takes off her clothes and slips naked into bed. It's dark and warm, safe. She curls around his body, pressing her chin into his gently rising and falling back, and waits to be saved from the disgrace of the night.

Twenty-five

*T*he casts are coming off today. Dr. Hotz joins them in the sunny yellow pre-op room, still golden from his trip to Florida (and probably from some maintenance at the tanning salon). As he greets them with that bored, gleaming smile of his, Anne hopes this will be one of their last reunions.

"How's Evan today?" he asks, looking down at the illegible scribble on his clipboard. It's obviously a rhetorical question because he pushes forward without waiting a beat. "Dr. Turvey noted here that the left foot wasn't as straight as the right one. Hopefully it's improved since then."

He honors them briefly with a glimpse of eye contact before returning his elusive gaze to that clipboard. "So today I'm going to take the pins out and then remove the casts. We'll call you in later."

"Dr. Hotz?"

"Hm?"

"Is it true that a lot of correction is lost by soaking the casts off the night before a cast change?"

"The amount of correction lost in a matter of hours is negligible," he says, visibly rattled. "Absurdly negligible."

"So there *is* some loss," Anne pursues.

His nostrils flare. "Some orthopedists are of that opinion," he says defensively. "I'm not."

"I hope that's not why Evan needed the operation."

"Evan needed surgery because the casting failed," he states coolly.

Or *you* did, she wants to shout. Instead she holds her tongue, worrying he might retaliate by mangling Evan's feet.

"Renée will take Evan into the operating room now—" he motions for the nurse to come over. "We'll call you in after I've examined the feet."

"The" feet, as though they aren't even attached to Evan! Just another pair of inconsequential, insignificant objects in his busy schedule.

The nurse gently removes Evan from Anne's arms. He gives her that half-resigned, half-beseeching look that precedes every separation from his mother. As the nurse carries him away his eyes stay on Anne, questioning and sad. Her spirits plunge.

"Did you have to be so antagonistic with Dr. Hotz?" Elie asks her, looking up from his loupe. He's brought some old coins and a magnifying loupe with him to keep him busy.

"He bugs me."

"Where did you get that information anyway?" he asks, returning his attention to the coin under his loupe. "About not soaking the casts off the night before?"

"Someone in the group," she responds neutrally.

"Everybody has an opinion," he mutters. "We shouldn't be second-guessing Dr. Hotz."

"What if they're not straight?" she broods, snatching the coin away from Elie so he'll pay attention to her.

"Careful with that," he scolds. "It's a 1793 Wreath Cent."

"I have a knot right here," she goes on, in an overwrought voice. "I just can't face another obstacle."

"Anne," Elie says calmly, "You'll face whatever you have to face."

*T*he nurse is standing above them, grinning. "They're off!" she says.

They follow her through the swinging doors to where Evan is still sleeping off the anesthesia.

"Evan's right foot is perfectly straight," Dr. Hotz declares, somewhat vaingloriously.

Anne rushes over to have a closer look. Both feet are still as swollen as dumplings and there's a lot of scarring, but since the shock of the last preview she's had plenty of time to wrap her head around that. And she's bought a vitamin E gel that Tami says is supposed to work miracles. Other than that, his right foot is virtually normal. The only obstacle now is the outcome of the stubborn left foot.

"They look so different from before," Elie comments, holding Evan's damaged little feet in his hands as though he were choosing fruit. "They don't look anything like they used to, even the left one."

Anne thinks Elie is being overly solicitous. He's settling. The left foot is slightly better than it was, but it's not straight. It still turns inward. She can appreciate that there's been some progress, but she feels the usual disappointment gathering momentum inside her and working its way up through her body. It looks like Evan will need more casting.

"His right foot is very encouraging," Elie goes on enthusiastically. "At least there's hope. Right, Anne?"

She nods mutely.

"There's at least something to embrace now," he effuses, overstating it. "It may not be happening as fast as we'd like, but his right foot is proof that they can be completely straightened."

She turns to Dr. Hotz, prepared to humbly defer to his expertise. "Based on your experience with other club feet, is this promising for six weeks after surgery? Could they still turn out normal?"

Dr. Hotz holds up Evan's foot for her to inspect. "You can see how it looks," he responds. "It looks pretty straight to me. In fact, it couldn't be any straighter than this. Is that what you mean by normal?"

She looks away, embarrassed. She doesn't even know what normal is anymore, except that it's always been crushingly important to her. She's made so many modifications along the way to allow for "minor" imperfections—scarring, swelling, underdeveloped calves—that her original concept has devolved into something quite different and inferior. She's been pursuing ambiguous ideals like "normal" and "perfect" for so long and with such plodding determination that she's rendered them virtually meaningless.

"The left one is going to take a little longer," Dr. Hotz is saying, "but I expect it to turn out exactly like the right one. And more than that—" he concedes, "I cannot promise."

Anne turns back to Evan and takes his right foot in the palm of her hand. She bends down and kisses it.

Dr. Hotz and Elie look at her queerly.

"What about shoes?" Elie asks Dr. Hotz.

"He should be fine with regular shoes."

"Regular shoes?" Anne repeats, loving the sound of it.

"Yes, regular shoes."

The clouds suddenly part. Regular shoes! She looks over at Elie, whose expression is one of relief.

"We'll keep an eye on that left foot," Dr. Hotz resumes. "I may have to recast it in another month, depending on how it heals. But we'll cross that bridge when we come to it."

*T*hey go directly to the mall, where they spend hours searching for a pair of regular shoes to fit over Evan's gigantic dumpling feet. All she could think about at the hospital was that Evan would finally be able to wear an ordinary pair of shoes. What she didn't take into account was how thick and misshapen his feet are. Nothing fits.

Everywhere they go they've got adorable leather slippers with pictures of bunnies and dragonflies. Evan will never slip his foot inside one of them, but Anne tries not to dwell on that. She's attempting optimism today.

The only shoe that fits over the swelling is two sizes too big in length. Anne doesn't know if it's possible for an eight-month-old to feel humiliated, but she isn't willing to take that chance. She is determined to find something he can wear without being ogled or ridiculed.

"What's wrong with these?" Elie asks irritably. Like most men, he loathes malls. "Does it really matter if they're too big?"

"He looks silly in them."

"I don't think he cares."

"Would *you* wear shoes that were two sizes too big?"

"I wouldn't give a damn if I spent all day in a stroller," Elie gripes. "Anne, his feet could be swollen like this for months. Deal with it."

This is always how it is with her and Elie. Whenever they're faced with a challenge, they turn against each other. They work at cross-purposes rather than as a team.

"He looks like Ronald McDonald," she sulks, yanking the offending Buster Browns off her boy's feet and tossing them back in the box.

Her good mood of earlier is on the brink of collapse. She'd had premature visions of slipping a pair of little tennis sneakers on Evan's feet, but as usual, reality has fallen short of her expectations.

"How about these?" the salesgirl suggests. She hands Anne a box of running shoes and then tugs her jeans up from behind.

She's wearing ultra-low-rise jeans that cut her at the hips. Two soft rolls of white flesh hang over her belt. She doesn't have the body to carry it off, but her boldness endears her to Anne.

The shoe is a size two. "This won't fit him," Anne says, discouraged.

"Let's try it first," Elie snarls, snatching it from Anne and trying to stuff Evan's enlarged foot into it. Evan squirms around in his stroller and lets out an indignant yelp.

"It's not that bad," Anne relents. "It's a bit too tight, but it's the best one so far."

"Maybe one size bigger," the salesgirl says brightly. She's brought out a dozen boxes already, all of them strewn around on the carpet; she seems as determined as Anne is to get Evan fitted with a decent pair of shoes.

"I think you're right," Anne agrees, smiling gratefully. "One size bigger might do it."

"*Inshallah,*" Elie mutters.

In the end, they decide on the running shoes in a size three. They're still way too long for his feet, but what matters is that Evan is wearing his first pair of shoes and is on his way to scaling that insurmountable wall over which await the perks and privileges of fitting in.

*I*n the middle of the night Anne wakes up with Harmony in her head. Bits and pieces of a dream come back to her. The church. Evan's big running shoes. People in the pews snickering at him. She reaches out for Elie, seeking his body for comfort. He isn't there.

"Baby?" she murmurs.

There's no answer.

"Elie?" Louder this time, in case he's just gone to the bathroom.

Still nothing.

She sits up and turns on her bedside lamp. Their room is empty. The bathroom door is ajar and the bathroom is dark.

She slides out of bed and throws on the T-shirt Elie was wearing earlier. Then she follows the smell of cigarettes down the hall to his office, where she can see a slash of light on the floor beneath his closed door.

She bursts dramatically into the room, expecting to catch him at something illicit. Instead, she finds him sitting in his leather club chair, gazing up at the ceiling with a bland, indolent expression. "What are you doing?" she asks him.

"I couldn't sleep," he alleges in a thick voice.

She notices a glass of scotch on the table next to him. "You're drunk," she accuses. "I can tell by your voice."

"This is only my second drink. I'm just tired."

"I hate when you smoke in the house."

"I can't drink without smoking."

She goes over to him and sits on his lap. "Then why are you drinking by yourself at four in the morning?"

"I have a lot on my mind."

"Like what?"

He doesn't answer.

"Are you having an affair?" she blurts.

"Are *you*?"

"Why would you ask such a thing?" she returns, puzzled.

"Why would you?"

"I'm not sure," she admits.

"Maybe because *you* are," he points out logically. "You've been very distant lately. Since the fall, in fact. And then our sex life . . ."

"It's Evan's feet," she defends. "You know that. It depletes me. I've got nothing left."

He swishes his drink around in the glass and takes a sip. She notices a syringe on the table, which he uses to inject water into his scotch. Next to the syringe are the coins he had at the hospital this afternoon.

"What's this one?" she asks.

"It's a Greek tetra drachma from 480 BC."

She reaches for it and holds it between her fingers. "Who's she?" she asks, examining the carving of a woman's head surrounded by dolphins on the coin's eroded surface.

"Arethusa."

"Was she a goddess?"

"She was a nymph. According to Greek mythology, she was bathing in a stream near Olympia when she was spotted by Alpheus, the river god. He fell madly in love with her and tried to abduct her. She was a maiden and she wanted to remain chaste, so she fled. He became obsessed with her. He took the form of a hunter in order to pursue her." Elie's voice is low and dreamlike. Anne closes her eyes and presses her head to his chest, like a child listening to a bedtime story. The more he talks, the drowsier she gets. She feels safe, protected.

"She was his prey," he continues. "He chased her relentlessly, until she finally appealed to Artemis, the goddess of the hunt and the protector of women. In order to save her from Alpheus, Artemis transformed Arethusa into a fountain. Alpheus was undeterred. He simply changed himself into a river and joined Arethusa, ensuring that both waters would flow together for eternity."

"How do you know that story?" she asks, lifting her head and looking up at him.

"Coins are historical documents," he says, his dark eyes luminous. "That's what I love about them. They give a glimpse into a lost time. They tell stories. It's my business to know the stories."

She sets the tetra drachma back on the desk and puts her head back on Elie's chest. "I dreamt I was in church and I was holding Evan up to the congregation."

Elie laughs softly.

"He had on his new sneakers and everyone in the church was laughing at him. It broke my heart." Remembering the dream, she feels a tear come to her eye.

"You're so sensitive," Elie soothes.

"I don't want my baby to know that kind of shame."

"He won't, Anne."

She buries her face in the worn terry of his robe and cries there for a while. "I love him too much," she whimpers.

That's the thing about motherhood—the stakes go up every day. The love and the joy intensify exponentially, but so do the fear and worry and that violent instinct to protect him from harm. There is an intricate, irrevocable shackle of commitment that tightens and clenches over time. Gradually, being a parent begins to feel like a kind of exalted affliction, burdensome and euphoric at the same time.

"You're a good woman," Elie whispers in her ear. His breath is hot and has the smell of scotch. She likes it. He caresses her hair.

She's glad she didn't wreck this thing she has with Elie. They're far from being a perfect couple, but they've got these moments.

"My father was there," she tells him, her voice muffled by his robe.

"Where?"

"In my dream."

Elie has a sip of his drink.

"When the swelling's gone down," she murmurs, "I still want to take Evan out West."

"I thought you'd abandoned that idea."

"I want to see my father again and I want him to meet my son."

Elie reaches for a cigarette.

"If you found out Ziad was alive, wouldn't you go back to Beirut to see him?"

"We've had this conversation before."

"We're married," she reminds him. "We only ever have versions of the same conversation anyway."

"It's different with my brother," he states adamantly. "Ziad was *taken*. Your father hasn't bothered to contact you in thirty years. He's made no effort. And you've never cared about seeing him either."

"Until I had Evan. Besides, I've always been curious about him."

"I just don't think it will serve any purpose," Elie cautions. "I think you'll be disappointed."

"I've got a father out there and I want to reconnect with him. It's a void."

"The kind of void you have can't be filled by another human being."

"I disagree."

"You thought having a baby would fill it," he reminds her.

"What *can* fill it then?" she asks him angrily, assuming he won't have an answer.

He turns his face away from hers and exhales a straight line of smoke. "God," he replies dispassionately.

"God?" she sneers. "You've never been religious."

"It's not a religious statement. It's a fact."

She lets his remark settle over her. It surprises her. And in fairness to him, she doesn't altogether reject it.

After a long silence, during which the only sound is of his breath releasing smoke from his lungs, she asks him what was on his mind that he should be sitting in here in the middle of the night, drinking by himself.

"I don't even remember," he murmurs. And she believes him.

Twenty-six

*H*er attraction to Declan is like a bad cold she can't shake. Just when it seems to be leaving her body it attacks again with fresh zeal, causing headaches and lethargy and a general malaise.

Perhaps this relapse has something to do with the fact that she read his column on Saturday. It was cocky to think she could read it without stirring anything up inside her. And even if she had considered the possibility, she read it anyway. It was called "Vexed and the City," a hostile piece about the astronomical prices of real estate in Toronto. He mentioned that he and his wife are looking to buy a new house in an esteemed downtown neighborhood where they've been house hunting for months. For a mere three-quarters of a million dollars, he ranted, he can invest in a generic three-bedroom with no closet space, an unreno-vated eighties bathroom and a yard the size of his son's playpen. "Seven hundred and fifty thousand dollars should at least buy me a linen closet and a downstairs bathroom!" he wrote. "After all, this isn't Manhattan. It's Toronto the Bland."

The article knocked the wind out of Anne. She never knew he was looking to buy a new house. He never mentioned it. They even had a conversation about where they each lived. He could have brought it up then. Shouldn't he have?

Of course it's all irrelevant now, but the omission over the course of all their encounters makes her feel duped and used. He probably never had any intention of letting her know him. It stings. She really thought there was something there—a connection, the beginning of a flirty friendship that could have lingered and distracted her for a while.

She's decided she should see him again. She can't let go of the idea that if he could see her one more time and she was a bit more forward—not aggressive, but *clear*—she could get him back. Not for an affair, but to want her again. It's the flirtation she misses. She feels lost without it. She thinks it's absolutely possible to sway him back. He had a vulnerability that she could have massaged. Given a second chance, she thinks she could coax him into something.

Something. She's not exactly sure what. She's convinced herself that she could step back from the brink of adultery at any point. It's the craving for his attention she doesn't want to give up.

She dials his home number, feeling bold and empowered. She gave up too easily. She always does.

You've reached the Grays. (Margaret's voice.) *Please leave a message at the tone*.

She hangs up, wondering where they are. House hunting?

The next morning she calls him at work. With swelling confidence she asks for his extension, thinking she'll get his voice mail and leave a sexy message. *Can't stop thinking about you*. Or something along those lines.

"Declan Gray," he answers.

The sound of his voice, live, startles her into mute embarrassment.

"Hello?" he says impatiently.

"Hi," she manages. "I, um . . . it's me. Anne."

A moment of silence precedes his response, and then, in a flat voice, "Hi, Anne."

Now that she's actually got him on the line, she discovers there is absolutely nothing in her head. She has no plan, no rehearsed speech. "How are you?" she asks him.

"Good. You?"

"I've . . . I . . ."

Her earlier confidence fails her and her voice dissolves into nothing, leaving a thick, awkward silence between them. It occurs to her that she could still save face, make up some bullshit reason for calling. She could ask the name of his surgeon or something.

"I've been thinking about you," she blurts, heedlessly exposing herself to a crushing rejection.

"You shouldn't," he says, and she detects in his tone a cocktail of pity and irritation. Maybe even some self-righteousness.

"No, you're right," she mutters. "I shouldn't."

"Listen, Anne," he says. "Our entire e-mail system is down here—"

"Oh. Sorry—"

"No problem. It's just that I can't really talk—"

"Right. Okay. Actually, I was calling to get the name of your new orthopedist," she babbles. "He sounded so knowledgeable about club feet and I was telling Elie about him and Elie said why don't we meet with him because neither of us really likes our current doctor . . ."

"His name is Dr. Hale. Calvin Hale. He's at Bloorview MacMillan."

"That's great. Thank you. And that's Hale? H, A, L, E?"

"Yes. Hale."

"Great!" she says, her voice false and overwrought, caked with bravado. "Good luck with your e-mail system."

"See you around, Anne."

She hangs up the phone with quivering hands and stands there for a few moments, too numb to move. His words slowly sink into her, like an ominous medical diagnosis.

See you around.

Her association with Declan Gray has been one long demoralizing assault on her ego. She has invested her energy, her hopes—things scarce and precious to her—while he was just going through some patch in his marriage, toying with her to soothe his manhood. Things are probably back on track with Margaret. They're house hunting. They're trying Ponseti. He doesn't feel emasculated or idle anymore.

Screw him, she thinks. Who needs his tortured alcoholic demons (probably an act) and his pretentious *Creideamh* tattoo. Celtic for *faith*! This isn't Dublin. It's Toronto the Bland. Screw his arrogant, self-important column and his contrived, pseudo-subversive persona. There isn't an authentic, sincere bone in his body.

Recovering her composure enough to locate her purse, she finds the Saturday house-hunting column she's been toting around with her ever since she cut it out and shreds it into tiny bits, feeling foolish and adolescent but slightly satisfied.

Dr. You greets Anne with a brusque handshake and sits down opposite her. He watches her for a while with an inscrutable expression on his face and then barks, "No tea."

"Yes. No tea."

"What is problem today?"

"I don't know," she responds, fighting tears. How can she explain to him the depth of emptiness she's experienced since losing the fantasy of Declan? Or the purposelessness and loss? "My head aches. My teeth hurt. My chest feels tight. My periods are painful and irregular. I don't sleep."

"Sounds like death very near," he says gravely, followed by an explosion of demonic laughter. "Just joking!" he says, turning serious. "Those are just symptom. What is *problem*?"

"My son has club feet," she ventures.

Dr. You's eyes narrow.

"I'm obsessed with someone," she confesses. "I know it's not a medical problem, but my body is so out of whack I thought maybe some acupuncture could balance my chakra or something."

"Obsessed with man not husband?"

She nods solemnly.

"First time?" he asks, writing notes to himself in Chinese.

"No."

"Many times obsessed?"

"Yes. Many."

He folds his hands together. "You are like a drug addict," he concludes, painstakingly enunciating each word. "Man does not matter. Could be any man."

"But this time was different—"

"Not different!" he growls. "Man is *substance*. Yes?"

"Yes," she concedes.

"Same as cigarettes."

"Right."

"Father absent?"

"Yes."

He nods triumphantly. "Very typical," he says, pleased with himself.

A first-year psych student could have deduced the same thing. In fact, a clever sixth grader could have too, but for some reason Anne's got to hear it from a second-rate healer who can barely utter a sentence in English.

Dr. You opens his drawer and pulls out a handful of amber-hued stones. He comes around his desk and stands above her. He has the smell of deep frying in his clothes.

"Carnelian and golden topaz," he says, laying the stones one at a time in the palm of her hand. "Crystal enhance emotional and sexual harmony."

"What about the acupuncture?" she asks.

Dr. You sighs. "Healing has many facet," he explains wearily. "Not just acupuncture."

"I don't understand how shoving some rocks in my pocket can help—"

"You are very controlling," he lectures sternly. "Just like man. Not open to healing process. Not trust me."

"I have too much yang," she reminds him.

"Yes!" he cries. "Too much yang!"

She arrives at her mother's to pick up Evan, feeling demoralized and dubious about the potential effectiveness of the healing rocks in her pocket.

"He didn't nap," Jean says, greeting her in the foyer. "He's a bit fussy."

She hands over Evan and he feels surprisingly light in Anne's arms without his casts.

"I've got a client in ten minutes," Jean says, gently nudging Anne out the door. "You were supposed to be here half an hour ago."

"Sorry."

"Did it help?"

"What?"

"The acupuncture."

"I didn't have acupuncture. He gave me these instead." She pulls out a couple of the crystals and holds them out to her.

"Rocks?"

"Yes."

Jean looks at Anne for a moment with a perplexed look. "How much did that cost you?"

"The session was seventy-five bucks. But the crystals cost extra."

"Oh, Anne," she says, her voice grating and full of pity.

"Oh, Anne *what*?"

"Never mind," Jean says dismissively. "I don't have time to start this."

She waves goodbye to Evan.

Anne takes a step toward the door and then turns back. "Mom, do you remember our old address in Harmony?"

"Oh, Anne—"

"You said no one ever leaves, so he's probably still living in the same house."

"Probably."

"I'm going to write him a letter."

"What are you expecting in return?"

"I honestly don't know."

Jean opens her mouth to say something, but changes her mind. Instead, she quietly mulls it over. She's staring at Evan. At last she says, "P.O. Box 1180, Harmony, B.C."

"That's it?"

"That's it."

"Oh."

She smiles wanly, seeming to accept the inevitable. Her cooperation surprises Anne.

*W*hen she gets home she puts Evan in his ExerSaucer and sits down at the kitchen table to write the letter. The ExerSaucer is the best thing to happen to them since the casts were removed. Evan's little legs fit perfectly inside the holes of the fabric and he's finally able to stand up. Dr. Hotz told them to use it as much as possible to strengthen Evan's legs and help him stand on his own. It doesn't hurt that it also frees Anne up to do other things.

With her father's address in her possession and Evan amusing himself in the first baby apparatus they've been able to use, her spirits begin to lift. She's looking forward to Elie coming home and decides to prepare a special dinner. She's going to throw herself back into this marriage. She's going to devote herself to him, or console herself with him, as the case may be.

She begins her letter: *Dear Father*. Then, deciding that's too formal, she starts again.

Dear Dad. Dear Toby. Dear Tobias. Mr. Biffin . . .
Finally, she settles on "Dad."

Dad,

This letter must come as a surprise to you, after almost 30 years. I'm 34 now, married and living in Toronto. I'm an artist. I've been thinking about you a lot since I had my son. His name is Evan. He's eight months old. I would like Evan to meet his grandfather. I think it would bring us all closure.

Please let me know how you feel about us coming to
Harmony to see you.

Your daughter,
Anne Mahroum

She folds it up, stuffs it into an envelope and sets it aside to mail first thing tomorrow.

*E*lie gets in hours after she's put Evan to sleep. The supper she prepared—a roast chicken with cream corn—is still sitting on the kitchen counter, cold and dry and hardening into dark yellow cement. She's got the TV on in the down-stairs den, but she's so agitated and furious she hasn't absorbed a word in over an hour.

She hears Elie tossing his keys onto the secretary in the foyer; then she hears him in the kitchen, running water and clanging plates. Finally he appears in the den, looking disheveled and unsteady. His eyes are red-rimmed and bleary, his tie askew. He's nibbling on a cold drumstick.

"Thanks for the phone call," she mutters, trying to keep her rage in check.

"The time got away from me," he slurs.

"I can smell you from here."

"I'll be upstairs then," he says, leaving her to her rage and indignation.

"I don't even get an apology?" she yells at his back.

He ignores her.

"Where were you?" she demands, chasing him up the stairs.

He's been acting strange lately; depressed and remote. He's always been prone to moodiness, but lately he seems to have sunk to a new level of despair. He won't say why. Unlike Anne, he prefers to suffer in silence.

He retreats to his office, but she follows him. "This isn't like you," she cries, feeling genuinely frightened. "Where were you?"

"Fuck off," he growls, collapsing in the swivel chair behind his desk. He puts the drumstick on his blotter.

"Who were you with?"

"Myself," he answers. "I went to the Avenue for a drink."

"Alone?"

He nods.

"Bullshit."

He shrugs, looking aloof. Her panic increases.

"Why are you doing this to me?" she whimpers. "Is it another woman?"

He rolls his eyes. "I said I was alone."

She stands in the doorway, not sure how to proceed. Her mode of attack seems to be fueling his indifference. Indifference—as opposed to rage—makes her very uneasy. Watching him now, she realizes he could have been anywhere tonight, with anyone. For the first time her vague musings and misgivings about his fidelity are starting to feel eerily well-founded.

"Why didn't you call?" she repeats, abandoning her anger for a whinier, more supplicating approach.

"I told you, I forgot," he says, unlocking the bottom drawer of his desk and removing his collection of B.C. coins. He opens the box and gazes lovingly inside, his expression changing like a kaleidoscope from reverence to satisfaction to anguish.

"I've been thinking about that Ken Schlittberg," he says.

"Schlittman," she corrects, taking a few steps into the room.

He picks one of the coins out of the box and examines it between his thumb and forefinger. "Isn't it amazing?" he goes on. "That he had this coin in his collection for all those years, probably never realizing what it was worth. And the whole time I was scouring the country to find it, keeping my eye out for it on all my travels, at every auction, on the Internet, in numismatic reviews. I'd just about given up, and then one day, out of the clear blue sky, the goddamn thing just falls into my fucking lap!" He shakes his head in wonderment. "It was right under my nose the whole time."

"It's a strange coincidence."

"Oh, Anne!" he scoffs. "Even you, the great pessimist and believer in nothing, has to believe it was God's hand in this. I was obviously meant to complete my collection."

"Yes, well," she points out derisively, "maybe if God hadn't been so busy finding you that coin, He might have been able to straighten out Evan's left foot. Or maybe He could have saved poor Ken Schlittman—"

"You think so small," he says harshly. "Which is par for the course, I suppose."

"Meaning?"

"You're devoid of faith. You think *you* control your world."

"Thank you for your assessment, Deepak. I didn't know you were so deeply spiritual."

Elie gets up, goes over to his liquor cabinet and pulls out one of his prize bottles of scotch. He lays out the crystal decanter and glass she bought him for their second anniversary, his syringe and a bottle of water.

"Maybe the cork's dried out," Elie remarks, apropos of nothing.

"What are you talking about?"

"It's an analogy," he condescends. "Our marriage is like a wine that's turned to vinegar."

The sudden possibility of his leaving her induces a violent wave of dread. "No one's forcing you to stay," she chokes, feigning bravado.

"No," he says. "I know that."

"Why are you so angry with me?" she asks him.

"Because you make everything difficult," he responds, turning to her with his drink in hand. "You drain the joy out of our life."

"Are you drinking to drown your guilt?"

"What guilt?"

"You tell me."

"Didn't you hear what I said?" he cries impatiently. "Why are you still grilling me?"

"Because you didn't come home after work tonight and you didn't even call to tell me you'd be late. I think I've got good reason for not trusting you."

"As do I!"

"For what reason?"

"Instinct," he says, with such precision it's like a spear through her flesh, directly into a vital organ.

She backs away from him, wanting to hide from his accusing eyes and escape the recriminating smell of alcohol on his breath. She can't shake the feeling that she's led him to this point; that her innocent flirtations have finally eroded the durable outer shell of their marriage. She's done damage. Her deception must have come through her pores.

She worries he's already retaliated. He can be a vengeful man. And he loves her.

Twenty-seven

She wakes up with something nagging at the back of her mind and realizes within moments of opening her eyes that she's forgotten to water her mother's plants. Jean's been in the Berkshires all week and she's coming home tonight.

"Is it possible to bring dying plants back to life in twelve hours?" she asks Elie.

He rolls over and yawns, fanning her with boozy morning breath. "Depends how far gone they are," he croaks. "You could try. I think ferns are quite forgiving."

"I could douse them and then trim off the dead leaves."

"She'll never know," he says sarcastically.

"Why didn't you remind me?"

"I forgot, just like you," he says. "I've had other things on my mind besides your mother's plants."

"I'd better go over there right now."

She moves to get out of bed. Elie catches her wrist. "I'm sorry," he says.

"For which offense?"

"The way I've been acting. Coming home late last week, not calling . . ."

"What about all the drinking? And the mean things you said?"

"Yes. All of it."

"What's going on with you?"

"I don't know," he says, running his hand through his thick black hair. "I guess I've been depressed."

"Why?"

He shrugs. "It comes and goes," he offers vaguely. "It always has."

"Is it us?"

"It's partly us. It's the boy. His club feet. It takes a toll."

"What's wrong with us?" she asks, as though she hasn't a clue.

"I don't think you're happy," he alleges. "You're not really present. And the sex . . . I seem to repulse you."

She swallows guiltily. "You don't repulse me."

"I don't turn you on either."

"You said yourself Evan's club feet are taking a toll," she defends. "I've got nothing left at the end of a day . . ."

He looks up at her with sad, defeated eyes. "Would you tell me if you were over me?" he asks.

"Over you? You're not some crush. You're my husband. I just got your initial tattooed on my flesh—"

"I don't want to be your Mr. Bovary," he laments.

"I've never read *Madame Bovary*."

"She despises her husband. She thinks of him as a buffoon and he sickens her. She has affairs . . ."

"Oh, Elie!" She flings herself against his chest and buries her face in the tangle of his hair. "I don't want you to ever feel that way! It's not how I feel. It's not . . ."

He clasps the back of her head and pulls her close. "I would rather you leave me," he mutters, "than have us wind up in one of those passionless, monotonous marriages full of resentment and regret."

"We won't," she promises, her voice earnest with conviction. But as she's uttering the words she wonders if

it's possible for even the best marriages to avoid a monotonous end. Year after year sharing a bathroom, a bed, a
child; revealing to each other the ugly underbelly of one's
character, the indecent thoughts, the embarrassing quirks
and foibles; trading cruel, indignant words that shave
something precious off every time.

Or maybe it's just her mind-set that needs adjusting. Maybe
she's been wrong in the way she's belittled and deemed inferior the comforts of marriage. Monogamy might not be
dangerous, but after a point, who wants danger anymore?
Besides, most flings combust into nothingness anyway.

Declan certainly didn't fulfill any of her fantasies. After
the initial explosion all the potential and possibility of their
affair faded like a rocket in the sky, leaving her wounded
and despondent where before she'd only been a little bored.
The lesson from Declan is that disillusionment is as
rampant outside of marriage as it is within it.

Elie kisses her forehead and releases her. "Evan's feet are
healing," he says. "It's almost behind us. We can't use that
anymore as an excuse for being complacent in this marriage."

Anne nods in agreement.

"Let's do better," he urges. "Let's make an effort to
rekindle this thing."

More nodding.

"I love you," he tells her.

"I love you too," she responds, meaning it. She wipes tears
off her face, wishing she could give up the tantalizing promise
of the unknown and just be happy with what she's got.

March has been temperamental, alternating between bouts
of mild weather and rain and then sudden binges of snow

and arctic cold. Today is a warm day. The sun reflecting off the snow is blinding. She pulls into a snowbank in front of her mother's house with a noisy crash, praying she'll be able to drive out of it later. She takes one step out of her car and her foot sinks into an ankle-high lake of dark gray slush. She knows what kind of day it's going to be.

Her mother's plants are in bad shape but may be salvageable. The ones hanging in baskets look the most promising; they must be the ferns. She has no house plants of her own—they don't fit with the decor—and therefore knows nothing about them. But her plan is to water them until they begin to straighten and bloom and then wait a bit and water them again.

Her mother's left a pitcher by the sink. There's a film of dust on it, which Anne rinses away. She starts with the hanging plants, first inspecting the soil to assess the damage. The dirt crumbles in her hand. Not a good sign. She stands on tiptoes and dumps almost the entire contents of the pitcher into them, until water is spilling out the sides onto the floor. The plants don't improve right away, as she'd hoped they would, so she plucks off the yellow and brown leaves in a feeble attempt to cover up her negligence.

Back in the kitchen she notices a red light blinking on her mother's answering machine—one of those old-fashioned things. (Jean doesn't trust Bell enough to succumb to its voice mail system yet, just as she won't trade her VCR in for a DVD player. She wants to be sure it's not a fad.) Suddenly curious for a small glimpse into her mother's life and bored with the tedious task of plant watering, she hits the play button with the innocent intention of taking down her mother's messages. Most of them are from clients wanting to book or cancel massages. *Hi, Jean, it's Marvin, I can't make next Thursday. Jean, it's Mary from the IGA. I want to book a massage for the morning of my daughter's wedding—*

Anne's got to hand it to her mother. She's really made a niche for herself with the middle-aged, middle-class set who don't feel comfortable going to spas and baring their imperfect bodies to younger, more attractive masseuses.

While the messages are playing, Anne goes into the pantry. She hasn't eaten yet and she's starving. She finds an unopened bag of chips and helps herself.

Jean, it's Polly.

The message stops Anne cold. She drops the bag of chips and rushes back to the answering machine.

You're probably not back yet—I think your flight gets in tonight—but I wanted to thank you for coming out west. Your support meant the world to me and I think it had an impact at the Tribunal. I won't stop fighting this and it's good to know you're finally behind me. I've missed you. It was wonderful to see you.

Anne stands in front of the machine for a moment, trying to make sense of the message, grasping for some rational explanation. A single thought comes into her mind. *Her mother is a liar.* She realizes she's gripping the table. Her knuckles are white and her whole body is shaking violently. There's an overwhelming dread creeping through her that something momentous and terrible is about to unfold. It feels as though her world is built on a frozen lake that is rapidly thawing and she's about to sink into its icy depths.

She collapses in a chair at the pine table to wait for her mother. She doesn't bother to turn on any lights, so that when the sun disappears and gives way to evening, she continues to sit there in the dark. Elie calls her cell phone, wondering where she is.

"I'm at my mother's."

"Still?"

"I'm waiting for her."

"Why?"

"I need to talk to her."

"About her plants?"

"Just put the baby to bed. I'll be home later."

He hesitates a moment and she's not sure if he's indignant about having to bathe Evan and put him to bed after he's already spent the day with him or if he doesn't believe her. Lately, there's been that current of mistrust flowing between them.

"What's going on?" he says finally. "You sound strange."

So that's it. He thinks she's with someone. "I'm at my mother's," she reassures him. "Call her home number and I'll answer."

"Don't insult me. I have some shreds of dignity left."

"I didn't mean—"

"I believe you, Anne, if that's where you say you are."

"I just need to talk to my mother," she repeats. "I'll explain when I get home."

She turns off her cell phone and tosses it onto the table. Moments later, her mother's phone rings. It's Elie.

"Just checking," he says lightly.

"What about your dignity?"

"I told you I only had some shreds left," he deadpans.

She tells him she loves him. His insecurity touches her.

*J*ean gets home shortly after nine. The hall light goes on, followed by the lights in the living room. Anne hears her gasp, probably at the sorry state of her plants. Then she enters the kitchen, first turning on the light and then letting out a startled cry at the sight of Anne sitting there.

"Anne!" she cries. "You scared the shit out of me!"

"Sorry."

"Why are you sitting in the dark? What are you doing here?"

"Welcoming you home."

She leans up against the doorframe, her hand pressed to her chest. "My heart is pounding!"

Anne doesn't say anything. Just sits there, staring at her mother with a sullen, recriminating look. Jean takes a deep breath and looks around the kitchen at her plants.

"What have you done to my philodendrons?" she asks. "And my lady slippers! My God, Anne! You've killed them all! Didn't you water them?"

"Polly called."

Jean blinks nervously. "What did she say?"

Anne gets up and goes over to the answering machine. She plays the message for her mother, scrutinizing her face as she listens to it. Jean remains stoic, impassive. Revealing nothing, as usual. But Anne can tell that her mother knows she's caught. It's in her eyes, her defensive stance. She's too still.

"You lied to me," Anne accuses coldly.

"I had to."

"You *had* to? That's crap. I've been waiting my whole life for you to tell me the truth."

"That's overstating it," Jean remarks.

"I've been pretty patient."

"More like disinterested."

"That's not fair, Mom. I just haven't wanted to bring up your past. It upsets you so much—"

"You're right," she acquiesces. "Let's just say our arrangement has suited both of us. You hate conflict. You hate anything that threatens your perfect life."

"Why did you go out West?"

"To help my sister."

"With what?"

Her mother looks cornered but resigned. "I'd have to start at the very beginning," she says wearily.

Anne shrugs. "I've got all night."

Twenty-eight

*J*ean quietly brews a pot of coffee. She brings Anne a mug, some milk and a bowl of sugar and then joins her at the table. They stare at each other for a while in silence. Anne watches Jean add milk to her coffee, two spoonfuls of sugar. She stirs it, has a sip and closes her eyes.

"What do you remember about Harmony?" she asks Anne.

"Swans. Orchards. Not much else."

"You won't find it on a map," Jean says. "It doesn't exist."

Anne is confused.

"It's a small community right next to Creston," Jean continues. "A secluded little oasis tucked between the mountains, right in that flat river valley where the Kootenay River enters Kootenay Lake."

She smiles nostalgically. "It's a breathtaking place, with snowcapped mountains and clear blue streams running through all this undisturbed open green space. But I remember that as a little girl I'd stare out our window at the fields of timothy and cottonwood and think how sinister it all looked."

"Why?"

"Because of the things that went on there."

"Like what?"

"It's a very private place. There's No Trespassing signs on the outskirts. No one's even heard of it. The people are secretive. They've always been, right from the beginning."

"The beginning of what?"

"Harmony was founded in the forties by a group of excommunicated Mormons."

"So it's a Mormon community. Big deal. Why are you so ashamed of that?"

"Oh, Anne . . ." she sighs. "You know I was married at sixteen."

Her face is pale and drawn. She's speaking softly. Anne feels slightly guilty for interrogating her after she's just come off a long flight, but not enough to let her off the hook.

"It was an arranged marriage," her mother explains matter-of-factly. "My father arranged for me to marry my uncle."

Anne gasps. It sounds archaic, brutal. Impossible for Canada!

"My mother was my father's half sister," Jean adds, with a deadness in her tone that gives Anne a chill. It's not just bleached of emotion, it's utterly barren of either pain or sentimentality. When she spoke of her family being dead to her, it wasn't the usual hyperbole. She meant it.

"We all lived under one roof. My father was one of the founders of Harmony. He had . . ."

Her voice stops short. She looks at Anne as though to say *I warned you.*

"He had *what*?" Anne presses, her heart pounding furiously.

"He had thirteen wives. My mother was the sixth."

Anne tries to absorb what her mother is saying, but something in her brain rejects the information. "What do you mean?" she asks, baffled.

Jean leans forward and speaks very slowly, as she would to a child. "Harmony is a polygamous commune. It's run by fundamentalist Mormons who broke away from the mainstream Church so they could go on practicing polygamy."

"Your father is a polygamist?" Anne mutters, feeling light-headed.

"So is yours, Anne. They all are."

At last, the revelation.

It takes a moment for her to fully comprehend. Her body is numb; she can't feel anything except the pounding of her heart. She has this sensation of watching the scene unfold from a distance. Anne sees her mother, nursing her cup of coffee. She sees herself, taking in the disturbing information. Her body is still and her eyes are wide, as though she's hearing a tantalizing piece of gossip about someone else. The words swirl around her head like mosquitoes, hovering in front of her but not biting into her flesh.

Hasn't she always known this, somewhere inside her? In that part of her head where the weird, incongruous memories that leak out into her dreams are stored? She probably didn't understand it then, not enough to consciously carry the knowledge into adulthood, but she *knew*.

"Sister wife?" Anne murmurs, her voice sounding strangely detached.

"Yes," Jean says. "Do you remember?"

"I don't know."

"That's how we referred to ourselves."

It's beginning to penetrate. The implication is slowly coursing through her, like a drug through her veins. She wonders if she'll be able to walk away from here tonight and go back to her regular life, unchanged.

An avalanche of memories suddenly tumbles into her conscious. Snapshots of her mother's strange behavior over the years, peculiar things she's said and done in the past. In the context of what Anne knows now, they make sense. Her violent reaction to that incident with Norrie and the way she'd implicated Satan; her penitent reaction to Ken Schlittman's death as though it were some sort of God-divined retribution for an unforgivable sin she'd committed.

"How many wives did my father have?" Anne asks.

"Only five."

"*Only* five?" Anne laughs out loud, not finding it funny so much as twisted. "I was the third," Jean says. "I was sixteen and he was thirty-eight."

"Was he cruel?"

She takes a gulp of coffee and sets her mug down. "No, he wasn't. There were a lot crueler than him, that's for sure. Like my father. In fact, there were moments when I might have loved him." Her expression dissolves into something softer, more reflective. "He used to call his wives 'his girls.' It made us feel special. I think he loved us in his own way."

"Tell me what it was like. Was it terrible?"

"Sometimes." And then: "I'm hungry."

Jean gets up suddenly and orders a pizza.

"My father married me off at sixteen," she resumes, returning to the pine table. "He would have done it sooner, but Toby wouldn't take a wife under sixteen."

"How noble."

"It was, considering that a lot of the men in Harmony had no qualms about marrying thirteen-year-olds."

Anne winces.

"I was so indoctrinated into that way of life, I hardly knew any better. In school, they taught us that we'd been called to celestial marriage. That it was our only purpose on earth. There were no other options. All we learned was to keep sweet and breed. And then we were yanked out to marry. It was hardly a decent education," she laments.

"But I didn't know any other way. I was brainwashed at home and then in school. There were things about polygamy that theoretically I could support. When I went to live with your father, the sister wives and I would often talk about how hypocritical the outside world was for condemning polygamy while they went on cheating on their spouses and having affairs. At least our men were honest and open about it. They didn't pretend to be monogamous."

"Weren't you jealous?" Anne asks. "Sharing your husband with other women?"

"Of course," she admits. "At first, when I was the newest, youngest wife, I didn't think it was so bad. I liked the sister wives. We were all close and there was a kind of unique camaraderie. The house was always warm and busy. Chores were shared. I thought there was a certain nobility in it, I suppose. It was selfless and self-sacrificing. I still had most of Toby's attention then, but when he took his fourth wife, I started to have my doubts."

"Why?"

"I was twenty and she was sixteen. She had no skills whatsoever. I had to train her to do all the chores I'd been taught. I felt like her mother. She was a kid. And she was pretty too. The prettiest one of us all. I remember one afternoon I walked in on her and your father making out on the couch. She was in his arms. I got so jealous! But you had to live with that sort of thing. I'll say this about him: he did his best to make a healthy environment. He was always encouraging us to talk out our feelings and our jealousies. As celestial marriages go, ours was a pretty good model, if you discount the toll it took on the spirit and morale of the women."

"Who did he sleep with?"

"We had a schedule."

"A sex schedule?"

"It was decided by who was ovulating at the time. We all had to abide by the Law of Chastity. Since intercourse is strictly for reproduction, the only time we were allowed to have sex was during our ovulation."

"Once a month?"

"Yes. And I remember Deborah—she was the one who came after me—got pregnant right away. That was tough. I had such a hard time getting pregnant. I started to despise her. I could be so mean to her . . ." She shakes her head. "It could be like that," she admits, sounding embarrassed. "The older wives abusing the younger ones. I did it, that's for sure. But then I remember he took the fifth wife—Lori—and I wasn't so jealous anymore, just demoralized. And angry. I felt middle-aged and worthless. It made me question everything about our way of life. That's the thing about polygamy. It slowly chips away at a woman's soul. It's a kind of emotional abuse."

At some point the doorbell rings and Jean jumps to her feet. She leaves the room and comes back carrying a large box. "It's late, you know. We could finish tomorrow—"

"When did you decide to leave?" Anne asks.

"The Church leaders used to say plural marriage was a 'polisher of the soul.'" She bites into her slice, tugging a rope of cheese off with her teeth. It leaves a splotch of grease on her chin, which she doesn't seem to mind. "It was drilled into us that obedience was the foundation of plural marriage. It was a sister wife's duty to let go of selfishness and pettiness. We were supposed to discipline our emotions; that's what your father was always telling us. Eventually, though, I started to get bitter about it. Some nights I could hear him having sex with one of the others and it began to disturb me."

Anne imagines having to share Elie with other women—in the same household no less—and it leaves her cold. But then she loves Elie. She *chose* him.

"I didn't just wake up one morning and decide to leave," Jean explains. "I grew more and more disillusioned over time. I started to think it wasn't a fair arrangement. I was pissed off that I hadn't gotten an education and that I was pressured to make a baby every year. Aside from the fact that I felt like a failure because I couldn't get pregnant the way some of the other sister wives did, I resented that it was even expected of me."

"Were you the only one who felt that way?" Anne asks, nibbling on a crust.

"For a time, I thought so. I remember I felt so isolated, like I was suffocating. I just wanted a normal life."

"How did you get out?"

"There was a woman," her mother remembers. "Her name was Eliza. She had a sister who'd escaped a couple of years before me. We wound up sitting next to each other one day at a hockey game at the local arena and we got to talking. She told me all about her sister, who'd been very outspoken about plural marriage before she left. There was a lot of talk about sexual abuse and that sort of thing. Anyway, this woman, Eliza, she told me how her sister had got out, and I guess it planted a seed.

"It wasn't until you were born that I made my decision to leave," she tells Anne, speaking in the calm manner of someone describing a movie they've just seen. "And even then, it took a few more years for me to muster the courage. If you hadn't been a girl, I might still be there."

"Is Eliza the one who helped you get out?"

Jean nods. "She drove us to Spokane."

"Is she still there?"

"I wouldn't know," she answers, shrugging. "When I left, I vowed never to contact anyone from Harmony again and never to go back. I closed the book forever and started fresh."

It's after eleven. At one point Jean glances up and says, "God, Anne, you've killed all my plants."

"I must have dozens of half brothers and sisters," Anne muses, suddenly prickling with curiosity. "My own blood out there."

And then something occurs to her. "Did you ever find out what was wrong with you?"

"Wrong with me how?" Jean asks, confused.

"Your fertility problems. In all that time, you only had me—"

Jean looks down, quickly averting her eyes. She doesn't respond.

"Mom?"

Silence. Still looking down.

"You were married to my father for fifteen years," Anne points out. "With only one baby. Obviously there was something wrong with you, maybe the same problem I had trying to get pregnant. Remember how long it took—"

Anne stops talking when she notices a tear slip off her mother's chin and land on the open pizza box.

"Oh, Anne." Jean's voice is full of anguish. She lifts her eyes. They're glistening with tears. "I didn't have fertility problems. It just took me longer is all."

"But one baby in fifteen years . . ."

Jean lets the silence speak for her. It takes only a moment for it to register and then Anne understands. "You had other children," she says, stunned.

Her mother's body begins to quake so violently it's like a convulsion. She covers her face with her hands. "I'm not proud of it," she moans. Even her fingers are trembling against her cheeks.

"Do I have . . .?"

Jean nods solemnly. "Two brothers," she whispers. "Thomas and James. I left them behind."

Anne gets up from her chair and starts moving around the kitchen like a caged animal. "How could you?"

Her mother stands up, leveling her eyes at Anne as though they could fire cannons. "I left my boys to save *you,*" she flares. "I had a choice and I chose *you.* I wanted you to have a normal life. I wanted you to go to school and fall in love and choose your own husband. I couldn't bear the thought of giving you away at fifteen to some old child molester. Or the thought of you suffering the way I was suffering, dying inside a little bit each day."

"Why didn't you take all three of us?"

She comes closer to Anne and grabs her hand. "They were ten and twelve," she says, squeezing Anne's hand. "Two boys who worshipped their father. They were believers. They had a good life. The day I was to leave, I waited for your father to go to work and then I told your brothers my plan. Of course I begged them to come with me. Do you know what they said? They said, 'Satan's got you, Mama! Satan's got you!' They warned me I'd burn in hell and swore they would never leave their father or Harmony. Once they knew, I had to go right away. I only had a moment, but I thought about the life that lay ahead for them and what lay ahead for you. And I left them."

Anne retracts her hand. "I don't know whether to be grateful or horrified."

"I saved you from a kind of hell you'll never know," she beseeches. "I saved you from being someone's concubine. It was sexual abuse, Anne, make no mistake about it."

Anne's head starts to throb. The space inside her skull can hardly contain all the information her mother is unloading. She knows she asked for it, but now she wants it to stop. She's got a dirty feeling, like she needs a shower to scour this all away.

"I couldn't have lived with myself if I'd handed you over to them," she says defensively.

Anne looks over at her mother and realizes for the first time that Jean must be impoverished inside, sustained over the years by nothing more than her mission to do better by Anne. She understands now why her mother thinks people aren't a cure for loneliness. She lived in a house full of people and yet must have felt utterly alone every day of her life.

It explains the flatness in Jean's tone and eyes when she speaks of the past. A mother must have to close down a part of herself in order to go on without her children. It makes more sense to Anne now—why Jean never made friends; why she isolated herself and withdrew from the

world. It was shame. The shame and unworthiness of
having abandoned her own sons. Or maybe she sacrificed
too much and had nothing left over to give.

Anne thinks of Evan and feels sick to her stomach. Yet
how can she judge? Her mother did it to protect her from
an unspeakable fate.

"This is too much . . ." Anne manages. "I'm overwhelmed."

"I told you. You see why it was better left alone?"

Anne shakes her head. "I don't understand how you
kept this from me all this time. Such a huge part of our
past—"

"There just never was a right time to bring it up."

"How did you . . ." Anne paces the kitchen some more,
trying to compose herself and organize her thoughts.
"How did you do it?"

"What?"

"All of it. How did you leave them? How did you start
over with no knowledge of the outside world and no skills
and no money? Weren't you terrified?"

"I wanted to be free," she explains. "I wanted you to be
free. That thought gave me strength. It was bigger than my
fear, I guess."

"But logistically, how did you manage it?"

"I don't know. I just did it. I stashed away some money
for a few years and when the time came, I just went. As for
the boys—"

Anne notices she doesn't mention their names.

"I imagined them grown up with their own homes full of
unhappy wives, and when I could picture them as men—
the bullying men of Harmony—in a way, it hardened my
heart toward them. Enough for me to leave anyway."

"I can't imagine how scared you must have been," Anne says, holding back tears.

"For years I worried I'd burn in hell," Jean confesses. "The truth is, sometimes it still crosses my mind. Usually when I'm lying alone in my bed at night, I'll think, *what if?* What if God just strikes me dead for having left my own sons?"

"Do you ever think about going back to see them?"

She smiles sadly. "I don't exist to them anymore. I committed the unforgivable sin. I ran away."

At this, Anne feels a stabbing of unprecedented tenderness and rushes over to throw her arms around her mother. She dissolves into compassionate tears. "I've always known it must have taken a lot of courage for you to leave," Anne says. "But I thought you were just leaving a small town for the big city. I never imagined . . ."

"You couldn't."

"You always said, 'Sins of the father . . .'"

"You're one of us," Jean states, her voice melancholic. "No matter how far away I got you, you're still a daughter of Harmony. It's part of you."

"Why did you go back to help Polly?"

Jean leads Anne to the living room, complaining of a sore back. She falls heavily onto the sofa and puts her feet up on the coffee table. "Come," she says, tapping the sofa cushion beside her. "Sit."

Anne sits down next to her and lets herself sink into the cushions. She is extremely tired. She'd like to get into her bed right now, snuggle up to Elie and forget everything she's heard tonight. He must be wondering where she is. His mind is probably leaping to all kinds of frantic conclusions.

Jean drops her hand onto Anne's lap and it feels very heavy, as though it's weighing her down, keeping her pressed to her seat.

"Polly started a political watchdog group," her mother explains. "Escaped Wives Against Polygamy. She spends her days lobbying and writing letters to the Justice Department, asking them to investigate the abuse that goes on in polygamous marriages."

"When did she leave Harmony?"

"Ten years ago."

"And she only contacted you now?"

"No. She's been writing me for years, ever since she left. I just wasn't ready to go there with her. I didn't want to disrupt my life with that stuff. I worked so hard to leave it all behind."

"Why now?"

"It wasn't just one reason," she says. "I guess I was finally ready. When you started asking questions, talking about going there, I figured it was time to revisit my past. It was unavoidable."

"Did she leave her kids behind?"

"No. She was able to get out with all five of them."

Anne decides not to pursue the subject of her two brothers. She never did want to inflict unnecessary pain on her mother. She's probably always known how much pain was already in her heart.

"Anyway," Jean says, with unconvincing levity. "We went to the B.C. Human Rights Tribunal. There were seven of us, all escaped wives. I didn't really say much. I was just there for support. Polly had filed a complaint alleging all kinds of abuse in Harmony. She's done a lot of research. I didn't even know about some of it."

"Like what?"

"Young girls are being trafficked between the polyga-mous communities of Harmony and Utah like slaves. B.C. is the only place in North America where polygamists can practice without being persecuted."

"But I thought it was illegal."

"Of course it's illegal," her mother snaps. "But their reli-gious rights are protected under the Charter. Can you believe that? There's actually concern that the Criminal Code's prohibition against polygamy might infringe on *the polygamists'* constitutional rights!"

"So the government is essentially protecting them."

"That was the gist of our complaint."

"And no one in the surrounding towns complains?"

Jean shakes her head. "The people from Harmony spend money in those towns. They're consumers. No one says a word against them."

Anne rubs her throbbing temple. "Have you got any Tylenol?" she asks.

"In the upstairs bathroom."

Anne runs upstairs and finds an expired bottle of Tylenol in the medicine cabinet. She swallows two of them with a glass of murky tap water. Her mother's words in her head. *You are a daughter of Harmony*. She wonders about the implications of that.

When she returns to the living room her mother says, "I've had enough for tonight."

Anne nods in agreement and reaches for her coat, which is draped on an upholstered armchair. "Thank you for telling me," she murmurs.

"How do you feel?"

"I'm shell-shocked," Anne says. "I always imagined

Harmony as this perfect little place where life was simple and peaceful. It's given me this kind of safe feeling inside, knowing that's where I come from. I just thought . . . you know, that it was like the name implies. Harmony."

"If it was like that, we wouldn't have left."

"I guess I need some time for it to soak in."

"I'm sorry I waited this long," Jean apologizes. "I have to admit, it's a relief that you finally know everything. I feel like a weight's been lifted. At the very least, I don't have that dread in the pit of my stomach that you might find out."

"I feel sad for you," Anne tells her. "For what you went through. I kind of wish I didn't know how much you suffered or what you left behind. I already miss that ignorance, you know? It will always be in my mind now."

"I'm resilient," Jean counters, perking up.

"I know." Anne turns away from her mother and goes to the front door. Then she stops and turns back. "Mom?"

"Mm?"

"Did he love me? I mean, did he even know me from the rest?"

"I'm sure he loved you the way he loved all his children and his wives," she says. "Because you were his blood, he was fond of you. Maybe even proud. It's a different kind of love from what you know. Did he spend time with you alone? No. Did he play with you and call you by a special pet name? No. It wasn't like that. He had dozens of children."

Talk about feeling irrelevant and inconsequential. Her mother's words leave her desolate, as though she's been freshly abandoned. Then it sinks in that her vain hope of returning to Harmony in triumph has been smashed once and for all. The self-appointed prodigal daughter will not be welcomed home by her daddy. She is as dead to him as her mother is to her boys.

Anne reaches for the door, desperate for air. Her mother's voice calls her back. "Anne," she says. "I've made a lot of bad decisions in my life, but I don't ever regret leaving Harmony, not for one moment. I look at your life, your marriage to Elie, your career. Especially Evan . . . and I know I made the right choice for you."

Anne smiles wanly in response. She's tired to the bone now, barely able to stand upright. Her limbs feel heavy, her head still hurts. She wants to get out of her mother's house, which feels something like the scene of a crime, with its dead plants and its musty odor of secrecy and lies.

"Do you still want to go back there?" Jean asks her.

The question irks Anne. Her mother sounds smug, as though Anne's devastation was the desired response. It makes Anne think her mother's main purpose in telling her all this was to prevent her from going back.

"I don't know," Anne mutters, closing the door behind her.

Outside, she takes several deep breaths of air. The cold wind in her face feels good for once. She tips her head up toward the sky, fearing that her mother has been irrevocably altered in her eyes.

Standing on the doorstep of the house where she grew up, the world looks suddenly ominous and unfamiliar. It's as though she's never stood here before, never gazed out onto this street with her back to this door. Never seen this sky, or this lawn, or that house across the street. She shivers and rushes to her car, unable to shake the disturbing feeling that her entire life has been a dream.

Twenty-nine

*E*lie wakes her up by roughly jerking her shoulder. She looks at him blearily and he frowns. He was asleep when she got home so she went into his office, sat in his club chair to think and passed out.

He's holding Evan, who's naked except for a diaper. Unlike his father, Evan is delighted to see her and greets her with his most charming grin, revealing his first tooth cutting through the gum.

"Mamama!" he bleats. He's becoming a real beauty, with that black hair, those deep green eyes and a good olive complexion, not quite as swarthy as his father but better than her sallow tone. He is the best of both of them, a perfect blend.

Elie thrusts him into Anne's arms and Evan's warm downy head and soft skin are instantly soothing.

"Where were you?" Elie wants to know.

"I was at my mother's," she responds, stretching.

"Until almost twelve? You spent the entire day and night there—"

"My father is a polygamist," she blurts irritably, in a tone stripped of emotion. "He had five wives, including my mother. I've got two brothers I didn't know about. She left them behind when we escaped. She wasn't in the Berkshires this past week—she was out west, helping her sister fight polygamy at the B.C. Human Rights Tribunal."

She clears her throat and then resumes.

"That's why I was there for so long," she explains, ignoring the astonished look on Elie's face. "My mother was telling me the heartwarming story of my childhood in Harmony."

"Harmony is a polygamist town?"

Anne nods solemnly.

"There's been some stuff in the news about that other place in B.C.," he says. "But I had no idea about Harmony."

"Neither did I."

"I wonder how many others there are?"

Anne shrugs. "I don't know who I am anymore," she says bleakly.

"You're exactly who you've always been," Elie counters. "Anne Mahroum. My wife, Evan's mother, an artist. We all have pasts we'd rather forget. Don't be melodramatic about it."

"I'm not being melodramatic!" she rants, melodramatically. "I'm embarrassed and ashamed, that's all."

"You've got nothing to be ashamed of," he assures her. "You're not the polygamist."

"It's in my blood."

"It's not a hereditary affliction. It's a choice."

Evan is tugging on her chain—the Tiffany heart Elie gave her last Christmas—cramming it into his mouth, using it as a teething ring. She strokes his hair, sniffs the swoop of his neck. He's as much a part of her as her own limbs and flesh. How did her mother do it? How did she have the hardness or the courage—whatever quality or defect is required for such an act—to sever herself from her boys, not only abandoning them to an unknown future but relinquishing her right to hold them, caress them, and kiss them ever again?

Elie crosses the room and reaches into one of the side drawers of his desk. He pulls out a thick white envelope and hands it to her.

"What's this?"

"Open it."

"A gift?"

"Not anymore."

She opens the envelope, which has the red Air Canada logo in the upper corner, and pulls out two first-class plane tickets. There's a brief moment of excitement, until she discovers the destination.

"Vancouver?"

"It was a surprise," he explains, sounding disappointed. "I've got an auction out West at the end of August. I thought . . . I figured we'd go as a family and then rent a car or take a train to the Kootenay Valley."

"Oh, El—"

"I figured I could go with you and be there for support. Evan's feet will probably be straight . . ."

She slumps over in the chair and starts to cry, tears trickling onto Evan's scalp. "You're not repulsed by this?" she whimpers, frightened.

"Repulsed? By *you*? Absolutely not. That's ludicrous."

"Thank you."

"I'm concerned about Evan though."

She looks up at him. "Why?"

"Well, I'm a Maronite and I believe you're a Mormon. So what does that make him? A Maromon? A Mormonite?"

It takes a moment for her to realize he's kidding. She punches his shoulder, grateful for the levity. "Can you leave me alone for a bit?" she asks.

"I'll get rid of these tickets," Elie offers. "Trade them in for a trip to the Caribbean or something."

"Don't," she says. "Not yet."

They leave the room and Anne indulges in a hearty cry.
Self-pity has a way of gaining momentum, feeding on
everything in its path—gathering up every old and new
indignation it can get between its teeth. Before long her
tears are spilling for Evan's club feet, for Declan Gray and
the grand love affair she thought she deserved. For the
father who will never know or love her.

A memory comes to her in which she is running toward
her father on the front lawn, flinging herself at him and
calling out *"Daddy!"*

He lifts her up and spins her around. "Hello, Angela,"
he says. Angela is the one whose mother has black hair.
She's Anne's favorite sister. She's Anne's age and her braids
look the same and since they're always together and they
all share the same clothes it's no wonder he's confused. But
Angela's front tooth fell out when she fell off the swing.
She's missing a tooth. Her father doesn't know that though.

He puts her down and she runs off without correcting
him. There are so many of them, it's no wonder he's
mixed up.

*T*he smell of pancakes eventually lures her to the kitchen.
Having cried for over an hour, her body feels hollow. She
realizes she's famished. Elie's made pancakes and fruit
salad and cappuccinos for breakfast. Evan is in his high
chair, pushing bits of pancake and banana around on the
plastic tray.

"You okay?" Elie asks, sliding a plate in front of her.

"Better."

"How many?"

He holds out the plate of pancakes, which she eyes hungrily. "Three," she says. "I'm starving."

He uses a fork to serve her and then brings over the can of maple syrup. Her cappuccino arrives next, with a heaping dome of white foam and chocolate sprinkles, which he grated himself from a bar of Lindt dark chocolate. (And he has the gall to call her a perfectionist!)

"Evan's left foot is looking good," he remarks, joining Anne at the table.

"I know. I was noticing it in the bath the other night."

"We might not have to do more casting."

Evan interjects, pointing to the chandelier.

"That's the chandelier," she explains.

"You remember I've got that trip to Montreal," Elie says, laying it nonchalantly on the table alongside the pancakes and the coffee.

"When do you leave?" she asks tightly. She'd forgotten all about it.

"Tomorrow."

The phone rings and she notices a look of relief on Elie's face. She gets up and answers it.

"Anne? It's me. Are you okay? How do you feel? I was so worried after you left last night."

"I'm okay, Mom."

She thought she might feel angry or awkward toward her mother today. She wasn't at all sure. But what she feels is a swell of sympathy, a powerful urge to protect her mother from further pain or injury.

"Do you need me to babysit?" Jean asks. "If you need some time to yourself—"

"I'm fine. Are *you* okay?"

"Me?" Jean echoes. "Why wouldn't I be?"

Her mother's stoicism pierces her heart. Her eyes fill with tears.

*E*lie leaves the next morning at nine. After the limo disappears down the street, Anne puts Evan down for his nap.

Once he's asleep she marches into Elie's office and plants herself at his desk. She starts opening drawers, searching through papers. Looking for what? As she watched him leave this morning she felt a pang of mistrust. It was an intuition, a troubling feeling that something is not right about this trip to Montreal. For one thing, he was very vague about his business there. He told her he was going to see about a potential new collection. What does that mean?

The bottom line is she has to find out the truth in order to protect herself and her son. Self-preservation. If she can't trust her own mother, who can she trust?

That's when she discovers the business card in Elie's top drawer, lying carelessly among his bills and correspondence. The name on the card is *Monique Cardinale, V.P. Blah Blah Technologies, 3050 René Lévesque, Montreal, Quebec.*

She apparently has nothing to do with coins, which means, logically, that neither does Elie's so-called business trip. Anne turns the card over and there on the back, in the unmistakably neat, flowery handwriting of a woman, are the words "cell" and "home" with two phone numbers written beneath them.

Anne sits there holding the business card for a long time, staring through blurred vision at that name. *Monique Cardinale.* She never would have imagined that catching him would be so easy; that nothing more than a woman's business card and a gut feeling would ultimately lead to his downfall. She's often thought he used his coin business as a way to meet and lure women, and this might be her confirmation.

In a way, she's insulted that he wouldn't have made more of an effort to hide the evidence. Maybe he forgot. Maybe he's in Montreal without the woman's phone numbers and he can't reach her.

Unless they've been involved for months and he knows exactly where to find her. It would explain the strange behavior that night he stayed out late without calling. Of course that's what it is. Isn't infidelity always the explanation? Her mind begins to wander, morbidly reflecting on the darkest possible scenarios. Suddenly, her bravado crumbles and her poised determination gives way to a terrifying reality. Her mouth goes dry and her heart seizes. She tries to swallow but her throat is clamped shut. She feels short of breath. *He beat me to it.*

Elie is having an affair.

The realization fills her with rage more than anything else; more than fear and sadness, even more than jealousy. Strangely, her first thought is of her father. At least with polygamy you know where you stand. As a woman and a wife in a polygamous marriage, you know exactly what to expect. It's all out in the open. She and Elie, on the other hand, only pretend to be monogamous.

She certainly can't claim her side of the street is clean. She may be angry with Elie for consummating his affair, but she's guilty of having made a play for someone. If Declan hadn't spurned her she might also be having an affair. She's no better than Elie. Not much better than her father either. Maybe there *is* a polygamy gene that runs through the blood; a hereditary, sexual insatiableness or a propensity for infidelity, the way one might have a propensity for being overweight or bald.

The men of Harmony have found a loophole for marital boredom. They've done so under the bold and irrefutable shield of religious freedom. They've put together a bucolic, insular little village that not only enables but legitimizes their sexual restlessness. Her father married five women and lived with them openly, sharing his body and passing himself around right under their acquiescent eyes.

Elie lied to her face and is probably with another woman at this very moment. She lied to Elie and had coffee and intimate conversation with another man; then she kissed him in his car, plotting how she could commit adultery without getting caught.

Her mother was right about the hypocrisy of the "outside" world, with its self-righteous principles and virtually unattainable ideals. Polygamy may be an unsavory practice, but the concept of monogamy is proving to be something of a farce.

Thirty

She hears the door open downstairs and freezes. *Elie's home.* She'll have to get out of bed and face this.

She looks over at Evan, who is happily munching on a cookie, and knows her hiatus from reality is about to end. She has virtually abdicated from life and gone into hibernation, languishing in bed with the ringers off and the blinds drawn. If it wasn't for having to prepare Evan's bottles and change his diapers she might have sunk thoroughly into despair. Only her maternal responsibilities have kept her hanging on by a thread.

"Anne?"

The house is dark and ominously quiet, but Elie must have seen her SUV in the driveway. She can hear him moving around downstairs as he goes from room to room, looking for them. "Baby?" he calls out from the stairs.

Evan starts bouncing up and down on the mattress, climbing over her to get to his father. Little traitor.

Elie bursts into the bedroom then, looking happy and radiant and relaxed. He sets his leather travel bag down and joins them in the bed. He tickles Evan and kisses Anne's forehead. "Don't you feel well?" he asks her. "How come you're in bed?"

She's rehearsed a multitude of dramatic scenes, but face-to-face with him now the will to confront him evaporates, leaving only a reasonable expectation of the truth and a certain measure of sadness and resignation.

"Who's Monique?" she asks, skipping all attempts at a gentle entry into this conversation.

His body contracts at the mention of that name.

"I found her card in your desk."

"I wasn't hiding it," he says defensively.

"Who is she?"

"She's a numismatist—"

Anne laughs smugly. "Was *she* your business in Montreal?" she asks sharply.

"Sort of."

"Sort of?"

"I met with her," he admits, with an edge of indignation. "But I was there primarily to meet with the Garfinkles."

"Who are the Garfinkles?"

"They've got a phenomenal collection. Over six hundred pieces they want to sell off separately. They're looking for a reputable dealer. They contacted me and I thought it was worthwhile to go meet with them."

"And? Are they going to give it to you?"

"Don't know yet. They're interviewing other dealers. A few in Montreal. I tried to convince them they're better off having the auction in Toronto, but they haven't made a decision yet."

"And Monique?"

"Not that I should have to explain this to you," he states. "But it *was* business—"

"She works for a technology company!" Anne flares.

Evan looks up at her with troubled eyes. Accusing your husband of philandering is tough to pull off calmly in front of your child. Evan is very perceptive. She's sure he senses when she's angry or sad, or when she and Elie are fighting. She doesn't want to scar him, so she smiles and pulls his nose and makes an effort at self-restraint.

"Coins are her hobby," Elie explains. "She's a collector."

"Was she buying or selling?"

"Buying," he says. "This feels like an inquisition."

"Since when do you make house calls?" she accuses. "You're not a traveling salesman."

"I'm flattered by your jealousy," he remarks. "I didn't think you cared this much."

She rolls over, turning her back to him. "After all our years together," she says softly, "can't you just be honest? Can't you tell me the truth? I've had enough lies already. I don't want any more lies."

"I don't think you're being rational right now. This thing with your mother has got you really fucked up."

"Don't use *that* to get out of this!" she cries. "They've got nothing to do with each other except maybe I'm not so willing to let myself be lied to anymore. I'm tired of living in denial."

"I think your mother shattered your trust," he patronizes. "And now you don't even trust *me*. You're looking for something, anything—"

"Don't psychobabble me, El."

"It's not what you think—"

She laughs harshly, cutting him off mid-platitude. Evan adds an angry "Mamama!" She hands him a loose strand of her hair and he settles back down, winding it around his tiny fingers, totally absorbed.

She turns back to Elie. "Just tell me who she is," she pleads wearily.

"She collects Canadiana. She saw the notice in *Canadian Numismatics* this month—"

"What notice?"

"That I've acquired the B.C. gold coin and that now I've got the only known complete set."

"And?"

"She came to see me at the shop, told me she was interested in buying my collection—privately, to avoid paying the dealer commission—and she left me her card."

"We both know you'd never sell it, so why did you have to meet with her in Montreal?"

"I might sell it."

"What?"

He looks away.

"What do you mean? How can you even contemplate that?"

He shrugs. "I don't know. I just . . . I don't know."

"Doesn't it mean anything to you?"

"Not as much as I thought it would. I could make a fortune off it."

"It's got no sentimental value for you?"

"I'm proud of it, I suppose."

"That's it? All those years you spent sulking over the missing coin—"

"I never sulked over it," he counters. "I had moments of wanting to quit, but I always loved the game. I always held out the hope that I'd eventually complete my collection."

"And you did!"

"Exactly."

She shakes her head, baffled. "I don't get it," she mutters.

And then she realizes: Elie is just like her. He's like anyone else who's ever desired something as though it were the Holy Grail and then, having finally gotten it, found himself utterly bored and looking for something else. He never really cared about the missing coin in his collection. What he valued most was its incompleteness. The distraction—no, the *compulsion*—of the chase.

He's always mocked her quests for fulfillment—the support groups, Dr. You, finding her father. How gratifying to realize that despite his self-righteousness they're exactly the same, she and Elie.

"I just figured it was like a second child to you," she goes on. "And here you are thinking of selling it to some woman—"

"A collector."

"Is she attractive?"

"Anne, please."

"Is she?"

"I don't know," he says, looking squirmy and uncomfortable. "I guess."

"That means she's hot," Anne deduces. "If she was ugly or fat or old you'd be thrilled to tell me so in great detail. When they're hot it's always, 'Uh, I don't know. I guess.'"

"Look," Elie says calmly, "when Monique came to see me—"

"You call her Monique?"

"I told her what my reserve would be if I ever decided to sell it at auction. She didn't even blink. She said that's exactly what she figured it would be and to give her a call if I ever decided to sell it."

"So then you *have* decided to sell?"

"Not yet," he responds evasively. "But I was in Montreal and I figured I'd meet with her and see how high she's willing to go—"

"You're lying!" Anne cries triumphantly. "There's no way you'd sell it privately. We both know you could easily generate a bidding war with a collection that rare and valuable. You'd be sure to get an outrageous amount for it at auction. Besides, you'd sell it through the business, so it's not like *you*'d be saving the dealer commission if you sold it privately—"

"Of course I told her all that," he says smoothly. "But this was my thinking. I could possibly get one point two million for it at auction, right? That would be significantly higher than my reserve. But what if this woman is really serious and she's willing to cut me a check for one point five or two million bucks? You never know with some of these wealthy collectors. I thought it was worth a meeting."

"Where?"

"Where what?"

"Where did you meet?" Anne asks impatiently.

"In the bar at my hotel."

"The bar?"

"Christ, Anne."

"How old is she?"

"How is that relevant?"

"It's very relevant," she assures him.

"I don't know. Fortyish?"

"Fortyish? As in closer to thirty-eight? Or closer to forty-five?"

He rubs his eye sockets in despair. "Forty-five," he answers.

"You're just saying that because you think it's what I want to hear."

"Yes."

"How did it end then?"

"She offered me a hundred grand over the reserve."

"She's got that kind of money from being the V.P. of a tech company?"

"Her husband is a successful songwriter. He writes songs for all those popular Québécois singers. They've got a place in the Cayman Islands, so they probably don't pay taxes."

"You know an awful lot about her," Anne remarks.

"Anyway," he finishes, "I told her if I was going to sell it I'd do it through a public auction. She wasn't offering enough to persuade me to sell it privately. And that was it."

"What time was it when she left?"

"Seven? Seven thirty?"

"Why didn't you tell me you were meeting this woman to discuss selling your coins?" she demands. "Do you understand that it's the information you withheld that makes this so suspicious?"

"Yes, I'm beginning to," he says miserably. "I didn't want to tell you that I was thinking about selling my collection. I figured you'd make a big deal."

"With good reason."

"The thing is, this Monique, she planted a seed with her offer. Now I'm thinking I could auction my collection and make a fortune and create a lot of buzz for the business. Think of the clientele I'd attract—the elite of the numismatic community. They'd come from all over North America. And then I can start building a new collection!"

"But don't those coins mean anything to you?"

"Sure, but . . ." His voice fades out. His eyes are unexpressive.

"So that's it?" she pursues.

"I haven't decided yet."

"I mean about *her*. Monique."

"Yes," he answers, relieved. "That's it."

She gazes at him for a long time. Scrutinizing. Surveying. Probing for clues, fine traces of betrayal. A flinch, a guilty gesture. Anything. But he's defended himself with impressive conviction and she finds herself wanting to believe him.

"Anne," he murmurs, "this is *me*." He takes her in his arms and holds her. It feels nice, being in his arms. She's missed him. "You never have to worry about me being unfaithful," he promises.

Evan, having finally exhausted her strand of hair, uses her hip to hoist himself up into a standing position. He teeters there a few moments, wobbly and proud, and then collapses on top of them, giggling.

A perfect family. That's what someone would think, peering in through the window. Yet for all she knows Elie might have fucked this woman in Montreal. Or maybe they've been having an affair for months. In the end, the absolute truth is really nothing more than an impenetrable defense. It's a tight story that can withstand relentless cross-examination.

It's whatever brings about happy oblivion.

Thirty-one

Christian Week—B.C. urged to charge polygamists in community dubbed "Canada's dirty little secret."

Anne is sitting in a restaurant on Queen Street, nibbling a panini and reading some newspaper articles that she printed off the Internet about one of the well-known polygamist towns in B.C.

It's Friday night and Elie has agreed to stay home with Evan, presumably so she could do some forging. Instead, she's sitting here immersed in newspaper clippings.

B.C. women's group asks government to stop funding polygamy. Cult's women slam polygamy critics. B.C. woman fears for daughter's safety in polygamist sect. Polygamists from U.S. using B.C. as safe haven.

It really is an amazing accomplishment that up until now she's remained virtually clueless about her birthplace. Anne's always known that she and Jean are pros at keeping reality at arm's length, but this revelation about Harmony is proof of how thorough and effective Anne's denial has been. And although she's taken her cues from Jean, it's fair to say that until recently she's never gone out of her way to pressure her mother for answers or to demand the truth. She's always suspected there was some mysterious and possibly sordid explanation for their hasty departure from Harmony. *But she never really wanted to know.*

And so now, for the first time in her life, she has to make sense of the scandalous legacy of her past. And once she makes sense of it, it remains to be seen if she can ever make peace with it.

As she reads she finds herself just as intrigued as repelled by her father's lifestyle. Not that she condones it, but she has a twisted curiosity about it. It's like a crime scene, something she has to see for herself. How does he live day to day? What are his wives like? What kind of father is he to all the dozens (hundreds?) of children he's got out there? She imagines him as a bully and a tyrant, even though that's not how Jean described him. It's just how she imagines all polygamist men.

The fact is, he can't be defined solely by that label. There must be other qualities and defects about him that make up the full man; that give him dimension. Intelligence, for instance. Or wit. Is he greedy, playful, cold, powerful, domineering?

She still wants to know.

Maybe she's supposed to hate him now and stop acknowledging his existence. Or maybe she's supposed to be self-righteous about polygamy and condemn it. Yet she keeps thinking about traditional marriage. *Her* marriage. The institution of marriage. Declan's marriage. Restlessness, it seems to her, is the common denominator. What constitutes a happy marriage? One faithful partner? Three faithful partners? Thirteen faithful partners?

The most accurate definition of marriage she can come up with is two people who irritate and loathe each other a lot of the time; who spoon and fuck and fight; who wake up morning after morning staring into each other's faces, smelling each other's breath—all in the name of companionship. Someone to go to the movies with and share the large popcorn. Someone neutral to blow steam at after a bad day. A wedding date, an ally, an enemy. Two people who have their own language, their own rhythm, their own rituals.

She glances around the restaurant, checking to see if there are any men with whom she could flirt. Her drug of choice: male attention. Her serial flirting is really all bravado, sustained only by the fact that she's married to Elie. Her confidence comes from having a man waiting for her at home.

Without the safety net of Elie she'd just be *dating*. She hated dating when she was single. The second-guessing, the insecurity, the desperation—it was exhausting. It was nothing like flirting as a married person. When she thought Elie might be leaving her she felt total panic and despair.

She considers that her flirting days might be over anyway. The experience with Declan knocked her down a few notches; her confidence has foundered. She managed to get bruised and humiliated and, in the end, being married didn't protect her from rejection. The only thing that could have spared her would have been not engaging with him in the first place. She could have left him alone. She should have.

Does her father get bored with his marriages? The question keeps nagging at her. She figures it must be restlessness that determines when he's going to go out and choose a new woman. Why else would he seek out a new wife every few years? Just when the relationship hits that post-fart phase he can simply start over with someone fresh and unexplored. He gets to experience all the good stuff again—the first kiss, the first touch, that reverence for what's unknown.

Isn't that why polygamy exists? She can't believe it could be for any other reason.

Outside, she hails a cab and, much to her surprise, finds herself blurting out an address that is not her own. The cab driver heads in that direction.

Not home. Not yet. First, she's got some business to take care of.

The driver drops her off on Jarvis, in a seedy area. Yet it all seems very logical to her that she should be standing here now.

She looks up and it's still there. The building they lived in when they first arrived in Toronto. She doesn't take her eyes off it.

It's drizzling and cold. She's shivering. She's waiting for memories to come toppling into her consciousness. She thought that seeing the old apartment building might trigger something long since buried in her psyche. She wonders if there were clues she's forgotten. Things her mother might have said in those early days in Toronto, about Harmony or about her father. Did she ever mention polygamy? It's possible she did and that Anne has blocked it from her memory. It happens to people all the time.

Inevitably, snippets from that era begin to trickle into her mind. Lost moments, fragments.

Will I ever see Daddy again?

Sitting at the fold-up card table in the kitchen. Her mother had bought it at the Salvation Army. It was where they ate. It was the kitchen table. The floor was olive green linoleum with burned patches. She can see it as clearly as if she were inside the apartment.

They'd been in Toronto a few weeks. She was just starting to understand that they weren't returning to Harmony.

She was confused about how things had been left with her father. Wouldn't he miss her? Why did he let them leave?

She remembers Jean shrugging in response to her questions.

What about Angela? Can I see her again?

Angela was her best friend in Harmony. They were like sisters. They *were* sisters.

Not unless she comes to Toronto.

That was Jean's answer.

Anne wonders what's happened to Angela. Did she marry a polygamist and stay in Harmony? Did she escape, like they did? She could try to find her. She could track her down. But what if a search leads her back there?

This is our new life. We can't go back there.

Why?

They won't let us.

Who?

The men.

Daddy?

Especially him.

And yet like all her memories, she has no idea if these fragments are accurate or if she's making them up on the spot. It's possible. Anything is possible.

Something else comes to her while she's shivering outside the old building on Jarvis. One night, Jean had a nightmare. She woke up screaming *"Tommy! Tommy!"*

They shared a bed. Anne reached out for her mother to comfort her. Her hand brushed Jean's cheek and it was sopping wet.

Why are you screaming "Tommy"?

I miss them. God, I miss them. She really let herself cry then. Anne held her, but she didn't understand. Jean cried all night, until the sun rose in the morning. She never told Anne why. She never explained anything.

Anne left those things alone.

Anne's head is starting to swirl. She thinks about all those people—her father, her brothers, Tommy and James. Angela.

What's become of them?

Her curiosity hasn't waned or abated just because she knows the truth about Harmony. If anything, it's the opposite. These people exist. They're real. There's a strong pull. It seems to her she wouldn't be human if she didn't have some desire to seek them out and reconnect with them; if she didn't want to know what they look like and how they live and whether they resemble her at all.

She knows the worst now and she despises what Harmony stands for. She resents the men—including her father and brothers. She pities the women, her half sisters and aunts and cousins. Yet she loves them all anyway, the way you love the parents who abuse you or the siblings you've never met. *Because they are blood.*

She forgives her mother. If not for Jean, she would still be there today. If her mother hadn't taken her out of Harmony she'd still be a prisoner. She'd be living a life of submission and obedience and repression. The woman she has become today would not exist; she'd probably be dead inside. How can women flourish in a plural marriage, forced to forgo education and start breeding early? Forced on men they don't love and then left to compete with other women for one man's affection and attention? She's certain that Harmony could not have nurtured anything but the worst in her—loneliness, jealousy, bitterness, fear.

Instead, she is free. She makes her own choices. Some days the life she's chosen brings out the worst in her—her marriage to Elie, the restlessness that led her to Declan, her self-righteousness toward her mother. Other days she rises to her best self—in her marriage to Elie, pursuing her passion for art, mothering her son, seeking fulfillment wherever she can. All these elements somehow manage to coexist, not perfectly, but in relative balance.

Who she is can now be defined by who she is not. That's why she's still compelled to return to Harmony, to see with her own eyes what she has been spared.

Thirty-two

"Over here!" Tami waves her over to where she's sitting. She's got one of those gigantic running strollers beside her that takes up half the coffee shop, and inside is Parker, eating a muffin as big as his head.

The place is noisier than a stadium. Screaming kids, loud talkers, a lineup at the counter—a typical Saturday morning at Starbucks. Nevertheless, Evan is sleeping in his stroller and the smell of coffee is wafting around her, both of which override any minor irritations. On her way over to Tami, she feels a wave of pleasure.

Happiness is this. Elie said that to her the other morning when Evan was playing between them in bed. Their feet were locked and it was warm. They were dozing on and off. Evan was babbling to himself, his adorable baby voice swimming in and out of her consciousness. "Happiness is this," Elie murmured.

"Hmm?"

"Virginia Woolf."

She was too sleepy to ask which novel. But at that moment it fit. In spite of everything that's happened, it fit.

Tami is still waving. Anne pushes her stroller in her direction, maneuvering it around all the other strollers. "I couldn't get the big comfy chairs," Tami apologizes as Anne arrives at her table.

She takes off Evan's hat and mitts very carefully, trying not to wake him.

"What are you having?" Tami asks. "I'll get the coffee."

Her generous spirit is endearing, the way it comes through her shiny blue eyes. She's one of those rare women who make other women feel comfortable, never inadequate, never in competition. In some ways she reminds Anne of her old friend Sharon.

She returns a few moments later with their coffees.

"It's been a while," Anne says, unable to remember the last time they saw each other. Was it the day Ken Schlittman died or at the club foot support group?

"I know it has," Tami agrees. "I've been . . . Darren and I have been through a difficult time."

"Really?" The thought of Tami going through a difficult time seems incongruous to Anne. Tami is light and fluffy and perpetually happy. She's whipped cream. She's a brightly colored balloon.

"I had a miscarriage," she reveals.

"I'm so sorry," Anne manages.

"I was nine weeks along."

"Oh. God. I . . ."

"I keep thinking it's my fault," she confides.

"You shouldn't."

"But I was so ambivalent about having a second child. I just wasn't all that excited about the prospect after what we've been through with Parker."

"That's understandable," Anne assures her. "But you can't cause a miscarriage just because you're uncertain. No babies would ever get born!"

Tami shrugs, unconvinced. "I was very anxious. Very stressed. I'm sure that had something to do with it."

"I doubt it, Tami. I was a disaster when I was pregnant. Talk about stress! But babies are resilient. It just wasn't meant to be. Not this one."

"The odd thing is, since I had the miscarriage, I'm now certain I want to have a second child."

"And you will."

"I hope so."

Just then a woman pushing a double stroller walks in. She has a newborn and a toddler inside it, both beautiful and healthy. Tami looks at Anne with a broken expression. "It's just so easy for some women," she murmurs.

Anne nods, thinking Tami's got a right to feel sorry for herself. Parker's club feet, then a miscarriage. It would shake the faith out of just about anybody.

Tami turns to Parker and kisses him on the nose. "I guess some women can't have children at all," she states. "I should be more grateful."

"You're allowed to feel sad—"

"Sad, yes. But the line between sadness and self-pity is very thin."

"Sometimes a little self-pity is warranted," Anne points out, in defense of her own recent wallowing.

"But it's so useless. Anyway, I'm sorry to have dumped on you like this."

"You've hardly dumped on me . . ."

Tami reaches across the table and touches Anne's hand. "You've become a good friend, Anne. You're a valuable part of my support system."

It takes Anne a moment to respond. She's been using support groups in lieu of friends for so long, she's forgotten that normal people lean on *friends*.

She lays her hand on top of Tami's and says, "Me too." Meaning it.

"I've been going back to the club foot support group," Tami says.

"But Parker's feet seem fine now—"

"Oh, they are," Tami effuses. "He's flourishing. His calf muscles are still underdeveloped but we've been thinking about starting him in martial arts, to build up his strength and give him some confidence."

"So why did you go back to the group?" Anne asks, wondering if Declan has been there but not daring to ask.

"I was so anxious when I found out I was pregnant," she explains. "I was worried about the possibility of having another baby with club feet. I needed a place to vent my fears." She smiles sadly. "Turns out I needn't have worried about that."

"It's probably as likely as getting struck by lightning twice," Anne tells her. "Having a second child with club feet, I mean."

"Do you think you'll have another one?"

"I doubt it," Anne responds. "Elie and I are good with one." She glances over at Evan, who is still sleeping like a little angel, and feels absolutely at peace with her decision.

"You don't mind that Evan will be an only child?" Tami asks.

"*I'm* an only child," Anne says, shrugging it off. "It wasn't so bad."

But as soon as the words are out of her mouth she remembers the truth—that she's got two brothers and God knows how many half siblings out west.

The realization, freshly acknowledged, disorients her. She goes quiet.

"Anyway, the support group has helped," Tami picks up. "Especially since the miscarriage. I guess just talking about things and having people who'll listen to me . . ."

"Exactly," Anne agrees, trying to pull her thoughts away from Harmony. "People who *listen*."

"I've started meditating too," Tami says, and Anne's ears perk up. "I joined the North Toronto Center for Meditation and Yoga. I've found it to be really helpful. I do a body awareness meditation with Zen Master Ha-Shoshi."

"What does that mean?"

"Instead of focusing on our breath, we focus on different parts of the body. Zen Master Ha-Shoshi says it helps the body function as a harmonious unit rather than as separate and conflicted parts."

Anne stares back with a blank face.

"Do you ever feel as though your head isn't even connected to the rest of your body?" Tami probes.

"Is it supposed to be?"

Tami chuckles, but Anne isn't sure what's funny. "Anyway," she finishes, "the meditating has really enhanced my body awareness. I feel much more in balance."

Anne finds a pen in her purse and scribbles the name down on a napkin—*North Toronto Center for Meditation and Yoga*.

"Evan seems to be doing better," Tami observes. "He's even wearing regular running shoes."

"They're way too big for him," Anne points out, slightly embarrassed. "There's still swelling. And his left foot isn't totally straight yet."

"I think Parker was worse off at Evan's age."

"He was?"

"Oh, definitely. We knew we'd need a third operation. There's no way he could have worn running shoes then. Right, Parky?"

She tousles his hair. He's a cute kid. He's got that whitish-blond hair that's so becoming on babies, with Tami's turned-up nose and big blue eyes. It's just his legs, which are still quite scrawny and dangle limply from the stroller.

"So I haven't seen you at the support group in a while," Tami mentions.

"I've actually been thinking about going back," Anne says, surprising herself. "To update everyone on Evan's progress. It's sort of a happy ending, I guess. It might give some of the others hope."

"It would definitely alleviate a lot of their fears about surgery. I can remember how terrified I was."

"Me too, although it feels so long ago now."

"We could go together," Tami suggests. "And afterward we can have dinner or a drink. A girls' night out!"

Evan wakes up then, rosy and grinning, revealing his one new tooth. Elie has been calling him Snaggle-tooth for the past few days.

"Good morning, little man," Anne gushes.

He lets out a high-pitched squawk and waves at her, and she's more certain than ever that he is enough; that he will bring enough joy and laughter and delight in her lifetime to make up for the siblings she's lost and the children she will never have.

"He's a beauty," Tami exclaims. "A real beauty, Anne."

She marvels that Tami isn't the least bit insincere, which is always Anne's first instinct about other women. Tami is good for Anne. She's like a salve on all her wounds. She bolsters her faith in women.

After they part ways, Anne veers off Yonge Street and takes a more scenic route home. The sun is blazing and much of the snow is melting before her eyes. It's early spring and the air has that wafting aroma of wet grass and muck and things blooming and coming back to life. She might even stop at the park and put Evan in the swing.

She turns leisurely onto Dawlish and heads for home. Evan is pointing at everything along the way.

"That's a tree," she answers. "A car. A house. A flower. The bushes. The telephone pole—"

She comes up behind an elderly couple strolling languidly with their arms linked. The old man is leaning ever so slightly on his wife for support. He's probably had a stroke or something. As Anne passes them she can hear the woman's ebullient laughter. The sound of their voices, intertwined and animated, trails after her down the street and she smiles to herself, feeling a sudden bloom of hope.

The following Monday night at the church, she and Tami sit down side by side in the circle. There are some familiar faces, some new ones. The people Anne knows ask about Evan and she gets to tell them triumphantly that the operation was a success and his feet are straight. She leaves out the small detail of his left foot, which will correct itself soon enough anyway. "There *is* an end," she reassures them. "I'm here to tell you, there's every reason to be hopeful."

Sharing Evan's progress is somehow restorative. It makes her feel like the luckiest one among the tragically unlucky. It's exactly the way she felt when she announced she was pregnant at the infertility group. A winner among losers.

"And at the end of the ordeal," she hears herself saying, "I think my son is better for what he's been through. We all are."

Doubt clouds their eyes. They're not buying it.

"Sure, I'd have preferred an easier way," she admits. "But Evan is so resilient now. He's tougher than he would have been." Then, quoting Declan from months ago, she adds, "He's got more depth. You know?"

"Depth?"

They all look puzzled.

"But are his feet *perfectly straight*?"

"Yes," she lies. "Perfectly straight."

Tami looks away quickly so as not to embarrass Anne. Bless her. She knows Anne is fibbing. Anne hopes this doesn't change her opinion of her, like that "oh no" moment in a new relationship when the other person commits that first fatal error—the irrevocable post-sex fart, the first glimpse of smothering jealousy, the revelation that he's got a name for his penis.

The chairperson calls the meeting to attention. Anne draws a breath and releases all the tension she's been storing in her body. She immediately relaxes. Her limbs get that liquidy feeling and her mind begins to settle. A warmth emanates from the center of the circle and envelops her. The first person to speak introduces herself as Julie. She's still wearing her maternity clothes and she has that glazed, postpartum, sleep-deprived look in her eyes (also known as the "what the hell have I gotten myself into?" look).

"My son is three weeks old," she trembles. "They told me in the delivery room that club feet were nothing to worry about, but now our orthopedist is talking about surgery!"

Tami and Anne exchange knowing glances. Anne considers that maybe she could become one of those women with a cause, a philanthropist who speaks out about club feet in support groups across the country. She could donate money to club foot research and devote her time to exposing the stigma around it.

Suddenly the door opens and everyone in the circle turns to see who's arrived late. Anne turns her head slightly—not expecting anyone in particular—just as Declan comes into the room. Her heart drops like a high diver plunging into the water from an unimaginable height. He looks infuriatingly gorgeous, his handsomeness enhanced by a deep, March-break suntan. His hair is a bit longer on the sides and he's wearing a backward baseball cap and a black ski vest. He looks almost superimposed against the abysmal church basement setting.

Anne quickly averts her eyes. He didn't see her. She doesn't know whether to avoid his look or to brazenly acknowledge him as though nothing happened between them. (Nothing *did* happen between them.)

She decides to greet him unapologetically; to make eye contact and smile and pretend she's as comfortable and natural with him as she is with anyone else in the group. That's when Anne spots *her* cowering behind him. He's brought her with him this time.

Margaret.

He grabs two chairs and inserts them into the circle next to Julie. He motions for Margaret to sit down and then takes her hand. Margaret is looking down at the floor.

"I've done some research on the Internet," Julie is saying, unperturbed by the disruption. "I've read about this Ponseti method—"

At this, Margaret's interest is clearly piqued. She lifts her head.

Out of the corner of her eye Anne can see Declan has noticed her. His expression quickly goes through the seven stages of that first awkward encounter following a thwarted extramarital affair: shock, denial, anger, bargaining, guilt, depression and finally, acceptance. He smiles halfheartedly. Anne smiles back.

She can tell he's caught off guard and that he wishes she weren't here. He probably assumed it was safe to return or else he's been coming for a while—possibly with Margaret—never expecting to see Anne here again.

He indiscreetly slides his chair closer to Margaret's in case Anne hasn't yet deciphered they're together. Julie drones on and on, sniffling, daubing at her eyes and nose.

Anne wants to scrutinize Margaret. Since she's unable to gawk openly, she settles for snatched glimpses whenever she can, pretending to be glancing at the clock on the wall behind Margaret.

She's not as perfect as Anne had previously thought. She's pretty enough, but she's very pale and drawn, with grayish circles under her eyes. She seems sad. She's got the potential for great beauty, but has a look about her of someone who's given up. Does she sense that her husband is bored with her? That he's got his eye on other women? That it's only a matter of time before he acts on one of his flirtations? Or is it her son's club feet that have finally worn down her spirit?

Julie finally wraps up her spiel and looks at each and every one of them with a desperate, beseeching look.

And then it's her turn. "My name is Margaret."

Anne looks over at her, intrigued. Now is Anne's chance to really examine her under the pretext of listening attentively.

"I think I've made a terrible mistake . . ." Margaret begins. "I chose not to let my son have the surgery, and now I regret my decision. It was selfish. I didn't have Sean's best interest at heart. I was terrified of the anesthesia and I didn't want him to be scarred for life—"

She pauses and looks over at Declan for encouragement. He offers nothing by way of support—not a smile, not a wink, not even a squeeze of her hand. He's probably angry with her. He must blame her for their son's thwarted progress.

"We waited too long," Margaret continues. "When the first casting didn't work, I still wouldn't agree to the operation. I hoped Ponseti would work, but we started it too late. We didn't have a good doctor at the beginning and now Sean is considerably older—"

Her voice cracks. She closes her eyes. In a soft voice, she says, "I worry I've ruined his chance at a normal life."

What a relief, Anne thinks. That she's just human.

*A*t the break, a cluster of club foot moms gathers around Margaret to console her. She has the kind of affable, Ivy League attractiveness that draws people to her; people who want to be part of her web, her world.

Anne imagines she's led a charmed life up until now. She probably grew up singing Christmas carols around the piano with her family. She was probably the Head Prefect at high school (and at the very least a cheerleader). Declan was probably her college sweetheart, the best catch on campus. Her son's deformity must be the first blight on her record.

Declan comes up behind Anne. "How've you been?" he asks, startling her.

She spins around, flustered to find him standing so close. "Fine," she responds, trying to keep a neutral tone.

"I didn't think I'd see you here," he admits. "I assumed your son was through the worst of it."

"He is. His feet are straight, thank God. The surgery was a success. He's wearing normal running shoes."

"Really?"

"The casts are off and the swelling is starting to go down. I think he'll turn out perfectly normal. I mean *they*. His feet. I think his feet will turn out normal."

"That's encouraging," he says. "I hope it's not too late for Sean. Margaret seems to think we've lost too much time. I told her we should have done the operation—"

"Sean is still a baby," Anne offers prosaically. "I'm sure it's not too late."

"I really didn't expect to see you here," he reiterates.

"I'm actually leaving now," she says, suddenly needing to escape the basement; to escape Declan and Margaret most of all.

"Not because of me, I hope."

"Of course not," she fibs. "I'm tired. I just came along with Tami. She wanted to come . . . we were going to have supper together afterward, but I'm feeling so exhausted."

"I'm sorry, Anne."

"Don't be."

"There was a pull right away when we met," he admits.

"It was a blip. Nothing more." With that, she turns away from him and heads toward the door. It would be different if Margaret wasn't here. She would construe his comment as an opening.

"Anne?" he calls after her.

She stops and lets him catch up to her. He looks nervously in Margaret's direction, making sure she isn't paying attention. Anne feels breathless, anticipating the long-awaited disclosure of his feelings.

"I just want you to know," he says, and her heart flutters a bit. "I never meant to start anything up with you. It was careless of me and I apologize."

Not at all what she wanted to hear.

"Was that an amends?" she snips, sounding more hostile than she would have liked.

A flicker of embarrassment shadows his eyes. "You know, Anne," he says, "you're no different from the rest of us."

"What's that supposed to mean?"

"It means we all get bored."

Thirty-three

*A*nne has agreed to meet her mother in the park for their first get-together since Jean dropped her bombshell. It's a sunny April afternoon, and although the park is a good neutral territory, the reunion has been awkward. It feels as if they haven't seen each other in ages, when in fact it hasn't even been a full month. Fortunately, they've got Evan as a buffer. They played with him in the sandbox for nearly an hour without exchanging so much as a word and now they're taking turns pushing him on the swing, still avoiding conversation except for the most benign banter.

"Is he warm enough?"

"It's fifteen degrees."

"But he's a baby."

"He's fine, Mom."

"Should he have a hat on at least? For the wind?"

"He's fine."

"He's grown a lot, eh?"

"We'll find out at his one-year checkup."

"What was he at nine months?"

"Twenty pounds."

"Oh, he's definitely bigger than that now. I can tell."

"He should be. He's three months older."

"Has he got more hair? It looks like he's got more hair."

"Mom—"

Jean looks over at Anne reproachfully.

"It's only been a couple of weeks since you've seen him."

"A month on Friday," Jean says tightly.

"His hair is the same."

"Did you manage all right?" she asks Anne. "Without me to babysit—"

"I haven't been working much. Only on weekends."

"I can take him this week," she offers. "If you want."

"That sounds good," Anne admits. "Maybe Tuesday."

"Whatever you like. I'm free." She kneels down in front of the swing and grabs hold of Evan's feet. "I've missed my baby," she says.

"He's missed you too. He said 'Nana' the other day."

Her face brightens. "How are his feet?" she asks, releasing him with a little push.

"We have an appointment with Dr. Hotz next week."

"You can barely tell he has club feet," she says. (Her choice of the word "barely" irritates Anne.)

"I think the left foot is starting to straighten out on its own," Anne says optimistically. "I think we're done with the castings."

Jean smiles affectionately at Evan and says, "Soon you'll be good as new." She stands up and turns to Anne. "You'll never guess who I ran into."

"Who?"

"Remember our neighbor from when you were a kid, that waitress?"

"Norrie?"

"I saw her at McDonald's in Scarborough."

"She was working there?"

"No, no. She was eating there with a couple of teenagers. Her kids, I guess."

"What were you doing at a McDonald's in Scarborough?"

"I had a reiki training at the Scarborough Missions. Didn't I tell you I'm studying reiki? I'm going to incorporate it into my practice."

"How did she look?"

"Who?"

"Norrie—"

"Oh. She looked the same I guess, only older and more beat up. She must be in her late forties now. Her hair was exactly the same. Bleached and frizzy."

"Did she recognize you?"

"No, but I definitely recognized her. I could never forget her face, not after what she did to you."

"God, you were hard on her," Anne remembers.

"She abused you," Jean responds matter-of-factly. "Besides, my self-righteous Mormon upbringing was still relatively fresh. I still believed in Satan."

Her voice fades and they both drift into their own thoughts about the past. Evan continues to swing, oblivious and enchanted.

"Do you think differently of me?" Jean suddenly asks. "Now that you know about Harmony?"

Anne's spirits deflate. She was hoping not to have to revisit this today. She was satisfied with their boring small talk. "No," she answers, without hesitation.

"Really?"

"It's been a lot to take in," Anne allows. "It was a shock. But none of it is your fault. You were born into it, just like I was. You only did what you had to do to save us."

"I just feel as though . . . as though maybe you judge me now . . ." She looks down at the ground, where she's digging the toe of her running shoe into the sand. "For abandoning my sons."

"No—"

"I figured that's why you didn't want to see me."

"I've just been processing everything."

"You wouldn't keep me from Evan . . . ?"

"Never."

She brushes away a tear and then rummages through her pockets for a tissue. She retrieves one and blows her nose. Anne gets a pang of guilt.

"If anything," Anne says, "*I* feel bad."

"You? What for?"

"I know I'm the main reason you left there. I'd hate to think you were lonely all these years because of me. Or that you traded in two promising sons for one disappointing daughter . . ."

"Anne," Jean says, sniffling. "Never talk like that. *Never*. You can't possibly think I was happy there."

"Do you think about them a lot?" Anne asks.

"In the beginning it was every day. Every *minute* of every day. Slowly, though, they began to recede. Now sometimes I wake up in the morning and realize I haven't thought about them in weeks or even months." She daubs at her eyes. "Talk about guilt."

It's on the tip of Anne's tongue to ask her mother: *Are you proud of me?* She still covets her approval. She knows Jean would tell the truth though, so she doesn't ask.

"Will you go out there?" Jean asks delicately.

Anne shrugs. "I can't answer that yet."

A hopeful gleam comes into Jean's eyes; she's obviously still trying to protect Anne from exposure to Harmony.

"Part of me really wants to meet them," Anne explains. "Especially my father and brothers. I'm dying to know if there are any resemblances. I want to see for myself if Evan looks like Thomas or James. Or my father. It's been almost *thirty years*. A part of me is still back there, you know?"

"I can understand that."

"And then another part of me is . . . repelled and embarrassed by them. I'd like to pretend they don't exist. Just sweep it under the rug, forget about it and move on."

"Can you?"

"I don't think so. There's this pull . . ."

"Did you ever write to your father?"

"A while ago, but I never heard back."

"Don't get your hopes up," Jean pleads.

"I won't. I've got no expectations."

"I don't want you to get hurt. You don't know how they'll treat you."

"I'm not looking for any relationships with them."

"What are you looking for then?"

"Maybe just another missing piece in the puzzle? Like I said, I'm not even sure I'll go back. The whole idea of Harmony gives me a sick feeling inside. I'm ashamed to be from there . . ." She shakes her head, confused. "I don't know. If I do go, it won't be for a while."

Evan lets out a sudden frustrated cry to let them know they've forgotten about him and that he's reached his limit in the swing. Anne lifts him out and takes him over to the slide. He studies it for a moment, gazing thoughtfully at the ladder and then at the kids already sliding down.

"Listen, I've got to go," Jean says, glancing at her watch. "I've got a client." She presses her nose to Evan's and says emphatically, "*This* is my boy."

Anne understands now that Evan has replaced her sons. "Mom?"

Jean looks up. "Hmm?"

"Are you . . . are you proud of me?" she blurts.

Jean looks at her strangely.

"I know on the outside my life looks great," Anne continues, "but on the inside I don't always have it together—"

"I think you're together," Jean assures her. "If you could just accept that your life won't ever be perfect, you'd be a lot happier."

"What's so wrong with striving for perfection?"

"Perfection is a myth."

"Anyway, I *am* happy."

"Good then."

Jean smiles and walks off toward the gates.

After she's gone Anne sits Evan at the top of the slide. He looks apprehensive, gazing down at the ground and then up at Anne for reassurance. He observes the other kids below him, playing in the sand and dangling from the monkey bars. Then he wiggles forward on his bum and with one jerky movement he manages to propel himself down the slide with his arms up in the air. Anne runs to meet him at the bottom, scoops him up and swings him around and around in the air.

It's spring and his world is beginning to blossom. He has escaped the confines of his casts. His legs are free and mobile. He'll probably walk soon. He might actually experience his first summer as a normal one-year-old boy. He points excitedly to the slide, gesturing that he wants to go again. Anne sets him back down at the top and releases him, letting him glide down by himself. He lets out a delighted squeal.

His joy is so infectious, it doesn't even bother Anne that her mother never said she was proud of her.

Thirty-four

*T*here he is, her boy. Black hair like his daddy, deep green eyes like a wine bottle. He waves to Anne and her insides melt. That's what it does to her, this love for her son. It turns her to hot liquid through and through.

Dr. Hotz steps aside and she rushes over to where Evan is sitting with his little legs dangling over the table, the faded purplish scarring on both feet, the left foot that still turns slightly inward, the slim, underdeveloped calf muscles. This is the reality after almost one year of attempting to correct the problem. The hoped-for outcome is still remote.

"It's looking good," says Dr. Hotz.

"Will he need more casting?" she asks. That's all she wants to know right now. She can live with all the rest of it as long as the worst is behind them.

"Not for the moment," Dr. Hotz responds. "I don't think it's necessary."

Relief! She glances over at Elie, beaming. He winks back.

"So what's the prognosis?" she presses, feeling anxious to wrap up this phase of Evan's life. His first birthday is approaching and it would be wonderful if everything to do with his club feet was finally resolved.

"The left foot is still turning inward," Dr. Hotz explains, demonstrating. "When he tries to stand, he's got a tendency to stand on the side of his foot—"

Oh no. Oh no. This doesn't sound like the tidy resolution she was anticipating.

"What now?" Elie asks.

"I'm going to prescribe straight lasts," he informs them. "It's an open-toe leather sandal with a buckle. The left one will have a flair and a wedge. Hopefully that will solve this problem once and for all."

"And if not?"

"There are a couple of options. Most likely I'd prescribe an ankle foot orthotic."

Anne remembers Tami mentioning the AFOs a long time ago.

"It's a brace," Dr. Hotz clarifies. "He can wear it under tennis shoes."

That image of Forrest Gump leaps into her mind again. *Run, Evan, run!*

"But that's down the road," Dr. Hotz states. "He might not need the AFOs at all. In fact, I think the straight lasts will do the trick."

"You do?"

"Absolutely. We're just fine-tuning here. Evan's made phenomenal progress."

"When should he start walking?" she asks.

"There's no precise answer to that—even for normal toddlers."

His use of the word "normal" as a way of excluding Evan punctures her heart.

"He'll walk when he's ready," Hotz continues. "I know of seventeen-month-olds who still aren't walking. Besides, the straight lasts should help."

"When do we get them?"

"They take about two weeks. I'll write you a prescription today. You can come back and see me about six weeks after he's been wearing them and we'll have another look."

He shakes Anne's hand, and then Elie's. "Congratulations," he says. "This is good news."

"It is?" she says, skeptically.

"He doesn't need more surgery or casting," Dr. Hotz reminds her, with an uncharacteristically warm smile. She notices a peppercorn between two of his upper teeth and for some reason it brings her great pleasure. "I'm very pleased with the outcome," he concludes.

"Who knew one of my best moments as a mother would be finding out my son only needs corrective shoes."

"We all have to adapt, right?" Dr. Hotz says, heading for the door. "You know that saying. We make our plans and God laughs."

*E*lie decides to take the rest of the afternoon off and spend it with Anne and Evan. "I'll cook," he says cheerily. He's in excellent spirits. She doesn't know if it's because of Evan's progress or his decision to sell his coin collection. Or something else.

They stop at the market to pick up a baguette and some lamb and some pastries. The day is shaping up nicely.

When they get home she retrieves the mail and joins Elie in the kitchen. With Evan perched on her hip she manages to sort through the usual bills and junk mail. Elie's *Time* magazine is rolled up in the pile.

"I'll take that," he says, and as he takes it from her one of the letters in her hand falls to the floor. She hands Evan off and crouches down to pick it up, noticing that it's her own handwriting on the envelope. And then she realizes it's the letter she sent her father weeks ago. There's a big stamp across it in block letters: RETURN TO SENDER.

No box has been checked off to explain why it's come back.

"What's that?" Elies asks.

"It's the letter I sent my father."

"Maybe he's moved," Elie muses, examining it over her shoulder.

"I doubt it. Where could he go?"

"Utah. Or jail."

"I'm sure he's still there."

"We could hire someone to find out."

Anne doesn't say anything.

"Or we could go ourselves," he offers. "We've got those plane tickets."

Anne looks up at him.

"I can imagine what it must be like," he goes on. "Finding out you've got two brothers. It's natural for you to want to meet them—"

"They may not want to see me."

"Of course they won't want to see you," Elie says pragmatically. "You're a sinner. You left there. But they can't stop you from seeing *them*."

"I'm not ready," she admits. "At first I only wanted go there and show off Evan to my father. I wanted to prove I'd accomplished something. Now . . . well, that seems absurd."

"Presumably they're not going anywhere," he says. "Nothing has to be decided today."

She leans her head against his chest. "I think I just need to be with it for a while," she says. "Either I'll wake up one day compelled to go, or the desire will leave me altogether."

She drops the letter in the trash, feeling surprisingly neutral about her father's rejection. She's disappointed, but in light of what she knows about him, she can't take it personally. That driving need for his validation, which began to take on a life of its own after Evan was born, has left her. If she ever goes back to Harmony it will be out of a healthy curiosity and a desire for closure.

"I'll go put Evan down for his nap," Elie offers.

Watching them leave, Anne gets a sudden surge of elation. She loves them both so much. Everything about her life today feels perfect. She wonders what people do when a good majority of their dreams have already come true and, just like that, her elation dissolves into panic.

She follows them upstairs and decides to plop into bed and also have a nap. It's drizzly and gray outside. A cozy, sleepy, pajama-wearing afternoon.

Elie appears in the bedroom. He sees her in bed and gets a hopeful look on his face. "Are you thinking what I'm thinking?" he asks.

"I don't know. Are you thinking of napping?"

"Guess again."

"Snuggling?"

"Nope." He jumps into bed and cuddles up to her. "I'll give you a hint. It's two words that rhyme with snow job."

"Very funny," she says, chuckling in spite of herself.

He kisses her, softly at first and then with a little more vigor. It's more than their usual closed-mouthed peck. She goes with it, willing herself to abandon her body to him, to let it happen.

She wants to be a wife to Elie. That's what she's thinking as he rolls on top of her. Maybe she had it wrong before, assuming that her eyes wander because her marriage isn't exciting enough. Maybe it's the other way around and the problem really begins the moment she sets her sights on someone *out there,* draining all her attention and energy, leaving nothing for Elie.

She remembers that story Elie told her about Arethusa and Alpheus—how Alpheus transformed himself into a river so he could be with Arethusa for eternity. The story ends there but, in real life, Alpheus probably would have gotten bored shortly thereafter. Declan had it right when he said it happens to everyone.

Yet that doesn't necessarily mean there's something better out there. What if the trick is to figure out how to go on swimming together for eternity *in spite* of the boredom?

Anne's been mulling over Declan's parting shot ever since that night at the support group, contemplating what he might have meant by it. It certainly ruptures the notion she has of herself as a tragic heroine searching for that elusive, perfect love. It means she's not unique and that her longings are ordinary—no deeper or more momentous than anyone else's.

Let's face it, there's nothing poignant or noble about boredom. Her mistake up until now has been confusing her own boredom with what she imagined to be an eloquent, smothering desire. Elevating it, inflating it and then losing herself in all the ensuing drama.

Declan could see through all that without really knowing her. A slap in the face in front of the support group would have brought her back to reality just as fast and with far less humiliation.

If nothing else, recent events have brought about the unavoidable revelation that the perfect, zealous, idealized love she keeps searching for doesn't exist. All that exists is what she has right now—her marriage to Elie Mahroum, a Lebanese numismatist who cooks great lamb and quotes literature and makes her laugh.

What a relief it would be to just look around and say *This is enough;* or to be able to give up on meeting her father or coaxing her mother's approval. Or perfection. Most of all, it would be a relief to let go of her quest for sexual oblivion that can only come in the form of a strange man who must stay a stranger in order to fulfill his promise.

She thinks freedom from her own desires might be a better pursuit. But there it is again. *Another pursuit.*

Elie's got her pants off. It's happening. They're making love.

She reaches around to his back and presses her hands against his skin. Her palm grazes that mole on his upper left shoulder blade. She smiles.

The sun comes out and their bedroom fills with light. She feels suddenly buoyed. All sorts of things come into her mind at once—a new idea for a table; a sudden inspiration to try that meditation class; a memory of that elderly couple strolling down the street the other day; a brief flash of Declan that carries nothing with it—no angst or longing or regret. And a surge of hopefulness. She hopes she can remember this tomorrow.

Elie is breathing hard. He's working at this. A moan escapes her lips and she realizes with tremendous joy and relief that it's starting to feel pretty damn good.

Acknowledgments

Special thanks to my friend and agent, Bev Slopen; and to Mom, Susan, Cousin Anne, Laura, Teresa, and H.P.

Photo by Miguel Cardinal

Harmony is JOANNA GOODMAN's third novel. She is the author of *Belle of the Bayou* and *You Made Me Love You*. Her stories have been anthologized and featured in *The Fiddlehead*, the *Ottawa Citizen*, *B & A Fiction*, *Event*, *The New Quarterly* and *White Wall Review*. She lives in Toronto.

harmony

JOANNA
GOODMAN

This Conversation Guide is intended to enrich the
individual reading experience, as well as encourage us
to explore these topics together—because books,
and life, are meant for sharing.

A CONVERSATION WITH JOANNA GOODMAN

Reader Beware! During this interview, the author reveals some key secrets in the novel. We recommend that you read this Conversation Guide after you've read the novel.

Q. Harmony *is your third novel. Can you tell us what inspired it and how you came to write it?*

A. Having my first child definitely inspired the premise of this novel. While I was pregnant, I was very concerned about having a healthy baby with ten fingers and ten toes. I also heard a story about a woman whose child was born with a dislocated hip and had to be in a body cast for the first few months of her life. This mother was such a perfectionist, she hid her newborn daughter from friends and family until the cast came off. Thus was born the idea of a perfectionist mother whose baby is born with a deformity.

Q. *Did you have to do a lot of research? Did the actual writing flow easily or was it a grind?*

A. I did do a lot of research, mostly on club feet but also on polygamy. But once the research was in place, the writing really flowed. I found it very easy to write in the voice of a perfectionist who also happens to be a new mother and an artist! The only glitch along the way came after I finished writing the novel, when I made a decision with my editor to change the narrator's point of view from first person to third person, to soften Anne's character.

Q. *In the novel, Anne struggles as a new mother to maintain a sense of herself as a woman, independent of her roles of wife, mother, and daughter. You're also a relatively new wife and young mother. Are Anne's joys and struggles ones you've also experienced?*

A. Yes, from the day my daughter was born, it was so important for me to still feel "myself." In other words, to feel personally fulfilled outside my home, to feel attractive, to have some kind of a life. Which is why I've stayed connected to my business and why I continue to write and why I still try to wear stylish clothes. No "mom jeans" for me!

Q. *Elie's background as Lebanese and a numismatist (rare coin dealer) is so unusual. What made you choose that background for him?*

A. A very good friend of my father is Lebanese, and his background and life experiences always fascinated me. I always knew Elie would be Lebanese. As for the coin collecting, the idea popped into my head years before I started writing *Harmony,* and I did extensive research on numismatics while I was in New York City. Basically, Elie's character has been alive and waiting for a story for several years.

Q. *Jean is one of my favorite characters. I particularly admire her courage in leaving her past behind and starting over, struggling for years almost all on her own to create new lives for herself and Anne. Yet, once Anne was grown, Jean gave up many aspects of her buttoned-down life and forged a looser, very personal style of living. Was Jean inspired by women you've known, or do you aspire to her midlife transformation?*

A. Jean is a courageous, ever-evolving woman. Because she evolved so much in her youth—from oppressed polygamist's wife to independent career woman—I felt it would be true to her character if her evolution continued well into middle age. I imagine—I hope!—that at some point in our lives we start to look for deeper meaning in the world than what we can find in our careers.

Q. *In addition to your roles as wife, mother, and writer, you also juggle work at Au Lit, the fine bedding shop that you and your husband run in Toronto. How do you manage it all?*

A. I have a phenomenal team of people in my life. My staff at Au Lit is more than capable of managing the business in my absence, so that I am able to go in just two or three times a week and offer guidance and direction. Also, my mother and husband are running the company with me, so we really are in it together. In other words, if I need to be at work, my husband can stay with my daughter. And for the first two years of my daughter's life, my mother was her part-time nanny. So we all three pretty much split the parenting/work duties among us.

The other practical answer to that question is that when I am deeply involved in a novel, I tend to pull my energy back from the business, which is a great benefit to being self-employed. I also only write at night, so I can be with my daughter during the day.

Q. *Now that you've published several novels, has the experience of writing changed for you? When you're dealing with page proofs, promotion, and contracts, etc., on a regular basis, is it harder to stay fresh and creative?*

A. Dealing with the business side of writing has no impact on my creativity. If anything, the idea that my novels are going to be published and (hopefully!) read, makes the whole process all the more exciting. When a novel has been published, and there's a good chance my next one will be published, I feel way more invigorated and inspired.

Q. *Can you share some of the reactions of your readers to your work?*

A. I am so grateful that the majority of the feedback I've received has been positive. Because I sell all my novels in my own stores, I get to hear tons of feedback from clients who read my books and then come in to shop again. What I hear most, and this was especially true of *You Made Me Love You,* is that my characters are so relatable and real. One radio reviewer actually said that reading the book made him feel as if he were sitting in a cafe, eavesdropping on an intimate conversation among the three sisters. He said he felt that he really knew these people, and that has been the most consistent reaction to my work.

Q. *What are you working on now? What are your long-term hopes and dreams for your writing career?*

A. I am working on my fourth novel, which is a love story set in the eastern townships of Quebec during the forties and fifties. Its tentative title is *The Seed Man's Daughter,* and it is a complete departure for me. First, it's a historical novel, and second, it's not a comedy! But I am absolutely passionate about it! I love working on it, love the research, love writing a love story . . .

As for my dreams for my writing career, I intend to keep writing novels and creating characters that excite and inspire me. Writing is my passion, and I look forward to a lifetime of it! I'd also like to see my novels on the big screen one day. I think *You Made Me Love You* would make a great movie.

Q. *As a Canadian writer, what special challenges do you face writing for a U.S. audience?*

A. I think the themes of my novels, particularly *Harmony,* are so universal that I cannot imagine my being Canadian could pose a challenge. For me, strong characters and a good plot can be set absolutely anywhere in the world and be successful. In fact, one of my all-time-favorite books, *The Colony of Unrequited Dreams* by Wayne Johnston, is about a Newfoundland politician from the fifties. I have very little interest in Newfoundland politics, but the characters and story line of this novel were so fascinating I couldn't put it down.

Also, practically speaking, are Canadians and Americans really all that different?

QUESTIONS FOR DISCUSSION

1. *Harmony* is about a woman who is also a wife, mother, and daughter. She is trying to remain true to herself while also being the best she can be in those many other roles. Do you find Anne believable, sympathetic, and likeable? Why or why not?

2. Anne's son, Evan, is imperfect because he has club feet, but all children are imperfect in some way. Discuss how your own mother dealt with your imperfections. Discuss how you, as a mother, deal with your children's imperfections. In what ways is your experience similar to, or different from, what Anne goes through?

3. Anne is ambivalent about the support group she attends, often needing it yet also disdaining it. Compare that to your own experience of support groups, whatever they might be.

4. Anne's husband, Elie, is not always perfectly supportive—helping out in some areas of domestic life and child care, not helping out in others; sometimes sympathizing with Anne's emotional turmoil, often becoming exasperated with her. In what ways do you find him

typical of husbands, and in what ways is he very different? Do you like him?

5. Anne is attracted to another man in her support group—Declan Gray. Why is she drawn to him? Do you find the author's depiction of this relationship realistic? Does it change how you feel about Anne?

6. Becoming a mother creates a need in Anne to know more about her own origins. Whether or not you are a mother, have you ever felt a sudden need to know more about your family background? Were there secrets in your family's past that you wanted to uncover?

7. Anne's mother keeps secret from her daughter the full truth about where they originally came from and the circumstances under which they left the small town of Harmony. Did you find her revelation shocking? Do you admire her for leaving and starting a new life for herself? Would you have made the same choice?

8. As many parents do, Jean makes a tremendous sacrifice for her daughter. Do you think Jean considers her sacrifice worthwhile? Is Anne grateful enough? What are children's obligations toward their parents who give up so much for them?